D0951237

S WELL

SWELL

A NOVEL BY CORWIN ERICSON

PUBLISHED BY DARK COAST PRESS COMPANY
SEATTLE, WASHINGTON

DARK COAST PRESS
3645 Greenwood Ave N.
Seattle, WA 98103 U.S.A.
www.darkcoastpress.com
info@darkcoastpress.com

ISBN-13: 978 0 9844288 4 7
Library of Congress Control Number (LCCN): 201192330
First Edition

Map of the Island of Bismuth illustrated by Lindsey Tibbott
and Rachel Blowen, designed by David Stone.
Cover design by Chris Jordan, Shipwreck Design
Text design by Charlie Potter

Distributed by Ingram Publisher Services

Acknowledgments

I am grateful to Susie Bright, editor of *X: The Erotic Treasury* (Chronicle, 2009), in which an excerpt from *Swell* was published as the story "Seagum." Thank you, Rachel Vogel, of Movable Type Literary Group. My thanks to the good people at Dark Coast Press.

Honorary Islanders:

Bethany Ericson, Tamara Grogan, Glenn McDonald, Amanda Nash, Parker Ramspott, Ann Tweedy, Dara Wier, Kimberlie Winter, Jeffrey "Reader Zero" Winter.

Contents

Part I

Part II

Part III

Bismuth Tourism Council
12 Commercial St., Bismuth

Dear Esteemed Publishers,

I write in my capacity as the now retired Director of the Bismuth Tourism Council to acknowledge our receipt of your gracious gift of the novel, *Swell*. I speak on behalf of the entire Council when I say how delighted we are to see such a tale set on our beautiful and historic Down East island.

Fisherfolk and whalers of Bismuth have gone down to the sea in ships and out unto the world for centuries. Family and friends eagerly await their return each time, not just for the bounty of the waters' harvest, but also for fresh stories that would often ease the strain of winter months and sustain them as heartily as a warm chowder.

Our rich heritage and traditions continue to thrive thanks to the undaunted courage of writers and artists who persist in patronizing our local culture. Though I have not yet met young Orange, I understand that his story of a boy finding his way in the world is wonder-fully representative of the strivings of the spirit and the imagination that marks all Bismuthians.

(cont.)

From the first saga-bard to dip his quill in squid
ink, to the great novelists of today, the literary arts
have long been vital to Bismuth. Ancient codskin vellums describe the epic journeys of aboriginal Americans from our shores to Europe, where they founded the
Northern Indian countries. Now, in the modern era, our
scribes have turned their eyes on Island life itself.

Swell, no doubt, knits a seamless net that unites our
earliest oral tradition with today's sharp-eyed scrib-
blers whose keen observation of our island's traditions
paired with their ears trained for lore produce a col-
orful portrait of a lively, exciting summer destination, indeed.

Just as Orange Whippey does in his story, visitors,
too, can come experience the adventure of a day fishing
at sea or relaxing on our scenic shores! Come see how
proud we are of our island's homegrown entrepreneurial
renaissance at Ely Pond, or perhaps pay a visit to the
salvage displays outside our Historical Society. You
may swap stories with Orange or other native Bismuthians during supper at The Topsoil, where they are ready
to delight with freshly-fried seafood at reasonable
prices. Stay over in one of our several inns or B&B's,
like the quaintly traditional Muffin Basket or The
Spouter, our newest and most luxurious lodging. Moorage
is available in our snug harbor for boaters.

Warmest island regards,

Eric Korangarson Bumpus,
(Ret.) Director, Bismuth Tourism Council

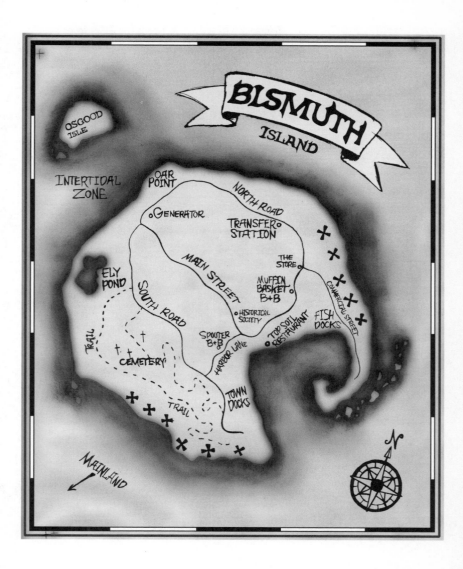

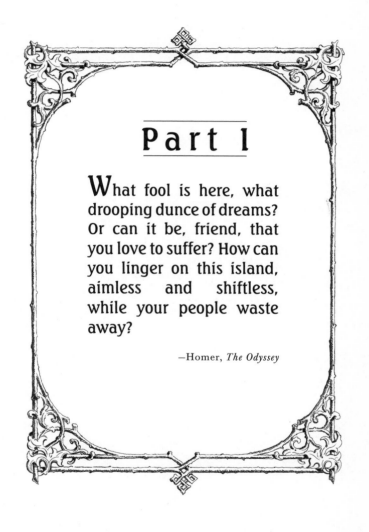

Part I

What fool is here, what drooping dunce of dreams? Or can it be, friend, that you love to suffer? How can you linger on this island, aimless and shiftless, while your people waste away?

—Homer, *The Odyssey*

CHAPTER ONE

Stranded and Conscripted

From my bunk, I found myself staring at the weepy ink of the Blue Öyster Cult tattoo that stained Donny's buttock. Donny Lucy was a repellent man whose sole topic of conversation was the genitals of various races and ethnicities. Some were prodigious, some were toothed, some toothsome, and a few had a unique tang that was best appreciated by he, himself. It's difficult to believe he'd done much field research into the subject. Down East islanders have a way of implying a worldliness that their biographies do not support. A few of us—well, many of us, considering that most of us are related in some way or another—have actual genetic links to voyagers to the archipelagos of cannibals and unclad princesses, and this seems to lend license to authoritative pronouncement where others might merely speculate. Donny had applied the speculum of his imagination to the orifices and organs of humanity with such vigor that he had lost sight of much else that the rest of the world considered suitable to discuss.

I was hoping hard that Donny was asleep, that his rhythmic motions were due to the waves. I was probably right, and he had probably moaned "motherfuck" and wiped his belly with one of the rank communal T-shirts due to a dream about maternal taboos and personal hygiene. Some boats have crews that are actually frisky masturbators. Masturbation is an enduring topic on most boats. Every single aspect of it, with the exception of the pleasure one might pull from it, is routinely discussed. But on some boats—say, one with a *fado*-crazed Portuguese—a beautiful night with flying fish and falling stars inspires the crewman to make his own arcing deposit overboard, as if to say, "I too am a resident of the Milky Way; here's my contribution to the sublime fecundity of the cosmos." In most retellings of this episode, this is the *pescadoro's* last thought before he's gored by a leaping swordfish.

A sleepless night spent eyeing a question mark on a man's ass is a philosophical night—*How did I get here, where am I going? Etcetera.* My mother says that when I got here, they called me Orange because I was a scion of harpoonists with a noble name that bespoke our lineage as natives of the island of Bismuth. And that it was rhyme-proof. And also that I was jaundiced at birth. Orange Whippey is a pair of names with plenty of precedence on our island. My nominal provenance can be found on ships' logs and public records stretching back to the early days of Yankee settlement here. It's my mother's job to answer the question of how I got here; it's my own job to say where I'm going, and all I can really say is that now that I'm in my late thirties, unmarried, and irregularly employed, I have come to realize that merely remaining alive is more of an achievement than I expected.

A surprisingly wide variety of namesakes are available to Bismuthians here off the North Atlantic coast. Our island has a winter population of just a few hundred people, but an impressive number of flip flops, Crocs, foul weather boots, and moccasins have trod upon Bismuth. We had actual natives here before the current versions of "native" arrived and gave them the Old World-crafted gifts of smallpox and Christianity. Nobody even knows what language the naturals, as the English called them, or the skraelings, as the Norse said, spoke or what they called themselves. The Northern Indians of Europe say that their ancient ancestors lived here—in fact, Snorri the Finlindian says his people, the Northern Indians, came from right here, when our little granite speck in the cold northeast Atlantic was taller, greener, warmer and the center of a bustling archipelago.

The way Snorri tells it at his occasional Bismuth Historical Society summer afternoon guest lectures is that his people migrated from Bismuth and the rest of the islands up through what would later become Labrador and Markland and Vinland and then east across the Arctic, fighting past Scandinavia, until they settled the northern coast of Europe and formed the countries of Finlindia and Estonindia way back in deep time. Their triumphs against the Vikings and Christians made them the most hated peoples in Europe for the most of two millennia, but their lack of assimilation into European culture had brought them into a sort of vogue here in the new century.

Snorri likes to visit Bismuth to maintain his ethnic claims of nativism, and I think he just likes it here more than he's willing to tell us—I can't see the profit in lurking about here otherwise. He speaks English better than many of my fellow Islanders, and claims to speak the language of every country that borders Finlindia, including the Estonindian dialect, and can communicate many significant gestures and vocalizations with bears and whales.

When I was a kid and still learning the nuances of island kinship and nativism—which was essentially us, the Islanders, who were divisible into people I was directly related to and people I was distantly related to, and them, the strangers, who could be broken down into many subgroups based on the regularity of their return to the island—Snorri and his ilk confounded my tidily bipolar sorting of the world. I think I first noticed him as the oddly dressed man with egregious eyebrows that reached up over the brim of his cap. I naturally assumed all such foreigners were so equipped and awaited puberty when I could sprout my own forehead feelers.

They didn't burst forth, thankfully, and by the time I could grow a reasonable mustache I had learned that in addition to Islanders and strangers, there were several billion other people on the planet who were all potential strangers whom I would never have to meet if I stuck it out here on Bismuth. Snorri wasn't the only Finlindian to spend time on the island. There are, presumably, brochures about Bismuth on Northern Indian travel agency shelves, but if you don't own your own boat like Snorri, this is an expensive destination involving an intercontinental flight, car rental, and a ferry ride, and then a stay at an inn or a mildly shabby rental house maintained by an uncaring person such as myself.

It's only been recently that another Northern Indian boat has frequented our waters. Unfamiliar boats, especially exotic ones capable of crossing the Atlantic, are watched like potentially rabid raccoons, so Waldena the Estonindian and her crew did not exactly sneak into our harbor. I hardly knew anything about her, though. She didn't seem like the ethnotouristic type. She and her crew drank at the island's only permanent restaurant, the Topsoil, where they gained a reputation for being cryptic and cold, which, considering our own legendary maziness and unamiability, is a significant cultural achievement. When I worked in the Topsoil kitchen, the waitresses hated serving them and found them stingy with tips, flirtation, and the English language. Waldena was the one who made me feel uneasy.

Her Estonindian hardboys were variants of a breed of masculinity I knew well enough already. She, however, snatched a little bit of my breath each time I saw her. She knew my name and that fact thrilled and frightened me unreasonably. Thoughts of beautiful exotic strangers who knew my name had sustained me through many kitchen shifts and fishing trips, but she was the first real one I'd ever encountered.

She and Snorri, like their countrymen, did not get along well. It's difficult for me to see the difference between an Estonindian and a Finlindian, but to them, it's as obvious as the difference between a Bostonian and a New Yorker, and one confuses the two at one's own peril. They're both the same race of people, inasmuch as "race" and "people" are meaningful terms. Their great schism lay in their treatment of whales, which represented the quintessence of cultural values to each of them. The Finlindians were pastoralists. They herded their whales and had domesticated breeds of them back before anyone in North American had even laid eyes on a goat. The Estonindians were hunters; as far as they were concerned, any domesticated fjord-bred Finlindian whale was a sad mutant aberration.

The people of the North Indies had maintained their traditional culture with much more zeal than their national neighbors. There were probably at least a few rune-covered centuries-old spoons in each Northern Indian kitchen from back in the day when people could really make spoons. Their language, which was mostly impenetrable to outsiders, was both antagonistically conservative—in the sense that old words died hard—and curiously round-heeled, since their lexicons would fall over, legs in the air, for anything new that came their way. So in the cutlery drawer next to the venerable spoonage—a good example of where English fails; we just don't have the vocabulary for the daily respect a Northern Indian has for proper utensils—were plastic sporks, which they kept for guests who wouldn't understand their spoons. Likewise for their spork-like language. They had no problem adding new terms like "cell phone" to the language, but returned happily to anachronistic phrases like "Hobomac spits in Loki's ear" for "wrong number." Their national languages had subdivided centuries ago, but they could seemingly understand each other the way a Mainer could follow a Cajun. I think their fervor for telecommunications might have its origin in their culture's automatic inclusion of all their history in so much of their daily life. Their cell phones were a logical next step from the rune stones and sagas that communicated to them across the gulfs of time. One of Snorri's devices was encased in yellowed ivory that I bet his ancestors had set aside in anticipation of the invention of mobile technology.

Even their names were a combination of the traditional and the progressive. Northern Indian surnames were post-parental; for instance, if Snorri—who, as far as I knew did not yet have a last name—had a daughter named Thora, his own name would change to Snorri Thorasfottir. Thus there were illegitimate parents—fathers and mothers with no last names—but not children. This practice is maintained in America by little kids who referred to their friends' parents as "Mrs. Larrysmother" and such. They loved proper names over there. Their houses, cars, and heirloom spoons all had proper names—some even had secret names which would only be whispered once in a lifetime. Snorri's boat, the *Honeypaws,* was like that. "Honeypaws" was just a nickname—he'd never tell anyone the boat's real name.

Snorri's claim to nativism on our island was backed up with his own translations of fragments of sagas and eddas that were themselves translations of vellums long lost to kleptomaniacal

Irish monks and Norse plunderers. The Northern Indian claim to coastal northeast America seemed like a case of wannabe colonialism to the rest of Western Europe until early twentieth-century linguists from Estonindia proved their language had origins in the Indo-American family instead of the Indo-European, like the rest of the Europe. Why the ancient Indians left Bismuth baffles historians. Snorri's explanations involve whales, bears, magic, and a quest for the Northern Indian version of El Dorado—Hyperborea, the mythical city of ivory and crystal hidden away at the North Pole. There's actually little Snorri tells anyone that doesn't start with a litany of Important Herring of Mythology or a sketch of what the world was like before the homo sapiens *arrivistes* paddled onto the stage.

Most of the Indians I know are people whom Snorri calls cousins and who think Snorri is a pedantic kook. My own family name is Whippey, as it was for my Yankee ancestors, who saw themselves as the original inhabitants of Bismuth. The Whippeys and Oranges of yore were whalers and some were even captains. Many were Quakers, which meant they saw their profit margins fulfilled by working indentured servants to death instead of African slaves. This moral high ground, along with our geographic isolation, gave us a sense of dominion over all the other peoples and creatures of the planet, which is why we pretend our current endemic poverty is ennobling.

There were Indians, and there are Yankees, but Bismuth has more exotic surnames on its gravestones than Ellis Island does on its customs logs. Not that there are many actual bodies in our graveyards. For every family plot with its listing headstones, there's a lichen-spangled marble cenotaph with a dozen names of sailors who died at sea. There's a cenotaph for Bismuthians who died trying to rescue those who died at sea. There's even a memorial for dogs that died trying to rescue the shipwrecked. There is a colored graveyard for Africans and French-Canadians. There's a praying Indian graveyard. After death became less segregated, Portuguese, Basque, Hawaiian, and Scandinavian names became as common on the stones as the Yankees' own biblical concordance of graven names.

I've broken some of the cardinal rules of island life. I probably should have died at sea, although that's not as popular as it once was. Or I shouldn't have come back from the mainland when I was finished wasting the state's money and my professors' time at Norumbega University. I should have fixed up my dad's lobster boat, the *Beothuk,* into a swordfishing charter boat instead of watching it rot through most of my twenties. If I were to remain here on Bismuth, unmarried and insufficiently employed, the least I could have done is be found frozen to death in my house after a winter of drinking Sterno. I left Bismuth for college in America because I just couldn't take it any longer on my island. And because it was mostly free. We have a high school on the island; all anyone has to do is get a B average, and a scholarship for the state university awaits. This is because we are both clinically disadvantaged and a cultural institution— and because there are so few of us that actually make it to college, the subsidy is chump change for the state.

The first complete rotation of my now cyclic discontent occurred when I came back to Bismuth because I just couldn't take it any longer in America. The continent was as big and stupid as my aunt's hairdo and my other uncle's gut. I was accustomed to people who were experts at being clannish and small-minded; I thought my classmates' callow attempts at bigotry and the school's attempt at bureaucratic insularity were laughably inept. I graduated in the late 1980s and returned that summer. The bequeathers of my scholarships should have been delighted, since their plan all along had been to enlighten us with culture and higher education. It's odd though; that's not how islanders see it. Getting an off-island education isn't necessarily a stigma—as long as one doesn't flaunt it—but returning to the island is somehow an automatic tragedy, as if the rest of your island life were a sequel that should never have been filmed.

Instead, it was my parents who fled the island, once I returned and settled back into the house, which they had tried to call "their" house for a while, but which I remembered as "ours." I'm third generation of Whippey here, which isn't that big a historic deal the way it might be elsewhere. It does mean that the house was paid for long ago and the mock-mortgage I'm supposed to be sending my father in Florida every month is just his way of opposing what he sees as my desuetude, though that is not the way he would phrase it. I oppose his opposition, naturally, by not paying him very often. I presume this relationship will continue until one of us dies, at which point we will have to re-negotiate.

I'm not the only member of my species here. Fishing is almost impossibly expensive as a small business on Bismuth and everywhere else in the Northeast. It was getting to be that one could count on fishing for providing severed fingers, bankruptcy, and divorce, but not a living wage. I crewed here and there, mostly with Mr. Lucy on his stupid boat. I worked in the kitchen sometimes at the Topsoil. There were other guys like me on Bismuth. There always were. Everyone likes to point out the Quaker captains' houses in town, but throughout history most Bismuthians were crew. Centuries after whaling ended and decades after fishing sputtered out, our island's population has thinned dramatically, and men such as myself are considered lucky to find work of any kind. Personally, I do not consider finding work to be any kind of luck at all and have probably said so too publicly. The one cardinal rule I could not break was that Islanders will always be Islanders, which is as much an ancestry as it is an albatross.

So, I do know something of where I came from, mostly because I hardly left. How I got to be on Mr. Lucy's trawler, the *Wendy's Mom*, skippered by Mr. Lucy—the scourge of my precious idle time—and crewed by his doltish son, Donny—my nemesis and companion since birth—is a tale of rescue and near-shipwreck that begins on an even punier granite speck.

Wreck Rock is reachable two ways: by boat, with difficulty, at high tide, and by mudshoe at low, but it's within shouting distance of shore. Wreck Rock's really Osgood Isle, named for the Englishman who supposedly stood upon it and declared New England to be rich in sassafras—which he thought was a cure for syphilis—and gold and enslaveable people and all his. It goes by Wreck Rock amongst locals for self-evident reasons. I'd had his island to myself since I'd unwisely decided to mudwalk out there and sieve for seagum.

The best mudshoes are made from old-school lobster traps and resembled snowshoes. Mine had been cardboard reinforced with more cardboard, and I had lost them mid-trudge. That muck at low tide is worse than quicksand, and I was knee-deep with my toes being bathed in snails' digestive juices before I realized the shit I was in. If there's one thing to be learned from Tarzan movies, it's that without a vine or helpful elephant, quicksand is lethal. The arrogant explorer has enough time to realize just what a horrible man he is, and, if he'd been more decent, a passing chimpanzee would have extended a branch to him. But he'd been a bad bwana, and, after a couple of gloopy air bubbles, his safari hat is the only thing that disturbs the dun porridge.

But we Bismuthians have spent centuries scrounging our shoreline, and although most of us can't swim, we do know what to do when the ooze has seized us: we lean forward and belly-crawl. Which is how I managed to lose my seagum gear and spend the afternoon covered in mud on Wreck Rock shouting and waving until Donny's sister noticed me. When she came back, Wendy Lucy told me that their dad was going out scalloping with the tide at about five AM, and he'd pick me up then. "How come you didn't crawl back?" she yelled across the mudflat. Which then became more or less my main topic for ponderment, until it was replaced by Donny's BÖC tat onboard the *Wendy's Mom*.

Wreck Rock is said to have gone missing a few times. It's just a jumble of gray rocks with a seaweed skirt, and within its cracks and more permanent puddles it's the home to any number of bitey, stingy, and pokey things—which, if I had died there, would have eaten and lived within my body for months as they attended to the final stages of my disassembly. I suppose some serious tide could swamp the rocks for some period, and bigger landmasses have been left off charts. It's certainly legendary on Bismuth, inasmuch that there are no historical records or witnesses to anything that is claimed to have occurred there. If the gulls could tell its story, it would be an epic of shitting and screaming, and their bards did indeed tell me that tale all through the daylight hours. The seagulls would probably have been the second or third stage in my disassembly. I imagine part of what they were screaming was their intent to start in on the soft parts of me as soon as I was too putrefied to defend myself. I challenged their sovereignty of the rock for a while, as I searched for artifacts useful to my survival, or which would at least distract me for a few minutes. I ascertained that the Viking runes remained nowhere to be found, never mind deciphered, that boxes of booze stashed there by prohibition-era Kennedys remained hidden, and that nothing even vaguely dubloonish was to be discovered.

"You could have just crawled back!" yelled Wendy again, "Why didn't you crawl back?!" Maybe she thought I was being petulant, but I was trying to figure why that hadn't occurred to me back on the mud. She answered for me: "You asshole!"

True enough. I would have said "idiot," but I couldn't muster much of a counter-argument. Wendy and I had once shared something more than a clinch in the old Korean War watchtower. I don't think she had ever liked me much in high school, but by the time I was twenty-five and back on the island, I had grown out of my adolescent uglies—my limbs were mostly even, my facial features fairly congruent, plenty of hair—and I hadn't yet acquired the paunch and hygienic decrepitude that middle-aged, single male Islanders usually exhibit. The same could have been said for her. The moon washed the concrete walls of the war ruin to a fleecy gray, the humid ocean breeze made undressing seem reasonable, and, well, there was beer and weed. But by twenty-five, we are supposed to be in the final stages of this sort of mating behavior; your destiny had already shipped you off-island, or you were going to stay and further your genetic line. Which is to say we were both old enough to know I should have been nicer to her afterward or at least spoken with her now and then since.

Throughout that day, as I explored the rock and made treaties with the gulls, I received visitors. Wendy came down the

beach again to test her rock-throwing skills. By her third visit, we were back on waving terms. Nathan walked by with his
dog and waved to me. Manuel and his guys chugged by on the
Manny's Girls and waved to me. Mitchell drove by in his pick-up
and shouted that Mr. Lucy would pick me up later, and I yelled
back that I already knew and, "Would you feed Rover for me?"
He waved. Rover is my cat, Mitchell is my neighbor. Late in the
afternoon, three strangers in kayaks, all women, paddled by.

"We could probably rescue you if we have to," one yelled. I
just waved.

"I'll report you, OK?" I said I was all set, but she was fussing
with her tricorder or cell phone or whatever it was on the lanyard she'd pulled from beneath her jacket.

"There's no reception," she shouted. I told her I was still all
set.

A little after dark, Mitchell came back and shined his truck's
headlights onto the rock from the beach. "Hey, Orange," he
called.

"What?"

"Where's your pot?"

"In the cabinet under the coffee maker."

"No, I found that, where's your weed?"

I couldn't really see why the seagulls felt they needed sole possession of the rock. They didn't do anything other than shit and
screech and flap around. They didn't have nests here, and they
didn't seem to be bothering with the mussels and such. Eventually, they grew accustomed to me and reduced their strafings
and bombardments to runs every five or six minutes. I didn't
know if a human skull would hold together long in the water. I
also didn't know if a hermit crab would grow to fill up a shell

that size. But I could see why the crabs were curious about me. They were willing to walk up my fingers and well up my arms, presumably to investigate whether they could make off with any parts of me for residences. The barnacles and I had relatively little to say to each other. In time, I realized I was going to be without anything to eat or drink until the next day. I figured, though, I'd gone twice that time without any sustenance and without even a conscious thought. All I needed to do was nothing—just loaf and sleep. What I hadn't factored into my equation was sobriety. One very important resource to surviving an entire night on a rock is alcohol. There were all sorts of substances that can get you by, but not on the rock. I made it though. My power to remain and do nothing has only strengthened over the years, even if my ability to sleep has deteriorated.

Sometime around dawn, after my night of surpassingly cold discomfort, the *Wendy's Mom* arrived. There's no real way to land at the rock, so Donny threw me a line while his dad kept the bow into the waves. I held the line and waded out a bit onto a slippery hump of seaweed. Then Mr. Lucy opened up the throttle and towed me away. That night had been one of the less pleasant ones of my life, but I was surprised by how much worse I could feel after having been dragged off the rock, through the frigid water, and onto the boat. Mr. Lucy figured I owed him a trip's labor for the tow and told me to go below and get dressed. Donny let me choose from the pile of rank, communal clothes and told me his sister said I was an asshole.

I don't know why God rammed an oar up Mr. Lucy's ass, but Mr. Lucy seemed to use it to his advantage. One could muse that it attracted some sort of telluric current, one that charged his plodding determination to wring every last drop of suffering from a day that was otherwise merely soaked in toil. As one of God's stiff and unbending agents upon the earth, Mr. Lucy saw to cultivating his rectitude into a salty pillar of disagreeability and impossibly regular adherence to an agenda of self-abuse that began long before dawn each day and ended each evening with the man making arrangements with his Lord to find the next day colder, rainier, and full of heavier things to make other people lift.

From what I know of dawn, it is an unaccommodating place where one's ears ring constantly, and gravity is twice normal. Its sky casts an ulcerous pink haze; the atmosphere enters one's body to give new life to every pain and ache that had ever resided therein. Those who arrive at dawn find themselves there too late or too early, beset by boiling stomachs and curdling brains, doomed to either wait for or rush to whatever burdensome beasts that they must carry to the far horizon of the land of the rising sun.

The lords of dawn are men such as Mr. Lucy. Their boats and trucks scrub away the shadows before them each morning, and they bide their time in the empty hours fashioning yokes and manacles for the unwary who stumble into their toils. They remember when dawn was hours earlier and when they had to kill a hundred Nazis every morning just to get to the percolator. They knew that if every young man in this God-fearing country would just get up at 5:30 AM and perform a modest flag ceremony, the upwelling of patriotism and personal pride would hasten Judgment Day upon us and we could get an early start on adoring Jesus in the afterlife before the tourists arrived.

Thus was I employed upon Mr. Lucy's trawler, the *Wendy's Mom*, despite my abhorrence of all manners of trials, toils, tribulations, and especially getting up early to go a-scalloping.

CHAPTER TWO

Smugglers on the Polk

T he Blue Öyster Cult symbol is an upside-down question mark with exclamation marks radiating from the shared dot at noon, three, and nine o'clock. BÖC was supposed to be America's Black Sabbath. In the 1970s, Canada evidently had not yet discovered Satan and had to make do with BTO, which I don't think had a symbol or an umlaut. Though they did share TCB—Taking Care of Business—as a motto with Elvis. Anyway, I don't get why we got the shellfish and England got their Satanic Majesties. This country, certainly the island of Bismuth, was settled by Europeans who were absolutely convinced of Satan's daily role in their lives and of the imminent apocalypse. America invented Rock and Roll by making the children of slaves sell their souls to the Devil and their songs to Elvis. But America invented Mormons and Scientologists too, and our Goths are found at Grimble's Cybercafe, not cathedrals. It's probably worth considering that music itself was considered the Devil's work by our grim ancestors. So I guess Donny was trying to make the best of his cultural circumstances when he got his tattoo.

Mr. Lucy broke my reverie on the enigma of American music's imprecise embrasure of the unholy and its influence on body markings of indigenous lower-middle-class white male islanders: "There's coffee."

I nuked my mug of water and stirred in the instant coffee. We Bismuthians take our coffee with sweetened evaporated milk poured from the canister. If you add vodka to the coffee and milk, you get an Irish Russian, which is usually made right in the mug and stirred with a fishy finger. Donny and I had drunk all his fifth the night before, so I had a virgin Irish Russian.

"We gotta go to the *Polk* today," Mr. Lucy told us. "Donny stays onboard. You go out."

The only pleasant thing about dredging for scallops is that they are not fish, so I was happy enough to skip the scallops. On the other hand, the *Polk* was real trouble. Back before the Navy used it for target practice, it had been a dutiful World War Two transport ship, too rheumatic to make it much beyond the coast. During the Korean War, when Bismuth had last been fortified (against, presumably, the North Korean Navy), the USS *Sarah Polk* ended its buoyant days and was run aground on a sandbank, where it was used as a watchtower for the Coast Guard. The Bismuthians posted there found the *Polk* to be a convenient waystation for smuggling, which by the 1950s—post-prohibition, pre-drugs—had become a fairly quaint operation of tariff avoidance. The government clamped down hard on this offshore free-enterprise zone and deeded the hulk over to the Navy to use as target practice. They blew holes in it for decades, giving it its present rusty cheese grater appearance. The Navy guns also opened up holes in the *Polk*'s hull that made for easy, enclosed parking for small boats and greatly facilitated its usefulness as a smuggler's depot. You could get tetanus from just looking at the thing, and you could get shot for going anywhere near it, as some windsurfers found out a few years ago.

Bismuth boasts fortifications from every single war, from King Philip's through the Korean. We were also rumored to be on the list of high-profile Homeland Security targets, and the fabled grant money for our self-defense was eagerly anticipated. I wouldn't have guessed that Koreans would be the ones to finally breach our defenses, but it was the Koreans who were waiting for us at the *Polk*. I don't think anyone would have guessed that after centuries of having little to offer the world other than arms for oar-pulling, Bismuth had something Koreans were willing to pay for in actual cash money.

We tied up on the ocean side of the *Polk* since the *Wendy's Mom* was too big to fit through the hull holes. Even though it was a slowly powdering hulk, the *Polk* was still larger than any building on Bismuth. About two stories up were a pair of guys with rifles pointed, I was certain, directly between my eyes. I would have hidden, but Mr. Lucy seemed to have expected as much. Being a target didn't seem to faze him.

"Those are our boys," he said, pointing with his chin. "And now you're the man." To make himself understood to strangers, Mr. Lucy, like many Bismuthian elders, had to pucker up like he was leaning in to kiss a gorilla between the bars at a zoo. This is because the seagum he chewed—the same stuff we were selling—induces neuropathy in a chronic chewer's lips. Our accent renders words like "are" and "our" and many other words mutually pronounceable as "ah," so context is very important in conversations with senior islanders. In fact, it probably takes a native listener to comprehend a native speaker. Not that it matters much. The weather, the condition of the boat, the price of whatever—everything is always unsatisfactory to guys like Mr. Lucy, so grunts usually suffice.

The Korean smugglers took a break from aiming their rifles at us and lowered us a rope ladder. There's no doubt that climbing the rigging is a skill embedded in the Bismuthian gene pool, but Mr. Lucy's elbows and knees had stopped following orders reliably long ago. I was to replace his son Donny, who had been thrown overboard in disgust last time, as the bagman. Bismuthians were probably among the first North Americans to ever lay eyes on Koreans, back in the whaling days. Perhaps some loose-lipped swabbie had disclosed our island's secret during an expedition to the Pacific and opened up this trade between otherwise entirely unlike cultures.

When Mr. Lucy had declared that I was the man, what he meant was I was the monkey. I climbed up the rope ladder and one of the Korean men helped me over the railing.

"You are the new American?" he asked in a measured tone.

"Sort of."

"And Donny, how is he?"

"His dad locked him in the cabin." The right answer, evidently. The Koreans brightened. We made our exchange. They gave me a plastic shopping bag full of currency and a small package wrapped in white paper and tied with twine like something from a butcher. I waited for them to ask me if I was going to count the money, since this was my first chance to play a scene I had watched in uncountable movies. They didn't; I didn't even know how much money there was supposed to be anyway, so I just shoved it all into the hockey bag I'd lugged the seagum up in. I realized too late that I should have been implying my readiness to hit specific nerve clusters in their bodies and break their bones with strategic karate chops, or that Mr. Lucy was prepared to vaporize them with a shoulder-launched missile.

The Korean who had been silently staring at me since I arrived took off his aviators. "You are a beer-drinking American?" Like his partner, he was gimlet-eyed, but I think he seemed more genuinely interested in my opinion about beer than intimidating me.

"Yeah, I guess."

"You drink German beers? You know many American beers are German beers? That the brewers use ancient German formulations that demand simplicity and purity?"

"Like Budwesier?"

"No, that is Czech."

The other Korean said, "We would like you to sit down there and to wear this blindfold." My time for dramatic headkicks and weapon-snatching was already over, so I did as I was told. I heard the sound of two bottles being opened. "In your own words, we would like you to describe the qualities of taste you perceive in each of these beers."

Both beers were presented cold and with a seemingly equal amount of head. One tasted familiar and pleasant, but when I considered it against the other, it seemed to have an almost cloying sweetness to it. The other beer, while initially tasting bitter, had a more rewarding flavor and left me feeling as if I'd just drunk a slice of astringent wheat bread.

"Now," asked my Korean publican, "if you were to choose a beer to drink more of, which would it be?" I indicated the bready one.

The two exclaimed to each other in Korean, and then the staring-master Korean said, "Take off your blindfold Mr. Orange Whippey! You have helped us, but we are still in disaccord. The beer you have chosen is from your own geographic region, it is called a small batch micropub brew. The other beer is a famous and common German beer. We compliment your palate and your senses of taste. However, we remain vexed as to whether German national standards have deteriorated, or whether American indigenous brewers have made advancements in formulations that had otherwise been unsurpassed in all of Europe for half of a millennium, or whether, in fact, this American small batch micropub brew should be more properly considered a German beer, despite its origin."

For the sake of comparative research we drank the rest of the microbrew growler and the rest of the German six. I felt cheerier, but my critical faculties did not improve. I went to piss over the side and saw Mr. Lucy in the boat. I waved. He did something with his arms that looked like yelling. Mr. Ill John produced a very nice looking bottle and said, "This is Japanese whiskey. Regrettably, it is superior to both Scots and Irish whiskies. The controlled conditions of the Japanese indoor peat bogs disallows some of the micro-organic flavoring agents that characterize regional whiskies; however, the purity and tastes cannot be rivaled."

I too plunged off of the *Polk*, but I think it was my own fault. I recall telling the Koreans I was going to make some coffee. Then I was cold and drowning and being pulled in to the boat by Mr. Lucy for the second time in two days. "Why can't you fucking kids keep the fucking money dry?!" he shouted and told me to go get changed. I let Donny out of the cabin and the smug prick offered me my choice of the rank, communal clothes.

CHAPTER THREE

Seagum

We Bismuthians have become experts in the multitudinous forms (or lacks of form) of various sea snots and marine mucilages and their relative worth in Asian markets. Somewhere, just over the horizon, there were factory ships with safes full of dollars waiting to buy up every depilation of the beaches' scaly dander; the carbuncles, worms, issuances, and repulsive undulants that the islanders had a particular talent for harvesting, due to the lessons of their ancestors in how to avoid them. It seems that the more nettlesome and gloopy they are, the more they fetch. Some are rushed into life-support chambers of the cargo holds to be delivered still quivering and secreting. Others are sealed up to ferment and further decompose what little cellular structure (or overabundance thereof) they once had into fizzing, bioactive delicacies.

Seagum, hauled up in sieves or sloughed off more properly piscine catches, is our island's specialty. It is denser than jellyfish but lacks even their animalian characteristics. Its particular link in the great chain of being is difficult to determine—too coagulated to be a liquid, too soupy for a solid, it doesn't even seem to belong to the kingdoms of plant or animal. As one early taxonomist put it, it was "known to produce an urticative fret in bathers." This is known to natives as "the hivies," which, along with goose flesh and hypothermia, and the uncountable methods of drowning, is among the many reasons we do not swim.

If you ever crack open a clam or lobster or really any of the ocean's many grotesqueries, at some point you are going to wonder about the first man to do so and how hungry he had to be. I figure it was the very first man to see one. You put a man and a pile of seagum—or frog spittle, or fish milch, or what have you—on an empty beach together, and by tomorrow he will have looked at it, poked it, rolled in it, eaten it, washed his hair with it, and tried to build a shelter with it. By the next day, he'd be trying to mate with it. Sure, maybe this is the vaunted ingenuity that has raised us above the rest of the world's creatures, but I think it shows us to be collective slow learners. Mistakes are made to be repeated—just look at us Bismuthians: we're still here aren't we?

Raw seagum is processed in a few stages. First, it has to be mashed. For the basic homebrew seagum, this is done simply with two buckets, a pair of waders, and a woman. She stomps side to side, not unlike the rolling stride of a seaman, squishing a bucketful of seagum with each foot until it changes from a gloppy blob to a pourable goo. The liquefied seagum is then poured into shallow, wide trays and left to dry for several days. It dessicates into a leathery film that is cut into strips and preserved in layers of salt and dried grass. Seagum is what gives us Islanders our distinctive slack and rubbery locution. Like betel and khat and coca, it's a mild stimulant that we chew like cud. It helps us haul in the nets hour after hour and gives us an unfounded sense of mild euphoria. It also slowly destroys the nerves in one's lips. Most senior islanders are unable to whistle or produce a pucker, making for a manner of speaking that most offislanders find difficult to understand and unpleasant to listen to.

For some of us, seagum-gathering falls somewhere between

wasting time and odd-jobbery—yet another way to make a boat payment or at least to ignore the payment-due notice. Donny's dad, Mr. Lucy—whom I disliked only a bit less than his fuck-headed son—showed an entrepreneurial zeal, unknown on Bismuth since the days of the grim Quaker captains, when he established the seagum trade with a pair of tight-lipped Koreans.

Thanks to my own lack of entrepreneurship, I found myself press-ganged by Mr. Lucy for occasional scallop dredgings and other low-paying forms of drudgery on the *Wendy's Mom*. It was usually a couple nights worth of toil and indignity on my part, and my pay was usually blown at the Topsoil before I even made it home. I was accustomed to Mr. Lucy's addlepated, inarticulable grudges and Donny's general repugnance; my own contribution to the *esprit de corps* was typically shirking sullenness.

But today Mr. Lucy seemed almost cheery; he had a hold full of scallops and a bag full of cash. He wouldn't tell me what was in the package he had taken from the hockey bag, and I noticed that he hadn't unwrapped it. On our way back to the island, I stood next to him in the wheelhouse and told him I'd never seen a Korean or any kind of offislander chew seagum.

"Tiger testes," he said with the poor lip control of a lifelong chewer.

"What?"

"The Koreans grind it into a powder and sell it as counterfeit tiger testes."

"People buy powdered tiger testes?"

"Yeah, it supposed to give'm a hard-on like a tiger's."

Donny asked, "Tiger hard-ons?"

"They snort the stuff and then fuck, I guess," said Mr. Lucy, "Supposed to make'm tigers."

This was news to us. "I'm gonna try it," Donny said. I'd been thinking the same thing. I was also thinking I was very grateful that I'd be off *Wendy's Mom* before Donny could begin his experiment in priapism.

"Don't," his father told him.

Mr. Lucy let me borrow his cell to check my messages. I doubted I had any, but I wanted to make a show of it, so Donny and Mr. Lucy would understand that I had a life beyond being dragged onto their boat. I was surprised when someone answered.

"Who's this?"

"Orange?" replied a groggy, familiar voice.

"Mitchell?"

"Hey Orange, how you doin'?"

"I'm fine, Mitchell, how are you, and why the hell are you answering my phone?"

"I just got up," he replied.

"Where's Rover?"

"Denise says she just fed her."

"Denise?"

Mitchell told Denise, "Say hi to Orange," and she shouted hey.

"You're just waking up with Denise Souza in my house?"

"Sylvie's here too."

"You're just waking up with Denise and Sylvie Souza in my house?"

"What are you, homesick? Where's your coffee filters?"

Hate and envy are curiously complimentary emotions that defy concise articulation. I handed the phone back to Mr. Lucy and told him I didn't know how to turn it off. We were still an hour or two off the island; I joined Donny in the cabin before

Mr. Lucy could assign me more chores.

Donny was using a shot glass and a cereal bowl to crush up a few strips of seagum. "Tiger cunt," he told me.

"What?"

"I got a tiger stiffy, I figure I'm gonna want some tiger pussy. You think this stuff would work on girls?"

"I dunno, does Viagra?" I replied.

"Viagra's for guys. Tiger balls could probably go either way."

"But this is seagum," I reminded him.

"Yeah, but you don't have to say."

"What are you going to do, tell a girl that it's not actually counterfeit tiger testes, it's the real thing?"

"I'll just tell her it's coke."

We used Mr. Lucy's drinking straw to snort the roughly ground seagum. I was a little giddy. It's not often in one's adult life that a brand-new drug comes one's way. It was something like fiberglass and rocksalt, with an afternote of low tide.

"Maybe we should have cut it with something," I croaked.

"I take it straight," testified Donny.

We huffed the other lines and hoped we'd filled our tanks with the tiger. I saw Donny's nose start to bleed before I noticed my own trickle.

"Tiger, tiger, burning bright!" I told Donny.

"Fuck yeah!"

We both ran our fingers around the bowl and rubbed the remaining powder on our gums. Donny was starting to fade in a red haze. Or, rather, every blood vessel in my eyes was bursting. I began to feel as if I were perspiring internally. My bones spun in their sockets. There was a hurricane in one ear and angry fleas in the other. I felt my windpipe go bullfrog and heard Donny rasp, "Cocksucking Christ!" as if he were a Tuvan throat singer. I spent my last moments of respiration clawing my way out of the cabin.

Mr. Lucy soon had us both in the cockpit with buckets of seawater between our knees. Speaking and thinking were impossible. I held my head in the bucket for as long as I could and then wept and sputtered as I tried to suck air through my engorged throat. Donny was similarly engaged. Mr. Lucy expostulated on our substandard humanity and locked himself in the wheelhouse. I could breathe, but my ribs were trying to wriggle out of my chest. I felt my eyeballs liquefy and trickle down the back of my throat. I wanted to purge myself, sea-cucumber style, by barfing my toxic internal organs out onto the deck. I held my head between my knees, wrapped my arms around my legs and felt my entire body puckering.

Then I felt something bumping into my forehead. The stuff worked.

Donny the Tiger was roaring, "Dad, Dad! It works!"

"You two fucking idiots stay away from me!" Mr. Lucy shouted from the barricaded wheelhouse.

I did not feel erect. I felt as if I had the very hook that would land the leviathan. I felt as if I could support all the troops at once. I felt that, if I ever pissed again, I would bore a hole in the moon. Leaping porpoise, cresting narwhal, electric eel, anything but a turtle gliding gently into the quiet deep.

An hour later we were heading past the breakwater into the harbor. Donny and I had kept to our benches and overturned the buckets on our laps. Donny was drumming on his with his thumbs. "I'm going to the fucking Topsoil as soon as we dock."

"Nobody's gonna be there this early," I told him.

"There's waitresses."

"You mean Mrs. Barrow?"

"Well, there'll be fucking tourists anyway."

"Yeah, like you'll be fucking tourists."

"Fuck you, Orange."

"You got a bone to pick with me, Donny?"

Donny launched himself at me, more bellowing manatee than tiger. Later, the bruises and cuts would remind me of his assault, but my initial impression was only of my face being pressed into the soft and stinking blubber of his chest, his sulfurous breath, and the sting of his saliva in my eyes, as his flippers bashed my head side to side.

I was still sitting on the bench, Donny astride me, flapping. I tried to heave him off my lap and felt instead an alarming sense of pleasure as my marling spike rubbed along his mizzen mast. This served to reverse our polarity sufficiently enough to send us back into our corners of the cockpit. I took the offensive next, figuring a headbutt to the bridge of his nose would be a strategic response; however, due to the pitch of the boat and my martial unsuitability, I found myself giving him a glancing wet willy as I pitched overboard.

I was lucky there were so many illegal lobster pots there, clogging the harbor approach. I was able to grab a buoy without foundering entirely. I yelled and waved and found myself unwilling to use the first person, screaming instead, "Man overboard!" It was a while before the *Wendy's Mom* began a slow, reluctant arc back to me. I found the most effective way to stay above water was to straddle a lobster buoy, as if I were riding a bike with a banana seat underwater. It was soothing. I rode and pedaled and paddled until Mr. Lucy circled the boat up and threw me a life jacket, hollering, "You're not getting back on my boat, Whippey!"

CHAPTER FOUR

The Angie Baby

I t's only about twenty minutes with no wake to get from the harbor entrance to the docks, but it's a hell of a walk. Bismuth's breakwater was our Great Wall of China, a half-mile-long stone wall that was built in the fat days of whaling to protect the harbor from storms and navies. It had later been fortified with barges full of rocks and huge piles of cement rubble from some off-island civic catastrophe. It afforded one a prospect from which to look back on the town and wish one was much farther away. I dogpaddled—with my newly stiffened daggerboard—over to it from the buoys and tried to dry off some. My wardrobe had, for the last couple of days, been an assortment of abandoned T-shirts and sweats from the boat. I took them off and lay them on the rocks to dry in the sun. I sat on the life vest down in a gap in the rocks to get out of the wind. My lingam was still good for surf-casting, and I was very uncomfortable with my level of exposure.

My altogetherness there on the breakwater wasn't altogether unprecedented. Our island lacked warm water and any stretch of sand pleasant or private enough to bare one's parts, but the breakwater's rocks and distance from civilization had a way of inspiring the youthful and exhibitionistic. I was neither. I wished there was a chart I could consult to tell me when my own personal high tide would ebb. So I laid there on the rocks, basking, with my gnomon seemingly stuck on noon, trying to think my way into de-tumescence. I thought about poor lonely Rover and how Mitchell might be at this very moment trying to trick her into the microwave. This was also a mistake, since thinking of Mitchell and Rover led to thinking about how the Souza sisters used to play mermaid out here at the end of the breakwater. Or were they playing siren? The fisherfolk of Bismuth, after days at sea among the worst squalor of manliness, felt very welcome when they returned to harbor on a warm summer afternoon. And they all knew how to find their binoculars in a hurry.

What else was there to do on the very granite slabs that had pressed into the tawny bodies of Denise and Sylvie? I took the situation in hand. My gaff, obdurately unpersuaded, seemed to have other ideas, or perhaps was finally free of ideas. At times, desperate ones, my brain has had me convinced that my body was a vehicle of pain and humiliation that I should just junk. At this time, however, the body seemed free of the mind's influence and was running rampant, as if it bore the very trident of Poseidon. It was resplendently disempowering. Ghostly Souza hands did not join my own.

I was bruised and soggy, and images of Donny kept intruding. My lips were bluing. There were crabs and buggy things everywhere. I was leaning on barnacles. I was a complete failure as a human being. My genetic line had no future. Some Europeans used to believe narwhal tusks served the same purpose as tiger testes. But the Arctic peoples knew better; they called them corpse whales, due to their pallor. I had that kind of stiff on my hands. I was actually whimpering in frustration when I heard my name.

I peered over the rocks and saw Angie on the *Angie Baby*

waving to me. "Heard you might need a lift," she called. There are very few degrees of separation between us islanders. Angie is Mitchell's ex-wife. The *Angie Baby* used to be his trawler. In fact, it's one of the nicest boats operating from the island. "If you can get over here, I'll bring you back to the docks. But hurry up, Orange!"

Angie, of all people. Why did the sea-gods, or at least Mr. Lucy, send Angie? There were so many other Islanders who did not trigger my vanity, my shame. I'd spent years cultivating the belief that this woman was my cousin. If she were my cousin, I could steal a few peeks now and then and continue to admire the way she'd never lost her youthful roundness, the curves that turn to crags and angles so quickly on so many islanders. I could sleep over on her and Mitchell's couch, and we could shuffle around each other in our underwear in the morning without too much fuss. If Angie were my cousin, the fact that toenail polish matched her lipstick and her habit of wearing only a sweatshirt, a bathing suit, and a kerchief for half the summer would merely be cute and practical; the way her brown pupils contrasted with the whites of her eyes in the same manner that her tan line contrasted with her pale skin when her suit slipped a little off her hip wouldn't fixate me at all.

I was grateful when the two of them split. It meant I could go back to drinking with Mitchell, quit showering before I went over. Angie had always been too competent for me. Too put-together. It was intimidating. People like her had too much presence of mind, too little self-consciousness. Well, maybe just enough—like just enough lipstick and enough poise to pilot her own boat.

Doing my best to crouch behind the rocks, I pulled on the damp sweatpants and t-shirt. I strapped myself into the life preserver and clambered down into the squishy seaweed and cold swirls of ocean. Once I was submerged, I took my tiller and tucked its tip under the preserver, hoping, absurdly, to preserve some dignity. After paddling over, I had some trouble climbing up the little ladder hanging over the stern.

"C'mon, let's go, Orange. We're drifting," Angie told me as she grabbed my life jacket and hauled me up. My limbs were stiff, the ladder meant for more sure-footed swimmers. Angie hauled me in over the side, grabbing my arm, the straps on my vest, and finally my very own windlass. "Jesus!" she said, surprised. The Lord's name was more than I could articulate at the moment. She got me the rest of the way in, but kept a firm handhold.

Entirely deprived of language, I gave her a look that was meant to communicate my appreciation of being rescued, my appreciation of the awkwardness of the predicament, my regret at imposing on her, my boyish vulnerability, my acknowledgement of the comedic situation and the fact that nothing like this had ever occurred before, my acknowledgment of my own virility and masculinity, my appreciation of her femininity and firm hand, my talent to be discrete, my ability to take care of myself after this was over, my willingness to sink back into the brine, a wry awareness of what I presumed to be our suppressed mutual attraction over the years, and a rueful apology for remaining friends with Mitchell—along with a sidenote of resigned awareness of the way we must all live in each other's pockets here on the island. I hoped the extra whites of my eyes expressed an urgent sincerity, and that their craquelment indicated an intriguing but safe degree of derangement.

If I'd been turned over, she would have had a perfect bouncer's toss handhold—one hand on the collar, the other on the belt.

Her grip, though, suggested I was not to be thrown back. If she were fishing, and I'd been a harbor seal, she would have been in a good position to gut me, chum the waters with my organs, and maybe pickle my pizzle for a souvenir.

But she was Angie, whom I had tried so hard not to think about over the years. She'd always been friendly but guarded, treating me a bit like the competition, someone prone to lead Mitchell down unpaved paths of dissolution and boorish bon-hommerie. There was never any profit to explaining to her that it had really been the other way around. Had I ever admired her unbashful way with a bikini? Certainly. Did I know that our friend, Laura, who did half the island's hair, barbered the fine brown hairs on the back of Angie's neck once a month? I did. And I had fully imagined running my lips down along those soft bristles, feeling them tickle the rim of my nostrils as I nuzzled her neck, taking my time deciding whether to continue kissing, licking, biting all the way down her backbone, or to take a tack and veer over her shoulder, maybe taking her collarbone be-tween my teeth on my way to the notch of her clavicle, where I would rest my nose as I unbuttoned her shirt and drew my face between her breasts, searching for the dot of perfume she would have harbored somewhere in that soft warmth.

Indeed, in my imagination, Angie and I had gallivanted more than a few times. Sometimes, poor Mitchell would have been relegated to an oarsman down below, chained to his bench. Sometimes I shared his shackles and Angie, the princess whose galleon we rowed, would slip below, point at me, and command, "Bathe him and bring him to my cabin,"—her cabin where she'd napped and frigged herself to the rhythms of waves and the oar pullers' straining, incessant sweeps. Thus I'd shoot a glance at Mitchell, my fellow traveler all these hard years at sea, as if to say, "Who am I to disobey the princess? I'll try to steal you some food from above."

Angie was a good sailor, with a tool for every job and a place for every tool. She was back from setting her wheel on "Thereabouts, slowly," and unwrapping a rubber before I could even get out of the preserver. I don't even know how her shorts came off. My yardarm seemed to go straight from her hand to her lovely cunt, without her grip ever lessening. She squatted across me like a coxswain and began her own rhythm, pressing my shoulders back to the deck to let me know that my role was to remain staunch. I pushed her sweatshirt and bikini top up to her armpits, bunching her breasts. I pulled her chest down toward me and snapped at her swollen pink-brown nipples. With a remonstrative palm to my front, Angie arched her back; she feathered and sculled, then bore down with long sweeping strokes that brought her clit right to my pelvic bone. And then again. A blush darkened her chest, and I felt the small of her back dampen with sweat. At last, I began to sense a familiar charge building within my body, a current channeling from the soles of my feet up the back of my legs, meeting the other current surging down from the back of my mouth, and then I was thanking every little thing that anyone has ever worshipped on this island.

We held each other's eyes in a softer grip than she'd started this off with, and I took a sounding right out of her skull. We were both trying to find words to say something more amorous than, "Thanks, I needed that!" A couple of smiles was all it took.

"There's juice boxes and chocolate milk and water in the fridge," Angie called from the bathroom—and it was a bathroom, with a bathtub even. "There might even be a beer if you look around." In the time it took me to choose water, she'd put herself back together. She handed me the driest, cleanest towel I'd seen in months. "I put a pair of Mitch's jeans and a sweatshirt on the bed for you. Take a shower, but hurry up because I have to pick up Moira from step-dancing class in half an hour." Moira was Angie's seven-or-eight-or-so-year-old daughter. They'd fitted out the trawler after the divorce into a mix of condo and SUV and lived aboard. It had sonar, a massive winch, and a good collection of Disney DVDs.

I didn't have a lot of experience being just what someone needed; the glow of it made me sluggish and hazy. I could imagine skippering Moira from school to lesson to birthday party, wearing bathrobes and sipping boat drinks with Angie after we put her daughter to bed. Never hauling a trap again. Slippers. Angie must have noticed me settling into my new life. "Orange, I'm not sure I even want to dock with you on board, never mind have Moira see you."

"OK, OK," I told her. The hot water was a delight just shy of Angie's attention. And the towel and dry clothes were some of my most coveted articles of civilization. If I could have added a good night's sleep, a decent meal, health insurance and financial security for myself and all possible subsequent progeny, I would have felt like a new man. I joined Angie next to the wheel as she piloted the boat into the harbor. She put her hand on mine and I felt my throat swell again. Soon, I would step from the boat onto a dock, then real paved land. A woman of real beauty and character would wave to me and say something fond. Someone would give me a ride home, and Mitchell would have cleaned up my house and left my refrigerator full of beer.

"Listen, I've got an idea," Angie said. *Yes,* I thought, *Yes, yes. I'll live in a cabin at the end of a wharf and you and Moira can stay on the boat. We'll give charter cruises to summer tourists. Moira will make them snacks, and I'll spin yarns about how ancient Bismuthians brought civilization to Europe and opine on how to make real chowder.* "I'm going to drop you off at the Topsoil dock first, so I can go pick up Moira at the town dock; that OK with you?"

"Thanks for everything," I said.

"If you tell Mitchell, I will actually kill you."

"Thanks," I said again.

CHAPTER FIVE

The Tender and the Hammer Maiden

I stood on the Topsoil's floating dock and waved goodbye, as I watched the *Angie Baby's* stern weave through the harbor's moored boats. I didn't have a dime on me, and I figured Donny was in the bar anyway, so I just stayed on the dock awhile. Ricky, the kid who ran the Topsoil's tender shared a joint with me, and I helped him ferry tourists from their boats to the restaurant.

Restaurants have come and gone on Bismuth in my lifetime, but the Topsoil is the only one that has become an institution. We have a couple places to buy coffee and muffins and such, a store that sells everything you should have bought on your last trip to the mainland, and for nearly three decades, the Topsoil with its oft-shuttered raw bar upstairs and restaurant down. It had a symbiotic relationship with the ferry, which delivered both its customers in twice-daily clumps and much of its supplies. Islanders ate and, more typically, drank there too, though not during the rushes at mealtime. In the off-season, the dining room was often open, but the kitchen was not. You could ask the bartender to pop a frozen pizza in the bar's toaster oven, and there was usually chili or chowder to be fortified with handfuls of the crumbled ship's biscuits from a bowl on the bar. Ever since I was a teenager I had been an irregular in the Topsoil's militia of native employees, which meant I got called now and then to fill shifts in the kitchen.

There's not enough room on any of the island's docks for all the visiting boats to tie up, so the harbor moorings and temporary maritime parking spaces were regulated more stringently than most enterprises on Bismuth. The Topsoil had always employed kids like Ricky to fetch people from their moored boats with a tender. Usually they were the sons of wealthy regular summer people who knew the island protocol pretty well and were presentable enough to shepherd tourists without making them hide their wallets. Ricky and his ilk usually looked like prep-school kids who'd slept a night or two on the beach. They had tans and attractively bleached hair, and they got their choice of the summer people's daughters. Their unofficial job was to act as procurers and fixers for native lowlifes such as myself. For years us seedy types had taken advantage of these quasi-concierges as mules and gofers, and the clever ones used the contacts they built up at school and ski resorts to maintain a decent trade in overpriced weed and shitty coke. Ricky wasn't much of a prick, and it was his second summer as the tender's pilot.

"All the rabbits have tularemia and there's a bounty on their ears." Ricky was telling me about a rabbit infestation on Slubbycunk, an island south of us. "They're supposed to club 'em cause the island's too small for a bunch of hunters with shotguns."

"Wabbit season, huh?" I waited him to respond with "duck season," but the current crop of teenagers know nothing about the classics.

"Good thing the monkeys are gone," Ricky said.

"Monkeys?"

"Yeah, they used blowguns on them."

"No way." I said, remembering the legend of Bismuth's monkey problem. Supposedly, a sea-captain's pet jumped ship back in the whaling days and found itself an unexploited ecological niche. It browsed the cliffs for seabird eggs, leading a mysterious and lonely life. When it spotted a whaling ship coming into port, the monkey would howl and wail at it from the cliffs. Over the years, enough other sea-captains' pet monkeys responded to his hail and jumped ship too, forming a monkey colony. It was said that the monkeys would guide captains into port on fogbound days with eerie howls. After whales were domesticated and the industry moved across the Atlantic, Bismuth hit hard times, and it was decided there was only room enough on the island for one kind of primate. "They didn't use blowguns," I told Ricky.

"Yes way."

"Nobody north of Ecuador uses a blowgun. It's un-American."

"The introduction of blowguns to North America led to the extinction of the monkeys; look it up," Ricky told me.

From where we stood, the harbor seemed free of monkeys, though I saw a rat under the Topsoil's pilings. I wanted to go home, but I didn't want to deal with Mitchell. I didn't want to deal with Donny upstairs either. Angie had already dealt with me, and the sense of emergency I'd felt earlier in the day was dissipating like chum in open water. Above us on the restaurant's deck, some kids were squirting mustard on potato chips and flinging them to the gulls.

Poor Ricky. He'd dropped his phone overboard earlier in the day and was stuck with just me and the marine band radio for conversation. He said there were messages he hadn't seen on his phone from a daughter he'd ferried yesterday from her family's yacht to the restaurant dock. We wondered if some fisherman would find his phone in the belly of a cod someday, still carrying plans for a teenage tryst. He'd asked another passenger to call the number, but they were on the wrong network.

The sun, as the tourists say, was over the yardarm, and I was fixed to begin my trek inland, where, I hoped, Rover was waiting patiently for me in her little bed—which I fashioned with my own two hands from a cardboard box—fending off the affections of Mitchell and his entourage. I was expressing just such a thought to Ricky when we heard the basso profundo glug-glug of the *Tharapita's Hammer Maiden* approaching.

"Oh shit, Estonindians," muttered Ricky.

Waldena's boat was a long open-sea catcher boat of a type mostly unknown in North America, though the narcopirates in the Caribbean prized them. Its black hull rode low in the water until it was at speed, then its hydrofoils extended, and the ship vaulted into warp drive. Instead of a flying bridge, it had an armored conning tower with narrow smoked-glass windows. On the foredeck was a military-grade harpoon gun, politely enshrouded with a Kevlar tarp for its trip into the harbor. As the boat cut its engines to drift into the dock, it sank even further into the water and pushed a slow surge in front of it that lurched the dock and made Ricky and I grab a rail for balance.

The Estonindians usually conducted their business with us far off shore, well away from witnesses. I knew myself to be an attractant for low-grade, personal dignity-eroding forms of trouble and wished I had cut my idyll on the dock short before their arrival. While I was considering my options, I found that, once again, decisions had been made for me below my belt. This time the legs were in charge, and I was already walking backwards up the dock's ramp.

CHAPTER SIX

Oysters in the Topsoil

S moking cigarettes is the only pleasure in kitchenwork. No matter the weather or time of day, nothing beats sitting on a milk crate in the alley, surrounded by garbage and grease, in whites soaked with gore and dishwater, and smoking. I had slunk up the ramp and found myself in the Topsoil alleyway out of sheer habit, I guess. All I'd been meaning to do with myself that afternoon was lurk about, and the alley made natural sense. I caught a couple dishers on break out back and was offered a smoke.

It was in the Topsoil's alley during my occasional bouts of employment in their kitchen that I first heard the Spanish and Portuguese cadences of complaint and suffering that inflected the speech of sailors trapped on shore in indentured servitude. My familiarity with this dialect of grumbling and staccato cursing helped me on the boats too. It felt like a fraternity of dirty-jobbers; our disgruntlement was a chantey anyone could whistle; its melody of boss-hatred and toil-grudging carried undertones of withered ambitions and abandonment.

Cigarettes themselves require no language. One is expected to offer tobacco and once the offer is accepted, actual work must cease. One sits on an overturned milk crate with knees apart and apron spread wide. One does not acknowledge the stinks arising from his self or his comrades or his environment. One's crotch itches palpably and is indulged. In the winter, on his plastic throne of indolence, the smoker is impervious to the cold. His body steams while he smokes, and his eyes wander from the trash barrels to the band of stars visible between the roofs.

In the summer, the smoker hears the waves, birds, crickets even. He does not allow them to beckon to him, since each night at work is longer than any land or sea voyage a man could endure and promises not even the dubious pleasure of a destination, and cash out is not for a few hours. The boss, ever in a state of kitchen-apoplexy, rarely pursues the smoker. To see his employees' hands idle is like seeing his own idol desecrated, so the boss learns to avoid the cigarette break, perhaps even enjoying the respite from his crabby underlings that being lonely at the top of the food chain provides. Waitresses are an even more rare sight by the Dumpster. The kitchen's alley, like the jailhouse or a ship's cabin, is a place that those who contemplate presentability do not breach. Waitresses take their tobacco in sharp draws at their station, in between morsels mooched from patrons' plates. The essence of being an islander is knowing one's place. I knew I always had a place wherever toil and discontent lurked.

As I was absorbing my alley-mates' attestations of who had been born by whore, bitch, and other forms of she-beast, I was summoned from within the kitchen's screen door: "Orange, is that you out there?"

I waved.

"We're in the fucking weeds, Orange. You want twenty bucks?"

"No," I shouted. I couldn't understand what made me appear so conscriptable. I'm an obvious shirker.

The cook came to the screen. "Look, we're slammed and we need another guy. What about thirty-five, just for the rest of the night."

I negotiated him up to fifty, just by staring at him blankly. It is my special talent.

"Good! Here," he said, handing me an apron and an oyster knife and pulling me inside toward the walk-in. There he pointed to a world of oysters. "We need these shucked yesterday. There's a big table slugging them down as fast as we can bring 'em out."

The thing about shucking oysters is they don't like it. They are alive and want to remain that way. They can actually fight back through active measures and passive resistance. In the bushel, they organize their ranks, with the most aggressive at the top. If one is foolish enough to look straight into the horde, one is attacked with a jet of bacteria-laden, allergy-inducing water, more properly known as liquor, directed right into one's eyes.

When fighting oysters, it's best to stay entirely engaged in the moment. Pluck one from the bushel, assess its particular weaknesses, swaddle it in a rag, cram a knife into its hinge like you're separating vertebrae, and twist the knife. The top shell is discarded (centuries of this practice have created entire shoals of oyster shells that have to be dredged from the harbor) and the quivery goo is laid bare. After repeating this process hundreds of times, one's fingers are smelly, abraded by the shells, cold, and eventually one hand stabs another with the oyster knife, thus confirming the oyster species' survival strategy against even tool-wielding hominids from the surface world.

But that's not the end of the line yet for the oyster. It remains alive, a pitiful and defenseless puddle lying on a sickbed that had been its redoubt moments ago. Some manage to slink away at this point, brave and foolish, believing perhaps that the shell was just an appendage that could be replaced. But there is no refuge for a homeless oyster. Once its shell is forced open, its fate is sealed. In a full-pitched oyster battle, they are borne on their dismembered carapaces to the cook, who fancies them up a bit on a platter, and then rushed to the floor.

The atrocities perpetrated upon the shellfish before they reach a table are actually only the excruciations that precede their execution. Waiting for them, circled around a table littered with the shells of their comrades, are drunken patrons whose sole intention is to swallow the creatures alive with a minimum of chewing. As the night goes on and the oyster-frenzy continues, the sounds of slurping and belching reach back into the kitchen, where the mollusks clamp their shells even tighter and try to bury themselves deeper in the silt.

Until there's a PBS special with an endoscopic camera, no one will ever know just what occurs to an oyster after its slide down a person's gullet. Most things that live in shells are stupid and stubborn. Too much so to just give up the ghost when they should. Once they hit the stomach, who knows how long they rage against peristalsis and acid? Horseradish, alcohol, and overindulgence have surely abetted plenty of oysters back up the esophageal escape tube, but that's as useful to the oyster as being blasted out of an airlock.

I would imagine that most shuckers entertain the fantasy of discovering a pearl. After so many, many tedious and unpleasant hours, something good ought to come from all this labor. Miners find gold, bricklayers wind up with buildings, shouldn't all this disemboweling produce something? And indeed, most shuckers I've spoken to claim to have found or known a fellow to have found a pearl. Yet not a single shucker has a pearl to show for their troubles. Cooks don't even bother to offer the possibility of a pearl as an inducement to their shuckers. It would be reasonable to assume that pearls were the product of a shucker's imagination, that the grunt who survives on the meager dregs of the economy's bounty after the tide has long receded might dream that not only would his toil produce something of significance, something of sublimity might even come his way. This would be reasonable to assume because the only thing those who suffer the shit jobs ever get is a lecture that they are lucky to be shoveling or swallowing shit. Yet, I knew that at that very moment, there were several women on the floor who had specially cultivated their tans to show off their cultivated pearl necklaces, which did indeed come from oysters. Just not the kinds of oysters the likes of workers such as myself will ever pry open. Those who eat oysters alive get pearls. Those who shuck them get squirted in the eye and infected cuts on their hands.

And perhaps I should be glad that the strangers, off-islanders, and summer people of the world cultivate their interest in oysters, because harbored within the benthonic depths of the unlit intestinal caverns of shuckers like myself lay hidden the only jewel a human can produce, a bezoar, so derived from the Middle Persian for "protector" and "poison." Like a pearl, a bezoar is formed around an indigestible irritant. It is marbled and complex to look upon. Also like a pearl and until very recently, a bezoar could not be extracted without killing its bearer. The ancients treasured them like narwhal horns—as an antidote to poison—the largest of them were valued as highly as meteorites and had the same mystical properties attributed to them. However, now that far more peasants are poisoned than aristocrats, bezoars have become relegated to cabinets of curiosities. For this we should be glad. Humanity, it would seem, has not yet come to induce and harvest bezoars from its underclasses, as it has with organs and hair and such.

CHAPTER SEVEN

Waldena, the Estonindian

At the end of the night in a restaurant, the wait-staff sit at a table to count their tips and complain. But there is no sitting, ever, in the kitchen, and much of the most odious work happens as the front-people flirt and begin their drinking. If a kitchen worker has somehow miraculously remained dry and un-smelly throughout the night, mop swill ensures wet socks, at the very least, for the trip home. I was mopping my way out of the kitchen toward the front when I was stopped at the wait station.

"There's still a table out there, Orange," Cindy, a waitress, told me. "One of them asked if you were still here, too. Bob told them you were busy."

They must have been big spenders—not a category of people whom I've associated with much—since most tourists were shooed away on weeknights, once Bob had judged they were no longer leaking enough money. I peered around the partition and saw Waldena, the only Estonindian I'd ever met who was willing to speak English, a few strangers I didn't recognize, and a midden of oyster shells. I waved to Waldena.

"Orange," she said, pronouncing both syllables of my name, unlike most Bismuthians, "I heard you're responsible for these delicious oysters."

I nodded and wiped my hands on my apron.

"Why don't you sit down, Orange? Oyster?"

"No thanks."

"Beer?"

"Sure." Bob and Cindy both scowled at me. Scullion sculchs do not sit with the guests. I squinted a bit at Bob, hoping to imply that if he had cashed me out when I asked, I would have been long gone.

Waldena could have been a figurehead on an ancient Estonindian longboat. She wore her long black hair in two braids that dangled down over her chest, one nearly nestled in between her breasts. Like most people from the North Indies, her eyes were the blue of ancient icebergs. Her sharp cheekbones angled up toward her temples, giving her face a slightly feline appearance that was encouraged by an upturned nose. She wore a black tank top that seemed to be a hybrid of neoprene and walrus skin and which revealed muscular arms that looked like she was born pulling oars.

The three men with Waldena didn't look like chatty types. They had the squint and thin-lipped snarl of men who didn't want to sully their tongues with the English language, much less be introduced to a native speaker. All three of them were big guys with at least fifty pounds on me. Each of them had black hair long enough for a pony tail and they wore identical barrettes with a complicated silver-work knot design to hold their hair back. At first I thought their thin gray sweaters were part of the uniform until I realized each had a different highly stylized animal pattern around the cuffs and collars. The collars looked exceptionally itchy. The men and I didn't exchange a word or even a direct look, but did manage to communicate our mutual hatred, as I imagined was the case with most men in the presence of Waldena.

"This is Oskar, Kermit, and Elmö," she said.

I did something of an internal spit take and had to rub some beer away that dribbled out of my nostrils. I just had learned either something very odd about Estonindian men or something even stranger about Sesame Street. Neither Waldena nor her Praetorians saw any humor in it. I waited until I had sorted out breathing, drinking, and speaking again and nodded to them.

"Orange," she said, and again her pronunciation of my name was unnerving, "did you know my people and Snorri's people, the entire Northern Indian race, had its origin right here in the coastal northeast of the American continent, uncountable millennia ago?"

"Ayup."

"You know what brought us to the part of Europe that became the Northern Indies?"

"You followed the whale roads," I said, using Snorri's oft-repeated kenning.

Waldena smirked at her po-faced crew and said something in Estonindian that I presumed meant, "See, he's not as dumb as he looks."

"But I imagine," she said, back in English, "you didn't know that the name of your island is in our national anthem."

She was right.

"We don't call it 'Bismuth,' of course. It's the Wind's Mouth, where we filled our sails for the journey."

One of her Muppets snickered. Waldena glowered at him and told me, "Children sometimes make a pun about farting when they recite those lines in the anthem."

"I thought Bismuth meant 'Land Kissed Twice.'" I did. My mother had often told me the North American Indians called our island that because it was kissed by the River Bis, whose waters drained into the enormous gulf our island sat in, and by the ocean itself. And then she would kiss me, which I was not going to tell Waldena and her sulky bruisers.

That cracked them up and cemented our animosity. Waldena's voice took a tone of amiable colonialism. "Each culture has their origin myths. My crew members here, this is the first time they've been to your island; they aren't sure what to make of our culture's humble beginnings. What would you say if I told you a whale road led us back here?"

I wasn't sure if she were asking me a real question or setting me up for a Estonindian version of a 'Why did the chicken cross the road?' joke, so I said nothing.

She gave me a harder look. "Do you know anyone else here who has heard the call of the whale?"

Again, I said nothing. 'I hear the call of the whale' is the sort of thing someone might announce as they went to take a piss off the side of a boat. She kept her eyes on me; I heard a peristaltic rumble from my gut. It seemed as if she were genuinely fishing for an answer, so I said, "Mermaid?"

Waldena looked perplexed. "You mean like in Denmark?"

"No, I, I don't . . ." I didn't even know there were Danish mermaids. I had said it because it had occurred to me just then that it might be nice to look her in her glacier milk eyes and say 'mermaid.'

The topic badly needed changing, so I asked them if they liked the oysters.

"Only when in North America," said Waldena, answering for all of them.

I drank my beer down, wondering why I merited a drink from a beautiful Estonindian who seemed to be confusing whale calls with last call at the Topsoil. I assumed she wanted to show her

boys some local color, hence the oysters, beer, and me, the au-
tochthon. Actually, I'm merely indigenous. My own raft of ancestors arrived here just a couple of hundred years ago. To jus-
tify the beer, I told them the legend about the largest lighthouse
in the prehistoric Western Hemisphere, here on Bismuth, and
how it could be seen from the White Mountains.

It was hard to tell whether they were rapt, bored, or just didn't
speak English. Rapt seemed least likely.

I heard Bob, the owner of the Topsoil, tell Cindy loudly, "You
can go when ORANGE'S table is clear."

"I gotta go," I told Waldena.

"That must have been a magnificent, enormous structure to
behold," she said, fluttering her eyelashes just a little.

"Yup," was all I could manage.

Bob must have shaken down the wait-staff for part of their
tip money because the wad of cash he gave me was mostly fives
and ones. Still, though, enough money to make a bulge in my
pocket was something of a thrill. I was standing in the parking
lot thinking I should have called home to check to see whether
Rover was taking care of Mitchell when I heard a car horn. It
was Waldena in a nice-looking Saab, which was a touch odd,
since I'd never met anyone from the North Indies who would
ever drive a Saab or Volvo—they'd been bickering with the countries of Scandinavia for eons. They probably didn't like Ladas
or Trabants either, but neither of those companies were doing
much business these days.

"Hey," I said as I walked over.

"You need a ride somewhere?"

I most certainly did want a ride from Waldena. "Where's your
crew?" I asked her.

"Back at the Inn. They are obsessed with the hot tub. It's their first time. We only have saunas back home."

"I could use a ride." I got in. I liked the Saab; most of the vehicles on Bismuth were janky unregistered pick-ups that reeked of fish water. "Where do you rent a Saab?"

She didn't answer. She'd been poking at a glossy little black slab that made me think of a tiny model of the monolith from *2001*. "All I can get is visual voice mail. I hate the American networks." She stowed the slab and lit a joint, dragged it, and passed it to me. I knew right off this was nothing like the kelpweed I'd been smoking with Ricky.

"Shit," I told her, meaning that I was really enjoying having my brain scrambled by a beautiful woman in a luxury car.

"Indeed," she said.

Her car seemed as if it might have been hovering some off the road. Or the weed was counteracting gravity.

"It's Estonindian hydro. Most of it gets sold to Holland. We've been growing indoors since the war."

"Ayuh," I answered, coughing, "the war." We drove a little while and smoked. It finally occurred to me that I should have been giving Waldena directions to my house, since I knew where it was. I let the thought pass; I was concerned we'd get there before we finished smoking.

"So," she said, "your old friend Snorri is in town. How is he?"

"I don't know, older?" Actually, I didn't know Snorri was around, I hadn't seen his boat, the *Honeypaws,* since earlier this summer.

"Did he introduce you to his new Korean friends?"

"He has Korean friends?"

Waldena stroked me lightly with one finger on my knee and took the roach from me. I had smoked most of it. "Yes, he does;

I think you've met them, too."

I was exhausted and too stoned for my own good. I thought about my new drinking buddies, Ill John and Chosen, the Koreans. Then I thought about their Kalashnikov and decided not to mention them. Waldena's wicked weed was like a Zamboni smoothing out the inside of my skull. My thoughts just couldn't get much traction. I should have been able to figure out she wanted something from me other than my company. Instead I was trying to figure out if I wanted her to touch my knee again. I couldn't tell whether I was experiencing lust or dread.

"So how is fishing with Mr. Lucy?" she asked.

I wondered if I should touch her knee.

"Catch any big game?"

I wondered if she were going to pass the roach back to me. It was going out. "Big lobster sometimes," I said.

"Hard way to make a living," she said.

"Got that right."

"But that's not all you do."

"Yeah, the Topsoil sometimes."

"I mean you and Mr. Lucy and his son Donny."

"Nope," I said and let it suffice, even though I wasn't sure whether I was agreeing or denying. I had mostly smoked all the language out of my head.

I didn't live too far from town, but I wasn't going to complain we were taking the very long way. We wound up at Oar Point, a sort of spit of land that surrounded Ely Pond, the lamprey breeding lagoon down at the ass-end of the island. She parked.

"Let's stretch our legs," Waldena said with a sensuous, dozy tone.

We got out and strolled slowly along the sand. I felt like I could pour over the landscape like the lunar light. Waldena said my name again in her lovely precise way. I turned to her, ready to swaddle her in lustrous touch and replied simply, "Waldena." It may have been just the moonlight, but I thought I saw a tiny apology in her eyes as she slugged me in the temple with something an awful lot harder than her fist. A black pelagic abyss opened up before me; I was going to dive right in, but I belly-flopped in the puddle next to it, instead.

CHAPTER EIGHT

A Special Terror in Ely Pond

I am a runny thirty-second egg in a hard-boiled world. I don't think I've ever seen a sap, a fedora, or been called a bright boy. But there's one thing I know how to do and that's wake up with a fulminating headache. A bad back makes you realize that every single nerve in your body is connected to your spine; a bad head, though, puts you in direct connection with the cosmos. Every noise, every photon, every speck of stellar dust strikes the brain's gray pulp like a war hammer. I knew from experience that my best defense in this sort of situation was to die as quickly as possible. I fell back on Plan B, which was to wait until the pain subsided just enough to begin whimpering and dry heaving.

After an hourless while, I began to add little pieces of the outside world to my interior painscape. I was horizontal, which was the best news so far. Something still felt wrong with gravity. I was pretty sure the Tabasco sauce in my eyes was sunlight. It was daylight again. I must have spent the night here. I'd been bashed in the head with, what, brass knuckles? Pistol-whipped?

"Orange!" I heard. That was me. Someone had correctly identified me. Good for them. Maybe later I'd wave to them and congratulate them on their perspicacity. I heard my name again.

It was Waldena's formerly sexy orthoepically precise diction. "O-range!" She wanted my attention. I didn't have any. There were a few more "Oranges" and then a nasty blow to my back. I prepared an executive summary of my situation: My arms are tied behind my back. I am lying on the bottom of a little wooden boat. The boat is floating. I've just been hit by a rock. Risking everything, I peeked over the gunwale. I was in a rowboat, anchored in the middle of Ely Pond, the lamprey breeding lagoon. Waldena stood on the shore. She threw another rock at me.

"Good morning, Orange."

"Guh," I uttered.

"What?"

What. I could say that too. Probably. I gave it a try. "What?" My head didn't explode. I could talk. Too bad; an explosion would have ended my headache quickly.

"That is all you have to say for yourself?"

I thought about it. Yes. That was the entirety of what I had to say for myself. But Waldena had good aim and an infinite supply of rocks. A few hit the rowboat and another hit me in the shoulder. I was further inspired to say, "Ow! Stop it!"

"Hearken! Nearly a complete sentence!"

"What the fuck?"

"Ah, Orange is back with us. You would perhaps like to know where you are, how you got here? If only you had been so verbally expressive last night. You're in Ely Pond, which I suspect you already know. I put you there so you would stop fucking around and start giving me some straight answers."

I honestly didn't even know what the questions had been. Evidently my answers came pre-bent. I felt sulky. "You hit me."

"Clever man. You know, last night, I was going to try some softer interrogation tactics. If you had just washed yourself up a bit after you got off work. The car reeked like garbage and bleach. I couldn't tell whether you were being evasive or stupid. Frankly, I lost the will and patience to try and coax you and didn't want to smell you or listen to you for the rest of the night. I got back to the inn much too late and barely slept three hours last night, thanks to you. And now its dawn and I'm back here again and I am even less patient. So let's save ourselves a few hours and you tell me exactly what I want to know. Any questions of your own before we start?"

"Is Elmö Cookie Monster's son?" Another rock. Christ, she had a good arm.

"Let's start with the last time you spoke to a Korean."

"I don't speak Korean."

Waldena picked up another rock. A nice skimmer. It skipped three times before it hit the rowboat. "What were you and the Lucys doing with the Koreans on the *Polk*?"

"We were selling seagum to them."

"Seagum?"

"It's the specialty of our island; it's derived from an ocean-borne organism with the consistency of. . . ."

"Shut up!" she yelled, raising the pistol. "Just tell me what the Koreans gave you."

I could guess easily that she would have shot me if I had said beer. "Money," I said. "I don't know how much." She appeared to be doing some math in her head. I knew how hard that could be; I didn't elaborate, so she could concentrate.

"What else?"

I thought about it. Money, then beer, then whiskey. Oh yeah, "A package."

"Money and a package," she said. "What was in the package?"

"I don't know."

"Where is it?"

"I put it in the bag with the money."

"Where's the money?"

"I gave it to Mr. Lucy."

"So where's Snorri?"

"How should I know?"

She reached down for another stone.

"No really, he hasn't been here all summer!"

"Of course he has," she said. "I saw him and *Honeypaws* a couple days ago."

"So where is he?" I asked. "What did the Koreans give you? Don't make me force you to tell me!"

"Orange! *You* are supposed to be telling *me!*" she said.

"I think I have a concussion."

Poor Waldena. She looked aggravated. "Let's try this: Where do I find Mr. Lucy?"

"Probably on his boat," I told her, "the *Wendy's Mom.*"

Waldena dropped her stone. "You people, even your boats are stupid." She put her pistol in her belt, took a phone from her pocket and photographed me with it, then walked to the Saab.

"Hey, wait!" I called.

"No, you wait." She got in the car and drove away.

I tell people the thing I fear most in this world is Clamato. I say I'm deathly afraid of being tied to a chair, having a funnel crammed in my mouth, and being forced to drink Clamato. Clam broth and tomato juice cocktail. It is a preposterously unlikable beverage. And astonishingly real—it's owned by a real multinational, has a marketing campaign, comes in juice boxes for kids, and cans of energy drink blend for God knows who. It makes as much sense to me as a nice warm glass of mayonnaise and ipecac before bed. It has the musky tang of menstrual blood; it looks like the product of a severe ulcer. Granted, chowder—clams boiled in evaporated milk—is disgusting too, but at least it was born from attempts to survive the winter. Clamato has somehow found its way to being a luxury product. It was brought to Bismuth by demented yachters who considered it an ingredient for boat drinks and is now stocked year-round at the store, presumably for the island's emetophiliacs.

I tell people this because it is one of the most horrid things I can imagine passing through my lips. Plenty of horrid things have passed through my lips in both directions, though. And my secret is that I think I could bear it. To let the world know that Clamato is kryptonite is something like telling an American interrogator that your innermost fear is to be scandalized by a sexy blond American woman in a miniskirt. While this may cause genuine acute anxiety, one suspects that the detainee could imagine worse fates.

On an island, the very epitome of a closed society, one guards one's vulnerabilities. One's weaknesses are divined and exploited from birth by fellow islanders. There's no point in trying to hide my laziness and general dissipation—my supposed moral turpitude and personal lack of accomplishment are qualities that have been described to me at substantial length throughout my life. But irrational fears that put one in mortal terror of having one's intestines unravel out of one's belly button are best kept private. Islanders, not surprisingly, tend to stultifying paranoias like agoraphobia. This type of fear is a sort of psychic blubber that insulates one against personal vagaries and environmental instabilities. One feels safe at home. Safety becomes the *femme fatale* that seduces with extravagant notions of preparedness and reasonableness. Until one has not left the house in years and has lost the ability to eat anything except Camp-bell's Chicken and Stars Soup.

This is not my affliction. Mine writhes right here, in Ely Pond. I did not become fully aware of where my pitiful little boat was anchored until Waldena had left. Initially, I was smug, amused at her underestimation of my ability to sit in a boat and do nothing. Then, without histrionics—not even an "oh my dear"—the cartilage in my knees melted and I fainted. Ely Pond is a lamprey breeding lagoon, as I knew quite well already, but had somehow managed not to mention to myself until now.

Lampreys have no lips, no jaws, no opposable fins, no scales, no decency. They are covered in toxic slime. They are self-pro-pelled intestinal tubes with a suction cup mouth rimmed with needle teeth. They attach themselves to anything lacking suf-ficient appendages to pluck them off. They suck the life out of their prey with a rasp-like tongue that shreds away the prey's skin and pulps the flesh with an anticoagulant chemical.

I recovered consciousness but not rationality quickly. My heart had simply decided to keep all its blood to itself for the time being. Wisely so, too. My first instinct was to huddle down on the floor of the boat—to hide. But the only effect of this was to bring me that much closer to the lampreys. I tried briefly to hover above the boat. I decided my best survival strategy was to sit quietly and motionlessly on the bench and try to convince my internal organs to come back to work. Eventually, I summoned up the courage to peer into the water. Oh there were lampreys. Oh, so many of them. Whatever they ate there in the pond, there wasn't enough of it. I could see several of the creatures cannibal-izing one another. Like the innards of a gutted mammothly cor-pulent sea pig spilling endlessly from its slit belly, the lampreys slid over each other in foul gooey loops. I puked, of course.

Several slued up to feed on the slumgullion. My arms were tied at the wrists and elbows, which made paddling with them even more out of the question. The anchor line was evidently too short to allow the boat to drift to shore. My hair felt matted, probably from dried blood. I tried not to let the lampreys see my injury.

Ely Pond isn't much of a pond; in fact it's actually a shallow crater. About a hundred years ago a humpback carcass had washed ashore here. Several hundred years ago that would have been a bonanza for the islanders, but by the early twentieth century, it was a massive, reeking, civic conundrum. The Bismuthians of that era decided to solve the problem with modern science, which, for them, meant a liberal application of dynamite. Every permanent resident of this island has their own version of what a truly horrible idea it was to blow up the whale, but back then, exploding animals still seemed progressive and clever. Ely Pond is the blast crater from the exploded whale. For nearly a generation, locals avoided that stinking, sulfurous marsh thanks to the whale stew that had been created. Even now it's not hard to find bone fragments in the piss oak and poison sumac.

Many years later, an enterprising islander laid claim to the pond and began to set up an oyster-ranching operation. As he was clearing the muck from the pond, he was daunted and disgusted by the number of lamprey that inhabited it. They had either arrived with the whale or shortly thereafter, to feed off it and the other animals it attracted. Each one he tried to haul out struggled like a fire hose. If he tossed it ashore to die, it slithered back to the pool—their coatings of mucous function like dive suits in reverse and they can survive out of the water for much too long. Holding them by the tail and whipping their heads against a rock didn't help much either. Brainless and skull-less, they were very slow to perish. It seemed the pond suited them very well. Instead of having to find the continental swamps and rivers they were born in, they made a shorter and safer trip to this pool, where they could breed in safe harbor. It took many more years for someone to figure out how to make a profit off of this squirming hell mouth by selling its contents overseas, where people have strange and perverse tastes.

I sat in the rowboat most of the day. It was character-building. My plan was simple: sit there and get sunburned until something happened. Don't rock the boat. I was deeply engaged in carrying out my plan when I spotted the Saab's return.

Waldena, looking quite more cross, yelled, "Mr. Lucy says you're hard to drown!"

"Well, I try."

"If I understood him correctly—which is very difficult, you know—he does not care in the least if you never take another breath."

"Why would he?" I asked, unsurprised.

"I showed him your picture and told him that if he doesn't give me the package, you wouldn't come back from this little fishing trip alive."

"So he didn't give you the package?"

"He said you have it, Orange."

"I don't even know what it is."

"That's what they all say," she told me.

"Listen, Waldena, I don't know what the package is; I don't know where it is; I'm wicked thirsty, and I don't think I can deal with the lampreys much longer."

"If you don't know where it is, and Mr. Lucy doesn't know, what do you suggest I do, Orange?"

"You should torture Donny Lucy. You'd enjoy it. He's a good

victim."

"And what would Donny Lucy know about this?"

"Nothing, probably."

"I think I will keep working on you, Orange. Let's be perfectly clear. I want that package in my hands before I see Snorri again. I do not want that man counting coup on me before I am done with him."

"What's counting coup?"

"As you Americans might say, it is a way to take the piss out of someone who deserves it."

Waldena picked up a boat hook from the side of the pond and used it to stir the water around. When she brought the hook up, there was a lamprey wrapped around it. "Catch!" she shouted, and flung it toward me. It missed. Nonetheless, I started to feel peaked again.

"I don't know anything!" I shouted.

"Did you know," she asked, stirring the pond casually with the hook, as if we were having a chat over a cappuccino, "that two English kings died from lamprey poisoning?"

I mulled this over. "They're not venomous or poisonous," I told her with the grave authority of a paranoiac.

"Overindulgence, Orange. They ate too many lamprey pies." She must have seen the queasiness win out over my feeble stoicism and took the advantage. "That's right, *pies*. Lampreys preserved in gelatin, floating, quivering there, as if they were still alive. You know how gelatin is made, of course, by boiling down horse hooves."

She got what she wanted. The thought of eating enough lamprey pie to kill a fat English king sent me into conniption. As I sputtered, she brought up another lamprey and tossed it at me. I could feel a scream of terror mounting within me. It was going to be a scream in a tonic register I had not achieved since before puberty. Only the jaw-fusing paralysis of fear saved me from complete demasculinization.

"Why don't you save me all this fish flinging and tell me about the package?" She could sense her enhanced interrogation tactics were failing her. I was losing my ability to speak. Out came the pistol again. "Do you know who Vedius Pollio was, Orange?

I shook my head.

"He was an ancient Roman senator who loved to eat fresh seafood and to torture his slaves. His villa was right on the water, and he kept a special pool filled with his favorite food. Lampreys. He kept the biggest and oldest of them as pets. They would wriggle to the surface when he called them, and he would decapitate a mouse and squeeze the blood and guts right into their mouths. Some grew as long and thick as your leg. But he wasn't always so tender. One night, when Caesar Augustus was dining with him, a servant dropped a goblet and broke it. Vedius Pollio had the slave's arms and legs bound and dumped him in the pool, to be eaten alive in the most horrifying manner imaginable. You know that they like to latch on where there's already an orifice, right? The anus, the eyeballs, and so on." She raised the pistol. "Where's the package, Orange?"

I was ready for the *coup de grâce*. I knew I could bear being eaten alive by lampreys if I was clean dead first. All I could do was stare at her and twitch. Waldena sighed theatrically and fired the gun several times. I remained alive and unshot. The dinghy, however, had a nice series of holes in the side just below the waterline. She waved to me and drove off. As the water surged into to the boat, I let my scream loose.

CHAPTER NINE

Mission Statement

Whenever Tarzan is being chased into a river full of alligators, he simply scampers across their backs, sometimes even apologizing to them. This would be the likely manner in which I escaped the sinking rowboat—skipping across the mucousy backs of the largest of the man-eating lampreys. I'm not positive that's how it happened. I simply cannot remember a moment of my escape. I was soaked though, which detracted from the lamprey-skipping theory. I may have just walked, since the pond isn't actually that deep. Regardless, it was a superhuman act that I am either too modest or too astonished to recall.

I sat on the bank of the pond, reassembling my faculties. I promised the lampreys that I'd return someday with enough dynamite to recreate the big bang that began their universe. I considered the natures of justice and retribution, and how I was unlikely to ever obtain them. Then I considered the nature of being stuck in the swamp end of the island with my arms bound. At first I thought I'd have to trudge all the way back to town with my elbows and wrists tied behind my back. All the beach rocks I could find were too smooth. Eventually I found I could saw the rope on the edge of a quarried granite block that was marking the edge of the parking spots near the pond. Waldena hadn't actually knotted the loops of rope around my elbow, so that wasn't too bad. I think maybe I was supposed to be able to get loose.

I figured it was about time for a few answers. I set off for town, hoping to find the *Wendy's Mom* and Mr. Lucy, if only to demonstrate to him that I was still breathing air. I would have been very pleased to find some dry pants. My jeans were chafing badly. The first thing I sought out was actually one of Bismuth's great secrets—a fresh water spigot and hose down by the docks. We don't tell tourists about it, partly so they won't use it up, and partly so we could sell them water by the gallon. I took a long drink of water and ran it over my head, trying to clean out the blood and pond muck, along with all the psychic residue of the lampreys. I had a little dozy sit down on the docks, and then a little lie down.

By mid afternoon, I could bear to walk in my now merely damp jeans and sneakers. I scanned the harbor for the *Wendy's Mom* again but didn't see her. I'd pass through most of town as well as by the Lucy's house by the time I made it home, so I started that way. When I got to the store, I saw Moira, who was sitting on a bench out front eating a popsicle. I waved to her.

Moira took a long drag off her popsicle and gave me a good stare.

"Grape?" I asked.

She showed me her purple tongue. "Mom says to bring you back when you show up."

"Why?"

Moira's popsicle was starting to slip from the stick. She expertly sucked the last of the color from it and tossed it in the wastebasket. "I don't know. She's angry or something."

"Wait a second," I told her and went in and bought a double-sticked grape on credit. I broke it apart and handed her half.

Corwin Ericson

We both removed the paper and threw it out. The first licks on a very frozen popsicle are tough—your tongue could cleave to it. We let them air a bit. "How's school?" I asked.

"It's summer."

"I know, but, like, do you like it? What grade will you be in?"

"C'mon," she said, and we started walking to the harbor. "Fifth."

"You're almost done, huh?"

"Two-thirds."

I knew that girls her age think men my age are astonishingly stupid; I had little evidence to the contrary to offer, so I gave up the conversational gambits and concentrated on eating the popsicle before it went gooey on my hand. It was good. I hadn't eaten since the Topsoil, the night before. Near the docks, we met a woman who waved to Moira and gave me a hard look.

"Moira, Honey, could I talk to you for a moment?" The woman and Moira stepped into a doorway and had a whisper. Then the woman gave me another hairy eyeball and left. Moira seemed happier.

"What was that?" I asked.

"She wanted to know if you were kidnapping me." She smiled, her lips were purple. Walking with a grungy codger was one thing; eating popsicles with a bad boy was another.

"Being kidnapped sucks," I told her.

"You could get kidnapped and chained naked to a rock by an evil prince and a sea monster would be coming to get you. But maybe Pegasus would rescue you if you were beautiful enough." She seemed to savor the notion.

"Pegasus is never there when you need him."

"Unicorns are really whales."

"Whales aren't really fish."

82

"But people won't believe them."

"Unicorns?"

"No, the people who knew that unicorns were whales. I already knew that whales were mammals. Pinocchio and Jonah were both kidnapped by a whale. My Aunt Mini's friend Snorri says his whales are too small to eat people. They eat kribble and they come when he calls them at supper. I go out on his boat you know. It's called the *Honeypaws* and it's named after his bear. Only it's not his bear's real name or his boat's name either; those are secret names. Once me and Mom and Aunt Mini and him all went out. My aunt was yelling at him because he kept talking on his telephone. My mom said he was talking to whales. He wasn't though. I could tell he was mostly texting. That's supposed to be like his job, though, calling whales on the phone or something. Sometimes he cries when he talks about bears. It's weird." Her "weird" was an expansive one that implicated most adult behavior, present company especially included.

"Lookit what he gave me!" Moira took what I presumed to be a mobile phone from her little back pocket. It was an off-white rectangle with three fuzzy little stuffed animals hanging from it. Moira held the phone like a hypnotist with a watch. "They're called 'dongles.' This one is a mammoth, this one is a raven, and this one is a polar bear. Here, but don't use it." She handed me the phone.

Her dongles were cute and well-made, considering. But what was interesting was that her phone bent like it was made of rubber. "Is it supposed to be like this?"

"Ayup and it's waterproof too."

I flexed it into a C-shape, then an S-shape. "That's cool," I said, handing it back to her.

"It's got shape memory and it can remember anyone I call

too. But right now it only calls my mom and Aunt Mini and probably Snorri. He gave me a big knife too, like a boat knife, but for girls, and with a sheath. My mom won't let me have it."

"That looks like your mom's boat," I said, pointing with my popsicle.

"How come you don't have a job?"

"I have a mission instead."

"What?"

"To find a package and to find out why other people want it."

"What's in the package?"

"I don't know."

"Do the other people?"

"I think so, but I don' t really know."

Moira stopped and thought it over. "Do the other people know where the package is?"

"They think I know where it is."

"But you don't even know what it is."

"Precisely."

"Why do you want the package?"

I stopped and thought it over. "I don't want it. Or I guess I don't. I don't even know what it is. I guess I want to know why they think I know."

"That's a stupid mystery."

"It's a mission."

"A stupid mission."

"Don't say 'stupid.'"

"Do you like my mom?"

I couldn't understand how Angie could wear the same gray Bismuth Yacht Club hoodie as the rest of us, yet make it look so soft and fetching. Maybe it was just because it was laundered.

Or how her face could be so clean, with just the right amount of lipstick for an afternoon on Bismuth Harbor. Or her legs, so smooth and tan—the big sweatshirt made her legs seem that much more bare. "This is good coffee." I told her, "How do you make it?"

"French press, dark roast, medium grind, no filter."

"Much better than instant."

"Orange, listen, you're a good guy, I think. Smelly, skinny, strange, slow, but essentially decent."

"You're making me blush."

"So why are you hanging around with those Koreans?"

Great, her too. I wondered why everyone seemed to know I was on a secret mission to the *Polk*, but nobody seemed to be aware of my recent detention in Ely Pond. That would have been the right time to be nosey. I was frustrated. "Listen, Angie. I've been shipwrecked, shanghaied, nearly drowned a few times, drugged, beaten unconscious, had lampreys flung at me, shot at, nearly drowned again, and I've missed a few meals, nights of sleep, and showers. And those are just the parts that don't embarrass me. I'd like to know why. So far, apart from you, the Koreans are coming out of this as pretty likable. Maybe I'd like to write them a thank you letter for their hospitality."

Angie rolled her eyes. "Well my sister says they're gunning for you."

"Gunning?"

"She says they say you stole a package from them."

"Jesus, the fucking package. They gave me the package. They gave me beer. They gave me money. I didn't steal anything. What's Mineola got to do with this?"

"I don't really know. She's up to something. She says the Koreans told her that you'd be taking the long walk soon."

"The long walk?"

"Till your hat floats."

"I kind of liked Ill John and Whatshisname. How does your sister know them?"

"Something to do with her boyfriend."

"Snorri? Shit."

"You don't like Snorri?" she asked.

"I like Snorri fine. I like every damn Finlindian. I even like their whales. Snorri's some kind of wizard though. All those polar bears and runes and yoiking. And your sister's a job of work, too."

Angie leaned across the galley table. I thought maybe she was going to give me a kiss. She sniffed me instead. "I'm going out to her island tonight for dinner. You smell. Clean up and you can come with."

"Why would I?"

"Because you want to know what's going on. And you like following me around."

That could have been an insult. I gave her my sad seal eyes.

She laughed. "I just want you to keep your hat on."

"I'm not wearing one."

"Maybe I'll buy you one at the haberdasher."

"Well maybe. . . ." Where could you go after "haberdasher"? It was a banter trump card. "I'll be back, cleaner."

"Come by at 5:30."

On my way out, I passed Moira on the deck where she seemed to be staging a scene from the Spanish Inquisition with her Barbies. Ken was doomed.

CHAPTER TEN

Gaeity

I wasn't going to have time to walk home and then back to town, and I didn't want to get stuck washing dishes at the Topsoil, so I used the public bathroom on the docks to wash up. Bismuth rented a cop every summer from off-island, and ever since he'd been told his cap might start floating if he kept trying to ticket cars from Bismuth's motor pool of un-inspectable vehicles, he'd taken to lurking around the public dock and bathroom. I felt a little bad for him. To shuck oysters is low, but to work for the town government here meant either high-minded volunteerism or taking a pitiful check from a bureaucracy that, in its isolation, had bipolar swings from plodding Ceausescu-era totalitarianism to Deadwood-style anarchy.

I was in my underpants, standing barefoot in the warm film of water that hadn't drained yet from the bathroom's concrete floor, having a sponge bath with the soap powder and easily melted brown paper towels when Officer Dewey came in to roust me.

"Sir, full body washing is not permitted here."

"Sorry, I was just changing into my bathing suit," I told him.

"No you're not."

I looked up at him, ready to argue that my JC Penny boxer briefs were indeed a bathing suit and imply that I was a man of leisure and not a local wastrel, when I had yet another terrible fright. This one wasn't paranoia, though I imagine there's a very long German word for it. I experienced withering self-pity by way of empathy. I saw myself through Officer Dewey's eyes. He—a twenty-something prick with a crew cut and muscles, full of dim-witted thoughts of the mastery of his own potential—was looking at a nearly naked scrawny pariah who should have made something of himself, or at least found a way not to be such an obvious bum in a public place. Moments ago, I had been a twenty-something prick, albeit with hair and without muscles. In just seconds, decades passed and hosts of opportunities were pissed away.

"Sir. . . . "

I crammed a handful of paper towels into my underpants and dried off my scrotum. "I'll be on my way."

His small act of cruelty was to stand there as I got dressed. I slunk past him in the doorway, ever mindful of the banality of uniformed evil and the necessity of not triggering a bully's predatory instincts. I didn't really have much of a way to be on—it was more of a wait to attend—so I meandered around the docks, occasionally bearing the baleful glare of Officer Dewey, who was probably trying to figure a way to have me exploded for being a suspected infernal device or just an unidentified substance.

Late that afternoon I met back up with Angie and Moira at the town docks to take a ride and pay a visit to Angie's sister, Mineola Bombardier, on her island for supper. To the locals, it was simply Mineola's Island. To the recreational summer boaters, it was taboo, and they learned to avoid it, like the *Polk*. On the maps, it was Gaiety, which everyone—locals and strangers—made an effort to avoid uttering. Gaiety is actually

Swell

the abbreviation of a much longer Indian name that supposedly means "that island over there." Before the Yankees arrived,
Indians of these parts had a variety of names for islands. Their
language could indicate complex shifts in derision and condescension based on degrees of rivalry and the current disposition
of the speaker. Long after the Indians decamped, a sportsmen's
camp was built there for the elite of the New York City Jewish
garment district merchants, and the name was contracted to
Gaiety—to encourage them to frolic. They rode out the summers
of Prohibition and the Depression on Gaiety. They made enough
of a presence out here to sire a few kids with the local Yankee
girls they employed as housekeepers and to ensure that a few
Yiddishisms would still be in use today on Bismuth. By the time
I was a kid, it was in ruins. The last time it had been inhabited
was during World War II, when the federal government fore-
closed on the camp and used it as a German POW facility.

Mineola Bombardier had bought it in the mid-1990s, flab-
bergasting and delighting the Bismuthians. For a local girl to
get off-island and marry rich was an achievement in itself, but
to come back and buy an entire island and then get rid of the
husband—that was revolutionary. Very few islands are owned by
actual islanders. We all loved Mineola, but from a distance. As
far as I knew, she hadn't stepped foot off of her island in years
and allowed few visitors. She helped herself to as much privacy
as the community could bear—it was a consensual act, after all,
helping her mind her own business so well. To thwart straying
tourists and pleasure boaters, Mineola hired various guys from
Bismuth to orbit her island all day long; when a strange boat
intruded into what she considered to be her territory, it was met
first by a local lobsterman doing his best to act spooky and inbred. If the boat made it all the way to her bay, her own security

89

force took over.

Despite her reclusiveness, her face and voice weren't ever that far away. Gaeity, Mineola's own island, was only a quick half hour from Bismuth and, fog permitting, usually within sight. Mineola had a curious and contradictory celebrity as a privacy pundit—her disembodied head appeared regularly via satellite on news and talk shows. She even had a syndicated column and something called a podcast, which had nothing to do with fishing. Privacy is a moot point for most of my fellow islanders. We pretend to mind our own business, but there's no such thing as anonymity on such a small island. On the other hand, we are roundly ignored by most of the rest of the planet.

We liked to hear Mineola's reifying homilies on modesty and drawing the curtains. Of late though, the gales of technical information and apocalyptic tone of her discourses had mostly just confused us. Our souls were in peril from birth, we all knew that well enough. Original sin and venality was our lot from the start. Toil and suffering was our purpose. If you tended your soul carefully enough, the toil would transcend the sin and a heaven-bound bunk was reserved for you. But, indeed, we venal sinners have some dominion over our souls here on Earth—for some of us, our souls were our one vendible commodity, the only important choice some of us might ever have. So how could our identities be stolen before we even got the chance to sell our souls, and, especially in the case of people like myself, why bother? What would happen to it? Would my identity wind up like someone's pet? Would it be eaten? Coffled into a chain of virtual slaves?

Mineola Bombardier, Priestess of Privacy, had the answers, even if I couldn't understand them. It was a fine evening for interisland visiting. I did feel a little princely accompanying

Angie and her daughter on the valiant *Angie Baby* as it made for her sister's sanctum. To be at the prow of a clean and decent boat and watch the waves part before me gave me a sense of purpose and destiny that was as exhilarating as it was false. But I was also feeling as swallowed and waylaid as the Biblical Jonah. I liked this particular fish and the way it made room for me in its belly. I suspected strongly, however, that once I was vomited from this fish, I'd find I'd been in another, larger fish all along. The fish would probably keep getting bigger until I found I was within a leviathan indistinguishable from what I'd thought was my whole world.

From the harbor approach, Mineola's island looked quaint—a weatherworn quaintness of abandonment and degradation that tourists expect from fishing communities here. But as we got closer, we saw that the ancient gray pilings and slouching docks belied an infrastructure of firm, unwormed wood and that the bracing beams that held the slanting shacks had been there from the start. It was camouflage, a movie-set version my own habitat.

Dominating Mineola's little sound was another big tough-looking catcher boat, the *Honeypaws*. Unlike Waldena's coldwater-black boat, this was white with rounder lines. Though it too had a harpoon gun mounted on the foredeck, its prow was built up with a brow of armor that made it look like it could butt its way through an iceberg. If Waldena's boat was a lurking wolf, this was a lumbering bear. Like the *Hammer Maiden*, it could leap up onto hydrofoils and ski across the ocean's surface. I could picture Snorri twirling a lasso on the foredeck as he rocketed between icebergs, rounding up his little dogies.

I knew this to be Snorri the Finlindian's boat from his many visits to Bismuth. He was a nearly perennial summer visitor who set up camp at the Historical Society building to show rune stones and tell the story of how the ancient Bismuthians who became his Northern Indian ancestors voyaged the whale roads from here, across the Arctic, fought the Vikings, and settled the icy wastes of the North Indies on the European continent. His lengthy, edifying tales of grim forbearance and royal grudges quickly bored children and adults alike, but some left with a sense of ethnic pride and a deeper understanding of heavy metal album cover art. I liked him and had been curious about him since I was a kid. He seemed the same age these days as he had in my childhood—impossibly old, but not particularly fragile. He was actually hard to keep up with when we took walks on the island, which is something guys who live on boats are not usually that good at. I think my dad thought Snorri was a hippy, but I'm not sure Snorri even knew what a hippy was, and besides, my father could smell a hippy almost anywhere, even though they hadn't really existed in decades.

Snorri hadn't been seen in these parts for awhile. I hoped he was well. Maybe Mineola had tamed him some. They were an odd pair. Mineola was a new kind of island captain who seemed like she lived at least several years in the future. Snorri seemed like he'd been to the future, but only because he'd lost track of time. I just couldn't imagine Mini joining him on the beach to yoik whale calls.

On the way over, Angie said they'd been getting pretty cozy together lately, and that last winter her sister had been to Finlindia on an ostensible business trip that she'd kept awfully mum about. Snorri was not a mum man, but he was cryptic. I figured that he might know something about his rival Waldena's fixation on Mr. Lucy and the fuckity package—I'd try to fish something out of him and get myself out of hot water. And then into Angie and her rich sister's good graces. It was a clever plan that involved two good-looking women. Foredoomed, of course. But I didn't want to muse on that quite yet. As we neared the harbor I came to feel immodest as the *Angie Baby's* figurehead, so I returned to the wheelhouse.

"You don't have to eat whale; I'm sure Aunt Mini will have something for you," Angie was telling Moira.

"I don't want to drink any old milk either; I hate it."

"You don't have to eat anything you don't want to eat."

"Uncle Snorri smells like old milk. He smells like a wet goat."

"That's not nice to say. Snorri says that old milk keeps him strong."

"It keeps him gross, and he won't even say what it really is. Orange probably likes it."

Where does old milk come from? Snorri guards his secret needlessly. I pray he'll never tell me. Native Bismuthians have strong stomachs thanks to natural selection (the seasick long ago starved to death) and the gastrointestinal calmative found in the freshwater springs that made our island inhabitable in the first place. Nevertheless I remain thoroughly untempted by old milk. We Bismuthians may consider a meal incomplete unless it's served with a brick-like ship's biscuit, but the food of the North Indies tends more toward endurance than store-bought survival rations. A race of people who, for centuries, went without any reasonable means of food-preservation produces a cuisine that dangles so far over the edge of rancidity, the rest of us no longer recognize it. The typical back story of an average Northern Indian dish begins with that which would have gone to the sled dogs. Then it is re-introduced into whatever bladder-like organ from whatever creature it once was. Bacterial agents are added to promote liquefaction over the long haul.

Then whatever it is is sealed away someplace dank and forsaken and left to stew in its own juices. On some distant feast day it is disinterred, and the children run for their lives. Presumably, the day after the feast day, the survivors marry each other and the next generation of Northern Indians is conceived.

"I like Yoo-hoo better," I said. "I don't think it comes from a mammal, though."

Moira said she'd had strawberry Yoo-hoo and it was OK.

The three of us were trying not to think about old milk when a naval-sounding siren made us all jump.

"I wish she wouldn't do that. It's not like we're Vikings," grumbled Angie.

Scores of birds flapped loudly up from the small bay—every living creature on Mineola's Island must have raced to their battle stations at the claxon. I went back on deck to ready the docking lines. At the pier, two of Mineola's security men wearing dark blue Cordura windbreakers with "GAEITY" printed on the back in large yellow block letters caught the lines and tied us off to the cleats. I have always liked this about boating. The necessity of tying up a boat has made for a grace note of welcoming. No matter where one is, if someone is on the dock, he will help you tie up. Except for Vikings, who preferred grappling hooks.

I think it was Moira who saved me from being frisked. I don't think children can resist running down a dock. Nor can a parent resist telling them not to. I was just trying to ingratiate myself to Angie when I trotted after the wayward Moira. The guards shouted at me to halt and I sort of did, mostly out of confusion. I turned back to see the two men reaching under their windbreakers for weapons and Angie right up in one of their faces. When in any kind of doubt, these kind of men mutter into their sleeves and stick a finger in one of their ears. This ritual action evidently calmed our two sentinels. A lifeguard would have just said "No running," and been done with it.

There was only room for four on the golf cart meant for transporting guests up to the house. I walked, while the ladies and the guards drove alongside me. I told them to go ahead, but I was told unaccompanied visitors were prohibited. On the way I stopped and gave my shoes a thorough retying just to let them find out how slow their cart could mosey. It wasn't far, anyway—a couple of unnecessary switchbacks kept the house out of sight from the dock and gave us something to look forward to. The house itself was as low-profile as a mansion gets. It was dug right into the hillside, right into the granite that made up the island, actually. From the front, long narrow windows of dense, dark glass glared at us from below the frowning brow of a roof entirely covered by grass and shrubs. I followed the cart around the back and found the rear to be three stories tall, facing a beautiful but oddly flat meadow, which may have once been tennis courts.

Mineola and Snorri were waiting around back for us. They pretended to be a little startled by our arrival. She hugged her sister and niece, leaving Snorri and I to shake hands.

"Greetings and welcome to Gaiety, Orange."

"Snorri."

"It's a delight to see you. How's Rover?"

Snorri's love and respect for my big furry coon cat Rover forgave any of his skaldic excesses, at least as far as I was concerned. He knew her from when she and I used to live near the Historical Society and I'd come home a few times to find them having private colloquies on my front steps. They were both usually pretty cagey about their time together, but I was glad she had the old gent for a confidant and trusted them not to mock me too much.

Once, Snorri divulged that Rover refused to believe in whales. Cats are generally equal parts hubris and curiosity. I suspected Rover of pulling Snorri's leg—she has the power to ignore things into nonexistence, but to ignore a whale she would have had to get started good and early, long before there was even any evidence to dismiss. There was hardly a cat on Bismuth that didn't come from an ancestral line of whaling cats. Coon cats from our parts had spotted blows throughout the Atlantic and Pacific from their perches in the rigging and done nothing about it. As much as they revered shredding up small animals, they rarely participated in the trying-out of a whale. I suspect that the Bismuthian breed of cats were of the opinion that all human endeavor was pure folly and their maintenance of plausible deniability when it came to whales was a form of signifying that belief.

"She's good—I hope. I haven't been home in days to see her."

"Rover can take care of herself."

"Yeah, but she might not feel like it."

Snorri gave me a long look with bloodshot gray eyes. His breath was a bit rancid and he seemed not to have acquired his land legs yet. His long ponytail was going from steel to ash and his alarming eyebrows had gone snowy. "Ha!" he exclaimed, "Indeed. 'Take care of yourself.' I hate that. A stupid North American way to say goodbye. It's an exile, is what it is. Enjoy your ice floe, old man."

It was a warm, breezy island evening. The sort of spell of weather that makes one forget entirely about the infinite winter. Hardly a single mosquito attended our *plein air* banquet.

Mineola, or perhaps her invisible staff, had prepared a fine supper for us. We sat outside at a round table with a linen cloth; green bottles of white wine and sweet cider sweated in the center, surrounded by a wreath of nacreous blue mussel shells. We began with bowls of perfectly clear fish broth upon which collops of blubber first floated atop, then melted and spread into a savory layer. Moira was given a hot dog with a knife and fork. She knew she was being patronized, but was willing to suffer. Next we had a salad of warm poached fiddleheads braised with chunks of salt pork on a bed of toasted island grains. Instead of the traditional Bismuthian cold summer cod—cod, potatoes, onions, and ship's crackers baked in evaporated milk and served cold in the summer, which I abhorred—we had slivers of whale sashimi with capers and toasted pine nuts on crispy bruschetta. It is actually illegal and genuinely impolite to eat a real summer meal on the islands without clams, so the steamers were no surprise, but the urchin roe/cedar vinaigrette in the *mirpois* was. Moira was delighted that French bread was served with the clams, and we were all perplexed by the foam that accompanied the baguette—we felt butterless and deprived, especially when sour cream was served with the new potatoes. The foam turned out to be a congealed froth of sweet mussels and seaweed. It was like an especially awful shake at McDonalds. Dessert was, as always, blueberry cobbler with a heavy dose of cardamom, a favorite spice of the Finlindians.

Snorri was more than capable of epochal silence, but not when there was a captive audience. This evening, however, he seemed sulky, and he was hitting the old milk pretty hard. At first I think we were pleased not to have to abide a disquisition on the ancestral lineage of a particular herring or the travails of the ancients as they sought Hyperborea, but we were so accustomed to leaving half-hour long chunks of time free to pretend to listen that we found ourselves struggling a little to fill the gaps. Moira had already been in adult company for far too long. She was tired of listening politely to our self-important drivel. She knew the formula for mixed adult dinner conversation: don't mention the other parent, try not to bargain too artlessly for better food and later bedtime, and don't interrupt grownups as they prattle on about doctors and furniture. But she was a Bismuthian too, which meant she carried the genes to hold forth no matter who the audience was, nor how small they numbered. As well, she'd picked up some of Snorri's bardic flourishes, which meant that she was learning that any moment in danger of passing into history unremarked could be enlivened with scraps of saga. She began to glow with the febrific heat of a pawky kid kept up too long in the presence of her boring elders.

As the crickets chirred and the cobbler congealed, she broke the seal on her word hoard in the form of a story about an Arctic island south of Hyperborea called Archangel Danger and the family of miniature mammoths that lived in burrows in the snow near a hot spring. She went on at great length, only pausing long enough to warn us to continue listening. It would seem there was a girl mammoth, possibly a princess, who became very lost and was stalked by an Odin-like hunter with a spear and two pesky ravens. She was rescued by a polar bear who turned out to be a man with long black hair wearing a bearskin. Together they hiked and swam all the way to his land, where it was summer and he had a warm barn full of sweet hay for her to live in.

When she finished, she told us the girl mammoth would live happily forever after in the world's nicest barn and then looked each of us in the eye, as if daring us to contradict her. I could see white all the way around her pupils—I would have believed

Angie if she told me her daughter had been possessed. Angie and Mini seemed as if they'd heard it all before, but Snorri seemed genuinely affected; tears welled in his eyes. He got up without saying anything and came and locked Moria in her chair with a bear hug for so long, she squirmed and gave her mom a panicked look.

Snorri sorted himself out, rubbed his eyes and snuffled his nose. He announced that it was the best story he had ever heard, a real Finlindian yarn, and said he was going to call it Moira's Edda. Then he stumbled a bit as he circled the table back to his chair. Propping himself on the chair's back, he told us he was off to prepare the sauna. He grabbed his tankard of old milk and swerved his way back into the house. One of Mineola's minions kept him from walking through the pane of the sliding glass door.

CHAPTER ELEVEN

The Sauna

Many of the structures at Mineola's compound looked as if they would survive a bomb blast and defy any sort of scrying. From her patio I could see that one outbuilding's lavish durability surpassed them all—the smoke sauna. Built from the prow of an ancient whaler, it was topped by a figurehead of a merdeer, a sort of mermaid with antlers, a creature from North Indian myth. It looked like a ship was cresting straight up from the ground, seized in mid-leap. Snorri had slunk off shortly after Moira's hitherto-unknown chapter of the Northern Indian saga to supervise the smoke-letting and scrubbing stage of the sauna's preparation.

The ancients of our parts brought their smoke lodges across the Arctic to the North Indies, if the likes of Waldena and Snorri were to be believed. It's easy to imagine their boats afire, sinking into the icy sea and a bunch of very warm Indians thinking that the frigid brine was a nice, cleansing relief to their superheated shipboard saunas as they drowned. A Roman general who had pushed far enough north to see the North Indian Sea wrote about flaming long boats in his memoirs. Some Northern Indian scholars have suggested that he had seen out-of-control sauna boats and not the Viking funeral ships that the Norse peoples would have us believe. Not many Bismuthians or other islanders of Yankee stock used saunas. Most of us were Christians with an apocalyptic bent, and that meant we were positive that witchcraft and licentiousness occurred within the sweat rooms. Stories go that the nasty old Puritans loved to trap Indians in their sweat lodges and let them bake to death. Saunas were enjoying a bit of a revival though, now that North Americans realized that the only thing going on in the sweat lodges were Northern Indians on the verge of heat stroke droning endless genealogical chants about their whale relations.

Even before she hooked up with Snorri, Mineola had been interested in the ways and lore of the ancients, and in the way of aging people all over the world, the two of them found enthusiastic common cause in easing the aches in their joints and stewing in their own juices for vague but encompassing therapeutic reasons. I had never stepped foot in a sauna, mostly because I'd never been invited, but the notions of sweating, endurance, and purification sounded much more like work to me than relaxation, so I'd always been wary of them.

"Snorri is making sure my staff have scrubbed away all the soot and that the sauna tea has been brewed correctly. He'll be back when he's sure the rocks are hot enough," Mineola told us. She added that we'd soon be joining him.

I told her that Snorri didn't seem as if he'd quite acquired his land legs yet, and Mini explained he hadn't had them for a while now and that he was sorely testing her patience. "Something happened to Snorri many years ago that just broke him. He's spent the rest of his life trying to be a new man, but there's a big black bear that still follows him."

"Literally?" I asked.

"Yes. Or no, imaginary. Well, if Snorri says he sees a black bear in the corner of the room, I believe he sees a black bear, but I don't believe there is a black bear."

"I've seen those bears, those corners."

"Actually, I don't think you have. Snorri's bear was or maybe still is real. He was very close to it. *Very*. Before he was a whale man, he was a bear man. He had a whole other life in the forest with that bear."

Mineola had real compassion for Snorri. I couldn't think of anyone else who would have tolerated bearlovesickness as well as she. I asked if his bearbride was the namesake for his boat, *Honeypaws*.

"I think so. I'm not positive. Snorri can be slippery with names and dates. I don't know how to describe his relationship with that bear. She was, I guess, like his pet, his daughter, his wife, and his foxhole buddy. He's got melancholia like a trick knee and when times get tough, he starts to maunder on about her. They broke up or she died—I don't really know, but it was something traumatic. He tells stories about her, but only when he's drunk and maudlin, and the stories tend to be vague and contradictory. I think it all happened years ago, but sometimes it's just yesterday to him. If it weren't for his work with the Whale Council, I doubt he would have survived.

"But, anyway, he's usually pretty buoyant; you caught him on a dark swing. I think something set him off recently. He was fine most of this summer. He'd been busy chasing his whales around the North Atlantic, stopping here now and then. Maybe it was Waldena. The two of them are supposed to be working together, but they can't even bear to be on the same boat, never mind cooperate."

"She's kind of a bitch," I said, still sore from our encounter.

"More of a witch, according to Snorri."

"A witch?"

"She's a priestess of a Thor cult that goes flying around the boreal forests and swimming among the icebergs, or so he says. I've heard she's been giving you swimming lessons."

"I don't want to talk about it."

"You and I are going to have a conversation soon," Mini said sternly. "Before you leave Gaeity, you're going to tell me what's going on between the two of you."

"I'll tell you right now. She's nuts."

"You're all nuts, that's why I have my own island. But I don't want to get into this now, and I don't want to have to get upset later." Mineola got up from the patio where we'd had supper and went in to join her sister and niece inside.

I thought briefly about how often I'd explained myself to upset women. My mother was probably the first; Mineola would be the next. Actually she didn't seem too upset. Just ready to be, if necessary. People who could plan their own moods frightened me. Mine just dragged me around on a leash, whether I could get my feet under me or not. Curiosity took me back inside. The sauna was ready.

"Orange, you'll be joining us, of course?" said Mineola.

"Do I have to?" asked Moira.

"Come on, it will be good for you; you haven't had a good sweat in weeks," said Angie.

"I don't want to with him," Moira said, meaning me. "I just want to watch TV."

"OK, but we'll miss you, and Uncle Snorri doesn't get to see you that often."

"I want to watch TV."

I suppose the ability to walk naked across your own island and be scrupulously unscrutinized by your staff and bodyguards is the ultimate act of privacy. You don't have to be modest because everyone is in on the act and bound by ferocious non-disclosure statements. The Bombardier sisters and I walked starkers along a footpath down to her sauna house on a tiny inlet just around the corner from her docks. To be with two naked sisters who fully intended to drape themselves on a bunk and work themselves up into a languorous but sweaty froth should have been more pleasurable. I, disappointingly, found myself stuck right between fight or flight, even though neither was appropriate nor desirable. I longed for some kind of displacement behavior; this would have been a great time to adjust my cuffs or re-knot my tie, or even just clean out my ears, but the same social conditioning that was nearly paralyzing me kept my fingers out of my orifices.

Mineola and Angie preceded me into the sauna house. They had similar butts, I was pleased to see. I was looking forward to harboring secret thoughts about the sisters until I felt the heat, then I was fully occupied with thoughts about my own safety. To say I felt the heat is insufficient. I felt the heat in the same way I felt Waldena's pistol butt concussing my skull. I felt it in the same way I felt influenza. I had baked roasts at lower temperatures. This wasn't the right crowd for a suicide pact, but there was little in this setting that suggested survivability to me. Snorri yelled something in Finlindian that I presumed meant "Close the door you stupid North American," and jarred me out of my spell. There were three tiers of shelves upon which to cook oneself; Snorri was on the top shelf in the corner—the hottest place in the room. It smelled like wood smoke and herbs—good for roasts—and, unfortunately, a bit like Snorri's old milk.

"Cleans out the toxins," he shouted, sensing our olfaction.

I was placed in the middle of the lowest shelf—"For beginners," Angie told me.

I tried to take shelter against a wall but found it was too hot to touch. Like a cat looking for the ideal spot in a room, I sensed that close to the ground, surrounded by as much air as possible, was the least stultifying place to try and continue my existence. For the next several minutes, I struggled to adjust to the swelter. I probably had more toxins within me to leech out than most people who had baked themselves in this oven. But some of my toxins were hard-won and I didn't necessarily want to give them up. I had barely moved a muscle, for fear of spontaneous combustion, yet my body experienced throes of febricity that I'd never felt before.

The women had taken their stations above me on the second rack. I was having too much trouble using my senses to understand what they were saying, though I could tell they were murmuring approval, giving voice to the easeful slackening they felt.

Snorri jumped down from his perch and took up the ladle. "Well, ladies and gentleman, I think we've taken it easy long enough. Let's get Finlindian." He dipped the ladle in to a wooden bucket made from a birch burl and splashed some of the sauna tea on the rocks. There was a crack like an explosion and a shockwave of botanically scented heat buffeted me. "Ahh, wonderful!" he declared and then did it again. This time he scampered up to the top shelf to experience the heat wave more fully. I, perhaps like the Buddha, considered the nature of mercy. There was none.

Snorri had evidently transcended into a meditative state himself. He chanted something that seemed like a litany at first but then became a dirge. The Bombardiers contrapointed his baritone drone with high-pitched yelps, in what I assumed was a traditional sauna yoik. Then Snorri went silent. For how long, I don't know, since time and sensibility were lost to me. He began a moan that rose to a wail and sank down to a keen punctuated by sobs.

As my own consciousness was eased of sight and a sense of the present, a vision of Snorri, or maybe, perhaps, of myself, bear-paddling under the glowing Arctic ice swam into my imagination. From what seemed like an abyss below, I heard the raga of whalesong. From the luminous yet ponderously vaulted ice above, I heard the cracks and groans that the old ice speaks with. Things of menace and things of beatification swam beyond the reach of my ken. Snorri brought me back either to the surface world or the inferno within when he un-beached himself off of his shelf. This time he drooped down off the upper bleacher and squatted on the floor in front of the rocks. He stood slowly and told Mineola something in Finlindian that I didn't understand, and then looked to me and said, "I cannot be the saunahost; I must go now." The waft of cool air from the door made my skin sizzle.

After a time, I struggled to my feet and looked at the recumbent sisters. Mineola said: "He's been that way since he got here."

"What happened?" asked her sister.

"His bear left him."

"That again?" said Angie. I looked to her for an explanation. "More heat, Orange," she said. "Pour some more tea on the rocks."

I did and was forced back to my bench. I hung my head well down between my knees and tried to breathe the air from just above the floor. I could no longer feel time pass. I watched the sweat drip from my nose and chin and form a black puddle that seemed somehow familiar. Angie and Mineola talked languorously, but I couldn't join them. One of them got down and ladled more tea onto the rocks. I heard the crack again, but it was all over for me; I was utterly wilted.

CHAPTER TWELVE

Up Late with Mineola

Below me, prickles of ice. Within me, a sense of cloudy disturbance, like squid ink dispersed by the distant stroke of a massive tailfin. Upon me, sleet and raking hail. I tried my eyeballs. Only one worked. Two polar bears stood above me, grunting lasciviously. I had been waiting below the ice for as long as I could hold my breath. When I put my snout just inches up into the air, I was snatched out of the water and dragged onto the ice. The bears were tenderly, expertly flaying me.

"He looks awake."

"Move over, I'll get his legs."

I closed the eye. A skeletal raven lit on my back. Its wing bones scraped between my ribs. I felt something I just could not identify—a sense of sickness and pain that was at the very same time relief and stimulation. Reason stormed back into my skull, and I realized I had just died. I opened the eye again. In the afterlife, I discovered that one lays unclad upon one's belly on the sand and grass. Two naked battle maidens kneel beside one. They, for eternity, one assumes, beat one's back, ass, legs with branches.

"I don't want to use up all these switches on him," said Mineola.

"He needs it. See, he's come to," said Angie, continuing to

birch me.

To use words in the afterlife turned out to be very difficult. A groan was as close as I could come.

"He's definitely awake. He needs to be rehydrated and needs some carbs. I'll get him a beer," said Mineola.

Angie said "Welcome back, Orange," and flipped me over. She drew the branches up and down my chest and legs, as if stroking me gently with claws.

I was not dead. As it turns out, in real life—in my very own life, even—naked sisters beat you with birch switches and then get you a beer. It was the first time I'd ever been beaten back to consciousness. I think I would have enjoyed it if I hadn't had to die first. I thought of stalwart well-dressed men in black and white movies lightly tapping the wrists of just-fainted young women. I thought of W. C. Fields in *The Fatal Glass of Beer*, in which he wore mittens while playing a zither.

Angie had got me back up on my feet and we walked back up to the house. I don't know how, but I was feeling chilly. I drank half of my beer at once and told them, "T'is a fit night out for neither man nor beast."

"You liked it," said Angie. Her sister smiled.

"What kind of beer is this?"

We talked lightly about our invigorated pores and our spent toxins and, after another round of beer, broke into Snorri's stash of pickled herring. I did feel a more pleasant afterglow than I would have expected from heatstroke and a beating. Moira came downstairs, looked at us and said, "Ew, gross." Geezers in towels eating cold vinegary fish. She had something there.

I was game to stay over and looked forward to crashing in the cushy guest room. I helped myself to the phone, just in case anyone decided to call me instead of kidnapping me. "Mitchell, what are you doing there at one AM?"

"I wanted to watch *Nova*, then I fell asleep. You have a better TV. What are you doing in Mali? Where's Mali?"

"What?"

"Your phone says 'Unknown Caller: Mali.'"

"It's in Africa. It's snowing. They have winter this time of year."

"You're not in Africa."

"I don't know. I might be. This is a strange phone."

"Why are you hanging around with my daughter?"

"Moira? What?"

"I heard you were all bedraggled and walking with Moira in town."

"I wasn't hanging around with her; I was just walking her back to her boat."

"Rover's been very snuggly tonight."

"Careful, she scratches."

"Not me."

"Well, good. Um, don't forget to change her water."

"Oh," said Mitchell, "I'll take care of your cat," and then he hung up on me.

Mitchell wasn't famous for his insight, but I was wearing what may well have been his pajamas and lying in a bed he'd no doubt slept in himself. A man can sense some things, I guessed.

I was still sleepless later that night but not too upset about it. I snuck a beer from the fridge and went back outside to watch the moon and ocean from the high ground of patio. Something big seemed to be lurking out there. I could see the moonlight frosting on its wake. Too bad the whole island was a non-smoking section. I heard a glass slider open and a "Hi," from behind me.

"Hey," I said, trying to make the one syllable sound inviting and adult.

"Wrong Bombardier," said Mineola.

"I'm sorry. I couldn't sleep. I figured I'd keep an eye on the moon for us."

"Thanks for your vigilance."

"Those guys on watch all night?" I asked, pointing down to the silhouettes of the guards on the docks.

"They sure are. Don't worry. They're discreet and well paid. As are my lawyers." Mineola wrapped her robe a bit tighter and sat down at the patio table with me. "I need to ask you a few questions, Orange."

"I. . . ."

"Not about Angie."

"Uh."

"My package. I don't want to have to ask you for it."

"*Your* package?" The Jesus fuckity package again. Recent negatively reinforced conditioning had made me a little fussy about packages.

"I know the Koreans gave it to you directly. Mr. Lucy says you never gave it to him."

"What do you know about Mr. Lucy and the Koreans?"

"I know what I want to know. And now I want to know about the package. Did you give it to Waldena?"

"Mineola, I don't have it. I don't know where it is. I don't know what it is."

"You know something? I might just believe you."

"Why?"

"Moira told me to."

I considered my unlikely alibi. A popsicle well bought, I

decided. "Listen, I know you've got a lot going on, but under-neath it all, you're an Islander too. I love to stay out of peoples' business Mini. I love staying out of businesses so much, I'm a socialist. But this package—your package, you say—suddenly I'm the expert. If you know what you want to know and you know less than I do, I don't see how you stay in business, because I don't know shit. Why don't you tell me something so the next time someone tries to feed me to the fish, I'll at least know why."

"Feed you to the fish?"

Mini always seemed mildly amused by my suffering and her whole tone tonight suggested she had more in store for me. "Waldena, lampreys, long story I'm not telling tonight."

"I"ll tell you. The package, it's not mine, it's Snorri's."

"Snorri's?"

"It's meant to be a gift for him—a sort of hospitality gift or maybe something diplomatic. I think Waldena meant to steal it."

"Why?"

"Her business," said Mini. "If I had to guess, I'd say she was counting coup on Snorri. Or maybe she just feels left out."

"Out of what?"

"A loop," she said.

"A loop?"

"A certain loop."

A certain loop. It sounded like an obscure film festival.

"Waldena says I stole it."

"She's not the only one."

"So why do I supposedly have this package? I can't Christly imagine what any of this has to do with me." It took some matu-rity to not whine *it's not fair* to her.

"Because the Koreans gave it to you because it was meant for

Mr. Lucy."

"And he says he doesn't have it?"

"He says you never gave it to him."

"How do you know all this?" I asked.

"Ill John is very concerned."

"How do you even know Ill John? So this package, it's supposed to go from the Koreans to Snorri? What's Mr. Lucy got to do with this?"

"He was the courier. He was supposed to give it to me, and I'd give it to Snorri."

"Why?"

"That's none of your business," said Mini.

"I wish. Why didn't the Koreans just give it to Snorri?"

"They . . . they're very thorough tourists. They're here . . . to be in *the certain loop*, and they want to show their appreciation and demonstrate their cultural acumen with this package. Sometimes they act like a pair of anthropologists and it can get annoying. You know the Sampo?" asked Mini.

"Sampo? No."

"Nor do I. The Sampo was known only to the wisest of the ancient proto-Finlindians."

"Mineola. . . ." I hoped she wasn't under the bardic influence of Snorri.

"No, it's supposed to be an enigma," she said. "One is not supposed to know, just to treat it with reverence. It's said to be many different things. All we know today is that it was very potent and worth stealing. Their stories are full of Sampo thievery and the trouble it caused. Astrolabes, orreries, whale jism, stills, perpetual motion machines, the goose that laid the golden egg. All Sampo."

"So the Koreans had the Sampo? That doesn't sound too

likely."

"No, I don't think anyone has *the* Sampo. Sampo has changed. Now things have 'sampo.' It's as essential a concept as whale-herding to the Finlindians. To understand something's sampo is to see something in the same way as a Finlindian."

"Is this like having a fashion sense?" I asked.

"Snorri says that just as in the Finlindian alphabet there are letters and sounds that cannot be expressed with the English alphabet, there are plenty of concepts that only a Finlindian can comprehend."

"So Snorri knows what it is?"

"I doubt it. Maybe. He'll never tell," she said, with resignation.

"I'm not sure I'm any closer to understanding anything."

"You're probably better off that way."

I rubbed my face with my hands and held the beer bottle to my forehead.

"Look," said Mineola, "the Koreans want to give a package to Snorri for him to bring back to his whale council, right? Whatever's in that package probably has sampo. I think the Koreans want to give Snorri's council a gift that shows they understand sampo. It would be a dramatic cultural connection if they could communicate via sampo, despite the fact that they live in different hemispheres, don't understand a word of each other's language, and don't have any mutual interests or even any rivalries."

"What's this got to do with tiger testes?"

"You mean, like, 'What's a piecost?'"

I knew that one. The same as a henway. "No, the seagum."

"That's how Ill John and Chosen get their trip to pay for itself. There's bigger things afloat than cock starch." Mini smiled to herself, savoring her coinage. "They and Snorri have bigger whales to milk, so to speak. Waldena, too. Snorri's got an idea for perfectly marbled miniature Kobe beef-style whales to sell to the Koreans. Waldena's obsessed with the Estonindian free-range whales and their noble pedigrees. I don't give a shit and only serve whale at supper to be polite. One thing the Northern Indians and the Koreans do have in common is that their societies are so old, they forget sometimes that there are easier ways to make money than hunting, herding, and trading, and that's why they need a North American like me around. If we can co-operate and play to our strengths, there's some serious money to be made, the twenty-first century way. Do something to bring people together and improve the world while we cash in. But we need that package first."

"Why?"

"'Why' is my question," she said, lowering the boom, "and I sort of hoped you have an inkling."

"I thought your question was 'where.'"

"My question is give me the package," she said sharply. "And your answer seems to involve sitting on my patio wearing my ex-brother-in-law's jammies and drinking beer."

I remembered reading an article about the island nation of Singapore. Evidently it's plagued by pajama-clad old duffers shuffling aimlessly around the city. I could do that. I decided to look for a pair of my dad's old flannels when I got back home. I'd probably need slippers. Mini's robe was a chin-to-ankle affair; I couldn't tell what she was wearing underneath. I wondered what her sister had worn to bed. And what was that out just beyond Mini's little harbor? I could almost see a bulge in the dark water. I thought of Angie's bottom rising up from the small of her back like the swell of a wake. . . .

"Orange! Sampo!" she shouted.

I guess I'd drifted a bit. I was tired of the whole thing. "It's late, Mini."

"When's the last time you saw early?"

I'd seen too much early recently.

CHAPTER THIRTEEN

In Bed with the Beargroom

I was very impressed with Mini's guest bed. It was vast and clean. It was almost too plush to pass out on. Almost. I had been dreaming about a woman the size of an island when I was woken by the bed sagging as someone crept in.

"Hey," I said, woozy, but ready for the right Bombardier sister. Before I could turn to face my bedmate, Snorri flung his arm over me, drew me in tightly and spooned me. Snorri was old yet bandy and well preserved by sea salt and maybe something bacteriological in his old milk. He nuzzled my hairline at the back of my neck and muttered what I assumed were Finlindian sweet nothings, while he flooded my nostrils with the reek of old milk gone even older. As I felt him draw up his harpoon, I slipped down out of his hold and onto the floor. He reached across the bed for me slowly, and I saw that he was still asleep. I regarded him from the floor. He was a goaty Silenus intent on my business. I don't know how that brought me to compassion. Maybe seeing the man in his primal state helped me see him as someone who hadn't learned how to be lonely yet.

After I slapped him awake and asked him all the questions one might want to ask an invading Snorri, I joined him in bed and we sat up with the comforter drawn up to our chins, drinking restorative beer and talking as the night gave up its ghost. He apologized for groping me and said that Mineola had told him to go mind his own business when he'd proven too drunk and pestiferous to sleep with her. He couldn't mind his own business, though, and in a stupor, wound up pawing me. I wanted to ask him about the sampo gift that Mini told me he was supposed to receive. I wanted to ask him about Waldena, counting coup, about Mini's big cash-out scheme, but he wanted to talk bear.

"I was a beargroom, Orange, and my bear left me. That's not supposed to happen."

I knew very little about the Finlindian practice of marrying bears. I did know that I wasn't supposed to know about it. It's an important mystery of theirs. Probably very sampo. I was prepared to listen honorably and not understand as the groggy satyr told me the story of how he had gone from bear to whale.

"My colleagues in the Council didn't know what to do. A bearbond is supposed to be for life. It's sacred. Finlindian beargrooms have had to deny their bears before for reasons of history and intolerance and the sometimes bad bear, but we didn't know what to do when the bear herself dissolved the bond."

"What happened?"

"We both liked the old milk, and she had been so wise and tolerant over the years." Snorri swallowed the lump in his throat and sat up straight.

"Did you know that I wasn't always a whaleherder? In my youth, I fought with the Forestbrethren. I lived in the snow and woods for years, fighting the Nazis and Soviets. Many of the Finlindian young men had gone to sea to escape the war. To stay behind meant conscription in one evil army or another. We who took to the woods had to adapt, to let the cold and the snow shape us, to join the creatures who were there before our ancient ancestors.

"Finlindians—all the Northern Indians—had always been

close to our whales, but it was the bears who showed us how to become whalers. It was the bears who taught us about our homeland and how to defend it from the wolfpacks."

"Most of us fought and lived alone. That's the way of the forest predator. We were hunters of men, as horrible as that is. The Nazis thought we were yokels at first. Actually, before they decided they wanted to annex Finlindia, we almost passed muster as models for their master race. There seemed to be a lot they liked about our hunting culture, but they turned to the Aryans instead. Wrong Indians. Later, the Germans and the Soviets said we were barbarians, demons even, as they lost more and more of their men to the forests of the Northern Indies.

I arranged my pillows so I could give the beargroom my full attention.

"Farther north on the tundra," continued Snorri, "where there were no forests to hide in, Northern Indian resistance fighters blended with the elk and reindeer—the best shepherds are barely distinguishable from their herds. Antlers are much deadlier when wielded by a primate, let me tell you.

"The Forestbrethren weren't demons or rubes, of course. We were savage because the forest is savage. We fought their dogs, their soldiers, even their slaves. We had to fight on the forest's terms, not mankind's.

The house was dark and still except for Snorri and I. We'd been speaking in hushed tones, but as his tale grew bloodier, a bur of ancient hatred grew on his voice.

"One day during the war, I was napping in a tree when I heard Nazi hounds running down a bear. Soon, an enormous brown, a great queen sow of the woods, burst through the brush and snow and stopped to make her stand at the base of my tree. The hounds were hot on her, and the Germans weren't far off. I could see dog gore and blood on her fur. She didn't have time to climb, I could tell. She growled and then surprised the hell out of me. Two of her cubs were with her! At her signal, they dashed up into the tree and joined me. I waved quietly to the cubs and we all waited together for the fight.

"In moments, the dogs were throwing themselves at the bear. She stove in dog ribs with hammer blows from her massive forepaws. She took hounds in her mouth and shook them like salmon. Their limbs were flung off their body from the force. Soon she and the snow around her were bloody red. For each dog she bust asunder though, another one got in a bite. And she was exhausted from running to save her cubs. She was slick with gore and draped with steaming dog entrails and still holding her ground when the human beings arrived.

Snorri's voice dropped down to a sinister whisper. "There were five Nazi soldiers tracking her. When they got to us, they let go the hounds they'd kept leashed. The bear simply brushed them all aside with one swipe. A hound was tossed all the way up to me and landed whimpering in a crotch. I slit its throat.

"The Nazis howled in rage and astonishment. They were already too close to the berserking bear to use their long rifles. She charged them and they fumbled at their holsters for their machine pistols. The cubs and I each picked a soldier. We leapt out of the branches and tackled them. I gutted, then slit the throat of one, then another. The cubs were unwilling to finish off theirs but had battered them insensible," he said, proud of the cubs.

"We had melted the snow with the blood of our prey. I heard the remaining injured hounds baying nearby. They would attract attention soon. The cubs were attending their mother, whose belly was gushing blood from bullet holes. She moaned

Swell

her death song as her cubs licked her face. I was washing off her fur with snow, and the cubs were grieving, when the rest of the dogs attacked again. One cub managed to run up a tree, but the other was ravaged by the war dogs."

He paused, as if he were having a silent moment for the lost cub, then patted me on the chest. "Our bond began then, as we watched the dogs kill her family. That first winter I had to carry her in my shirt as I tracked and killed the invaders. By the next winter, she could tow me on my skis.

"This cub grew up and became the bear I married," he said, with incongruous brightness. "But before then, we had something of an unconventional relationship—though, I think the war made all of us break many rules and taboos. Normally, a beargroom gives up something like soldiery to live contemplatively in the woods with his mate, to be an example for both peoples to learn from. But, like I said, it was the war and nobody was going to live contemplatively for some while. The cub was young, and I didn't have a home to bring it to. I did not think at all at first that I would marry this bear.

"She stuck with me through the winter, growing and growing. We fought side-by-side and sought warmth and shelter together. By that summer, she was bigger than I."

Snorri paused again and turned to me as if he expected questions. I finished my bottle of beer and said, "Your big bear-bride?" as a prompt.

"In summer, the Forestbrethren bands and single hunters gathered together to feast and exchange information. At the camp, some beargrooms thought it unseemly that I was with such a young bear and felt it was sacrilege that we were fighting partners. I was supposed to take care of my bear, not to expose her to such evils as we fought. They had left their bears behind and pined for them. I could not disagree with them, yet this was a war to defend our very culture, and I felt we all had to make adjustments.

"The Beargroom Council met there at the summer camp to consider our relationship. When they heard my testimony about how my bear and I had met and joined forces, they understood that I had no choice; that I had been chosen by the bears and that I must marry my bear and make things right. So, of course, I did in a beautiful ceremony attended by all of the men of the camp.

"Well, that war ended, and slowly, we Forestbrethren emerged from the woods to rejoin the world. I had no family to return to. I had no land to work. I went to working at a whale ranch on a fjord as a whalehand, work that came to take me out to sea several times a year. My bear stayed behind, of course. Over time, she was blamed for killing some of the ranch's dogs, and the owner of the ranch told me that he could no longer accept the honor of hosting such a noble warrior.

"We moved inland, back to the forest, where I hoped she would be happy. Many others had moved to the forest as well, and they were disturbed by having such a beautiful and powerful creature among them. I couldn't always be there to explain that her taste for blood and old milk had come honestly, since my work as a whaler and cultural ambassador had me traveling across the Atlantic to these very shores, often right to Bismuth, where the ancients began their journey across the Arctic. I cannot help but wonder if we would still be together if I had been there more for her.

"One day, I returned to my home in the forest and found my bear was gone. Her housekeeper said she'd become unruly and violent. Members of my council felt that I should not have left her alone as often as I did. I wish now I had cared more for her, maybe brought her on my travels. She never did get to see many of her own kind, and, in her loneliness, she drank more of the old milk than I ever did. Maybe I should have stayed in the forest with her. I didn't know then that my calling would be on the waves and not among the trees. I just heard on my way over to Bismuth that another beargroom, a man I'd trusted with my life, had been feeding her for the past few months and that she'd been seen hibernating in his barn. Maybe, as soldiers sometimes find, my bear and I were better battlemates than housemates. We loved to wrestle, I can tell you that."

At that, Snorri crossed his arms and gripped his shoulders hard in an auto-bearhug. He stifled a sob. I waited a bit and watched him squeeze some of the despair out of his body. "What was her name?"

Snorri barked a short bitter laugh. I had forgotten myself and asked a very rude question.

"Sorry, I forgot."

"That's OK, Orange. I know in your culture it means that you care. Sometimes I called her Honeypaws."

Snorri relaxed his grip on himself and closed his eyes. I thought he had fallen asleep, but after a minute or so he continued his story. "That was all a very long time ago. When I met her I was nearly half your age now."

"You still miss her, huh, guy?"

"I don't know what it is. Sometimes a little bear cub wanders into your memory and that's all it takes . . . it keeps an old man humble, I suppose."

I couldn't really square Snorri with humble, but I saw his point: Your suffering isn't done yet. I almost wanted to smooth out his eyebrows and tuck him in. His tale was told and my night was over. Long over, actually, it was late in the morning, and I could tell the house had been up for a while. I went downstairs with my head zooming. I felt like the wedding guest in the "Rime of the Ancient Mariner," stunned by the sailor's harangue.

"Snorri still up there?" asked Angie.

"He just dropped off."

"What were you doing?"

"He just climbed in with me. We were talking."

"You two are pretty cozy," she said, making it sound like a warning.

"We kept a harpoon between us."

She gave me a dubious smirk, but I think it was meant more for my entire perplexing and annoying gender than just myself or Snorri. Or our harpoons.

Mineola joined us. She looked fantastic and absurdly well composed. "I just did my bit for CNN this week. I'm not sure when they're airing it."

Her sister asked her what it was about.

"Keeping your clicktrail clean and hard drive hygiene in the workplace. Boilerplate stuff."

Moira and Angie were itchy to go; I supposed I'd better get on to talking with Mr. Lucy. Mineola supposed that was a very good idea.

At the dock, I marveled at the enormous fake Christmas trees that were Mineola's antennae. Standing there right next to the other white pines, they looked outrageously artificial. That's how it's done, though—an array of fake trees lets you tell everyone else what to do and stay invisible yourself.

Just as we were ready to cast off, one of Mineola's bristle-headed goons shoved a clipboard into my hands. "You'll need to read and sign this, Sir."

"What's this?"

"The standard non-familial binding non-disclosure statement."

"I don't think so."

"Yes, you will. Sir."

He was preparing to talk into his sleeve when Angie told me to just hurry up and sign it. "Everyone has to."

"What if I don't?"

"The slow boat to Guantanamo, knowing Mini," said her sister. "Just do it, we have to get back."

I signed. Thusly I sold that much of my soul to the sauna of Gaiety.

Part II

I do not know your hidden destiny; all that concerns you interests me. Tell me then if you are the realm of the prince of shadows. Tell me. Tell me, ocean, (me alone, so as not to sadden those who have yet known only illusions), whether the breath of Satan stirs storms which arouse your salt waters to the heavens. You must tell me; I would rejoice to know that hell was so near to man.

— Comte de Lautrémont, *Les Chants de Maldoror*

CHAPTER FOURTEEN

The Yankee Circumciser

When Angie took us back to Bismuth on her boat I saw the *Wendy's Mom* moored in the island's harbor. Mr. Lucy must have been out and back already. We cruised by her, but nobody was on board. We get a couple of seals in the harbor now and then in the summer. One paced us back to Angie's berth, even rolled onto its back and waved at us. We waved back. It was an auspicious welcoming, even though I knew it just wanted fish. I resolved to give Rover an entire can of tuna when I got back. I was even looking forward to the smell of it on her fur when I finally got to sleep in my own bed.

I didn't know how to leave it with Angie. But her usual busy self took over as soon as we got past the breakwater. She even told the seal to hurry up. Moira was on the phone with I don't know how many other girls, renegotiating her ETA. There was no place for me in their schedule. Angie surprised me when she pulled me close and whispered: "We're going to have a nice little supper all our own soon Mr. Whippey," and gave me a full-bore kiss.

I was smiling to myself as I rode to the Lucy's on the back of a pick-up full of traps and lines.

Wendy wouldn't open the screen door for me. "He's in his shed," is all she'd say. I went around back. Mr. Lucy's shed was older than Mr. Lucy. That's not unusual for a house around here, but the houses were built to last. Sheds and shacks were made out of leftover building materials and boat parts. Most of the aging Bismuthian fishermen spent a majority of their dry time in their sheds, resolutely not repairing them.

Sheds are inevitably full of the ass-ends of things and stuff banished from the house. They hold unquantifiable amounts of the useless detritus of island life that isn't quite used up yet. The real secret to an island shed is that it's as full of sentiment and ghosts as an old toy chest. Island geezers aren't necessarily toughing out the frigid winter out there—sometimes they're weepy with memory, unable to look past the old paint cans they used to paint their dory so long ago.

Mr. Lucy's shed smelled like a sampling platter of toxic leftovers. As most of them do. I'd been on board with him enough to recognize his own particular brand of reek. I saw him before he saw me. He was in the open doorway, taking the sun, and reading a book. He looked small there and oddly professorial in his black plastic frame glasses. He closed the book, took off his glasses, and gave me a good slow squint. Then the churl spat, or tried to, anyway.

"You're an asshole, Orange."

"Could be."

"Waddayawant? Run outta seagum?"

"I got to talk to you."

"Done talkin' today. Took my teeth out already."

I looked past him into the gloom of the shed. I couldn't tell if it were a boat or a coffin that I saw inside.

"What did you tell Waldena?"

"That North Indian bitch?"

"Yeah."

"Nothin'."

"I don't think so," I said, unsure of how to press him further.

Mr. Lucy laughed, or at least it seemed that way. With his poor lip control and no dentures he could have been gargling his Irish Russian.

"Where's the package?" I asked him fair and square.

He laughed some more and even gave his knee a slap. "You come here just like her—'Where's the package old man!'—Ha! She shows us a picture on her telephone! It's you sitting there all grouchy in Ely Pond!" His laugh went from a gargle to a serious rearrangement of the phlegm in his lungs.

I was just so pleased he was amused. "She had me kidnapped; she had a gun on me."

"Listen, you let her do that to you, you deserve what you got. I didn't appreciate you settin' her on us, you know." He paused and smiled. "You in that dinghy!"

"Christ, I couldn't do anything about it; you're the one going around lying about me and the package!"

"You think I'm gonna flap my gums to any bitch that walks in here with your little picture? None of her business."

"You could have saved me a lot of trouble."

"Your trouble. Not mine."

"You know, Mineola says it wasn't meant for you. You were supposed to give it to her. It was supposed to be a sampo gift from the Koreans to Snorri."

Mr. Lucy pulled his drinking straw from his glasses case in his pocket. He held it between his teeth and puckered his lips around it with his fingers and then took a good sip of his Irish Russian. "Snorri and Mineola, eh?"

"They want it."

"Mini knows where to find me. Snorri's an idiot. Says he

crossed the ocean inside a whale."

"Ill John's pissed."

Mr. Lucy fussed around a bit with his glasses and straw. "I ever tell you 'bout Ill John's dad?"

"Please don't."

"You know I was in the Navy in Korea, right? A submarine. No air, submarines. No room to think. We were chasing Chinese subs all the time. They were chasing us. Christ, men got better sonar on boats in the harbor right now, just to find fish for tourists." Mr Lucy wiped his glasses again and paused so long, I was startled when he spoke again.

"It's no Cary Grant movie, I tell you. You'd think it would be interesting to see what's underwater, but there ain't a single window on a sub. Christ knows why. Everyone's always wanting to know: What's that? They spot us? That a good echo? A bad one?

"All that ever happened was there'd be a big thud. Some officer does a bunch of math. We all twirl dials and wheels. Levels go up and down. Everyone gets worried, and you're supposed to be very quiet. I never knew what the fuck was going on. We could have been right here in the harbor for all I knew.

"One day, the echoes are going back and forth. Maybe fleets of submarines. Maybe all the Chinese, Russians, and Japanese joined forces. Everyone's going crazy. Suddenly, 'Wham!' And it's not just some bump. We been hit so hard the hull's buckling. Then, wham, again and again, a wicked pounding. Half the men are screaming, holding their bleeding ears. The other half are shouting 'Shut up!' Everyone's ears and noses are bleeding. We're blasting up to the surface. Men trying to climb up each other's backs to claw open the hatch before we even strike air."

Mr. Lucy reached out with his straw and poked me in the hip, the only part of me he could reach.

"Listen, guy, we crest so hard, we're airborne for a minute, then we splash down again. The hatches are undogged. We clamber out. We're all over the submarine, clinging to anything, and the sea is foaming all around us. Just as we're getting our shit together with life boats, something else breaches hard.

"Straight out of the water comes a roaring whale, angry like no man has ever seen before. The crew is hollering a reeling of terror; I can hardly hear anything over the pounding of my heart. The whale lands hard on our bow, crushing it. We run to the tower, scared right past fright. Then we see something Christly crazy. The whale is circling our sub and it's got a line around it and a brow full of spears like it's been dogging a giant sea-porcupine. I tell you this, Orange: there is a man standing on the beast, holding on to the harpoons. He is driving the whale round and round us bellowing, 'I am the Yankee circumciser!'

"Most of our crew just plain faints. It's too much for them. It had only been a couple generations ago that my family put down its harpoons. I still got some of them right here, in the shed. Woulda given anything for a good Bismuth spear to finish the thing off.

"Anyway, nobody's making for the lifeboats, since it seems safer on the sub even if it's a goner. The whale is leaving a pink glowing wake. Its blood is mixing with the phosphor. The man plucks off a harpoon and hurls it at us. Our captain empties his sidearm at him. Nothing. The whale is circling tighter and tighter and our sub starts to spin in the maelstrom its making. We weren't going to be floating much longer. The man is windmilling his arm around, whooping, 'the circumciser!'

"Our sub is leaking fuel and the fumes are choking us, but we can't go anywhere. I see my chance and scoop up a floating harpoon. The whale and us are spinning in opposite directions, so it's hard to take a bead. I was aiming for the man, but it plunges into the whale instead. A good strike at any rate. Not like I'd been practicing in the sub." Mr. Lucy paused to rearrange the gravel in his craw and took another sip with his straw.

"I must have hit the head of an old harpoon with an explosive tip and raised a spark, because next thing you know, a sheet of blue fire spreads from the whale's head right over the man and all across its back. It keeps circling while the man becomes a screaming torch. The fire feeds on our fuel and the oil leaking out all the whale's jabs. Soon we're eddying in a ring of fire spread by the flaming monster. The whale gets wise that there's no more man on him, and dives down to quench its flames. And that's the last we seen of it, though we could see it left a tunnel of fire down into the deep." Mr. Lucy took out a handkerchief and wiped his chin and gave me a level stare.

I couldn't help myself and asked, "And the man was Ill John's father?"

"No, I don't know who that was. Johnson Kim was on the boat that rescued us eventually."

That was maybe the most monstrously huge big fish story I'd ever heard, and I was loathe to ask another question, but I did have my mission still. "Mr. Lucy, the package, the sampo. . . . "

"No such thing."

"There is too."

"Maybe I ain't done with it." Then he raised himself and went into the shed, closing the door behind him.

CHAPTER FIFTEEN

Winslow Homer and the Price of Tartar Sauce

Ill John announced: "Orange, we were discussing the cultural significance of Bill Gates' purchase of Winslow Homer's painting *Lost on the Grand Banks*."

Listening to Mr. Lucy had worn me out. I had been standing at the end of the Lucy's crushed-shell driveway thinking about how a bit of gray weather in a summer afternoon could be a relief to the rigorous glare the sea and the sun enforced. Some smudging is restful. These fleecy thoughts led me to more germane matters—my mission and how a nap was seeming increasingly utile and possibly sampo. *Mistakes were made; mission creep was experienced*, I testified before the imaginary tribunal. If being underemployed on a wearying summer's day on an island does not merit a man such as myself an afternoon nap, I'm in the wrong business, I reasoned. Minding my own business hadn't been working out lately, though.

My chief ally in all matters of dormancy had always been Rover. She was a genuine connoisseur of the afternoon nap, and a brave temporal explorer of napping at other unorthodox times of day as well, such as when she was already asleep. I tried to see my environs through her eyes. I spied the grassy mound that had once been part of the harbor fortifications and now was

135

strolling ground for tourists. It featured granite and earthen nooks that held soft heat like the Topsoil's bun warmer. I was already drifting there, half-asleep, when Ill John waved to me from the driver's seat of a big old Chevy Suburban parked on the roadside near the Lucy's house.

He and his yet-to-speak-English partner, whose name I'd yet to remember, were unpacking bags of food from the Topsoil. They had brochures unfolded on their laps; kraft bags and Styrofoam containers and cups lined the dash.

"We are staked-out, and while we attend Mr. Lucy, we are having a picnic of taken-out food and discussing whether our imaginary visions of this region, which we developed in admiring the artwork of Northeast American painters Winslow Homer, Albert Pinkham Ryder, Andrew Wyeth, and Edward Hopper, compared to what we see here while we are actually on this island. And our dinner is delicious. Please sit in the back seat and share it with us. Also, please tell us where Down East is."

These two did not look like they were gunning for me, as Angie had put it. It would have been ridiculous for me to run away. I was weary, but maybe it was time to treat with them. Plus I was hungry. I got in the back seat, and told them, "Down East is just down from here and to the east."

"And where would it be if we were not here right now?"

"That would depend on whether you're a native or not."

"We are not."

"Then it just means the continent and the islands near it."

"And if you are a native?"

"Much could be considered Down East."

"You are saying, perhaps, that it is a culturally idiomatic concept that does not translate well?"

"It's actually about which way the wind blows, but a way of

seeing things, yeah."

The two men were doing a decent job of ethnotourism here on the island. The old Suburban was definitely island in provenance, and their Red Sox caps, hoodies, and jeans looked local enough, except a little insufficiently slept in. Ill John's partner's assault rifle seemed out of place, though, as did their Ray Ban aviators.

Ill John's partner ate a bite of sandwich slowly, as if he were chewing around something, then he spoke to his partner.

Ill John translated and elaborated: "We are also enjoying comparing the Pinkytoe Crab Salad Sandwich to the Lobster Roll. Both are served on rolls for frankfurters and both are shellfish mixed with mayonnaise sauce. Both are white-pink and sweet. Yet their mouth feelings are different. The lobster roll has a resistance to the tooth that I enjoy, while Chosen appreciates the tastes of delicacy and gentle texture of the pinkytoe. He believes it would blend well as a milkshake."

"Chosen appreciates the pinkytoe?" I asked.

"Yes the native crab of your northern waters. So named, as the Topsoil person has said, for the traditional method of fishing used. The children of the fishermen dangled their smallest toes in the water to catch crabs for their fathers," said Ill John.

"Did you do that as a youth?" asked Chosen.

"Never."

"Many islanders are said to have lost their toe as children."

Someone at the Topsoil had been pulling their legs about pinkytoes, a type of crab Islanders used to eat as a last resort, but which had become faddish in America recently. "I've still got all eleven. What are you guys doing here?"

"We are waiting for Mr. Lucy."

"He's right there," I said, pointing to him.

"Yes, we are waiting for him to finish."

"What, lunch?"

"No, for him to finish with the package we trusted with him."

"So you know he's got it? You know what it is, I'm sure. You know I gave it to him? What the fuck? You know what I been through?"

"Hellanback?" said Chosen.

"Where's that?" I thought it was another island.

"Hell and back," Chosen said more carefully.

He spoke more English than I thought. "Maybe not back yet. Don't you want this package back from Mr. Lucy?"

"No," said Ill John, "we want the package to take its natural course to its recipient, Snorri, the Finlindian."

"What's that supposed to mean?"

Ill John said, as if it were obvious, "We did not anticipate Mr. Lucy's extra possession of the package; yet, we are prepared to observe Mr. Lucy's possession of it and how it may affect him. Also the additional tacks this package must take to achieve its course are unplanned and interesting, and we may be affected too by the spirit of this enterprise." He seemed mildly pleased his plan had been complicated by Mr. Lucy.

"The sampo."

"Perhaps."

"I've been affected."

"Yes, we know. Waldena, the Estonindian."

"So now you're just waiting to see which way the breeze blows?"

They conferred. "Yes, so to speak."

"I don't really want to be any part of this."

They spoke again in Korean. "Chosen and I have a saying," said Ill John. "Every man must pull his own island."

I sat back in my seat to think on that. "You guys chew any of the seagum?"

"It tastes terrible, and it makes my lips numb," said Chosen.

"You islanders are addicts?" asked Ill John.

"No, well, there are some, but I just chew it now and then. When you have to work all night and stuff. It's more like coffee you can chew."

Ill John held two big Styrofoam cups over the seat to me. "Here, would you like to have our coffees? We have been unable to acquire the taste for coffee, and we find that the coffee here is much worse-tasting than the coffees we have had in North America."

That was a good start. I took both cups like they were the paddles to a defibrillator. "So, like, tiger testes?" I asked.

"Many substances are sold as powdered tiger testes in Korea, including ground-up insects and caffeine pills," said Ill John.

"You don't have Korean Viagra?"

"Erections are still in the hands of amateurs in Korea. Men are reluctant to put their penises under medical control."

I supposed that sounded reasonable. "The seagum must sell for a lot back home."

"Not really," said Ill John. "It makes the visit more interesting though."

"Fuckin' A."

"Fuckin' A?" said Chosen.

"It's like 'wicked pissa,'" I said.

Chosen had met his idiomatic match. "Oh—because of the erection and the difficulty of urination," he said.

"Nope." I didn't explain, since I didn't want to tell him that I had no idea why I had grown up believing these phrases were the proper way to express approval and enthusiasm. Also, I was uncomfortable talking about erections.

"You understand that we are here for more than seagum?" asked Ill John.

"Yeah, I think you want Snorri's whales, right?"

"We are prepared to open a discussion with his whaling council. But we have become involved in another endeavor involving whales and Snorri and even the Estonindian witch."

"Waldena?"

"Yes. Snorri the Finlindian says she is Waldena the Witch," said Chosen.

"Yeah, that sounds right. I think they hate each other."

"Now we must all cooperate along with the woman from Gaeity on something that will pay us all very well and even be a boon to your island," said Ill John.

I recalled Mini grilling me after supper on her island and her implication that there was a bigger scheme in play with the Koreans than the seagum and sampo whatsit package. I wondered why they wanted to tell me about it.

"Boon." I said, not expecting them to be forthcoming. "Bismuth still has to be way out of your way. Why bother coming all the way here—you could have met Snorri in Europe."

"It is . . . ."

"A working vacation," Chosen finished for him.

"Yes, we had admired this part of the world for years before we established the seagum trade with your Mr. Lucy. Just visiting as tourists is unsatisfying. We like to engage in the lives of people here, to see things as an Islander might. We, Chosen especially, have been researching the arts and cultures of your region since college. You should see Chosen's bookshelf at home: Phillips Lovecraft, Waldo Emerson, James, King, Hawthorne, Mather, Rowe Snow, Maud Montgomery, Allen Poe. Books about blueberries and potatoes. Many collections of coastal seascape paintings. He has a special blanket on the wall that he traded for last summer."

"A crazy quilt," said Chosen, "with lighthouses and lobsters. It is authentic."

"We would like to try lobstercatching. Do you do this?" said Ill John. "With a pot-hauling boat—yes?"

"Yes, but it's not my boat—you already know Mr. Lucy."

"We asked him once; he did not answer."

I supposed there must be lobster boats to charter. But not pots. They'd have to crew with someone. If they didn't get in the way too badly, taking the Korean guys out would be like having free labor. I would have been quite willing to let the Koreans work in my place for a small fee.

"Do you guys want to try working in the Topsoil kitchen? It's very authentic. I could make some arrangements. It might involve a gratuity. To me, that is."

"No, thank you," they said in unison.

"Perhaps, Orange, as a native, you can tell us why this tartar sauce costs so much when it is clearly composed of common ingredients and does little to complement the taste of the fried clams we have," said Ill John.

"It's like a tax for tourists that the Topsoil charges."

Ill John nodded sagaciously. I was pretty certain he had an intuitive understanding of mark-ups and middle men. I continued to help them eat their lunch. They were smart not to have ordered the seafood salad. I'd seen the tub it was kept in, in the Topsoil's walk-in.

"We have ordered well?"

"Any American would have known to get more napkins."

"That is noted." Ill John and Chosen spoke for a while in

Korean. Ill John turned back to include me in the conversation. "So, you are familiar with the works of Homer?"

"A little."

"His paintings, we were saying, show more tendency of Modernism than Regionalism. Do you agree?"

I shrugged. Nobody had ever asked before. Summer people painted on Bismuth. Painters painted Bismuthians painting their boats. I heard there was one guy from New York that spent years here, winters included, trying to get the color gray right. You can't ask a native about Regionalism though. It's like asking the proverbial frog if his bath is boiling yet. Regardless, I appreciated being asked.

"What fascinates Chosen and I is that so many of the sea paintings of your region after the American Civil War show all these empty boats or individuals adrifting. Yet the most exciting painting, which we look forward to seeing one day at the Museum of Fine Art in Boston, Massachusetts, on the continent, is Copley's dramatic *Watson and the Shark*. What happened during the period since it was painted during the American Revolutionary War and when these painters began depicting lost moody boats and castaways?"

"What guide books do you guys read in Korea that includes art criticism?"

Chosen smiled. Ill John said, "None, but we might write one. This whole region has a fascinating aesthetic history, even if it is now. . . ."

"Rundown," said Chosen for him.

Rundown was the very word for Mr. Lucy's shed. "Rundown, no shit. Listen, Ill John, your dad knew Mr. Lucy during the war?"

"Yes. They met in a naval rescue."

"Is it true about the whale? Who was on it?"

"What whale?"

I began to explain the story Mr. Lucy had told me in the shed about the submarine and the whale, but then my instincts caught up to me. I had long since stopped believing or disbelieving anything Mr. Lucy, and frankly most of my elders, told me, since the island is essentially a corroboration-free zone. One does not have to apply to a mainland agency to get a poetic license, though they do have to be renewed frequently. Mr. Lucy was probably just keeping his current when he told me about the Yankee Circumciser.

"Storytelling is a very important tradition on your island, innit," said Ill John.

His "innit" was an attempt to use Indian dialect. "Yankees don't say 'innit.' Only Indians—Native Americans, not Northern Indians."

"Ah, but we are not Yankees. You have forgotten that visitors do not have the same cultural prohibitions that natives follow."

I didn't have anything nice to say, so I ate a fried clam.

Chosen asked, "It is part of your culture, though, storytelling? We admire it. I have read a great deal about the supernatural storytelling traditions of northeast coastal Americans. We find speech hard to induce from your neighbors, but also we find that their stories continue for great durations and contain hidden barbs. And also, the elderly of your island are especially difficult to understand, even if they are storytelling at length."

"What can I say? We have a lot of time to kill. And bad reception, too."

"Maybe we can help with that," said Ill John.

"Killing time? OK, good luck." They didn't realize they were in the presence of a master. I'd killed more time than I'd lived through. I'd killed entire histories. My life was a shooting gallery of time.

"No, reception."

"Oh. I gotta dish now, anyway," I said.

"For your telephone?"

"No, TV."

"Why are these called Clam Fritters, and not Clam Dumplings? Are they good in soup?" asked Chosen, holding what we in the Topsoil Kitchen had always called a Clam McNugget.

"I dunno."

"Would you like to eat it?"

"Sure." I took it from him, and as I ate it, I began to feel like an ape in a zoo, taking a banana from a visitor.

"Would you like to tell us an island story? We would be curious to hear it," said Chosen.

"No matter how true it is," said Ill John.

Their interest in paintings of people falling overboard and the forlorn boats of yesteryear reminded me of the dory races that had lasted here on Bismuth even until my youth. Though by my time they had devolved into drunken scrummages, the dory races were once an important competition between the tribes, families, guilds, sects, and factions of our island. It was a sort of combination of Northwest American potlatch ceremonies and a life boat drill—a way of bleeding your opponents dry by exsanguinating yourself first. On the first Sunday in May, Bismuthians gathered to cripple and sink each other's boats with generosity. Each crew in this regatta would be obliged to carry their dory full of gifts from other crews across the island, launch it, and then row it back into the harbor. If they made it back to the docks, they'd get to keep the gifts in the dory. You couldn't just give another crew a boat full of rocks, since the quality and extravagance of your gifts signified the status of your crew, just as much as your own crew's ability to haul the goods home.

A few decades ago, the Quakers had dominated the dory races for many years. Their chapel still bears evidence of their supremacy. Since many of the more durable gifts included sacred icons, idols, statuary, and even relics, the Quaker Chapel had become a museum of pantheism. Finlindian ursaphernalia, a birch bark canoe, a vast unthrowable spear made of horn named "Lay It in Your Lap!" from the Estonindians, a right whale skull, and the thigh bone of the ancient giant, Glooskap, from the American Indians hung from the rafters. Along the walls stood a statue of the walkingfish god of the Dagon, stitched from hides and skins unrecognized by Bismuthian lay-scholars, a cairn of holy sauna-stones, a suit of lacquered horseshoe crab armor, the island's first internal combustion engine, a totem pole of famous Northeast Yankee writers, a narwhal pizzle, and an Egyptian sphinx made by the island's Masonic order.

As a kid, I found myself in the Quaker Chapel fairly often, and as we all sang "Michael, Row the Boat Ashore," I enjoyed musing on one of the more modest bits of booty—on a shelf was a seemingly empty bluish Ball jar. It was said to contain all the greatest treasures of the tiny people of Bismuth, whose puny boats never stood the slightest chance in the dory races, yet who bravely and stupidly entered every year.

The minister there told us kids that the races had ended because the crews had become too vain. They had gilded and decorated their boats so lavishly that they didn't want to sully them any longer by participating in the spectacle. So instead, they rowed them to the great waterfall at the edge of the ocean and pushed them off into space.

I've since learned that a rivalry between the Yankee Quakers and the Portuguese Catholics had ruined the whole thing. One year, the Portuguese gave the Quakers what they said was their most sacred statue, an eight-foot tall figure of St. Cephalus, carved from native granite by a Portuguese sailor blinded in a flying-fish attack. St. Cephalus was one of the more deformed saints, who performed miracles even though he was debilitated by an enormous head and tentacular-like dewlaps.

The Quakers managed to portage the huge idol in their dory across the island but the top-heavy saint sank the boat just off shore, killing two of the Quaker rowers. Divers still visit the statue today. The Portuguese were horrified by the deaths of the Quakers and, ever since then, feasted the Quakers with paella teeming with squid, octopus, and cuttlefish every year on the anniversary of the race.

The caption on the wall of sepia photographs in the Historical Society building called them the "Dories of Yore." This was the phrase in my mind as Ill John considered the empty boats and the collective depressed psyche of Northeast islanders in the mid-nineteenth century.

I told my Korean interlocutors that I didn't know any stories, and anyways I wasn't in the mood.

CHAPTER SIXTEEN

A Twelve Pack and the Lucky Lady

I'm not sure I had ever killed an entire afternoon in a car going nowhere before. At least food was served. By the time it started getting cool and breezy, I had tired of playing an immobile tour guide for Ill John and Chosen. Plus I was jangly and a little green at the gills from drinking their coffees and eating their fried clams. While they patiently observed Mr. Lucy's house, I refined my mission: Go home and be done with this business. Pet my TV. Watch my cat. I told the Koreans so, and Ill John said that he wasn't yet ready to pull up his stakeout. I bid them happy hunting and made my way back downtown, hoping to catch a ride back to my place.

I stopped into the store to use the bathroom and therein hatched a plan that would lead directly to personal fulfillment: Buy a twelve-pack of nice regionally brewed beer and a pack of cigarettes. Give bottle number one to whomever gave me a ride home; I'd drink number two along with him or her, preferably her. By bottle number four, I would be Orange, Laird of Bismuth. By six, I'd be ready to solve the quandary that most plagues members of the leisure class—shall I sleep on the couch or go upstairs to bed? An excellent aspect of this plan was that there would be more beer for tomorrow.

The reason that this required a plan and not a mere purchase is that I didn't have any money on me, which is why I didn't plan to buy cheap cans of 'gansett—shoot the moon, I figured. I can't steal from the store; its existence is tenuous and we were all engaged in a silent conspiracy of good will to convince the owners to keep it open throughout the winter. I could have walked out of the store with just about anything else I wanted on credit, but the owners forbade all the good stuff like beer and cigs unless actual cash was surrendered.

I waved to Donna at the register as I walked out, already feeling nostalgic for my plan, which, though simple and well considered, remained an impossibility. I met Ricky, the kid who ran the Topsoil tender, coming in. He had money, he had to. He got more tips than most anyone else on the island. And he was friendly and sympathetic to most endeavors that included drugs or alcohol. And he was probably legal too. I described my plan to him, emphasizing the immediacy with which I would remunerate him, as well as the nice cold beer I would immediately render him upon receipt of the twelve pack.

Ricky concurred that this was a fine plan and even went so far as to go into the store to buy the beer, instead of just loaning me the money. When he got out, he took a bottle of the nice stuff from the case, popped the top with the opener on his key chain and handed it to me. "On the house," he said. I had a long smug pull before it occurred to me that Ricky had modified my plan and that now he had eleven beers, a pack of smokes, and I only had one beer and it was half gone.

Donna banged on the inside of the store's door and told us to beat it. Ricky asked me if I wanted to smoke some bowls. I allowed that might be something worth doing, though I should probably have gone home.

"Actually," Ricky said, "I gotta get back to work. You want to just smoke on the tender?"

I also allowed that although I ought to go home, I could probably bear to watch Ricky work as long as I did not have to remain sober, nor work myself. It would be easier on me, I cautioned him, if he also did not strain himself.

Bob, the owner of the Topsoil, did not share this opinion. When we got back to the dock where the tender was tied, someone must have ratted Ricky out for dereliction of duty, since Bob was on the radio ranting almost the moment Ricky turned it on. Ricky was politely contrite in a way that only well-bred offislanders can manage. He told me he, himself would open the floodgate of the dinner rush and that within a couple hours Mrs. Barrow, the ancient waitress who had worked there since before food was invented, would be radioing on the sly to ask him to bring in the tourists more slowly, so things would be less frantic on the floor.

There were actually worse ways to kill an evening. I don't think drinking with my cat would have been an improvement, though I really should have started home earlier that day. I held the boat steady a dozen or so times as veiny-legged, knobby-kneed geezers in pastel shorts clambered down their yachts' ladders onto our taxi. The worst was a return trip where Ricky and I had to play hospital orderlies to get a hostile yachtsman flushed with sunburn and cocktails back up his ladder. But even then, his wife gave us a twenty. It was a nice switch for me. Usually I lost dignity and money. Here, they lost dignity and I got paid.

It was around eleven and we were on the last pair of beers and idling out on the far end of the harbor when Ricky got a cell phone call. He turned his back to me and hunched over the outboard motor to give himself a sense of privacy. I could hear him quickly assenting to several things. When he finished I asked him how he'd found a new phone on the island to replace the one he'd dropped overboard.

"Look, dude, it's like this," he said with quiet urgency, "she gave me this phone. She calls, I come."

"Who? And don't call me dude."

"I . . . I don't even want to talk about her. But I have to go now."

"OK but can you drop me down the town docks instead of the Topsoil? It'll be easier for me to find a ride there."

"I mean I have to go *now*. There's . . . a window."

"A fuckin' back door, I bet. Who is she?"

Ricky looked concerned, spooked almost. Determined, though. Little Ricky had found himself a Mrs. Robinson he couldn't quite handle, but he was definitely going to try—again. Or so I presumed.

"I got an idea," he said. "That's Bob's boat, the *Lucky Lady*. I've got the key to the hatch. He's not going to sleep out there tonight, especially if I've got the tender."

"So?"

"So you could crash there and I can come pick you up after."

"After?"

"Yeah."

"When's that?" I was dubious.

"I could leave you at the breakwater."

"Not a chance."

He was already heading to Bob's boat. "Ricky, just take me back. What's that going to take, half an hour?" He looked desperate.

"Here," he said, and gave me a sandwich bag with around

half an eighth of weed left and the little wooden pipe shitty with resin we'd been using. "And he's got a full bar with a beer fridge." I held the baggie and pipe but didn't put it in my pocket. Ricky delayed a moment and then grubbed out the tip money from his pants pocket and handed me the wad.

"Oh good, I can throw a boat party." What was I supposed to do? If it came to an oar fight, I'm not sure I would have won. My brain had gone soft and beery anyway.

I'd been on Bob's boat before; it was kind of plush. Sometimes there were parties after work there, especially if there were new, cute waitresses around. I looked at Ricky, ready to tell him to fuck off. There was smoke coming out of his ears; I could smell his wires frying. I was a fool and then some, but I was feeling lazy and avuncular. "Fuck. OK. But right after, OK?"

"Right after. She won't let me stay long anyway."

I didn't wave as he motored off to his assignation, not that he would have noticed; he had the scent bad and would have swum to her if he had to.

Bob's boat, the *Lucky Lady*, was a cabin cruiser, something over 30 feet. It was pretty typical of the pleasure boats moored in the harbor, but back in the early 1980s when Bob acquired it, it was considered a little too big for the island. Ricky had given me the key for the hatch on a red and white bobber keychain so I let myself into his pleasure palace. The way Bob tells it, he got the *Lady* off a dead cocaine cowboy.

The story goes he's trying to close up the Topsoil, but a hard-partying trio won't get the hint. There's a Colombian or some kind of Central American guy—short and ugly—Bob emphasizes. Bob is tall and paunchy now; he was probably swank in denim bell bottoms and a blow-dried beard in his prime. With the

Colombian are two beautiful young women from, as Bob figures it, New York. He says they had to be escorts. Bob winds up sitting with the three of them at the bar after closing, doing some lines. They run out, but the Colombian says he's got a stash back on his boat.

They're all real well lit so it sounds like a good idea to the four of them, and Bob takes them out to the cowboy's boat with the Topsoil's launch. According to Bob, he wanders into the cabin to find the head. He opens a stateroom door and nearly has a heart attack—the room is packed with bales of money. Shrink-wrapped bundles of pure, uncut greenbacks.

Bob is truly disappointed because now he feels burdened— he's obliged, he says, to steal it. There you are, an honest man, a Boy Scout even, and you have to begin a life of crime just because some gangster is too buzzed to hide his cash. So, he tells the threesome he's sick and leaves on his launch. He comes back to the restaurant, slaps himself sober and makes his ninja plan. Before dawn he paddles back out in an inflatable and sneaks on board. There's nobody there. He checks the rooms—no cash. He's disappointed but relieved of the responsibility of having to steal that much money.

A week later, the *Lady* is still moored in the harbor. The harbormaster has noticed. Bob rows over for another visit and nobody's home. He doesn't think anyone's been there since he went and found the money gone. He waits a few days, pays yet another visit and finds her title—it's registered to someone in Virginia. Another few days and Bob has signed the boat over to himself and now it's his.

The best part of the story comes weeks later. Bob says he finally had time to take it out of the harbor. He goes to use the head and discovers the Colombian's severed head floating there in the blue chemical solution of the toilet. Bob adds as a coda to his story that he thinks the girls did it, maybe they were assassins, and if he'd stayed any longer on the Colombian's boat, he'd have been killed too. It was only his decision to steal the money that saved his life.

CHAPTER SEVENTEEN

Waldena in Balsam and Hashish

It was good and late. Ricky was unsurprisingly absent. I never did believe he was coming back. I had gone to lay down for a while in the bedroom that had once been filled to the ceiling with bales of cash money, thinking to replace its absence with my presence would be amusing. It wasn't—it felt like I was gently rocking in a crypt and it made me feel queasy. Bob's bar was like an adult orphanage. Midori, Cointreau, Irish Mist and so on—all absurdly undrinkable. The promised beer fridge held a six of Buttwiper and my brain was already too wet to get excited about it. I opened one out of pity—just to give the six a reason to exist. I went topside and stretched out on a bench on the rear deck. Only the smallest of waves were still awake and chattering against the hull. I could hear a shushing roar of surf from out past the breakwater and the sporadic clangs of halyards against aluminum masts from the dozing sailboats moored in the harbor.

It was chilly; I found a hoodie from the life jacket compartment under the bench. It had a silhouette of a poodle on the back and said "Black Poodle, Bismuth ME," which was meant to be an inside islander joke on the dog logo of a wealthy island's restaurant that had become fashionable with the tourists. A thick creamy moonbeam floated on the surface of the harbor; it ran from Miss Moon, herself, right to me on the *Lucky Lady*.

Sometime during the small hours, I spied the glint of moonlight on a ripple of water. The ripple resolved in to a wake; something pretty big was swimming just underwater. I was able to track it as it meandered around the boats slowly arcing on their mooring lines. I figured it for a harbor seal, cruising for leftovers. It kept a heading for me, just like my moonbeam. Soon I could hear it parting the water but could see nothing other than the highlights of the wake. I felt the stern dip a little and realized it had climbed aboard. Seals do this when they think you're holding. They can be bullies.

There, on the stern deck stood Waldena. There, on the stern deck stood Waldena, clad only in moonlight and a heavy coating of transparent grease. There, on the stern deck, stood a beautiful Estonindian woman, unblushingly naked and greased, who had recently kidnapped me and menaced me beyond all reason. I should have jumped overboard. Instead, I gawked.

Waldena wiped her face then squeegeed her body by running her hands over her breasts and belly. Her hands parted to skim each buttock. Then she wrapped her fingers around her thigh and pushed downward as if she were taking off her stocking. Lampreys do something similar to slough off their mucousy coatings, but she was significantly less repulsive. She raised a hand as if she were going to wave, and then flicked a gob of grease at me. Some of it splatted quietly on my chest; I bent my head to sniff it. The unguent had an aroma of balsam and hashish.

"Towel," she said. "Orange, close your mouth, and go get me a towel."

I wondered why I should take orders from this woman. She was as vulnerable as someone gets; she had been very mean to me; and she hadn't yet even said hello. So I fetched her a towel.

After blotting herself a bit, she handed me back the towel, now moist and bewitchingly fragrant. Before I could check myself, I held it to my nose and took a hit off of the pheromonic and hallucinogenic musk that clung to it. Waldena smirked. "You haven't even said hello."

"You're supposed to ask for permission to board another man's boat."

"Did you?"

She had a decent point. And she was glistening in the lunar light. The water beaded from her slickered skin and each dot of sea held a pearl of moonlight. "Happy birthday," I told her.

"It's not my birthday."

"We call what you're wearing a 'birthday suit,'" I said, "because it's what you were born wearing."

"That's not what we say. But children born wearing fur or cauls are special to us."

"Would you like a robe? I bet Bob has a few."

"If it would make you more comfortable."

I went and pushed the hangers around in the bedroom closets. Shorty kimono, smoking jacket, and a nice après-skinnydip robe. I brought it back out top; she took it and wore it negligently. I wondered if there could be anything on Earth more intimidating than a dangerous, undressed woman.

"So," I said, "going visiting?"

"I come in peace." Waldena turned away from me to face the town and reached within the robe. She opened a finger-sized ivory container and held out a nicely rolled joint.

"Where. . ."

"The pocket of my birthday suit."

I was flummoxed, "I'm not so sure. . . ."

"Just get a lighter."

156

I did, of course. An assassin sneaks up and tries to drug me? Of course I'll help. We exchanged the joint quietly, until I said, "That's not Vap-o-Rub, is it?"

"No," she said, opening her robe so she could dredge two fingers through the film that still slicked her belly, "It's a secret, sacred preparation we have used since the time of the ancients to swim the cold, dark distances. I'll have to leave before it deteriorates—it gets rank and starts to run in the daylight." She puffed. "It will probably ruin this robe."

I've read about the witches of Massachusetts; Hawthorne says they flew to their sabbaths on broomsticks. Later scholars suggested the women's broomsticks were phalluses lubricated with hallucinogenic grease, and that the flight was metaphoric, though still pretty visceral. Long distance swimmers coat themselves with a gloop called channel grease to keep the cold and jellyfish and all the other stingy and nasty things off of them. Waldena's form of witchy goo seemed to nicely split the difference.

"How did you know I was here?"

"I checked a few boats; it was not difficult."

"But how did you know?"

"A little boy told me," she said, arching a brow.

"You mean birdie."

"No, I do not."

God, that boy had to be Ricky. He was probably tied to her bed or something. Served him right. "Well." I puffed on the joint. I'd never smoked weed like Waldena's before. I'd never felt so conclusively massive, yet so likely to fly away. "Well then, how come?"

"To see you. To ask you a few more questions."

"Are you going to throw me overboard?"

"I bet you'll fall off all by yourself tonight."

We smoked the joint down.

"Listen," she said, "you think I'm some kind of thug. What I'm doing is important."

"A sadistic Northern Indian ninja witch whale huntress Thor cult priestess coated in hallucinogenic grease."

"What?"

"I don't think you're a thug."

Waldena seemed as if she were checking in with her astral projection, pausing in a way that suggested time was flowing differently for each of us.

She toyed with the robe's sash. "Thugs worshipped Kali, I believe. Stranglers, weren't they? A knotted cord to the throat? And Thor cult is not that accurate. The Norse had plenty of deities who had to be introduced to the Northern Indian deities when we arrived in Europe. There were the original Arctic ice giants, the Norse gods, the deities that accompanied us from North America to Europe, the Christian deities that seeped up from the desert, all the local gods and spirits, the animal and monster gods, venerable ancestors, the Roman gods the Vikings brought back with them, and there are plenty more too."

She leaned in close. "I am sworn to a god you might translate as Thor, but the worship is much more sophisticated than I think you are implying. Besides, this is Thursday, his day, and a full moon. A woman with responsibilities like mine does not just sit quietly and light candles on his night."

I must have looked worried. She smirked. "I am not going to sacrifice you, Orange."

I did not know the name of the emotion I felt around Waldena. It was a new one on Bismuth. I think she brought it with her the way her ancestors brought their gods eastward on their migration. It was a sense of pleasant imperilment, like I was sitting on the edge of an abyss, whistling and swinging my legs, knowing perfectly well the cliff was crumbling.

"Oh calm down, Orange," she said coyly, "I am here on business. Mostly."

"So, what then? You're a businesswoman, a spy, a smuggler, a pirate?"

"I'm not a spy or a pirate. I'm a cultural ambassador."

"And I'm the mayor of Bismuth."

"Nice to meet you, your honor."

I would have stood and bowed to play along, but I was experiencing a powerfully clement gravitational collapse. The smoke, the aroma of Waldena's deliquescing salve—part blubber, part deep forest, part cannabis—warming from her body heat, and the homey scent of brine and mild decay that was the harbor on a summer night conspired with the waves to make me feel tremendously open to suggestion and equally unlikely to act on anything.

"As a cultural ambassador, I travel on behalf of Estonindia to places like Bismuth to promote our culture and help people understand our history."

"Make allies, open new trade routes. . . ."

"Exactly, Orange. You can imagine a hunting culture is difficult to maintain over millennia; hard simply to survive, and hard now that the character of both hunter and prey have been sapped away by civilization." She drew up a knee, parting the robe, and smeared a circle on her kneecap. Her pronunciation of my name still thrilled me.

"We human beings can do two things pretty well when we set our collective will to it: adapt to our environment and change our environment. When the Northern Indians decided to leave here and follow the whale roads to the north we didn't know we'd arrive in the North Indies—Estonindia and her little sister, Finlindia—many generations later. We were hunting, and we kept getting farther away from our homeland, until we passed the point of no return. Then we became Arctic people." Waldena pinched a layer of fat on the inside of her thigh. "We adapted. We grew insulation. Animals in the Arctic evolve faster than anywhere on the earth. Forget finches and tortoises—just look at polar bears; they were brown bears just a few thousand years ago.

"It is because the environment changes, of course. The glaciers advance and recede over and over. When they ebbed, the big beasts flourished and North America was home to the biggest, hairiest animals on the planet. When the slow ice tide came back in, the animals shrank.

"In the Arctic, we learned how to climb over and swim under the ice from the bears and walruses. We learned the whales had done the same and learned how to hunt for the squid from the sharks."

Sensing an oncoming saga, I interrupted the ambassador and asked her if she wanted a beer. She said she wanted something as sweet and potent as could be brewed here. I got us Buttwipers and settled back in to hear the rest.

"We found the way to Hyperborea. It may not have been real, but the route we discovered and the world we found there was more fantastic, more sublime than a city-oasis in the frigid wastes. We wouldn't have discovered it, or even made the voyage if we hadn't learned the umweltern of the Arctic."

"What's the umweltern?"

"You don't have a good word for it in English. It's the sensorium one lives within; the world that is just your own."

"Like mood or point-of-view?"

"No, it's much more encompassing. It's the sum of everything perceivable—in a way it's the subjective realm each of us occupies. Our umweltern are very similar because we share the same senses. We think they're quite different because of our cultures, but most of what we know and see is translatable between us."

Waldena was holding forth, and I liked it more than I should. If my professors in college were more like Waldena, I'd be a genius. Or dead.

"But the umwelt of a polar bear and the umwelt of a tern are very different, even if they're both sitting on an iceberg. Their senses and needs are quite different but they converge on the same fish each of them wants to eat. The fish has its own umwelt, the iceberg yet another."

"You're saying the iceberg can sense things?"

"I can hardly describe the umwelt of an iceberg to you this evening. It's not something for words in any language. I could yoik it, maybe. Icebergs—they grow, they calve new bergs, they sing, they take voyages. Anything from the Arctic that has any life in it at all is attracted to an iceberg. Modern people see cities, blocks of buildings, cathedrals when they see a herd of bergs. When moderns see Hyperborea, it's a city above the clouds that the stars themselves are moored to. The stars pivot around the legendary city like boats at anchor.

"The ancients couldn't see cities in the north. They had no concept of city in their umweltern. They saw crystal mountains, vast walls of forest—they were mirages and hallucinations, of course, just like the moderns who trudge on and on to the city that they will never find."

"But you're saying your people discovered a passageway to this mirage city that wasn't even a city?" I was seeing Waldena, nude, behind the crystal wall of a transparent palace. I shook my head to fix on her sitting in the boat again. She didn't seem to notice.

"My people discovered they were on a voyage. They changed their minds many times about their ultimate destination—Ultima Thule, as it turned out—but the realization that the voyage was more important than the destination, that's not something many peoples discover.

"The voyaging helped us adapt and learn. There were infinite passageways. We found them in the icebergs.

"A berg is like a planet, wandering the sea instead of the space. It pulls life toward it—shelter for the tiny creatures, hunting ground for the larger ones. They are habitats that house the skeletons of animals from all of history. There are arteries that you and I could swim through side-by-side that vermiform the bergs. Animals use them as caves, as escapes, they ride inside the bergs like passengers on a ship. The tunnels are so slick and twisting that many creatures have died within them, leaving ancient bodies still being consumed by the slowest of microbes. They would hide boats from times before times, boats built to scales for giants and dwarves. Tusks unreasonably long. Some bergs have crevasses that allow one to climb all the way to the bottom of the sea within the berg.

"As the bergs furrow the seabed, and the water surges through the tunnels and chambers, as the wind whisks around the peaks and ridges, a slow, primal music is made. The tides and waves provide a steady rhythm. The birds sing atop and the whales moan from below; the foot of the berg dragging across the ocean floor makes the sound of an orchestra besieging a symphony; over time their skirmishes resolve into what sounds like a coordinated battle. If you listen long enough, the battles come to tell the stories of peoples—eddas of tribes and nations, sagas of herds and flocks.

"It took us generations to learn how to hear this music. It's slow. Compositions just reaching their crescendo now were begun in a time of giant shaggy beasts. We had to learn how to master coldness and stillness. Bears had taught us how to wait for almost unendurable stretches at a breathing hole to spear a seal. The whales and wind had taught us to listen for voices from vast distances from the land. We had to learn to wait through snowblindness, through *kayakangst*, to learn to float alone, silently, unthinkingly, and break free from the time kept within our bodies to hear the slower music of the bergs.

"You probably know the story of the Hyperborean king, the frost giant that herded icebergs—he whiled away his days frivolously pushing the bergs around like enormous chess pieces, killing time until he could attack the Norse deities. We tell this story differently. In our tale, he is a sorcerer and a conductor. He is telling the story of the whole world from before the beginning and after the end with the music of the bergs, like an orrery of symphony halls and stadia orbiting in the compass-killing North. That's part of the Northern Indians' umweltern; we don't know the story of the world, but we have heard part of it being sung."

I could hear a few halyards clanging and a motor chugging in the distance. Waldena settled into a silence. I tried to hear the music of the spheres above but knew it wasn't anything for a quick listen. The sky had filled in with sidereal detail, and the fogs, birds, bugs of my planet were gone; earlier, I had felt imbued with gravity, now it was dissipating. I felt as if pathways through the atmosphere were forming, tempting me upwards; I was light-footed but still heavy-headed. I had been enchanted;

I was being reeled up to the dome of the sky, an ancient micro-fractured skull with uncountable trepanations.

The telling and the listening had set us both adrift. We orbited slowly in our own eddies; Waldena's breathing had become loud and regular. I thought it sounded like a prenatal yoga exercise. That aperçu made me realize my head was out of the ether and back on Bismuth. I grabbed Waldena's slick foot to pull her down or up from whatever pelagic or celestial realm she was lollygagging in.

"Hey. Hey! I forget. Why did you swim here?"

"Umwelt," she said, after a long prenatal pause. "You needed to hear the big picture."

"I think you've told me a lot, but I'm not sure you've told me anything."

"The package, Orange."

"Ah, the sampo."

"The sampo," she said mockingly. "Oh, Snorri. He doesn't deserve it. His people don't deserve it. It should be ours."

"The package?"

"You know Finlindian wizards used to feed their bears hallucinogenic mushrooms and then drank their urine? It condenses the drug."

It actually wasn't that hard to imagine Snorri with a mug, tailing his bear, waiting for it to piss. "So the package is that important?"

"Probably not. I don't think I even want it anymore. It's the trade we want."

"What trade?"

"What do you mean, 'what trade?'"

"I mean, what are you talking about?"

"I told you this was all about the survival of our hunting

culture, right?" she said with hypnagogic testiness.

"Oh yeah, you're the Ambassador."

"The Finlindians want to destroy our culture, replace it with their insipid ranches and stupid trained whales. We had been selling the Koreans whales for years; now they want whales of their own. They say they were whalers before we were. All they ever did in Korea was wait for them to wash up on shore. You buy our whales, you're buying a free-range creature that has lived a full life in the world. You see our brands on their haunches, you know you're buying something that's lived a rich, natural life. We breed them and let them rove in pods of their own; we only harvest the healthiest, strongest creatures at the peak of their maturity. Finlindian whales are disease-prone dwarf sperm and pygmy melonhead minkes that beg and roll over for their krill-kibble.

"The Finlindians keep their whalestock in pens in the fjords, breeding them fat and docile. They're probably breeding miniatures for restaurant aquariums. Their whales have no sense of the breadth of ocean; they've never dived for the big squid or called to a pod thousands of miles away. It's cruel, Orange, it's cruel to keep a whale like that." She shook her head sadly.

"As opposed to hunting them down on the open sea? That's not cruel?"

"Exactly! These are powerful hunting animals. Cages destroy their spirit. They need to remain in fighting trim to be worthy of an Estonindian hunter. We wouldn't sell anything less. If Snorri brokers a deal for the Finlindians to drive a herd to Korea, it will destroy our trade with Korea. We don't have many customers anymore—we need that trade for our way of life to survive."

"What about North Korea? A whale would go a long way there."

"No, not *juche*."

"*Juche* and Sampo—it sounds like a boat drink."

"What is a boat drink?"

"A leisure-class cocktail. So, the package, the sampo. . . ."

"It's just a bribe from the Koreans to the Finlindians. Probably some Korean scrimshaw or maybe chocolate. Sampo is important to all of us Northern Indians, but Ill John and Chosen are exaggerating its importance. It's a game they're playing, like cultural flirting. They are more like cultural stalkers than tourists."

"You tortured me for that? The Koreans know I gave it to Mr. Lucy, you know. He was lying."

"I didn't torture you," she said sharply. "You torture yourself. I was here to do what I could to disrupt their meeting. I wasn't going to pick a fight directly with the Finlindians—they're our brothers and sisters. Now it's too late. There's going to be some shame in store for me when I get back. All I could do is count a little Finlindian coup to remind them they're supposed to be hunters."

"What do you mean 'a little Finlindian coup'?"

"You know what counting coup is."

"I thought it was more like playing tag with a stick."

"You're thinking of Plains Indians on horses. If I have to go back to my whaling council in Estonindia and report that the Finlindian council got the Korean whale trade, I will at least be able to say I taught Snorri and the Finlindians a lesson."

"What was the lesson?"

"You might as well stay out of it. Let us just say respect for tradition."

"Fine by me. Why are you still here, though? Bismuth, I mean."

"The Estonindian and Finlindian whaling councils have decided to cooperate on a joint research venture and my council wants me to stay in this region to watch over it."

"So, Snorri, too?"

"As you islanders might say: aye yup," she said, drawing the word out for maximum sarcasm.

I was going to ask something more about her research venture when Waldena stood and shrugged off the robe. Once again I lost control of my jaw muscles and could only gape. She stepped over to me, greasily and sublimely bare. She tossed her braids in back of her and ran her palm from her clavicle, between her breasts, down to her pubis. She scooped out a dollop of grease from her belly button with her fingertip and poked it in my mouth, like a lurid eucharist. She told me she had to go before it wore off, then leapt daintily overboard. I saw her swim under the hull of a moored pleasure boat before I lost sight of her wake. Later on, I closed my mouth and swallowed.

CHAPTER EIGHTEEN

Field Trip to a Dead Whale

The *Honeypaws* is all fender and hull armor. Snorri cut the engine and let it drift until it bumped Bob's boat like a milk-drunk bear cub wanting more from mom.

"Ahoy, Ranger Orange, great explorer!" he shouted, waving.

Waldena's visit had left me with more of a soft, powdery lunar impact crater than a hangover. I spent the rest of the night dozing under the stars waiting for Ricky to come back and pick me up. I wondered what Waldena had done with him. She probably hadn't eviscerated him to haruspicate her god's will. More likely she gave him the time of his life, and then more so. He was probably crouched in a corner somewhere worrying about his vital essences.

I tied *Honeypaws* to the *Lucky Lady* and noticed that Snorri had brought Moira with him. "What are you guys doing here?"

"We're going to America!" said Moira.

"We are taking a field trip to the mainland," said Snorri. "Would you like to come with us?"

"No, thanks," I said.

"Come on. Don't worry, Uncle Snorri already said we won't go in any stores or anything. We're going to go see a dead whale! Way underwater!"

The two of them looked like they were skipping school. "Have fun."

"What, you have plans?" said Snorri.

"I'm waiting for a ride."

"I'm your ride."

"Why are you going to look at a dead whale?"

"For the sake of Moira's cultural and scientific education."

"You said *revenge*," said Moira, savoring the idea.

"Well, yes. My council suspects one of our whales has been rustled. But this will be an educational trip. So, how about it?"

"No. I don't want any more education, especially about dead whales."

"Oh come on, you need your horizons expanded."

"I don't need a dead whale on my horizon."

"A little surly today, aren't you?"

"I didn't get much sleep. Or supper, or breakfast—or lunch, depending on what time it is."

"You probably shouldn't be drinking that can of beer."

"There wasn't any coffee served."

"Oh Jeez, you're like my Dad," said Moira. "Beer and cereal is *so* gross."

"I have snacks, Orange. Come on board; I'll feed you, and you'll learn something while you help me out. We've got some serious talking to do, and you might even stand to make some money."

Snacks? Money? Ricky was never going to pick me up. My only alternative was to get on the marine band and make a big fuss, guaranteeing trouble from the harbormaster and Bob, whose boat I'd been squatting on. I told Snorri that I supposed so and went and fetched the remaining three Buds from the fridge. I battened the *Lady* and clicked the padlock back in place on the hatch's hasp. Moira granted me permission to board *Honeypaws*, and we shoved off. I went down to the boat's galley with Moira as Snorri took us out of the harbor. She and I found nothing but jars of pickled herring and incredibly dry, thin crackers. I was hungry enough to eat it; she wasn't.

"I think I might have seen the *Hammer Maiden* leaving harbor very early this morning," Snorri told me when I left Moira on the rear deck and joined him in the wheelhouse.

"Yuh, you mighta."

Snorri beetled his bushy brow at me and asked me for a beer. We sipped our brunches for a while.

"You know why Waldena is so surly?" asked Snorri.

"Parasites?"

"The Estonindians have a national inferiority complex."

"I doubt she'd put it that way."

"It's true," he said with regret. "The Northern Indians were one people for long after their arrival in Europe. It was an ethnicity that spread from little Bismuth here, all the way across the Arctic and into Europe. By the time we'd balkanized into warring countries, our rivalries were so bitter it was only the common enemy of the Vikings that kept us from each other's throats.

"In time, the empires of Europe: Rome, Christendom, Germania, Russia, the Germans again, the Soviets, the EU, all found reasons to annex the Estonindians. For long periods, centuries even, they had to tend to their own culture in secret, while slaving for their conquerors. It's been barely 150 years that they've had borders worth defending. It's all that blood-letting and cultural hibernation that makes them bitter and defensive."

"Understandable, I suppose."

"Throughout their history, they've had to slink back to the Finlindians to get what they need. They could have marched back, proudly, to join us, but they're too stubborn—they just beg, borrow, and steal from us instead, convinced we're withholding something important from them, sure that the snow is always brighter on our side of the gulf."

"That sounds a little arrogant."

"Ha! At times, their country has been so awash in blood and gore that they've even lost their own language! Everyone knows the Finlindians are lexicologists, but they might not know that we're word wizards because we've had to tend to our words—and the rest of the Northern Indians'—so long and so far, like I told you, from here, up through the ice, down into the continent of religions and empires, and then all the way through all of time. We had words! Forged steel! Boats! We know who we are. We can yoik on any subject; we can go generations without eating a vegetable, we can swim. . . ."

"Snorri, I. . . ."

"You're right, of course. We are also modest and generous. Our nets are flopping full with fish for our fellow Northern Indians. Our meat pits are more like meat mounds, and our cultural coffers overspill tradition and history to spare.

"You know, when their lugubrious, nameless giant of a national epic hero wanted anything, he'd swim to Finlindia: 'wolves ate my horse,' 'we're out of seeds,' 'I need a sword,' 'we forgot how to talk,' 'our fire's gone out,' 'we ate all our reindeer,' 'the dogmen are chasing me,' 'a witch stole my penis.'"

"His penis?"

"We forge him a new one from sacred ore we'd carried in our sauna ships all the way from the coast of North America. We cast delightful spells all up and down its shaft. We bury it in mammoth dung to let it mature. We give it a name so wonderful, we mourn the loss of the name from our language.

"Off he swims, the oaf with his cock. Is he happy? No. He's

the prototypical Estonindian; he can't be happy, even with a big new Finlindian prick.

"Down south, there's a series of maidens and nymphs that he's crushed or impaled to death. He's supposed to use his phallus to plow and plant all the land, but the Estonindians miss spring for a few decades because he can't stay stiff enough to scratch a decent furrow. One winter the sense of failure is so overwhelming, it doesn't even snow, and he decides to put an end to himself. He's a giant, so he's hard to kill. He figures the easiest, cleanest way to do it is to just jump off the side of the earth. But of course, he can't find it, and he swims back across the gulf to ask us directions.

"The cooler minds of Finlindia prevail. We teach him something peaceful and practical—whaleherding. He's bad at it, but we let him be. When we visit his fjord to check up on him, the penis is gone. He's got a story about whales but none of us believe him. He yoiks 'sad, lost penis' so well, our sun goes out for months. He curses his own legs for not walking him to the edge of the earth, and they take umbrage. They run away and leap off the earth without him, and he bleeds to death."

"Well, that's. . . ."

"Of course he cannot even die right. He's caused us all so much misery, he's chained to the gates of hell, where he sets the tone for new arrivals by yoiking 'torment' and 'frustration' and 'penis' unto eternity."

At "eternity," it seemed as if Snorri had said his piece. Warily, I waited a few minutes to see if the conversational coast was indeed clear. "So you're saying Waldena's got penis envy?"

"Thursdays are her sabbath, Orange. She and the rest of her cult worship on the day you call Thursday. You know what Estonindian witches do on Thursday nights with full moons?"

"Swim to the moon?"

"The rites are a bit more visceral than that."

"What?"

"She's not his handmaiden for nothing."

"Hammer maiden."

"Exactly."

"Exactly?"

"Listen, the Estonindians need periodic re-assembly. It's our role as Finlindians—their older brothers—like it or not, to go find all their bones, their penises, their words and rebury the people in the right order so they can come back whole again. They are still our sisters."

"With penises."

"Not all of them." Snorri then said he was going to check on Moira. When he returned he had his leathern flask of old milk. "Partake, Orange, in the ichor of Finlindia."

"Ugh. I don't even know what animal—no wait, I don't even want to know."

"Your loss. It's both bracing and a direct link to the history of our culture. I won't tell you how it's made—there are secret rites involved—but I can tell you some of the bacteriological agents in it are from a line older than our nations. A bit like your American pioneers' sourdough, I imagine."

I shuddered.

"Oh come on, what do they say in your country, 'cowboy up'?"

"They say that down in Red Sox Nation. Up here in Down East we say 'old milk is revolting.'"

Snorri took a long pull. "Just a cordial, then."

Moira joined us in the wheelhouse, wrinkling her nose at the aftercloud of Snorri's liquid patriotism. "How much longer?"

"We have barely left the harbor, Boo Boo."

"Boo Boo?"

"That's what you call bear cubs, right?"

"No."

"What about Yogi?" he asked.

"Yogi?"

"She's too young," I told Snorri. "But she's got a point—where are we going?"

"We are on course to the submarine pens of the Oceanographic Institute on the mainland. It will take around an hour. Our approach is going to be a bit tricky. When we get near their bay, we are going to meet another boat who will guide us in."

"Why? That's an easy harbor. No shoal or anything."

"You are forgetting that I'm not an American citizen and that the submarine pens are full of nasty military secrets. My colleague will escort us through security. Just stay calm—the Americans panic easily these days."

I suppose the *Honeypaws* has a low profile. I suppose that since it wasn't up on its hydrofoils blasting away with the harpoon cannon, and Snorri wasn't chanting a yoik about running minkes across the wide blue lonesome, the entire U. S. Navy hadn't noticed his approach. Still, I had the strong sense that we were risking a fully immersive experience at the waterboarding spa in Gitmo.

Snorri had been on his odd-looking telephone, making arrangements. Our native guide to American military security waited for us in a Boston Whaler out near a welter of moored boats at the outer edge of the harbor. He took us on a long, elliptical route into the docks of the Oceanographic Institute. We were obliged to tie *Honeypaws* up at one of the outer docks— she was just too big for where we were heading. Moira, Snorri, me, and a guy named Mr. Bagsadarian, who told us to call him Bags, took his Boston Whaler from there and continued under the docks. Soon, we were underneath buildings in a canyon of pilings that continued inland much further than was apparent from the harbor.

Well under the docks of the Institute, hidden within the submarine pens, is the Office of National Deep Submergence, which Bags explained was recently appropriated by the Office of the Vice President and no longer beholden to the namby-pamby agendas of the tubeworm-fellating scientists in the Oceanographic Institute above.

Bags of ONDS was a Mr. Seville Bagdasarian. He was conspicuously a "Mister," here among the titled ranks of the Navy. His hair was too long and he didn't call Snorri or I "Sir," which I took as a sure sign that he was some kind of spy or special ops. I got the sense that the Office of National Deep Submergence may well have been an undisclosed location—why else would everyone from the founder of the CIA to the president's dad live near here? It's not because they like shoveling snow all winter. This was likely one of the country's back doors, a taxi stand for trips to locations of hitherto unheard of undisclosability. This made me feel a bit smug, since my island is hardly ever disclosed and I seemingly already had a head start on the VIPs away from whatever catastrophes the continent could prepare for us.

Well back under the piers, we tied up at a floating dock and went inside a weathered unmarked door that opened to what looked like a utility closet too small to hold the four of us. From there it was a bolt hole in the floor down a staircase that took us under the water level and to a watertight door with a vault-like lock. Bags poked in a security code and led us in to a conference room with a white board and a big picture window. The room on the other side of the window was dark, but from what I could make out, it looked like a small TV studio with bucket seats. There were three Danishes on the conference table and a small sideboard with powdered creamer and a stack of Styrofoam cups, but no coffee machine. We ate the stale pastries. Bags fussed with some type of digital projector. The white board showed a field of not quite oceanic blue and the word "WAIT" fluttering across its surface. Eventually he quit whatever it was he couldn't start and addressed us.

"Welcome to the Baphometric Orientation Room Exercise. Today we will learn the basic operational parameters of *Alousia*, the Plutonic Depth Class Submergence Vehicle."

"Can we skip this?" asked Snorri.

"Yeah, I guess. It's just a bunch of specs and pointless advice on what to do if you're about to be crushed." Bags gave me and Moira a once-over. "Look, I've been down with Snorri, he knows the drill. You two are going to need a bit of orientation though. Let's get some preliminaries of Baphometric exploration out of the way. You'll each get a waste liquid bottle and a diaper if you want it—you'll have to change into the diaper before we enter the *Alousia*. . . ."

Moira looked aghast.

"It's a seven-hour dive," said Bags.

I was horrified.

"And there's no toilet. In fact, there's only three seats at all, and I can't see how we're all going to fit."

Moira volunteered to stay behind, and I mentioned plans I'd already made to breathe air on the surface world that afternoon. Snorri brooked no dissent.

"I am not wearing a diaper," said Moira, nearing tears.

"Me neither. And I don't like it underwater."

"How do you know?" Snorri said, "You've never been."

I could tell Bags was feeling deprived of his arsenal of sarcastic similes, due to the presence of an actual, teary girl. "I'm going to go change," he muttered.

Snorri tried to rally us with gambits about science and opportunities. Moira stood firm, with significant moral support from myself. Mutiny was underway when Bags returned sporting a cool-looking white jumpsuit with lots of pockets and an insignia patch on the chest.

"Look," he said, "scientists wait for half their careers to go for a ride on *Alousia*."

A patently unpersuasive argument.

Bags took our measure. "We're going to breach protocol," he announced. "Bathroom visits will be allowed."

"You just said there's no toilet," I said.

"There is no toilet on the *Alousia*. There is a bathroom right through that door. It's where I changed into the jumpsuit."

What Bags and Snorri had neglected to tell us was that the actual *Alousia* was currently sinking downward from its mothership, already well on its way to the abyssal plain off of Georges Bank that was our ostensible destination. Our personal destination was next door—the *Alousia* simulation chamber, a reproduction of the Plutonic Class Submersible Vessel, from which Bags would be remotely operating the thing. Exact adherence to the actual expedition was mandatory in the chamber, from diapers to decompression. An allowance so devilishly transgressive as a bathroom visit would be made only under the mantle of absolute secrecy. No food was allowed, no exceptions (ants), and we could wear the jumpsuits if we wanted to, which we did.

Moira changed into her jumpsuit in the bathroom, while Snorri and I changed up in the conference room. Hers was way too big, but she liked it anyway. She loaded the tubular pen-pockets on her left sleeve with several plastic coffee stirrers. Bags went into the room I'd taken for a TV studio on the other side of the picture window and turned on the array of controls and monitors.

When we joined him in the oversmall room, he explained further that *Alousia* was an ROV PCSV, and then was obliged to explain even further that the *Alousia* was a small submarine-like machine—a Plutonic Class Submersible Vessel—and it could be piloted from right here in the submarine pens—it was a Remotely Operated Vessel. On shallow missions, it seated three individuals. But because this was a special hardened military craft, it could travel much deeper in the ocean than the other more publicly-known vessels, like its civilian cousin, *Alvin*. When *Alousia* was sent on a dangerous mission, she was usually unoccupied and operated from a station like this, or more typically from a simulation chamber aboard her mothership, which was disguised as a tanker running under various flags of convenience.

The room beyond our conference room was supposedly an exact reproduction of the *Alousia*—the TV monitors were in place of the vessel's own portholes, cameras on the vessel itself allowed those in the simulation chamber to see the same thing someone would see from on board. This whole set up here, under the docks, below the Oceanographic Institute, was a secret training facility unknown to the scientists above.

Normally when operating the craft remotely, as Bags was about to do, the crew made every effort to pretend they were actually inside the submersible vessel. That meant they spent hours, sometimes days inside it, mirroring the entire mission. Everything from operating the blurp guns and vacuum hoses, to simulating hours of decompression as the vessel returned to the surface. Bags did not mention whether the remote submariners simulated the bends if they rose too quickly. He also did not mention what sort of missions the *Alousia* was used for—I was hoping to hear about covert visits to sunken Lemuria and the retrieval of alien artifacts. Nor did Bags, or Snorri, say why blatant security risks such as me and Moira were allowed here at all. I was too savvy to ask, and Moira was too naive, but, as native islanders both, we could sense when to shut up and mind our own businesses.

"I've always had time to settle into the spirit of the descent—I've never joined a mission already on its way down before," Bags told us. "It helps the imagination if you can adjust to the dark and time."

I was finding adjustment difficult due to the fact that the *Alousia* was a three-seater and Moira refused to sit on anyone's lap. Snorri got shotgun, Bags, the driver's seat, and I was wedged into the alleged cargo space next to the rear seat, occupied by Princess Moira. Man is not meant to sit with his knees touching his nose, not to mention doing so however many millions of fathoms underwater we were pretending to sink to. I found it odd to think of water vertically. It had always seemed so thoroughly horizontal. Water likes going downward, I supposed.

Moira wondered to us whether a dog had ever been onboard and found it a shame they weren't allowed. She further wondered whether any dogs had ever seen the bottom of the ocean. Laika, I told her, was a Russian dog who'd been in outer space before either of us had even been born. We hoped he'd had a window seat. Our own windows were TV screens and in the hour that I sat there courting deep vein thrombosis, they showed an utterly bland static, which turned out to be a perfect representation of what water looked like underwater.

One of the more disappointing things about the whole trip is that we did not thunk onto the seabed at the end of our descent. I like that scene in submarine movies with all the rivets apop and the crew reduced to pure primate terror. The underwater is on TV almost every night. Coral reefs, sharks, squid, shipwrecks—it's just aboil with action. As it turns out, just past the continental shelf, it's more PBS pledge-break territory. More boring than even the shipless surface. Bags actually suggested I make a donation to the Oceanographic Institute.

The abyssal plain, Bags told us, is a desert. Snorri added that the Arctic is a desert. Moira countered that the Gobi, for instance, was a desert chiefly due to its lack of water, and that deserts were not the kind of place where she could throw a snowball or drown the moment she opened her mouth. Bags unhelpfully reminded her that her lungs would be too compacted to breathe enough water to drown, and that her whole body would just squish in seconds anyway. Not that she could get out and walk around, he added. The ground wasn't actually ground—it was more like a porridge of snow and dandruff. He said that we should just shut up for a second and watch the portholes.

I couldn't be certain I was seeing anything but water and more water, but Moira and Snorri both said they could see the marine snow. Bags said it was from little pieces of dead fish and even tinier pieces of stuff like krill and less apparent creatures. They die and whatever minerals their body once contained continued to sink until it settled into the silt down here. The silt was the realm of the holothurian—rarely observed, gooey, eyeless (and limbless and everything elseless) creatures that resembled nothing from the surface yet outnumbered all the ants and worms of the world combined. He said that they were like the vast herds of mites that grazed our skin, snuffling up the dead cells. This was a cruel thing to tell tightly packed people.

We were deep, I was told. Deep down over an invisible cliff on an invisible plain that contained nothing sightworthy in the first place. Yet we were homing in on a gray smirch that was just becoming evident through the collodial haze.

"I don't need to tell you three that what you are seeing is absolutely confidential and not to leave the submergence vessel," Bags warned.

Moira and I looked at each other. I think we had both reached the conclusion that the only secret we could perceive was that the underwater was much more boring than TV documentaries had led us to believe.

"That's it, it's definitely her." said Snorri.

"The transponder is still going strong," said Bags.

Throughout our descent, Bags and Snorri had been telling Moira and I about whalefalls. Whales, according to Snorri, die all the time. Bags had added that instead of disintegrating into slowly sinking biological confetti like the marine snow, dead whales just sank right down and settled into the silt before they really began to rot. He said there was a secret map at the Institute marking the locations of hundreds of whale corpses, or whalefalls.

"Why's it secret?" asked Moira.

"Everything we do is secret—national security. Anyway, who wants to have to explain why you're monitoring rotting whale corpses?"

I remained unenlightened. "But, why, anyway?"

"So that they won't be disturbed."

"But why monitor them?"

"Ah, a whalefall is like an oasis here in the pelagic wastes.

They take over a hundred years to decay and communities with hundreds of different species—some unique from fall to fall—form around them."

"Why?" asked Moira. I recalled that Snorri had dubbed this a scientific mission and imagined Moira's re-creation of the rotting corpse for a school science fair. She was still too young and bloody-minded to be girly about decomposition. I hoped her school custodian ordered enough bleach for the coming year.

Bags told her, "They're the only thing to eat for miles around. By the time the carcass is entirely consumed, several generations of lots of different kinds of creatures have passed. The whalefall is the only home they'll ever know. It's like they're on a spaceship that's going to take centuries to get to another solar system, and it's only the great-grandkids of the original colonists that get to arrive at their destination."

"But it's not going anywhere," said Moira.

"It's traveling through time," said Snorri.

"The great-grand shrimp and worms and crabs and such, they hope they can find yet another whalefall and move on to that one, before their lines die out. Whole species moved across oceans of water and time this way," said Bags.

"Gross."

"No! It's beautiful—it's evolution, it's the mystery of life and it could be answer to the sustainability of the human species.

"Imagine these whalefalls as models of undersea arcologies for our own species. Even if humanity is reduced to a few underwater colonies, they could imitate the whalefalls and use their limited resources and dwindling technology to build just one more arcology that would sustain them for just enough time to allow the next generations to build the next arcology. If they built it from resources that would somehow sustain them, the way the worms both live in and live off of the whale skeletons, they could potentially move across the oceans and eventually repopulate the continents."

"What happened to the continents?" I asked.

"Oh, you know. Nukes. Plague."

"You're certain about this?"

"Sir, I am a Christian American. Of course there's an apocalypse. And sooner than later."

Hell, bring it on, I thought. My chief worry about the apocalypse was that it was going to happen a few days after I died, and I'd miss the whole thing.

"Like Atlantis?" asked Moira.

"Atlantis was a big city," said Snorri, "above ground. This whole nonsense about it being underwater is a recent invention."

"Well, even if the whalefalls don't help humanity survive, it's nice to know that there will be something going on after the nuclear winter and photosynthesis has had its run," said Bags.

"Like the black smokers!" said Moira. "We saw a movie about them in school! Is this the ship?"

"No, this one's too covert. That was the other one. But *Alousia's* been to see the thermal vents too. Hold on, now, things are going to get a bit tricky."

We were maneuvering to hover over the whalefall.

"There's red grass!" said Moira.

"Tube worms," said Bags.

From out of the turbid murk, *Alousia's* spotlights showed our first vivid glimpse of color. The tube worms formed a pelt over a vaguely whale-shaped mound. It seemed each cilium was swaying and waving to the other, like congregants in a chapel awash in fellowship. The worms clung along the ordered pews of the vertebrae and fluttered like tells from the vaulting ribs.

Long-limbed pale crabs cruised the crowd as deacons passing the plate, while clouds of ghostly shrimp fluttered among them all. Bags angled the spotlight to bore through the biotic squall we stirred up, illuminating the sacristy within the cyclopean skull. Eels leered back lidlessly, mouths agape, priests interrupted mid-scandal.

Undoubtedly, it was another hellmouth, another vagina dentata, another bear trap, more than a slight hint at the illimitable horrors that await whatever's left of our selves after our mortal suffering concludes. The whalefall, the thermal vents, the sulfur seeps, each a case of a man coming too close to guessing at the sublime, as if passion plays and deathbed scenes were not enough to sate his need to take his torch and descend, descend to stand in the fringed cloacal gateway and peer through the keyhole.

Yet there was a harmony here at the alpha and omega. The creatures were the landscape. The rude redness of the undulating worms was hypnotic; the eels and crabs seemed enthralled, swaying in a rhythm too gentle and supporting to be trusted. I noticed Moira and I were rocking slightly in sympathy.

"It will stay like this for years," said Bags, mollified.

Snorri broke a timeless, queasy quietness: "This isn't the picture you showed me."

"That picture was from last year," said Bags.

"There's no flesh left at all."

"Just tiny shreds of gristle, but there's lots of tissue and oil that leeches from the bones."

"I could see the rune in the picture from last year."

"Let's see it again," said Bags. He moused around his laptop a bit and the *Alouisa's* portholes became a storm of visual static before they showed a new scene of carnivores harrowing the carcass. Our deep submergence vehicle was also a time machine. It was a year earlier, according to Bags, a much more violent stage in the whalefall's afterlife. Shadows of sharks passed over a field of much longer, more active grass.

With his finger on the screen, Snorri traced the rune that showed the whale was indeed his council's. "Rustled."

I was looking for the branded rune when I saw that the grass was not the waving mat of red fingers from before. It was a gorgon's head of hagfish. I lurched forward and hit every button and switch I could come into contact with, while yelling, "What's that!?"

"Hold steady!" hissed Bags as he changed the porthole screens back to the present decompositional garden scene we'd been watching. "What was that about?"

"I felt something," I said.

Moira somehow sensed my need for her complicity. "Maybe a colossal squid."

"Nothing out the windows," said Snorri.

Just because we were playing aquanauts, sitting in a closet watching a year-old movie about a rotting whale, didn't mean I was going to abide hagfish. They have no business imposing themselves on my existence. They are not going to be on my ark; they are not in my book. I have unicorns in my brain and their only job is to roam the forests and clomp through the shallows, stomping and spearing any thought of hagfish into paste.

"Anyway, that was from when I visited it last summer," said Bags. He turned back and gave me a nasty stare. "We'll stick to the present, so there won't be any more disturbances."

"Show me the antenna," said Snorri.

Bags said he was reversing his slurp guns and shovelfuls of sediment were blown off the furry skeleton. We could see a strand of cable there in the silt.

"Antenna?" I asked.

Snorri said something in Finlindian about Estonindians so obscene, it didn't need translation. "That was ours. The Estonindians are boat thieves and whale rustlers. You're all witnesses."

"Why's there an antenna?" I asked.

"It's not retrievable; it's too big and heavy for us to pull it up ourselves," said Bags.

"We don't need it anyway. I just need to bring back documentation," said Snorri.

I tried asking Moira: "Antenna?"

"Somebody killed the whale?" she said. "Was it Waldena? Did she harpoon it?"

"Just to watch it die," said Snorri.

"Why?"

"High seas piracy. Ecological delusion. I needed to come check on this, but I wanted you all to see it, too. Waldena has gone too far. Probably hag rode it to its grave. I don't even know this poor whale's name—the prototype team kept shoddy records."

"Snorri, what the hell are you talking about?" I asked.

"This whale here—this carcass—was part of the prototype pod. Orange, Moira, you can keep a secret, right? I would not have brought you down here, otherwise. This is serious; you cannot tell anyone."

I crossed my heart, a gesture lost on Snorri. Moira didn't even respond. She was wise enough to know that she wasn't supposed to keep secrets about what happened when weird old men got her alone.

"A few years ago, our whaling councils—this is supposed to be a joint-venture between Finlindian and Estonindian governments—began to fund research into cetacean-borne telecommunication. With help from Mr. Bagsadarian here and his office, and especially *Alouisa*, we identified a small pod of whales that were regular travelers on these waters. These are wild whales, but we branded them like our own pods, so we could identify them.

"That group is what you Americans would call humpbacks. I think they were a bad choice—many of them are already monitored, and they're sort of easy targets. They are master vocalists though, and that is why their species was chosen first, because of their propensity and talent for long-distance communication.

"After we marked them and defined their territory, we installed antennae in some of the strongest of the whales."

"Why?" I asked, "So they can listen to the game?"

"Do not be clever, Orange, this is a serious enterprise as well as an opportunity for you. But you are right. The antennae are for reception—telephone reception. We've developed a way for ordinary cell phones to work out on the open ocean—no satellites, no dishes, just your own pocket phone. The only restriction is that one has to be within range of the whales carrying the antennae. We call that the Whale Network, and it works, well, swimmingly so far. For the actual Whale Network, the one we're monitoring now with *Honeypaws* and the *Hammer Maiden*, we are using semi-domesticated belugas, which are more tractable and much easier to breed. Once we finish field-testing it this summer, we'll go into production mode and sow the northern waters with augmented belugas carrying antennae and repeaters. The belugas are much smaller and so are the actual antennae, which resemble . . . oh what do you call them? Yardsticks.

"Bags has been in on it from the start—we go way back to when my bear bride and I kept our eyes on the Soviets along the Finlindian border. But the rest of his team thinks we are just

researchers from Europe and are not aware of the entrepreneurial aspects of the network."

"So, what's with Waldena?"

"She knew about this early on and felt she had some coup to
count before her country became involved officially. She must
realize I will not let this stand."

"Why do you work with her now?"

"The Estonindian council thinks she is the woman for the
job. She has *Tharapita's Hammer Maiden*, a crew of tough guys
at her disposal, and she has been hunting in these waters long
enough that she knows them better than any other Estonindian
whaler. Plus, I do not think they like me and were happy to have
her plague me."

"Well I don't like her, she's mean," said Moira.

"And violent," I added. "Though, I don't know. Maybe she's
complex and troubled."

"She is a witch in a Thor cult and you are a fool, Mr. Whippey.
Do not believe a word she says."

I shrugged, and Moira elbowed me in the ribs.

"I hope you see why it is so important to remain extremely
discreet about this. A great deal of money and time has been
invested, and, if you cooperate, you stand to make some money
yourself."

"Me too?" asked Moira.

"We will work something out," said Snorri, "Just say nothing
about the Whale Network to anyone."

"I'm going to tell Mom."

Snorri thought about it. "OK. Mineola knows all about it and
has probably told Angie already."

Bags announced that we only had around ten minutes of bottom time left before the ascent and that we should be quiet and

let him work. Moira kept trying to take up more of the space we were supposed to be sharing. Her elbow was sharp and persistent. I think she was trying to take advantage of her little-girlness, and there was no reason I saw that she deserved an inch more room. I'd been folded up for hours and was surely developing lethal blood clots, and it was only my manners and stoicism that had kept me from claiming my proper physical space. She seemed to have constant needs—craning for the window, rooting for a different color pen, the water bottle—all she seemed to do was reach and twist like she had the hivies.

So it wasn't my fault that Snorri missed decompression. Moira had virtually forced me to pinch her—she refused to understand that the pinch was part of an autonomic defense reaction that I had little conscious control over. I wish she had just taken the hint and let me be a full-sized adult, but, no. Whatever alliance we had shared during our trip was sundered when she loudly accused me of pinching, and neither Bags nor Snorri—both also full-sized adults—defended me. I did not start it.

"I've got a taser and chemical restraints," growled Bags.

"Tase her and give me the sedatives," I said.

"He keeps shoving me," added Moira.

"I have not! She's been. . . ."

"That's it! Enough!" said Bags.

The rest of our trip was aborted. Bags ejected us from the simulation chamber and told us to wait in the conference room. He was short-tempered and annoyed that he had to cede control of *Alousia* to the back-up team on board her mothership for the sub's ascent. Snorri was sniffy about it too.

"How often does a man get to genuinely decompress?" said Snorri. "To sit there and know that your time and depth has been perfectly calibrated to the restoration of your body? The bends are a very painful death."

The bends. I had the bends. I had to limp to the conference room because there was no blood in my legs.

"Herdsman or hunter," Snorri continued, "you still have to learn how to wait. And it's not often I get to wait so productively."

"Jesus fucking Crackers, Snorri, it wasn't real, and you had all the room you wanted in front."

"You should be thanking me for this experience."

"I'm hungry," said Moira.

I did not regret missing the opportunity to sit in the stupid pretend submarine for two more hours looking at what water looked like underwater while Snorri re-aligned his molecules.

"We could go to Friendlys," said Moira.

"I have snacks on the boat," said Snorri.

"Herring."

I said I wouldn't entirely mind Friendlys.

Snorri said we weren't allowed offbase and that we had to get back to Mini's anyway.

I thought about jumping ship and absconding to the mainland. Its preoccupation with busyness and its unquantifiable impediments to peace of mind weren't much more daunting than the sleigh ride I'd been dragged on so far. Still, though, it was the continent, and one of my few pleasures is hating it. Just knowing that all eighty billion of its landlocked inhabitants could be rendered completely insignificant by standing on the island and facing seaward is a fine thing that no stranger will ever understand.

Poor Moira though. The continent held everything she did not. For any island kid, no matter how privileged, life is full of constraints and prospects denied, even if all you want is TV reception and a trip to the mall every once in a while. What's worse is you're not alone. You and the rest of the kids that you're damned to know your whole life all want offisland too. Every few years there's a terrible fever of discontent on the island and not all the kids recover from it. The adults expect them to resign themselves to the same traces they've toiled in, and the kids who had the fever worst write letters of resignation and go offisland without ever reaching the mainland.

In the end, we milled around the conference room, inspecting the cabinets for leftover snacks or loose pens we could take. Bags was on the phone with his colleagues on the mothership for around half an hour until he could come and escort us out of the harbor on his Boston Whaler. It wasn't until then that Moira saw fit to mention that she was overdue back at home, and that she hadn't told anyone where she was going.

CHAPTER NINETEEN

Castaways

Nobody in the whole history of yelling at me had yelled at me like Angie Bombardier. The only reason she hadn't murdered me on the spot was so she could preserve her moral superiority. My inferiority, along with an ample catalog of character flaws, was well explained to myself at high volume and rapid pace, accompanied by multiple jabs of the finger to my chest. I really should not have tried to explain that I felt that her daughter Moira had been more complicit in kidnapping me than me making off with her. I should not have introduced the word "kidnapping" into the dialogue. "Not my fault" was not a phrase I had been allowed to complete. I should have known better. I should have thought about the safety of her daughter before anything else. I should have called Angie. I should have asked more questions. I should go entomb myself in the *Alousia* simulation chamber. I should go feed myself to hagfish. I should have had better judgment than a drunk, whale-fucking coot and a fifth grader. I should consider myself gloriously fortunate that law enforcement had not become involved, that Mini's security guards weren't practicing their enhanced interrogation tactics on me with phone books while I barfed into a fertilizer bag cinched over my head. I should be aware that Bismuth was going to get smaller and smaller until I could bear it no longer and that there were a number of short piers available for long walks.

It hadn't been until we were back on the *Honeypaws*, on the way out of the mainland harbor, that Moira had told us she was AWOL. I hadn't really understood the significance of this, since AWOL was more or less my typical MO. Snorri and I agreed that replacing Moira on Gaeity ASAP was our best plan. Moira seemed to take sly pleasure in watching us dither—she already knew better than us how much holy hell we would soon be facing.

I suppose that, after beating our retreat from Gaeity on his boat, I should not have lost my shit on Snorri, though I was mostly glad I did, and he certainly deserved it. It galled me beyond reason that he was trying to suggest he was not the true culprit in this field trip turned fiasco. I am willing to admit that his windpipe was not the right place for my forearm, and that I ought to regret the fire hose of recriminatory verbal pissing that I treated him to. But it was his fucking fault. By the time we'd made it back to Bismuth and Snorri dumped me at the town docks, I was still full of ugly swagger, and he was sulking, so I felt like I'd won something. Of course it was the feeling that I'd lost everything that had set me off.

I sat out on a hidden corner of the dock, leaning on a splintered, tarry piling. Seeing a dead whale was supposed to have been that day's defining moment. Instead, I had kidnapped a little girl who was nearly forced to wear a diaper in the presence of three grown men showed her a murdered whale, proven my complete and utter unsuitability as a partner for Angie, and then brutalized an old man, just because I was frustrated. The fact that I'd meant well meant nothing. I didn't want to hide here on the docks all night. I didn't even know why I was hiding. Probably because I kept weeping. I didn't want to go home, I didn't want to get drunk, I didn't want to be sober. I didn't want to be alive and didn't want to make the effort not to be. Above all, I did not want to be Orange Whippey, Idiot of Bismuth.

I had decided to sit on the docks until I felt toweringly sorry for myself. Then, I figured, my next terrible decision or act of abysmal judgment would be evident to me. But, of course, even my plan to be the sorriest man alive was ruined. I'd been moping for at least an hour when I heard someone whispering, "Dude, dude!" It wasn't the seagulls, or the staring little tourist kid being pulled away by his mom. There was nobody else around. "That you, Orange? Down here."

I rolled over and peered between the boards of the dock. It was low tide and resting on the soupy clay eight feet below was a nasty oarless little wooden dinghy holding Ricky, the kid who ran the Topsoil taxi, and whom I had presumed had been sacrificed to pagan gods by Waldena.

"Ricky?"

"Yeah!"

"Don't call me 'dude.'"

"Sorry."

He actually sounded especially sorry. "What are you doing down there?"

"Sitting in a dinghy."

"No kidding."

"Yeah."

"Do you need a hand up?"

"No, I'm just going to wait for the tide."

It was going to take more than a full moon's worth of tide to raise his spirits. "You been there a while?"

"Since this morning. I guess."

"Where were you last night? I was stuck on Bob's boat."

Ricky looked stricken, like he'd swallowed a sea nettle. "I . . .

I can't say," he said weakly.

I knew it. He'd been bewitched. "Let me help you up."

"No. It's OK. It feels safe here."

I wondered what Waldena had done to him, but didn't want to ask, since then I'd have to explain what she'd done with me. "Tide's not in til after dark, you know?"

"I know. Hey, you still got my pipe?"

"Yeah, but I'm keeping the bag."

"Would you mind just packing it and then giving it to me? Keep the bag, that's fine."

It seemed merciful, so I packed it tight and even removed a couple seeds for him. I found a wide enough slot between the boards to drop it down into his little boat.

"Thanks," he said. Then after a bit, "Do you have a lighter?"

"Nope."

Ricky sighed. I hoped it was clear to him I wasn't going to go asking for matches. He looked bad. Pale, drained—a creature that belonged under the docks.

"Were you crying . . . ?" he asked.

I could tell he had a tough time not ending his sentence with 'dude.' "Why, what did you hear?"

"There was, like, a puddle."

I told him it wasn't me; he let it go, unchallenged.

"Where's the Topsoil tender?" I asked.

"It's back fine. I came here after, I guess."

"You still got a job?"

"Yeah, probably. I didn't even talk to anyone."

Ricky and I had a lot to not talk about, yet neither of us seemed to be on our way anywhere else. I could only see him by lying flat on the dock and looking with one eye through the slats. It made conversation awkward.

"Summer's almost up," I told him. "Labor Day's coming."

Ricky looked out on the harbor, as if Labor Day were floating just beyond the horizon.

"You gonna go back to school?"

"I don't know."

"You gonna keep renting here?"

"I stopped paying a while ago. They already got my last month's and security and they're never giving back my security, so why pay?"

He was right. Nobody ever got their security back here. At best, it got counted towards a down payment to reserve a place for next summer. There was no way he'd be wintering here. It might have seemed romantic to him at the moment, but he didn't have the fortitude to commit to that kind of melancholia. Besides, he was too young and handsome. The girls go for those bleached curls and beachworn Oxford shirts. He actually held one of the best summer jobs on the island. I was probably the only living being who didn't pay him a tip for his taxi service.

I think the best summer job probably was Bismuth Yacht Club sailing instructor. Their afternoons were spent on Sunfishes coaxing teenage girls in bathing suits out of the harbor and beyond parental supervision. The boats were invariably flipped, and only a few of the young ladies returned in tears.

"My buddy worked at Potemkin Smeerenberg this summer. I might go with him next year," said Ricky.

"At a whaling camp?"

"It's a tourist thing. People come to be whalers for a week or something. My friend says the first-year guys have to work the blubber ovens, though."

"The try pots. They're supposed to reek."

"You know about the Vault?" he asked.

There was one in the Topsoil. Every skeevy islander had thought about it at one time or another. "No."

"My friend says there's the Doomsday Vault on the same island as the whale camp."

"What is it?" I asked.

"It's for all the countries to use for before the apocalypse. It's like this deep freeze mineshaft. All the countries are filling it up with stuff people might want after the apocalypse, but it's got to be kind of small, like DNA and seeds."

"How are people supposed to get up there at the end?"

"They aren't. It's just for stuff. All the languages and instructions and seeds and stuff will be there for afterward."

"Who would know where it was?"

"They probably wouldn't," he said, settling back down. "Nobody even knows it's there now. Maybe some people would be trapped inside it when the airlocks closed."

I took a good look at Ricky down in his pitiful little boat. It wasn't hard to work out a scenario in which he and his Smeerenberg summer love found themselves in the vault and repopulated the human race. For many generations everyone would look slightly like Ricky.

"What?" said Ricky.

"I should go."

CHAPTER TWENTY

New Friends on the Princess Pea

I'd walked back to my house after chatting with Ricky in his dinghy. It was nice to see my cat, Rover. We hadn't spent much time together lately. She and I had what was left from Ricky's bag of pot, ate a can of soup and a bowl of kibble, watched *Jeopardy*, and were asleep before the sky was dark. Consequently I awoke more sober and rested than I expected. All night in a comfortable bed, my own even—I thought I ought to do that more often. It seemed to come to most people more easily than me, but it felt pretty natural. I was wondering what I'd do about coffee when my phone rang. The caller ID said "WhaleNet," which I couldn't place. I answered it on a whim.

"Mr. Orange Whippey?"

Not enough people call me "Mr.," so I said yes.

"This is Chosen, your Korean acquaintance."

"Howdy."

"'Howdy!' America! Ha! Howdy Doody is very strange. Is he related to your Yankee Doody? Is Yankee a puppet also? No he is a historic legend. Northeast, but not coastal. Right?"

"It's 'Doodle,' actually. What's up?" I asked.

"We have a job for you! Are you ready to work?"

"No."

"We have rented a native lobster boat, Orange. We would very much like you to be our companion on it. It has less controls than a car, but the boat owner insisted we have a local on board to pilot. We mentioned you, and he said, 'OK, I guess.' Will you be our pilot? We have the ship right now."

"If it's for lobsters, it's a boat, not a ship," I said.

"Will you be the boat pilot? We have fifty dollars and a picnic for you."

"Today?"

"Right now!"

"OK, I guess."

"Please find us at the town dock soon."

"Coffee."

"What?"

"Fifty, a picnic, and a coffee-to-go," I said.

"A coffee-to-go? No worries, mon."

"Wrong island. We're the one with the worries."

Even if I don't have dreads or a nice accent, I do still keep island time, so it was a while before I made it down to the docks in town. Chosen was waiting for me with a Styrofoam cup of coffee gone cold. He was wearing a garish Tyvek New England Patriots windbreaker and looked more like a jerk for it—and therefore a little more convincingly native.

"Which one?" I said, taking the coffee from him and drinking.

"Over there, the white boat, *The Princess Pea*. You see my partner there on board?"

Oh, yeah, the *Pee Princess*. It had been owned by a few guys I knew. It was the fiberglass equivalent of a rusty old pick-up truck. "Who's with him?"

"We have a passenger for the day. She is attractive; you may like her."

"A passenger?"

"She pays us three hundred dollars for today. For a boat ride and a story!"

Three hundred dollars. You aren't supposed to be able to turn a profit in a lobster boat before you even leave the dock. Not much of one when you get back with a full load, either. "A story? What's going on?"

"I need to speak with you before you board because we have already begun telling the story to her and we need your help as a native storyteller and pilot."

Fifty dollars, a picnic, a coffee, an attractive woman. All for a story. I could handle this, I supposed, even if it was early and I was still sober. "So, what's the scam?"

"Scam? Like crime?"

"Yeah."

"We are not criminals," he said, as if he'd practiced the phrase.

"No, me neither. What's the deal though? You said we need to get our story straight."

"It is not a straight story or a true story. John and I discussed it yesterday night. It is supernatural, eerie. It is about an absent mountain and creatures from below."

"Cool."

"Yes. Will you help us? We need a voucher."

"You don't need a voucher, you need a poetic license," I said.

Chosen looked a bit confused. "We need you for verisimilitude, a native to vouchsafe our story."

"That's what I just said."

"Good! The first things you need to know is our audience is a New Yorker and that John and I are Native American Indians."

"Wait, why are you selling her a story? No, wait. You're Indians?" I asked. They had black hair, but. . . .

Chosen said, "We told you that we have been reading the supernatural literature of the northeast coastal region of America, yes?"

Yeah, I remembered.

"We are fans. Korea has an ancient tradition of ghost stories. Yours is much more modern, just the last two centuries. Ours has many ancestors and demons, yours has many monsters and preposterous events. We like the guise of the reluctant exaggerator. We want to explore and exercise in your narrations."

OK, I got it. Spinning a yarn sounded like fun to them. Chosen conducted me toward the boat.

"Yesterday, we had not even thought of the opportunity. We were planning on playing the roles of lobstermen. We had just rented the *Princess Pea* and were scrubbing her when we met that woman there, Lettie, the New Yorker. She approached us and asked if she could buy a lobster. We had not caught any. Then she asked us if we were natives, and John said, yes, we were native Americans. She said, Indians? and he said yes. She was very pleased. We spoke a bit about lobsters. She said she was going to buy one and make a film about herself and her boyfriend eating it. Her boyfriend was in bed trying not to be seasick. She said she was a kind of storyteller and had come to Bismuth Island to find stories about people from here to tell on camera. She was having a working vacation before Labor Day. She wanted to have the experience of being told about the island by natives. She was delighted we were Indians."

"Yeah, but you're not," I said.

"We know. She seemed eager to believe us, we were surprised. So, she has paid us to go lobstering and learn stories about the island from natives."

"Whose pots you guys hauling?"

"I do not know."

"What designs are on the buoys?"

"Designs?" asked Chosen.

There were lots of floats hanging around the docks and on the boats. I showed him how each person's buoys had a unique pattern. Chosen was very impressed. He had thought they were traditional decorations. I told him if he touched the wrong buoy, his chances of catching some buckshot were very high. Chosen said he did not want to disappoint her—I suggested telling her that there was a red tide alert and no lobstering was allowed. I didn't mention that such alerts didn't apply to lobsters. Red tide is just such a good, powerful excuse to use on strangers. Raw shellfish with poisonous bacteria. Nobody asks too many questions.

Red tide sounded fine to Chosen. "So, please remember that my name now is Uncas and John's name is Chingachgook, and he is my brother, and that we are Native American Indians from Bismuth all of our lives."

"So, what, I'm Natty Bumpo?"

"You may wear the leatherstockings," he allowed me.

"I don't think so. You're going to have to change your names to real Indian names."

"Those are real."

"Nope. Now you are . . . Franklin Mint. And he's Ronco." Nobody on a boat went without a nickname. We Islanders exercise our Adamic privilege regularly, even when we weren't very inspired.

"And who are you?"

"Ahnge," I said, emphasizing the island monosyllabic. "It's a special name that repels all nicknames."

"Ahnge, aye yup."

"Try to sound less like an actor."

"I will try. Ahnge the Beerslayer, let us meet Lettie."

"It's pronounced 'Beeahslayah.'"

The *Pee Princess* was looking quite a bit cleaner than her surrounding boats at the dock. Ronco, the Indian formerly known as the Korean Ill John, was wearing a a black nylon jacket with the spoked-B Bruins logo. He was chatting up a thin woman with wiry henna hair who looked like she was in her later twenties. Franklin Mint, who had been born, I presumed, as Chosen, and he had a quiet word, while I lurked on the dock. Ronco-John then waved me aboard.

"Orange, you already know *Franklin* and I from your youth upon the island. This is Lettie. She is a documentitian from Manhattan, New York City . . . the mainland." His accent had taken on a John Wayne-ish quality.

I could have told Ill John—Ronco—Manhattan was an island, but I didn't mention it.

Lettie shook my hand. "Documentarian," she said, "producer, actually. I'm glad we're going to have this opportunity!"

"Ayuh," I said. Nobody says "opportunity" to me without actually meaning trying, unpleasant, unpaid work. But she was kind of pretty in a freckled, red-headed but not Irish sort of way. She seemed professionally curious.

"So your partners. . . ."

"Ronco and Franklin."

". . . Say you were fishing since before dawn. Did you have a good haul?"

"I suppose."

"What did you catch?"

"Uh, schrod?"

"Mmm. I used to eat that when I was a girl. Schrod with crumbs. It must be fascinating!"

"Schrod?"

"Fishing! Out before dawn on the rough, cold sea; lots of hard, dangerous work. You guys," she said, gesturing to the three of us, "are the kind of honest, rugged guys that make this country what it is," she said, making it evident she'd never met a fisherman.

"Well . . . it's in our blood," I said.

"Has your family always fished?"

"Sure. All our families."

"And now you and your friends own this boat together, huh?"

"Yup. Me and Ronco and Franklin Mint on the *Pee Princess*. Been in the family for years."

"Whippey family. Franklin and I are brothers in another family," said Ronco.

"Yeah, there's lots of Indians here," I added.

"You're Indians and he's a Yankee, right?"

Ronco did a terrible "ayuh." "Natives."

"Oh that's perfect!" said Lettie, obviously enthused about the ethnic angle.

"So, you're from New York? You have a cigarette?" I asked.

"No, gum."

"No thanks. I have gum."

Lettie said, "Your partners have kindly offered to take me on a short fishing trip, just so I can get a feel for things here. I was hoping you all could tell me what island life is like, maybe some fishing stories."

"What show do you produce?"

"Well, it depends on the footage. It would be great if there were celebrities here, but that's OK because I don't really do celebrity stuff that much. If maybe one of you gets hurt on the boat or if there's a storm, it could be a sort of fishing reality thing. Or if there's like a haunted lighthouse or something we could do a segment of *America's Most Haunted Islands*. Or we could do a *Trading Boats* type thing where we redecorate your boats. Do you guys know any addicts? I bet the island would be good for a *Regular Joe Detox* episode."

"I want to decorate the boat," I said.

"This is a fishing vessel, not a boat." said Ronco-John.

"I like the ghost one," chose Franklin.

It was decided that we would decide later. My best-friends-forever, Ronco and Franklin, had offered to circumnavigate the island and "expose island hospitality." Our island had a famous circumnavigator back when I was a kid. One summer he made it his mission to circle the island in his sailboat every single day. This isn't that hard to do, but shouldn't be done in heavy weather. After his seventh or eighth rescue, the harbormaster padlocked the guy's O'Day to its mooring. The next summer he wasn't back, and people said that he was dead from cancer. His orbiting summer was, I guess, some kind of slow surrender to the gravitational pull of the island. Not that my new partners knew that story—I was curious to hear what sort of supernatural story they had for Lettie.

On our way out of the harbor, Lettie told us that she had got her start as a videographer during 9/11. New Yorkers claim ownership of everything, including the apocalypse. I bet she even went to the afterparty. She said we must have known people who drowned. I told her islanders like to talk about drowning about as much as heavy smokers like to talk about cancer. She said she knew someone who had just died of cancer and AIDS. She also knew several famous people I'd never heard of before and had been to parties on some of their roofs and that there had been DNA and bone fragments found on some of those roofs after the World Trade Center attack. Indians, she said, had built some of the towers. She said it was important to join up and show support. She said her videography career began when she realized how important it was to make things known to other people around the world. In her role as a producer, she got to travel all over and work with people to share their stories. She said it was beautiful here but needed better cell phone coverage. Her muffin was unsatisfactory this morning and she knew fellow producers who traveled with bagels. There's actually a good bagel place on Fire Island, she said. The best pizza was to be found some place in New York near where an avenue and a street intersected. It was all about the water. New York water was essential for pizza and bagel dough. Other people disagree but are wrong. Most of her friends lived in Brooklyn. The isolation of the borough concerned her. She knew someone who used to be a fisherman in Alaska. Or maybe he worked at a cannery. He made a lot of money one summer. He was her ex-boyfriend. Her boyfriend now was back at the B&B recovering from the ferry trip. She was going to get a massage when she got back to town, and, no, she hadn't heard the old island maxim "suffer and be silent" ever before.

CHAPTER TWENTY-ONE

The Indian Boys Reformatory, a True Story

"**D**id you know that part of Bismuth is missing?" I asked Lettie.

"You can't find it?"

"No, we know where it is. Mostly. It's somewhere near the Fens and the Leif Ericson statue in Boston. The Bismuthians sold everything from Mount Bis along Bismuth Downs, up through the swamp to the city of Boston to use it as fill. There's supposed to be a plaque on the street there thanking the residents of Bismuth for their dirt."

"Where was it?"

We were passing out of the harbor and beyond the breakwater. I pointed out Wreck Rock. "Right there, that's the mountain's stub."

"Are there pictures of Mount Bis from before?"

"No, and if you weren't a stranger, I wouldn't have even mentioned it. Bismuthians don't like to talk about the mountain; they're still too superstitious."

Ill John, AKA Ronco, pointed with his chin: "You see yonder mountain?"

Lettie scanned the horizon with her hand shading her eyes. "Yonder?"

"Yes. It is new."

"A volcano?"

"No, it is Ted Williams' sludge," he said.

"What?"

"It is dredged from the bottom of Boston Harbor to make a tunnel. And then put here to make a mountain."

"Why?" asked Lettie.

"The people of that island were paid to take that dirt and keep it on their island forever."

"Why didn't Boston just leave the sludge underwater?"

"It is poisoned by Boston Harbor water. The city wanted the harbor to be cleaner."

"What happened to the people on the island?"

"They are members of our tribe," said the newly coined native. "They have moved to Florida."

"A lot of my tribe did too," said Lettie.

"You are Indian?" asked Ronco.

"No, Jewish."

"The Jewish are a tribe?" asked Franklin, née Chosen.

"Twelve different tribes—God's chosen people," she said.

"And the Jewish North American Indian tribe are the Mormons, yes?" asked Ronco.

"No? I'm not sure. I think the Mormons are like the Celtics—all white until a few decades ago," I said.

"No. I am sure," said Ronco. "They migrated from Palestine across the Arctic Circle and down into North America. Guided by angels. It says so in their book."

Before either of my Indian friends could ask about the religion of the ancient Celtics, or the Yankees or the Knickerbockers, or the Redskins and Red Sox, I changed the subject and asked Ronco if some of his ancestors hadn't lived on Mount Bis.

Franklin answered before Ronco could. "Ted Williams is buried there."

"Not on Mount Bis," I said.

"No, of course. He is buried in Ted Williams Island Mountain."

"That's not entirely the case," said Lettie. "His head is cryogenically frozen in Florida."

Was she on to us?

"But I think Roosevelt's tomb is on Campobello Island, Isn't it?" she continued.

"No, I have been there," said Ronco, "It is just his monocle, cigarette holder, and the skeleton of his dog."

"He was just a summer person," I added.

"So your ancestors lived on the mountain?" Lettie asked. "Was it a reservation?"

"No, there were no white people yet," said Franklin. "The mountainous people warred instead with the lowlanders and the mainlanders. They were miners instead of fishermen."

"Miners? What did they mine?"

"Bismuth."

"Oh yeah. Why?"

"They traded it for mussel shells."

"Why?"

"Mussel shells were like dollars. They made great middens of shells in the mineshafts to save for later. They were frugal," explained Franklin Mint.

"Middens in mineshafts?"

"Yes, it is disappointing they did not also have compound interest."

"But the mines were haunted, right?" I said.

"Quite cursed." said Franklin.

"But they're gone?" asked Lettie.

"There are said to be shafts that went below the roots of the mountain, down under the water line—Tunnels and caverns where Franklin and Ronco's ancestors hid during raids and brutal winters."

"Our ancestors told legends of shamans who descended into the mountainous bowels and never returned," said Ronco.

"They became nacreous pale creatures that learned the language of the whales," said Franklin. "They sang with them in hooms and thrums. They were said to travel impossible distances—to distant shores and the icy wastes in the north. Maybe through cracks in the planet, maybe in the bellies of whales."

"Mmm. The ancestors made sacrifices to them. Maidens, first-born sons, tribal enemies and that ilk," said Ronco.

"And in return," I said, "the creatures from below guided whales to the island, where the original islanders would swim out, spear them to death and drag the carcass to shore."

"The waters were fouled with gore. Sharks would come. The tide would be red for weeks from the slaughter," said Franklin.

Lettie asked if she could interview a shaman. Franklin said they were gone with the mountain.

"Wasn't there a reform school on the mountain?" I asked.

Franklin Mint and Ronco didn't answer. I guessed they might not know what a reform school was.

"The Indian Boys Reformatory. It's where the whites sent orphan or otherwise undesirable Indian boys to learn the salubrious effects of industry and obedience."

Neither of my fishing buddies seemed ready to elaborate on the reform school; I supposed the next bit of telling was up to me.

"After the glory days of whaling had waned, and before the mountain was sold for landfill, most of the Indians here had moved to other Indian islands or to the mainland. The Yankees couldn't see the profit yet in these islands, so they used them for dumps and prisons—A leper colony here, a POW camp there, maybe some pasture islands of merinos. They saw the islands as the outermost margins of civilization, not the point of origin, like the Indians here and the Northern Indians think.

"The reform school was built into the entrance of an old mine shaft carved from the side of the mountain. The Stony Lonesome for boys with no place to go anyway. The Quakers who ran it had a delusional zeal for discipline and self-sufficiency that would make a modern North Korean proud. In fact, the entire continent believed entirely that beatings and toil were to be passed down from the richest, palest people and distributed among the masses of indigenous and immigrants, thus making us all the very model of Christianity, to be smiled upon during the final judgment."

"The reform school?" prompted Franklin.

"Well, it was around the time of the Civil War. The Indian boys sentenced to the school were charged with raising sheep and gleaning from the abandoned mines. The merino wool was actually a reasonable source of profit then, and an island is a pretty easy place to be a shepherd. When the boys weren't tending the sheep or sorting through the tailings, they were supposed to be memorizing their Horn Books or attending chapel service. It was a miserable life, but nobody was ever happy in those days.

"There's nothing on an island around here that can kill a sheep, other than an islander. Or so they thought then. One summer they started to find mutilated sheep bodies out in the pastures.

"It only made sense to the school's bosses to blame the boys since they were Savage urchins who, at best, were born to pull oars for the Quaker captains. And the boys probably should have, too. They never saw a cent of the profit from the wool at the school and they lived on food as meager as a sailor's half-rations. The killings spread to the rest of the island's livestock and the Bismuthians responded by blockading the reform school, setting watches on the cavern doors of the school that had been chiseled from the granite mountain.

"The islanders told stories of *loups-garous*. The boys themselves were stripped and searched for signs of shape-shifting. The island's pastures were emptied and children were kept indoors. By summer's end, Bismuth accepted the obvious; wolves had swum to the island and were quickly depopulating it.

"Even a few rabbits can destroy an island, but predators like these were worse than a hurricane. The islands can't sustain them so there are no native populations. Actually, there are no wolves at all anymore, anywhere. And this is why—humans are much worse. The Bismuthians gathered on a fall day just before the foul weather started. They armed themselves like villagers in a Frankenstein movie. Even the Indian boys were conscripted to burn out the wolves.

"They knew the wolves denned on the mountain and one morning they encircled the base of it, and with as much alarum as they could scare up, the islanders forced the mountain's animals to the summit. Then they lit a ring of fire around the peak and stood guard below to kill any wolf that tried to flee the conflagration. Then they ran for their own lives, since lighting their own island on fire was a much worse idea than they had anticipated.

"There are accounts from ships at sea that they could see the fire from all up and down the coast, and by morning the island itself was ringed by gawkers by the boatful. The Bismuthians were lucky, so to speak. The fire never really made it to the harbor, where most people lived. Rather, it spent itself burning the island's pastures and woods, which had already been over-grazed and overtimbered anyway. Still, the smoking stump of their island was a sore sight. The fire must have descended into the mineshafts of the mountain, since the smoke never abated."

"There was a reform school on that mountain, right?" reminded Ronco.

"Well that's what I'm trying to tell you about. Keep up. Like I said, it was the Civil War; the mainland was pooling with blood. That winter after the wolf-burnings, nobody on the continent had the slightest thought about islanders. Not even the school's Quaker masters. Once the wool tribute stopped, the school was conveniently forgotten. Their teachers had taken to sea to dodge the draft. The Bismuthians were too concerned with their own subsistence and besides, they kept their backs to the smoking mountain. The Indian boys had the dubious freedom to fend for themselves.

"During the course of that frigid winter, the boys took to roaming the island and terrifying the village. Islanders did what they always do in hard times—shun the outsiders and refuse to share. The boys' raids lessened as winter deepened. They must have holed up in the shafts and caves below the school. Maybe they tried to hibernate—people say the Indians knew how. But the mountain never stopped smoking.

"Come spring, as the islanders were first shaking out their quilts, the continent remembered the island. The Army sent engineers to Bismuth to survey the still-smoking mountain for sites to fortify against the Confederate Navy. They were told the reform school had been closed—and maybe it had, but nobody had told the starvelings the engineers found at the mountain. Hardly a word could be cadged from the wretches that remained. Bodies were found in bunks as if they were shelved for cold storage. Graves had been dug out and long bones were found by the cast-iron kettles.

"The revenants who'd survived had surrendered their senses and could make no account of the winter. And it's easy to imagine the Islanders, the Quakers, the Army—everyone—weren't too eager to hear it anyway."

Lettie hadn't checked her cell phone for life signs in a few minutes, so I figured it a story well told. My friend, Franklin Mint, didn't seem satisfied though. I could sense he was hoping I'd leave off somewhere good for him to pick up.

"Many of the boys were still missing," he said, in a tone that insinuated ancestral knowledge of the unspeakable. "Not eaten, not dead. Disappeared into the fetid blackness of the shafts, hauling all record of their existence along with them. Legends say the boys found the shamans—or the creatures the shamans had become—and joined them in their lightless sanctuary below.

"The years that followed the American Civil War also saw the end of whaling as Bismuth knew it. And without whales and sheep, the people saw less reason to live on the island. The villagers whispered sinister stories about the mountain and chose to ignore stinking tendrils of vapor and the luteous glows that sometimes escaped from the crevasses. Rumors spread of cacophonous flutings and groanings from the unwholesome chasms and of lightning that lingered too long on the summit's rocky knuckle.

"Islanders were careful not to speak of a curious phenomenon that occurred each summer near where the mountain sloped sheer into the sea without so much of a strip of sand to skirt it.

Still, a professor from an important mainland university who had summered here for years became curious about the annual turbulence. Curious because it occurred on the solstice and curious because he had read weird accounts written by mad scholars and suspect fantasists of other such unseemly disturbances of the natural congresses of fishes and men."

Franklin's language had purpled dramatically, like the sea before a disastrous gale. His story was creepy enough, but the transformation that was coming upon the Korean skald was really starting to give me the willies.

"It was said that when the sun finally set after its longest shine of the year, that any islander who trod the mountain would not return. That foolhardy fishermen found abominations in their nets. That children were snatched and replaced with changelings who developed gill-like deformities. The ancient Indians who let slip dark hints told the professor that shrill piping and rumbling hooms throbbed through curséd Mount Bis on that evil night each year, making its very pebbles dance primeval steps of inhuman choreography. The natives insinuated that the shamans of yore still lurked the mountain's roots, though they had long ago shed their humanity. They warned that ever since the forsaken boys of the reformatory disappeared into the ramifying mine shafts, the solstice had become a dire day marked by tragedies and accidents. 'Do not linger here upon the solstice,' they admonished. 'Sublet your cottage to tourists that week.'

"On that shortest night of the summer, as the aurora borealis shimmered, the old professor took his walking stick and equally-old-but-equally-curious dog and slipped from his cottage, telling his sleepy wife that he was going to make astronomical observations. She warned him to stay away from the mountain and the moiling pool that formed annually below it. But he was a true Nineteenth Century scholar and was certain that, along with his dog and stick, reason and skepticism would ward him from supernatural bunkum."

Ronco pitched in: "It must have been a difficult walk for both, since none of their six knees bent well any longer. They were driven by a curiosity, by the gravity of the sublime, an impish perversion that has always driven mankind to consider beyond what simple reason would allow."

Franklin nodded sagely. "What drives men into the depths of lurking madness? What is worse; to traipse blindly into a horror that should not exist, or to court it, whether through necromancy or imagination? The professor chose his fate, of course, but how is it his highly-praised organ of reason allowed such a choice? Here is what we do know: When his wife awoke in the morning and found the professor had not returned from his observations, she sent searchers. He was discovered, alone, that afternoon, shuffling along the mountain road. He collapsed into the arms of his rescuers and did not utter a word for more than a week as he convalesced. When he did speak again, he had lost most of his talent for rhetoric and reasoning. He could only blurt warnings and bizarre gabblings that did not suit the once proper and staid man at all.

"His wife would never say a word about the man; she simply kept caring for him and telling those concerned that he had fallen ill and deserved their prayers, while keeping the key to his sickroom on a ribbon around her neck. One of my ancestors was a servant in their cottage, and it is from her that my family has preserved his story. She gathered from his ravings that he had hiked the mountain to a flat cliff that hung over the ocean. He sat there to listen to what he supposed was the wind whooshing through the boulders and cracks and marvel at the spectral light folding luminously across the sky. The aurora seemed to have an anti-shadow in the waves, which fizzed with phosphorescence as they convolved upon themselves, forming a surging whirlpool below the beetling crag.

"His thoughts had wandered among the stars and waves so it seemed a surprise to him when he noticed the wind's roar had taken on distinctive trills, like the undertones of a thousand bull rushes. A deep counterpoint worried its way to his earbones through his bottom. He noticed his dog had gone rigid with attention and soon he could not even hear the waves, only the piping and wooming that was devouring his mind.

"He saw a swirling in the inky water just beyond the undulating black bladderwort and felt compelled to clamber downward to it, despite the fragility of his age. His dog began to growl but would not join him.

"Any man who knows the sea knows to expect grotesqueries. The professor may not have been an islander, but he was of coastal stock and a free thinker, besides. Maybe it was his education and sophistication that prevented him from dying of shock at that moment. Perhaps it was the utter inconceivability of what he saw that allowed him to stagger away. But his sanity did not return from the mountain with him, nor did his dog.

"For men of reason and intellect know better than to see those same qualities reflected in an animal's eyes. Moiling beneath the spume were pale creatures with griseous brows that surely contained thought. Slatches in the waves showed them to be the size of dolphins yet without their sleek and resilient skin. The professor thought more of insect larvae than piscine hunters. Their bodies suggested bulging tubes of tallow; the tailfins were strangely articulated, and their lateral fins were more like hands with attenuated, webbed fingers.

"Several creatures rose to the surface as if they were standing on pedestals. What shocked the professor most was not their repugnant bodies. It was their wall-eyed stare, both unhuman and disturbingly familiar. It was the wide, chinless jaw with the curiously rubbery lips and the corpse-like pallor of the creature's face, and the uncanny attention they fixed upon him. What shattered the mind of the poor professor most entirely was their request: 'Give dog.'

"He said later that at the time he could not even begin to question why he was throwing his beloved dog into the seething water—he said that he had still been in their thrall even after he'd been found. His dog yelped and snapped at him, pulled into the depths before it could even drown. The last thing the professor could recall seeing was his loyal friend moaning with fear and betrayal, trying to bat at the sickly smooth heads of the creatures with his forepaws as something tugged from below."

I had stopped breathing a minute or so prior. I was afraid to look at Franklin. Ronco was smiling with pride. I renewed my vow to never swim again.

Lettie looked aggrieved. "He killed his dog?!" When none of us defended the conclusion, she asked if we didn't know any shorter stories about houses with lights that went on and off and creaking floorboards in the attic. I did, but they were all true and not worth mentioning.

CHAPTER TWENTY-TWO

BBQ Squid

Turns out, we blew it with the story. As the only real native around, I felt I was qualified to judge, and I deemed it magnificently eerie. Lettie, on the other hand, grumbled it was nasty and old fashioned. She couldn't get over the dead dog. Her lack of appreciation cast a pall on us and transformed us from salty raconteurs to three creepy guys she was trapped on a boat with. Ronco had promised a "water picnic" earlier, but she was having none of it. A boyfriend awaited her at the inn. A cell phone potent with runes of busy-ness and personal significance was waved before us. An insufficiency of bars was declared. The danger of interfering with Lettie's immediate destiny were made plain: the likeliness of our televised celebrity was diminishing with every second we failed to promptly deliver her back to the island.

I think it was when Ill John shucked his Patriots jacket that he also doffed his Ronco persona. Franklin slipped back into Chosen by simply turning silent. I suppose his feelings were hurt. His story had deserved a better audience. As Lettie grew more anxious, the Koreans grew more distant, and I realized I was witnessing an important evolutionary moment—Ill John and Chosen had taken an important step in adapting to the island; they had assimilated the fluidic, unexplainable concept of "island time." Island time is endemic but meaningless among islanders; it only becomes apparent when strangers wield their own sense of time and significance. Island time then begins to calcify around them, suspending the irritant in a way that makes them continue to feel glossy and valuable, while rendering them inconsequential. Lettie's attempt to summon the persuasive power of the Manhattan Minute must have catalyzed the Koreans and revealed to them the complex nuances of inaction and delay that make up island time. Needless to say, the no-wake rule of the harbor was well-anticipated and applied with a sense of stately conservation as we gurgled dockward.

Lettie took to the foredeck to recuse herself from our company and do something in her lap with her thumbs and an electronic device that wasn't as interesting to watch as it might have seemed. I had hoped to impress my salty, rogue sexuality upon her by coiling a line on the deck and offering observations about the quality of the weather, but Ill John and I wound up with our lips in each other's ears, trying to whisper over the engine noise.

We were looking at Lettie's back as she sat on the deck and leaned against the cabin's front window. She was wearing a blue-and-white striped jersey and a black bra or maybe bikini. Lots of tourists wear bathing suits under their clothes. Presumably because this island is so paradisiacal that one never knows when one will feel so joyful that one must fling off one's clothes and swim. When I was a kid I wore trunks under my pants for an entire summer, waiting for that very feeling to overcome me. I got a rash and new underwear for school that year, but that was all.

Since the dock and Lettie's slouching boyfriend had been in view for some time—and would continue to be so for some time due to our negligible pace—our guest seemed a little more pacific. Her boyfriend, she said, wasn't partial to the water and hadn't really recovered from the ferry ride. But he did own his own apartment in Manhattan. She said that even though Manhattan was on the water, there wasn't much aquatic about it, except in some restaurants. She praised the plaintalking authenticity of us islanders but didn't think we were telegenic, especially the geezers.

After we tied up to let her off, I watched her climb the low-tide ladder and thought she was still kind of good looking even if she was from New York and had a seasick boyfriend. I liked the way she carried her sneakers instead of putting them back on. I told myself it was her way of telling me that the key was under the mat, for later.

My mind was getting so watery that my only lingering thought as we pulled out again was of Lettie's soles. I forgot to follow her up the ladder and back to my life, whatever had become of it. Ill John must have noticed. He told me not to be forlorn and that good supper and a pleasant evening was before us. But my needs extended beyond good supper.

I watched the two of them converse in Korean; Ill John seemed to be coaxing Chosen out of his sulk. It was soothing to see them rally, and I settled a bit. Their fondness for Bismuth life was disconcerting, but it gave off a nice little contact high. I shouldn't complain, I thought. Here I am on my own island in my own harbor, where I knew at least two names and a nickname for every rock in sight. These people actually want my company and are fully aware I have nothing profitable to offer them. We roamed the harbor, presumably in search of a good place to lay out our metaphorical blanket and begin our picnic, and I tried to re-assemble what had been my plan, since I was somewhat convinced that I had once felt a strong sense of purpose and was currently experiencing mission drift. Men need plans because their lives are what happen when their plans go south.

There was the still enigmatic sampo gift. At one point it had seemed life-threatening and desperately serious. My anticipation of supper had tidily replaced my dread of the sampo. There was Angie, whose ire was going to dog me forever. I felt lousy about running our potential relationship aground before it had got much farther than Mini's Island. I should have known better than to get between a mother and her cub. Snorri's worries about his whale and antenna were much too perplexing to become my own worry. Waldena was well worth thinking about, but my mind seized up between fight and flight whenever she made it to my forebrain and gummed up all my mental machinery. I tried to concentrate and project my will into the future. I should expect things of the world and anticipate them and integrate these things into what was expected of me and my own personal aspirations. But I kept leaping to what seemed like an inevitable conclusion—if I were lying on my own couch, in my own home, right this very minute, there would be no need for a plan. But plans are plans, especially other people's plans.

"So what's the plan?" I asked them.

"Delicious barbeque, Korean-style," said Ill John.

You can't shock me with a squid; I've seen too many. The ones we fish around here are like children's hands with eyeballs. Sorting them can be difficult. If I think about them too much, I have to go sit down—I've never been completely comfortable around tentacles. They're slithery and intentional when fish are merely random and floppy, and plus squid piss black ink all over you. I know they have cousins who are much too large and smart for their own good. I've heard tell that the summer after the Cape Cod Canal was dug, it clogged so badly with migrating squid that cutters had to go out dragging heavy cables to slice through all the entangled tentacles and make the new canal navigable again. I don't suppose many species out there have humans digging a giant shortcut to their mating grounds for them.

I've seen them vomited from fish. I've chopped them into a slurry of chum. I've watched their torpid limbs stiffen terminally mid-grapple as they try to crawl from the freezer holds. However, this was the first time I'd seen them so flat and well-organized. While Chosen set up a Hibachi that hung on a bracket from the side of the boat, Ill John produced a leather attaché case that opened from the top. Inside it was divided with expandable file folders that Ill John flipped through with his forefingers.

"These are unavailable in your hemisphere," he told me, "but common in Korea. Chosen already selected the right ones for this evening. He began preparing them this morning. Here is another good one, please be careful."

I took the squid he was showing me. It was light, tan, stiff, and flat. It looked like an old sandal. "See, it still has all its limbs and eyeballs. Many are damaged, even counterfeit. See the two longer tentacles? They are the favorites for children to chew. One is used to deposit sperm."

Ill John re-filed the squid. I figured his system probably wasn't alphabetical. I thought about Korean kids chewing their favorite tentacles, and then I tried to unthink the thought.

"I am not the chef, though, and perhaps Chosen is not either. He is an artist, a scientist. You Americans think you invented the barbeque, but we were grilling animals before this continent even had the wheel."

The attaché case folded open further to show an apothecary of jars and bottles labeled in Korean. Each was strapped in with a leather band or bundled in a handkerchief. "I have been curious about Tartar sauce since we first tasted it here," said Chosen. "What do the Turkmen have to do with Bismuth? Their ancestors were masters of the grass sea, not the ocean.

"Upon your revelation that the Topsoil makes it by mixing mayonnaise and relish, I was disappointed."

"You should see them make Thousand Island dressing."

"Furthermore," said Chosen, "it does not contain tartaric acid, which would be helpful for the squid. As I sought to prepare the liquid for the squid, I reviewed other materials in your store. I found that tonic water contains a cure for malaria and that club soda does not contain a sufficient amount of bicarbonate of soda. I had been told that the English translation for what I wanted was Lyle Water however, and I cannot buy such a thing."

"Tonic water's a mixer for boat drinks. They call club soda 'sparkling water' at the Topsoil now. If you want a Coke or something, you can say 'soda' now, but we used to say 'tonic' and sometimes still do. Just don't say 'pop.' I've never heard of Lyle Water. But I meant to ask, do you guys have any beer?"

They had played their lobstermen role too well. All they had was a case of Bud cans. At least I was helping to contribute a sense of realism. Whenever Donny and I drank cans on his dad's boat, we always shotgunned the first one by punching a hole near the base of the can. Donny, however, was a dick; whereas I was gallant and cosmopolitan. I opened mine properly and made sure I took at least five minutes to sip it down.

Chosen resumed his disquisition. "What was necessary was lye solution. I considered making the lye by soaking wood ash, but that too is hard to find here."

It was true. Only God knows the last time there was a hardwood tree big enough to cut for cordwood on the island.

"In the shop I found the solutions I needed outside of grocery. A drain cleaner contained more lye than I could ever use. Baking soda powder for sodium bicarbonate. Do you say 'making math' here? I thought the verb was 'doing.'"

"Why?"

"As I counted my change from the clerk, he asked me if I was 'making math,' where I thought I was 'doing math.'"

"He said 'meth'—crystal methamphetamine—poor man's crack made from store bought chemicals."

"Ahh. Why, when you have seagum?"

"The grass is always greener," I told him.

"What?"

"The next drug is always better."

"Well, indeed, because the next drug was very helpful." Chosen showed me a glass jar full of a yellow-gray liquid that fizzed a little when he wiggled it. He opened it and offered to me to smell. It made my eyes water. *Snorri*. This was old milk.

"This is old milk," I said, handing it back quickly.

"Yes! From Snorri! We have nothing like it in Korea!"

"Nor here."

"It is perfect, and Snorri assures that it is entirely organic," said Chosen.

I never understood the consolation of "organic." All the most horrible things in the world are organic.

"Snorri would not explain the ingredients, but I think I understand the principle. This is an animal's milk that was going to become a cheese when a bacteria was introduced. However, both the milk and the bacteria used are very strong and they continue to fight each other, instead of adapting to being comfortable cheese. Snorri keeps them in chaotic equilibrium secretly.

"After Snorri donated his sample of old milk, the preparation congealed in my mind. The opposing forces of lye and soda, once distilled, could be made cooperative. The old milk assists in the unlocking of squid protein structures while adding an element of the uncanny. And finally, we make it personal!" Chosen held up a vial of pink powder.

"Bismuth! Right from your island! I saw the pink stomach preparations in the store next to the calcium carbonate tablets and had the idea. It is a regulating force to the wildness of the old milk and the combativeness of the lye and soda, while adding a calming pink hue to what I have named the Bismuth Squid Relaxing Juice!"

I demonstrated how mature and open-minded I was by not jumping overboard.

The charcoal briquettes were nearly gray to the center, and Chosen was ready to grill. He pulled a plastic bin out from under a bench and peeled off the lid. "The squids soak in their tub for most of the day." He swirled the liquid. "The squid relaxer was hard to devise. First versions of it. . . ."

"Exploded," interjected Ill John.

"Yes. But this," he said, as he held up a dripping squid and laid it on the grill, "is an elixir."

At that slap and sizzle, my stomach contracted like a child's fist.

"The relaxing juice bloats the squid body enough to make it good for chewing. I will grill it for approximately ten minutes to sear the outside and add the flavors of charcoal and smoke, while making the skin somewhat crisp and sweet. Sometimes this squid is eaten with a sauce of garlic and chilies, but Ill John has a special surprise."

Ill John had a big ceramic baked bean pot. "This has been in my family for generations. My mother is very unhappy it has left Korea. She gave it to me so I would remember her and home."

He opened the lid and held the pot before me. "See? Real kimchi!"

I imagined gulls dropping from the sky, simply from the stench of the stuff. I felt dizzy and febrific, but not at all hungry. Somehow, Ill John's sentimentality and Chosen's sincere enthusiasm, when combined with what they considered supper, had unmanned me. I felt my lower lip tremble and my throat swell. The film in my eyes welled and spilled down the sides. I tried choking down some beer, but it wound up in my nose. Chosen stared at me, and I felt Ill John's hand smoothing my back. "It is OK, Orange. I brought a sandwich, just in case."

That had been a real mom-and-apple pie moment for the Koreans, and I was annoyed with myself for not appreciating it. I had buckled, I supposed. Underslept and unmoored. I was grateful to Ill John, and I didn't want to be. I really did need to sit quietly by myself on the foredeck and eat a turkey sandwich slowly. But it bothered me that he knew me well enough to suggest it. The only thing to do was pick myself up and eat squid like a real man.

Ill John and Chosen were ready to help me save some face. Everybody with a boat knows the liberty of no witnesses. Usually it's just license for hedonism or at least bad personal grooming, but I thought my ex-lobstering partners were being remarkably humanistic about it. Chosen offered a choice of tentacle or body. I chose body. He gave me a finger-long strip around an inch wide that had been siped like a balding tire with cross-hatched grooves. Considering its origin and recent history, it wasn't all that bad. In fact the same piece continued to be not all that bad as I chewed it for the next several minutes. I wasn't sure whether I was supposed to swallow it or not.

"Chewy," I said.

"I grilled four," said Chosen, "have all you want. You sure no tentacle?"

I was sure. The two of them promptly broke off their choice of tentacles from the stack of grilled squids. Chosen chomped his down, while Ill John worried one like Eastwood with a cheroot. I let my wad soak into a swallowable bolus in the pouch of my cheek. Another beer helped.

"So that was a wicked story," I said.

Chosen beamed. "In college, I took 'Supernaturalism in Coastal Northeast American Literature' in the English language. Lovecraft was best. I kept the books. I read King in English now. Ill John likes Poe."

"I didn't know people in Korea read that stuff."

"There are many important writers from this region," said Chosen.

"I don't think I've read any Korean books. Not that I read Korean."

"Not much gets translated. Many Koreans study English literature, some study American."

"There is a big American Army base in Korea. We tire of big Americans quickly there," added Ill John.

"Here, too," I said.

CHAPTER TWENTY-THREE

Donald Slips a Mickey

The sub-woofing "thug-thug" of a fishing boat takes a few seconds to catch up to the boat itself, but the waves have a way of pushing sound forward, and sometimes it heralds rather than explains an arrival. I heard something like it: distant concussions with a rhythm, maybe even a military backbeat. My skin horripilated while I braced irrationally for a rogue wave washover. It was all sonic. The sound of muscly, sluggish propulsion—an overbored engine lurching forward on too much throttle—resolved into a drive and drop of fuzzy guitar growls and whomping percussion that mimicked the whooshing slatch and rattling slap of a longship riding and crashing on steep gray waves.

This was Estonindian black metal dub. Music for wounded bears as they shrugged off tranquilizer darts. A genre so conclusively suicide-inducing, blue-ribbon Congressional panels were afraid to listen to it. If Francis Scott Key had been a ninth-century raider whose head was still throbbing and clanging from an ax-blow to the helmet, standing with one hand braced on the dragon prow of his longship watching his enemies' tarred warships burn in an uncanny blue bituminous haze, while unseen galley slaves chanting the stroke rumbled the ship from below, he may have closed his eyes, thought of Ragnarok, and composed an anthem like this.

The loury drone that underlay belied a bass drum thumping

away at smothering rapidity, like adrenalized mastodons stomping out a tachycardiac wardance. Snatches of phrases, usually snarling exhortations to stroke harder, blew in and out of the lumbering music; it was music for weeks of sleet on the open sea, for the anthemist to wrap himself in a reeking wool cloak and keep his ax close. Soon the galley slaves would be dead of overwork and starvation and he would have to pull an oar himself if he ever wanted to see his own linden-graced shores again. It was music of the cold, countless waves of the middle distance, well past the point of no return.

Yet here it was in our harbor in the form of the *Hammer Maiden* sluing toward our little *Princess Pea* on a slow but irredeemable collision course. We banged hard to port as she arced in the other direction. Chosen flipped open a compartment under the deck's bench and grabbed his Kalashnikov. Waldena was probably lucky his attention was split between the collision and rescuing his alchemical cooking kit. Waldena herself was right there on her deck waving both arms, shouting "No!" I think maybe I was too, but I was shouting to her boat, while she was shouting to Chosen.

We grazed each other right around amidships, which was healthy piloting by Ill John. The *Princess* took a good body check and a bite out of her gunwale from the *Maiden* and left a ragged smear of chalky white paint along the whaler's dark hull. Had our angles been off just a little, the *Maiden* would have foundered us like a hibernating bear sow smothering her cub. I couldn't help noticing her black opalescent paintjob and the unibrow-like louvers beetling over the smoked amber windows of her conning tower. This was a wicked boat that picked tubs like ours out of her teeth. We were lucky to have bounced off her.

We do-si-doed back to neutral corners, while Chosen kept a
bead on the *Maiden*. Ill John backed off to an idle to see if she
were pursuing us. She was beginning to orbit back around when
her engines and music cut. She lifted a bit as her wake passed
under her. Waldena kept waving to us in a jerking semaphore
and yelled, "I've been tampered!"

"What?" I yelled.

"I'm . . . Jesus Fuck!" she screamed. Then followed up in ranting Estonindian with what I presumed was her assessment of the
desert god's son's shameful intramural relationships, as well as
how his turpitude was directly responsible for her current state.
She concluded, "I need help!"

We huddled. "You know Waldena, right?" I asked the Koreans.

"We would be fools not to," said Ill John.

"You can still be fools even if you do," I said.

"Orange!" she hollered. My goose pimples grew back.

"If we leave her for the harbormaster, she'll hunt us down and
kill us," I said.

"We are proper mariners," said Ill John. "We must have
honor."

We came around and puttered down to her. As we came alongside, she told us to use bumpers.

"We are not tying up," yelled Ill John. He held a coiled line
in his hand. "You have had a boating accident. Take this and we
will tow you to shore."

He tossed the line across her foredeck. Waldena snatched it
and flung it back. "You will not!"

"You are not in distress?"

"I'll swim back before I get towed in by this thing!"

I think all three of us paused to entertain private thoughts
about the contradictory needs of dangerous women.

"So . . . ?" said Ill John.

"So, fuck!" Waldena looked more cross than engine trouble warranted. If she wasn't hopping mad, she was at least tap dancing. She was wearing a tank top and I could see that a flush had spread up from her chest to set her arms and face aglow. Her eyes were far too open and sweat soaked her hairline. I put my hand on Ill John's arm like he was going to help me cross the street.

"I think she wants a ride," said Ill John.

"She's a pretty good swimmer," I said. "Maybe she should just swim to shore."

We tied up, bumpers and all. Waldena dropped anchor, two anchors in fact, and spent a piece of time battening the *Maiden*. Ill John and I differed on whether she was fastening or fascinating. She stood a good chance of catching some hell from the harbormaster for illegal parking. Once the boat was theft-proofed, or whale-proofed, or whatever her inordinate security protected her from, Waldena leapt down from her boat onto the *Princess's* foredeck, dropping down to one knee to soften her landing. This brought her face to face with Ill John and I in the wheelhouse. She put both her palms on the windshield and gave us a hard stare until the glass fogged over. She was clearly in distress, and, therefore, so were we.

Waldena was radioactively pissed off. It was hard to tell who was to blame, since most of creation had been itemized and cursed in an accelerated sputter of English and Estonindian. Held to particular account were the Island, Snorri, the Lucys, me, the Koreans, and the ocean, all of whom had collaborated to produce this pitch of botheration. I don't think any of us, even Waldena, could have anticipated the effect she soon had. Ill John gunned us toward the dock, flouting the wake rule.

Chosen hurriedly packed up his cooking kit and then sat on it, clutching his AK. I found myself gnawing on my knuckles. When Waldena paused her diatribe to cross her eyes and knees and exhale hard through her nostrils, Chosen said something to Ill John in Korean that suggested he had figured something out.

"What?" I asked.

"Tiger testes."

Oh God. "Seagum?"

"What?" asked Waldena.

"Seagum," I said.

"Tiger testes," said Chosen.

Waldena looked frustrated and perplexed.

"A white powder?" asked Ill John.

"Not cocaine?" she asked.

I had an insight: "Not Donny Lucy?"

Waldena pinched her eyes to arrow slits. Her flush empurpled. I felt her teeth grind. Or, no, I felt my own teeth grind. I was growing confused, and her agitation was infectious. Our cockpit had become a pheromonic funk hole; we were all gasping.

"Donny . . . Lucy . . . not. . . ."

Waldena was too incandescent to finish speaking. I took a towel and soaked it over the side. "Here, put this over your head. It'll help us calm down."

She darted me with an angry one-eyed stare and then draped the wet towel over her head like a wimple.

The rest of us gawked. It was odd to have so much empathy for a woman in the throes of arousal. I'd always wanted to know, but I'd imagined the context differently. Arousal was the wrong word, anyway. Waldena had set off a panic in us all and triggered some awfully dangerous instincts. Provocation maybe was the better word. A big fish had got away not long ago, and now we'd landed another one, and none of us, fish included, were done fighting. I had nothing overtly evil in mind, and my partners were supposed to be honorable mariners. That's why I didn't feel insulted when Waldena pulled up a pant leg and took a knife from her boot sheath. Two men can be a hazard—partners in crime—but three men are the beginning of a pack and the end of reason. Lettie had known this, probably had some Mace ready the whole time. She even led our pack for a short while. Her cell phone, her waiting boyfriend, her dissatisfaction all served to remind us of how to behave. Waldena was a wounded wolf who had just noticed that the deer she'd been hunting so scornfully had begun to cooperate. We were squid-eating deer, though. We weren't a threat.

"Don't worry," I told her.

"I will worry all I want," she said with her teeth clenched.

We reached the dock quickly, but just before we tied up, Ill John reversed the motor, dropping it just enough to keep us from drifting in with the waves. "Spill," he said.

Waldena glared at him.

"Tell us the story."

"Let me off this boat right now!"

"Tell us what happened," ordered Ill John in his best DMZ border guard voice.

"Mind your own business."

"Exactly. You are in our own business."

Waldena was probably sussing us out like a pool shark. Our heads were the billiard balls. Chosen, however, had a pretty persuasive pool cue, and the only duel she'd win against him was a kegeling contest.

"The chum buckets of Bismuth will be filled with chunks of Snorri of fucking Finlindia and Donny Lucy of buttsucking

Bismuth." She paused to clench her entire body. A spasm was presumably condensed to a tiny, dense diamond and stored away to be spent later. "Maybe I will think of a way to feed them to each other. And you three will be in the chowder. Dock this boat."

Ill John gave her a good, solid, island hairy eyeball.

"I have three hard Estonindian crewmen waiting for me in town. And, like the Americans say, they do not truck with this island shit."

If a person could go cross-eyed with just one eyeball, she did. "And they are simmering in the outdoor hot tub on the back deck of the Muffin Basket Inn drinking bloody mimosas! Fuckers! I pay them! For what?!"

"What is wrong with your boat?" asked Ill John.

"The *Maiden* has a screw loose and a fouled shaft, thanks to Snorri. He is a saboteur and a bearfucker. Or he wishes. His prick is too tiny."

"A screw loose, indeed," I said.

"Foul shaft!" she growled.

"And what made you so unseaworthy?" asked Ill John.

"You tell me," she said.

We explained the relationship between Bismuth and the tigers of Korea.

"He said it was coke." Waldena endured some kind of internal weather. "Give me those beers."

"Why Donny?" was what I really wanted to know.

Waldena stood upright, seemed as if she were about to stretch, or maybe stab me, handed me the can she'd emptied in a gulp, and then sat back down with her knees to her chest. She still held her knife, but wasn't exactly brandishing it. "He said he wanted to trade. He said he had the package—the sampo."

"What did he want for it?" Donny Lucy? Fuck.

"Oh Donny Lucy is the big gigolo on little Bismuth, is he not? He calls me up, says we can have 'a little bite' at the Topsoil. Says he has something he knows I want; he can hardly wait to give it to me. Donny is a . . . you don't have the word in English. A kind of sea-ape. A sort of unevolved merman that masturbates very often."

Ill John stood by the wheel, goosing our slow drift. Chosen held his AK in his lap.

"So you went on a date with him?"

"Do not mock me, Whippey. I do what must be done. Dinner with that oaf was a price I thought I could afford to pay. I suppose the seared skate punches were not bad. A chantey is a work song here, right? He says you sing one about him—"From Pawtucket to Bangor?""

"It's not about him. It's supposed to be about an old pirate."

"It is a stupid song. He winks at the bartender as he sings it. At that point I was glad I had told my crew to stay at the Inn."

One night when we were at sea, Donny took it upon himself to perform this song as freestyle gangsta-rap. Whenever he couldn't think of a rhyme, he'd say "Donny Lucy, Yo!" His dad came out of his bunk, slapped his son's head, and confiscated our beer and seagum.

Waldena continued, "So he goes to the bathroom and returns saying he has left me a present in the 'Buoy's Room' and promises that it is not shit. He says to hurry up, there is coke. I believe him, since I know Americans do their cocaine in the bathroom. I am a busy woman, and I thought sniffing a line will get me off this island even faster because it is a breeding factory for imbeciles. But it was too late. I had become an imbecile myself. Donny is so eager for me to open my present, he is snickering as

I go to the bathroom. There on an old paperback book on the toilet tank is a line of what Donny says is coke. I do the line and look for the package. Nowhere, of course."

"He was trying to slip you a Donald, instead of a Mickey."

"Give me another of those horrible beers.

"Your Donald walks right into the Buoy's Room, asks me how I like it. I'm getting ready to tell him I have something much more interesting than waterboarding to show his country if he does not give me the sampo-gift. Then the Donald-coke hits me like a man-o-war sting. I think I tried to vomit through my eye sockets. He says he has my package 'right here, baby,' so I kick him as hard as I can right where he is pointing, simply out of instinct. I cannot say I remember leaving the restaurant. I could not even have a thought until I got to the *Maiden*. Then I suspected I had been tampered."

"You mean dosed. Tampered is for containers."

Waldena hugged her knees and clenched the knife's handle. "I mean the boat was fucked! Sabotage! I went a short way out into the harbor before I realized it was the *Maiden*, not me, that had been tampered. I was wrong, of course; it was the both of us. She would only steer to starboard; I hoped the top of my arc would get me far enough from Donny to collect myself. That is when I saw you."

"What was with the abominable snowman marching music?"

"I was trying to focus my thoughts. We use the music to stun whales when they are close to the boat. It destroys their echolocation. I thought it would help boaters stay away."

"Was Donny, like, lying on the bathroom floor, moaning—"

"Enough! I do not know! Put me on the dock now!"

She'd spilled enough to satisfy Ill John, evidently. He goosed the *Princess* and let her drift in. "And enough dilation from you," he said. "That sampo gift was not for you, not for Donny. It was for Snorri. And he will receive it tomorrow. Enough divagation. Tomorrow we meet again."

Waldena jumped to the dock. "Enough of my ass you pricks. My hind is the last you will see of me."

"No, not your hind," said Ill John.

"And why is that?"

"We will bring Snorri. You and he may reckon."

Waldena gave us ex-lobstermen a look just like Rover did that day I really shouldn't have given her a bath.

She began to walk away; I waved and tossed her a line, shouting, "Hey, tie us up!"

CHAPTER TWENTY-FOUR

Brief Redemption

Angry ethnonationalists with foul shafts and screws loose. Divagations of sampo. Squid tentacles softening in what looks like fizzy strawberry milk. Waldena's hind. A rotting whale. The sun was set and a dimness was upon the land, and I was standing all by my lonesome on the town dock, scratching my balls and slowly realizing that I was unchaparoned. Waldena had set off to moil her crew in the Muffin Basket hot tub. The Koreans had wished me goodnight and made plans to meet tomorrow before they motored off to wherever they'd been keeping themselves. That left me to my own devices, devices that hadn't seen much use lately. Freedom was perplexing.

Thank God my feet don't overthink. The walk from the dock to my house was a mile more familiar to me than my own body. Lefty and Righty were taking me home without even asking. Good for them. The rest of me came along, gradually comprehending where I was headed.

Until I arrived, it seemed strange to have a home at all. Did Waldena have a cozy cottage in Estonindia? Did she neglect to mow her lawn for the month of August? What did Chosen's kitchen look like? It seemed unreasonably mundane to be a lifelong resident of the ol' Bis.

While I walked, I tried to savor the nostalgia and anticipation for this place I'd sought to flee much more often than to return. Sometimes it seemed almost unreasonable that I had a house at all. I grew up in the house. My parents didn't drink Sterno. Mom was almost entirely sane. Dad, like most island men, used to have eleventy-seven different jobs; often, it would seem, all at once. I went away; I came back. I went away; I came back. My parents learned not to be disappointed, and my mother in particular came to learn that it was better to assume I was alive and just as boring as ever, even if she hadn't heard from me in over a week. We really were out of reasons to bother each other by the time they announced they would not endure a single 'nother winter on the island.

I didn't think they would like Florida, but they were hooked up with a mafia of snowbirds from these parts. I imagined them all in ugly shorts and pastel sun visors standing around an alligator eating ducks at the golf course water trap, discussing the profligate idiocy of Florida culture, disgusting the natives with their seagum-loosened lips and habitual parsimony. I was supposedly paying my father the same sum in rent that he had once paid monthly before the second mortgage was paid off. I hadn't though, and apart from a few hints about their condo association fees, he'd let it slide. The lack of grandchildren made visiting with me much less interesting—they began each summer intending to drive up, but hadn't made it much past Georgia in recent years. I'd never been to their condo.

Rover looked mussed and bed-bodied. "Daddy's home," I said quietly. She sniffed my cuff and walked down the hallway to sit and stare at me from the kitchen doorway. "*Your* daddy's here in *his* home," I told her more loudly. She seemed disinclined to spring into my arms and slobber me with kisses. I said, "Stay back you vicious cougar!" And she did. "Well, looks like

Mitchell's been feeding you, at least." She showed me her butt-hole and walked with a crooked, peevish tail up the stairs to where she could be observed ignoring me all the better. "I hope you bought beer," I told her.

I had lordly plans to find the joint I thought I might have stashed, then sample each of my mod cons as my sobriety slipped away and mild euphoria was gently replaced by oblivion. The joint went unfound, unsurprisingly. And, following Rover's lead, I felt more lordly spurning my shower, clean clothes, and TV/VCR/DVD in favor of the couch. I'd see what havoc or at least what degree of shedding Rover had left for me upstairs later. I didn't care if bears were denning down cellar. Maybe I just felt too displaced to sleep in my own bed. As soon as a bit of my drool on the throw pillow had activated the smell of Rover and smoke, I was out.

When someone knocks at the door, you're supposed to get up and open it and say hello. Or some variation thereof. It was the variations that were confusing me. I could lie right here and shout, "I'm not home!" or "Who is it?" or "I am my own personal savior." What was it that polite people said? Then there was the whole apparatus of locks and security chains to worry about. Only I'd lost my key long, long ago and there was no chain. The knocks continued. I settled on yelling, "Coming!" but only because my butler had the day off.

"I didn't ever have to knock before because you weren't here, but Dad says your light was on."

Moira.

"I'm coming in. You look gross," she said, opening the storm and sidling past me.

Rover gave her the big hello she'd withheld from me. Moira got down on knees and elbows and the two of them rubbed cheeks. Then they fairly scampered down to the kitchen together. I followed, feeling big and dumb.

My fog hadn't cleared at all yet. I watched Moira haul out the big bag of cat food, wrapping it with both arms. She scooped a mugful from the bag into Rover's bowl. As Moira changed the water bowl, Rover crunched her kibble, purring through her nose.

"You want some coffee?" I asked.

Moira told me a "no" that came from a deep well of exasperation with grown-up men.

I looked around. I didn't have any, anyway. My first clear, self-diagnostic thought was that I was going to have a big headache soon.

I rubbed my face and scratched my head. "Where's your dad?"

"Home."

"This your weekend?"

"Mm-hmm."

"Where's your mom?

"The boat, I guess. I can call her."

"Nope, I was just asking. She still mad?"

"She says it wasn't really my fault, but I should know better."

"I meant at me."

"You hurt her feelings. She said she was dumb to trust you."

"I didn't know; I thought we were just going on a ride."

"Aunt Mini is still yelling at Snorri."

"Well, tell her I'm sorry."

"OK."

I opened a few cabinets and the old dishwasher, just for the sake of it. Still no coffee. "Can I come over your dad's with you?"

"He said to bring you back, as long as it was you."

"I am. Probably."

Mitchell rented a decent house near me. He crewed instead of skippered these days and didn't appreciate it. Moira was his every other weekend and on every Wednesday with an R in it, or some such schedule.

"You're wearing my jeans," he said.

He was my height and several waist sizes wider. I'd had trouble keeping them up the past few days. His belly and grizzly beard began after he and Angie separated; they were becoming his defining characteristics.

"You drank all my coffee."

"I was out."

"I was pantless." I couldn't figure whether we were going to fight or he was going to make me coffee. We had his pants and his ex-wife's ire in common. "Thanks for taking care of Rover."

"No problem. I'll make some coffee."

I was redeemed.

Mitchell even had cigarettes, but I passed—it was too early, and I'd seen enough stars the previous night. He'd heard two fairly different versions of Moira's voyage to the bottom of the sea. I gave him a third version, emphasizing Snorri's blameworthiness and Moira's safety.

"That doesn't make any sense," he said.

"I probably left some parts out."

"No, I mean, a dead whale. Who cares? You sure he was saying 'antenna?'"

"Yeah, I saw it."

"You sure it was Snorri's whale?" said Mitchell.

"He showed us the rune, said there were rustlers."

"So Snorri call the sheriff on his rustlers?"

"Yeah right. He must have thought it was Waldena; last night—"

"Waldena the Estonindian?"

"The same."

Mitchell was at the counter scraping wet coffee grounds from a paper filter he meant to re-use. He looked over at me at the table and said, "Let me just tell you now that you don't have a lick of sense."

"So I've been told. Anyways, she says Snorri sabotaged her boat—it must be revenge for the whale. She was shit howdy."

"What are they up to?"

"I look like I know? I try to stay out of their business, but I can't. Why me?"

"Poor Orange. You got something they want."

"I don't. They thought I did. I even thought I did for a while."

"Maybe they just like you," Mitchell said, allowing for the improbable.

"The Northern Indians think Bismuth is their omphalos, their point of origin. All the stars rotate around Bismuth. They climbed up out of the center of the earth right here and went on to settle the world. But they're suckers for nativism. They'll claim they were here first, but I think they get off on hanging around with us. We're a new sort of native to them. We're an island full of sidekicks for them."

"You once said your parents were the first members of your family to ever live offisland. That's pretty native, I guess."

"I'm glad I'm not from a Sherpa family."

"The who?"

"An entire ethnicity of sumpters."

"Whatever, Whippey."

I had a broader point to make about ethnic primacy and nativism, but wasn't up to the rhetorical task. I told him about Korean tiger testicles and snorting seagum instead. Leaving out,
of course, the story of Angie hauling me aboard. I could tell he
was very interested in Waldena's extreme unction. Maybe he
was just on his second pot of coffee.

"So you cut it?"

"Donny didn't, but don't, Mitch."

"Why?"

"It's bad medicine. Our ancestors must have known. Christ,
our parents probably knew. The island is too small, that's why.
The wisdom of the ancients, you know?"

"Still."

"You'll regret it," I warned.

"You should probably take a shower."

CHAPTER TWENTY-FIVE

Sampo in the Shed

Ill John looked around, asked me if I'd decorated the house myself. Mostly my mother, I told him.

"Do you think of yourself as an ideal islander, Orange?"

"Ideal?"

"Your people have been here long enough to form an ethnicity—the Yanks."

"I prefer Yankee."

"One who yanks or one who has been yanked?" asked Chosen.

"You're the yanker."

"In any case, you seem very much a product of your environment. I think you may be very well adapted," said Ill John.

"Well, thanks."

"That is not completely a compliment," added Chosen.

"Well then take it back."

"It is not an insult, just an observation," said Ill John.

"OK then, but I'm still not going to make you any coffee."

"We are all set," said Chosen.

"You're all set? You guys are getting good."

"All set," said Chosen, "was a hard term to understand. But it is like 'OK,' yes?"

"You could still want more and be OK, but if you're all set, you're OK because you don't want any more."

"OK," said Chosen.

"We are all set with this. Bestir yourself, Orange," said Ill John. "We must leave."

"All right."

It would seem we were done with our lobstering career. The Koreans were back in their hoodies, and the ride was the Suburban we'd luncheoned in a few days ago. Myself, I was much cleaner and felt much more comfortable in my own jeans. I sat in back on the wide bench and we took a short drive down to the Lucy's.

"You so sure this is a good idea?"

"We are not ready to say whether it is good or not," said Ill John.

"I still don't get what I have to do with this."

"You are the pivot point for the sampo-gift and the native we trust. We met you when you tendered the first handoff, now it should continue its course with you."

"Wouldn't it be easier if Snorri came, and you just gave it to him?"

"Not at this stage," said Ill John. "We gave it to you. You gave it to Mr. Lucy. Mr. Lucy should have given it to Mineola Bombardier, who was to give it to Snorri. The sampo stalled at Mr. Lucy, and that was unanticipated and perhaps important."

"What am I supposed to do?" I said.

"Nothing. It would be better if you did not speak."

I didn't know what to think of that. I guess it suited me.

"You are all set?" asked Ill John.

"OK, I guess."

Donny bust open the kitchen storm door like a seagull trying to look tough. His head bobbed forward and he held his arms out, bent up at the elbow, forming a W. I knew Donny well

Corwin Ericson

enough to know that this meant, "What, what!?" He telegraphed angry confusion easily.

Ill John stepped out the car and summoned all his posture and authority into his chest. Donny flapped over, squawking, "The fuck?!"

"Fetch your father," said Ill John.

"Motherfucker!"

"Mr. Lucy should be the only mother fucker here."

Donny was parsing this when Mr. Lucy came out. "Get inside," he told his son.

"It's fucking Orange and his fucking fag friends."

Ill John withered Donny with such a dominating glare, I suspected drill-sergeantry in his past. The two Lucys tangled in the doorway as the younger retreated and the elder advanced.

Mr. Lucy was wearing a green plaid flannel shirt tucked into his faded green Dickies, which were hitched up to mid-rib with suspenders. He rooted around his pocket, found his partials and installed them into his jaw. To speak comprehensibly after a lifetime of seagum-chewing requires one to keep one's lips in something of a moue; Mr. Lucy looked like he was expecting a kiss as he squinted at us.

"What's Whippey doing here?" he said—or tried to say—sharply.

"He is here to felicitate."

"Facilitate," said Chosen.

Felatiate, I thought, but did not utter.

"Jesum Crow. Come on."

We followed Mr. Lucy around back to his shed. The wide door sagged on its hinges and scraped the granite cobbles as he dragged it open. Briny mildew and turpentinic vapors watered my eyes a bit. He shuffled between the workbench and the little dory flipped over on sawhorses that took up most of the shed's interior to pull on the cord for the bare bulb hanging above the bench. There was only the one lawn chair in the shed; we stood around the upturned boat that was either being reconditioned or demolished—it was midway through either one of the processes and probably had been for years.

We stood and stared, each testing the others' mettle to stand and stare. It seemed like a fair match. As the felicitator, I felt obliged to break first. "Well?"

"Well, what the hell you boys want?"

"We discussed this last night, Mr. Lucy," said Ill John.

Mr. Lucy grunted. He leaned down on the boat to rest his forearms and elbows. Then he straightened and pushed some old bolts around in a dirty Chock Full o' Nuts coffee can. He plucked out a couple of the rustiest, dropped them on the floor and kicked them under the workbench.

"Well . . . ," he said, then thought better of finishing his statement. Instead he lined up a few tools on the bench. He considered a paint brush that had been curled into a crusty brown ringlet by dried varnish. A dead fly was added to an ashtray with butts from another decade.

"Well what?" I said.

"We heard 'bout enough outta you, Whippey," said Mr. Lucy.

I didn't know if the Koreans had realized that an island geezer has the ability to fart around in his shed until long after the heat death of the sun. Which is presumably when Mr. Lucy would finally get around to finishing some of his projects.

"Why don't you explain it again, boys. I'm not sure I follow."

"Mr. Lucy," said Ill John, "when we last paid you for your seagum on the *Polk*, we included with the payment a package, which you had agreed to give to Mineola Bombardier, who had agreed to, in turn, render the package to Snorri, the Finlindian whale herder."

"What's that fuckin' dinghy gonna do with it?" he muttered.

"It was a gift, as I had explained previously," said Ill John.

Chosen elaborated: "It is an important gift because we feel that it demonstrates our insight into Finlindian culture, particularly the concept of sampo. We hoped that as cultural ambassadors we could use this gift to signify our comprehension of the subtleties and unmentionables of his culture. This would help us broker a successful trading relationship and inaugurate the herding of North Indian Atlantic whales to our peninsula, where such stock is valuable in our seaports."

"You make it sound important," said Mr. Lucy.

"Its perfect unimportance is what makes it crucial," said Ill John.

Mr. Lucy side-stepped from between the bench and boat toward the shed's dooryard where the fraying webbed lawn chair held open the door. He sat down with some difficulty. His pant legs rode well above his white socks. "I'm sorry kids, I don't got it."

"Yes, you do," said Chosen, "it is right there."

Mr. Lucy took the contradiction sitting down. Unfazed, he said, "Well I ain't done with it."

"How long?" asked Ill John.

"Could might be some time," said Mr. Lucy. "Can't really say."

"Should we wait here while you finish?" asked Ill John. "Help elucidate matters for you?"

"Wouldabeen done if Donny hadn'tabeen in such a rut. Stole it from me."

Mr. Lucy took out his reading glasses from the case in his shirt pocket. He picked up a thick, worn paperback and showed us where he'd bookmarked it. He appeared to have around forty pages to go. "I already knew the fish dies at the end. And the ship sinks."

"This book," said Ill John, "is the defining totem of your island culture. From the islands come men of tragic obsession chasing sea monsters that resist the lumber of symbology by never divagating from their own essential savage natures. The monsters remain monsters, make the men into monsters. Men can only be true men among monsters. A German literary critical term for masculine monster lust would be apt. Men love their monsters; in the end they explode together. Only the men most full of doubt and words outlive their monsters, and it is an unbearable burden for them."

The book was beachworn, slept upon, sneeze-inducing. Infinities of rings belied its shadow life as a coaster. Summer humidity and winter furnaces had plumped and shrunken its pages like a fisherman's face. The browning edges of the foxed and dog-eared pages were perfect camouflage for the shed; it was as much a piece of Mr. Lucy's world as the brass oarlocks that dangled from the shelf bracket—a piece of island umweltern whose ubiquity made it a familiar relic, its cover still iconic, the eponymous monster still, after all these years, a perfect summation of dread and desire.

Ill John was dead right. This book was both product and symbol of our island ways. Our history, our families, even our property tax assessments were affected by this book—the one book read by both Islanders and strangers—the book that told us it might just be better not to go down to the sea. It had so permeated every space of private and public thought on the island that it was hard to imagine a shelf without it. From the Christian Science Reading Room storefront window to under my very own pillow, that book has never been far from any Islander's eyes.

I remembered the day it made me understand the very nature of family and community here. Not only has every Islander lost family to the water and its monsters, but we all know Islanders whose lust for monsters exceeds their means, or who have met their monsters, done nothing about it, and live now in moiled shame. That wasn't my revelation though. Kids already know all about monsters. It was when a friend was telling me his cousin had regretted wearing denim cut-offs when he was a beach extra in the film of the book. I too had a cousin in that scene. In fact, as years past, I came to learn that everyone had a cousin in the film that could be spotted if one paused on a particular frame in the beach scene. How many cousins could one have, I began to wonder. I had cousins to spare, some of them who really were the children of my parents' siblings. Cousins are one thing all Islanders have in common. Even only children can have cousins. Cousins aren't limited by blood or intermarriage. Many of us knew each other perfectly well as cousins but were at an utter loss to explain our familial relationship. And all of them were in the beach scene, screaming, frothing up the water, losing their floats, shouting for their children.

Ill John and Chosen began to converse in short, quiet Korean. Maybe even argue.

"He can finish? Maybe quickly?" Chosen asked me in English.

"I didn't know he read books," I said.

"It would be best if he finished reading the book," said Ill John.

"He knows how it ends; the whole world knows how it ends," I said.

"Ho!" shouted Mr. Lucy. He held up his right index finger and licked it with deliberation. Then he turned a page. "You boys are disturbing my afternoon."

The Koreans whispered to each other. "Let us attend him," said Ill John.

"Wait, you mean?" I asked.

"It is important to finish reading books."

I was getting the vapors from the turpentine fumes. I wondered what could be more boring than watching Mr. Lucy read. "You got to be kidding."

Ill John frowned. "Perhaps we have overestimated you, Orange."

I thought maybe I could get Chosen's AK from the Suburban and make Mr. Lucy read faster with it, which was a stupid idea. It wasn't even worth blurting out the ending, since everyone knew. I looked around at the eddies of rusty jetsam that covered nearly every surface of the shed. This would be my fate. I would be stuck here decomposing in this shed until an archeologist's trowel tinked on my bones. I'd be written up in a dissertation on early twenty-first century Northeastern Islander suicide-by-boredom rituals; Mr. Lucy's shed and Mineola's sauna hut would be reconstructed as worship chambers where Islanders practiced the dark art of killing time. Mr. Lucy would be the high priest; I'd just be a novice who obviously couldn't go the distance. It wasn't fair.

"Tighten up, Orange. I have your back, OK?" said Chosen.

I moaned; Mr. Lucy told us to shut up, with more spray than say. The Koreans had surely endured horrific stress-position desensitization training in the army I presumed they had served in. Sitting still, or leaning anyway, was nothing to them. Mr. Lucy, he had a book for Christ's sake. What did I have going for me? Politeness? Patience? Strength-of-character? It was subtle theater, each of us trying to outbore the other through shades of inaction, and I supposed I was a mere spear-carrier in the production. I locked my knees and pretended I was getting paid. That which doesn't kill me only makes me older.

Mr. Lucy turned a page slowly. I watched rejectionist wasps that refused to believe in glass bonk against the pane. The sill below was mulched with the chitin of prior generations of fellow apostates. Outside more wasps labored to caulk every crevice of the window's warping frame with a mud of their own making. Maybe they were charged with the immurement of the indoor wasps. Maybe the founders of the shed wasp line had transgressed the rules of waspdom so shamefully that they and their descendants were doomed to eternal captivity. Were they an edifying example to the free-range wasps?

The summer my father sold me to Mr. Lucy—or got me a wage-paying, character-building job, as he liked to phrase it—we got stranded when the oil pump blew on the old *Wendy's Mom*. Donny and I were still too young and full of complaint to be committed to any kind of productive makework, and the real work had to be suspended while we waited for a tow back. I was in a sulk simply because I was on the boat in the first place, but when I realized that we would make no profit at all on this outing and that the one zillionth share that I was entitled to would not be forthcoming, I caught a bad case of the mopes. Donny contracted it quickly, and the combined power of our whines induced Mr. Lucy to try and distract us with big fish stories and tales of the heroic skippers of yore. This bored us further, and we suspected it of being educational, which quickened our truculence.

Donny and I, along with every other kid on the island, had been telling shark jokes to each other all summer. We had a good routine going with the landshark. We had ganged up on his father and were drowning his stories with an improvised call and response version of the sketch. On each iteration we traded roles so that we could take turns announcing ourselves at an imaginary door: "Candygram," "mailman," and "plumber" gave way to more familiar island figures like Mr. Loomis, a hated teacher, Denise and Sylvie—the sisters already on our pubescent minds—and then more strangely, realer monsters like King Kong and Godzilla. This disgusted Mr. Lucy, who grumbled we didn't know how to tell stories or even listen, just to shout out stupid phrases. We succeeded in bothering Mr. Lucy sufficiently well enough to transfer the burden of the sulk onto his shoulders, leaving us in good moods, blithering around the boat like over-caffeinated goats.

It was Donny who began screaming, "Shark, shark!" Even I thought it was in poor taste, given how thoroughly we had beaten the landshark joke into the ground. But he persisted, and sure enough, even Mr. Lucy saw the fin. It was huge and oddly floppy. In fact, as it slapped slowly back and forth, it didn't seem to be taking its role as supreme monster of the sea seriously. We were motorless and dragging a sea anchor, which functions as a sort of cross between an anvil and a kite, so we could neither escape nor give chase. Eventually the wind and waves brought us and the lollygagging fish closer. It was indeed huge and frightening, just as the shark should be. Its head was vast and gray and more like a sea boulder with eyes than a predator's snout. In fact, given its lackadaisical lolling, it seemed more like a hazard to navigation than to life and limb.

Donny and I were frantic. Every single shark encounter we'd

ever heard of ended in dismemberment at the very least. Any second, it would bite the boat in half and gulp us down like oysters. Donny begged his dad to get the rifle. He armed us instead with a boathook and a gaff, which we brandished like harpoons. The shark was barely moving, neither predator nor prey. We wondered if it were wounded or sick, like the parasite-addled dolphins that insisted on killing themselves on our shores now and then. Man-eating sharks were canny though, capable of making ambush plans and certainly capable of playing dead.

By the time we arrived at poking-distance our fear had mostly dissipated. The fish was still oblivious or laying in wait. As the tide of my excitement ebbed, I noticed something profoundly disturbing. No matter my perspective, no matter how hard I looked, the fish had no body. It had a head half the size of the *Wendy's* hull and then just nothing. It had been bit off at the neck—pinched off, maybe, since I couldn't see any gore and its skin seemed as if it had been clamped together to seal the wound. Donny and I had convinced ourselves that we were witnessing the best, most topical monster of our lives, yet we were looking at something much more frightening, otherworldly even. Universal laws were broken right in front of us. Somehow, as if surviving as just a head weren't preposterous enough, it had managed to move its fins up near its jaws, so it was still able to propel itself. An anti-cherub from the pelagic underworld biding its time until it chose to pull us down to fish hell.

Donny was holding his dad's hand shamelessly. I suppose the only thing that kept me from exploding into chunks of chum was that I just could not fully convince myself that I was seeing what was clearly right off our starboard bow.

"Sunfish. Moonfish, maybe," said Mr. Lucy.

Sunfish? Moonfish? Sunfish were the first fish I learned how to throw back. Sunfish nibble toddlers' toes and flit around under docks. Sunfish were insignificant freshwater fish that some summer kids called crappies, for God's sake. Of all fish on the planet, this was the least like a sunfish I could imagine. A fish from the moon seemed as reasonable an explanation as anything else.

"What happened to it?" asked Donny.

"Nothing. That's just the way they are."

"Its body . . . ?" I said.

"Yer lookin' at it."

"But what happened?" persisted Donny.

"Nothin', I said!"

Donny was right. Something happened to it. Or the laws of nature were not enforced as strictly as we'd been led to believe.

"It's just a head," I whined.

"It's a sunfish," snapped Mr. Lucy. "They eat jellyfish. Look at its mouth."

Its mouth was beak-like, hardly suited to man-eating. Jellyfish made sense, since they were obviously creatures from beyond—the right meal for a giant floating head.

"Are they smart?"

"You'd think," said Mr. Lucy, "but look at it."

Donny was preparing to harpoon it with the boathook. I had to admit, now that I was getting used to looking at it, that it lacked menace. I felt threatened by the mere fact of its existence, but it did look kind of goofy, and one certain mark of a stupid animal is if it sticks around in the presence of armed teenagers.

In the end, it did nothing about us, and we did nothing about it. Donny and I both felt that authorities should be notified, that others should know that sea monsters were stranger than previously imagined. Mr. Lucy hardly mentioned it to the guys that towed us in.

If enough generations of wasps pounded their heads against the same point in the window pane, would it break eventually? Why not just fly out the door?

"I knew it," said Mr. Lucy, as he gave the back cover a gentle spank, "the fish always dies."

"Did you think it would end differently this time?" asked Ill John.

"Never read it before. Never will again, neither. Probably."

"It's the captain that always gets it in the end," I said.

"Don't be clever," said Mr. Lucy. "At least the captain sticks with it to the end. It's the talky guy that always lives to tell the tale. That's what's wrong with books."

"The captain as his own Jonah."

Mr. Lucy scowled. "It's not enough I just read a book for you?"

I was sorry.

"Why did you never read the book before?" asked Chosen.

"Never had the time; knew how it ended."

"Why, now?"

"You know, my dad once gave this guy's grandfather a ride across town in a wheelbarrow," said Mr. Lucy, indicating the book's author and presumably not the title monster.

"Why, and what is a wheelbarrow?" said Chosen.

"A wheelbarrow, son, is a cart with one wheel that you push."

Ill John pantomimed pushing a wheelbarrow for his partner.

I tried to signal 'don't get him started' to the Koreans, but they both ignored me.

"And the reason why," continued Mr. Lucy, "is 'cause they

wasn't sober much at all. The old man used to be a summer visitor and was a famous souse. My dad said he had a skinny little mustache and he could talk fancy till the fish drown. The boys thought he was a queer and a pinko, but they liked his stories and let him drink with them at one of their oyster shacks in the evenings. According to my dad, the island was supposed to be dry then, thanks to the temperance crazies, so nobody was supposed to be drinking. Fishermen made more money bringing whiskey in from Canada then they did on fish then.

"Anyways, one night they're all blind and staggering and this guy says he's gotta get home to the wife, only he can't walk and wasn't sure where the home or wife was. But, he says, by happy coincidence he's doing research on an essay he's gonna write called 'How to Get Pushed Home in a Wheelbarrow by Fishy-Smelling Drunks' and that his buddies would be contributing to a great and important cause if they was to push him home. I suppose you might already know they made it into a short subject some years ago."

"Edifying," said Ill John.

"Well here," said Mr. Lucy, giving him a fishy eye and then the book, "I don't need it anymore. Woulda been better if the shark ate 'em all."

Several minutes later, I was headed to the docks in the Suburban with the Koreans. Mr. Lucy had hollered to Wendy to get her to bring lemonade to us in the shed, and she had hollered back that we could piss our own lemonade, so we left, and not because we didn't have cups.

"Next?" I asked.

"Next, Snorri," said Ill John.

"If you knew he was just reading the book all along, why

didn't you just take it from him?"

"We discovered we were making friends with Mr. Lucy."

"This makes you guys buddies? What, a book club?"

Chosen turned to face me from the front seat and handed me the book. "Only your friends steal your books, Orange."

CHAPTER TWENTY-SIX

Reeled In

I scanned the harbor for familiar boats. In the summer the harbor gets cluttered with pleasure boats, and the harbormaster has a lucrative cash trade going for overnight mooring rights. He patrols his waters in a decent Boston Whaler and carries a shotgun and a nasty-looking dog to remind the tourists that he is more than a meter maid. Today there was a preposterous yacht anchored inside that should never have been let into the harbor. I couldn't figure why a ship that size bothered with islands. It probably had more flushing toilets aboard than we had in all of town.

Maybe it's good that the aristocracy comes to demonstrate their finest and most agreeable floating castles to us now and then. It might do us good to see the baronial daughters sunning in their bikinis through our binoculars. Maybe someday I'll be rowing by in my muscular, hardworking, seaworn way and a bikini top would flutter from a pair of well cultivated breasts, and I would snatch it from the air before it became sullied by our yacht-discharge waters and present it to the young Miss in a manner that irresistibly combined my rustic charm and native grace. She would be terribly curious about Island men, having been forbidden to even look at us by her father, yet intrigued by her sea-chambermaid's nearly primal enthusiasm for social congress with the strapping fishing-lads of Bismuth, such as myself.

"I do not see *Honeypaws*," said Ill John.

"Me neither. I don't see anyone worth looking for or avoiding."

"The coast is clear," said Chosen.

"So you guys don't need me right now, right?" They both peered over their aviators at me. My indentureship had not yet concluded.

"We will have to go to Gaiety," said Ill John. "We will take the *Princess*."

We found their rental boat tucked in among the lobster boats and trawlers at the commercial wharf. We shoved off with a notable lack of picnic baskets; Ill John did a serviceable job of extricating the boat from the welter of lines and double-parked rust buckets.

We made our way in a glugging trundle to Mini's island. I thought it would be just delightful if her sister were not there, but I hadn't seen the *Angie Baby* anywhere around Bismuth. It was clear at sea; the continent a mere smudge of fog and toxic out-gassings. Snacks were not served.

I was telling them about the nerve tonic/soda drink Moxie, and how the bartender at the Topsoil had once lost a bet on it. He was an offislander and claimed that Moxie could not be mixed with anything alcoholic and remain potable. Me and a few guys were making our way through the Mr. Boston well bottles, trying the gamut from rye to gin in a series of undrinkable highballs and baroquely poisonous island ice teas. We had hit on a contender with Jaegermeister, only I felt the flavors were too similar. The bartender pulled out a dusty greenish bottle from the cabinet under the register. It was absinthe, he said. We all knew it was illegal, but none of us knew why. It was the lonely unicorn of liquors. All the rest of the booze got to repopulate the continent after prohibition was repealed, but absinthe never made it off the ark. We were all very pleased with ourselves. The green liquor made earthy swirls in the brown, fizzy Moxie. We knew we were supposed to do something with a sugar cube, but not what. We added ice and, hey, it wasn't bad. Much better than cough syrup and better than either of its components on their own. It was dubbed a "Mabsy," and we never drank it again.

Ill John was describing some of the improbable liquors distilled by, as he called them, "prison campers from the North," when we noticed both the *Honeypaws* and *Tharapita's Hammer Maiden* moored off of Mini's dock. A cocktail that ensured a hangover.

I told the Koreans that judging by the quality of the sunlight and the color of the water, and especially the presence of the two vessels, that the forecast for Ragnarok or Rapture was medium-to-high, and we'd be wise to heed the squall signs. Chosen told me it was a good thing they were with me, otherwise I'd never get anything done. It wasn't worth re-explaining that nothing was exactly what I'd wanted to get done.

"Shouldn't we at least call ahead, maybe find out first if we need to call the Coast Guard?" I asked.

"We should not need to call first. Mineola Bombardier knows we are here," said Ill John.

"We could fire a flare," I said. "They might appreciate a cease-fire. You're cultural ambassadors right? Just like them? You could stay here and host a summit and I could take the *Princess* back."

"Why are you so reluctant?" said Ill John.

"We're all looking at the same boats, right?"

"This is an excellent opportunity."

"To not and say we did."

"Orange, you may understand that others may have agendas to which you are only a codicil?"

"Right, it's none of my business. You've seen the light. You can just give me a beach ball, and I'll float home from here."

"Yet a codicil can be a crucial addendum."

I was fed up with my inability to distinguish between palling around, doing a favor, and being press-ganged. They'd sort of sweet-talked me with flummery about destiny, but here I was, literally being taken for a ride by a pair of mooks. Albeit bilingual *flâneurs* with a decent sense of adventure.

"Tell me honestly." I said to Ill John, "Why bother?"

"You know that Mineola Bombardier is a spy, right?"

"Here I thought she was a cultural ambassador too. Who's she spy for?"

"Herself. She is a fisherwoman for information and has her hooks in the jaws of many."

"We're being reeled in?"

"We have casting rods ourselves," he said.

"So you figure you're both pulling."

"Perhaps, so to speak. But you remain the Yankee."

CHAPTER TWENTY-SEVEN

The Thing

norri told me that Angie wasn't around. He'd been there to catch our lines and help us dock. He was cooling his heels seaside, he said, since Mini was otherwise occupied.

"And your tan is well?" asked Ill John.

Snorri raised an eyebrow. "Tan?"

"Cooling the heels is working the tan, right?"

"Mini won't let me in until I talk to Waldena," he said, pointing inland then to the *Maiden*.

"Where is she?" I asked.

"Waldena won't get off her boat. She says, 'Not while Mini's got the Varangian Guard here.'"

"Why's she here?"

"Followed me here to kill me, she says."

"And you?"

"She would never leave the harbor alive. I have resources and assets."

"A Mexican stand-off, then?" I said.

"No Mexicans," Chosen observed.

"What are we supposed to do?" I asked.

"Arrive with all the answers," said Snorri.

The three men waited for my response.

"Well that'd be something."

We watched Waldena busy herself with boatwork while we tanned our heels. Snorri said he'd learned important lessons about immobility when he fought with the Forest Brethren. He said you could waste hours, even days of immobility if you succumbed and moved just an inch.

I hadn't thought about why we didn't just walk up to the house until I heard the whine of Mini's golf cart. She was being chauffeured by one of the Gaiety Varangians. In her straw hat and blue smock, she looked dressed for a bit of aristocratic gardening—ordering the servants about while she clutched some blossoms.

"I've figured out how to get rid of you all," she announced. "You need to have a Thing."

I barely suppressed my groan. Things reportedly lasted weeks; Islanders who hadn't uttered a word all winter would stemwind for hours about the failings of their peers. Our island had kept up this tradition of self-governance since time immemorial and some people claimed that it was our ancestors who brought the practice to the Old World. However, World War II had been the end of all Things on Bismuth. After that, no one person could manage to remember all the laws and debts, and the surfeit of uniforms that accumulated on our island during wartime had so many conflicting and hermetic notions about jurisdiction that any sort of peaceable assemblage of authority figures was a farce anyhow. My father said that the end of Things had made us all good Christians—we just gave up sorting out morality and ethics for ourselves and declared we were all sinners, therefore we were both absolved of all guilt and free from any further bonds of self-reliance.

"Excuse me, a Thing?" asked Ill John.

"An ancient tradition," said Snorri, "where the tribal leaders gather to decide disputes. Today, all the first-world countries do it in parliaments with elected members."

"Yes, Korea as well. South Korea, anyway. And here?"

"Here they do it with think tanks."

Snorri made it sound like an insult, but I liked the sound of think tanks. They seemed science fictional.

"And who would be in our Thing Tank?"

"It's just a Thing," said Snorri.

"So, who?"

"Us, I guess. I propose we sink the *Maiden* with all hands on board."

"That's not how it works," said her chauffeur.

"If you agree, we may hold the Thing on my patio this afternoon," said Mineola.

"How are Things decided?" asked Ill John. "Votes?"

"Either a king or votes, depending," said Snorri.

"Is there a king?"

"I think it would only be fair if we voted," said Snorri. "And that Mineola should get two votes, because this is her island."

"Ow!" yelled Mini, yanking on a piece of plastic that had evidently been wedged deep in her ear.

"That was Waldena," she said. "She's been listening on the Bluetooth. She disagrees."

I looked over to the *Maiden*. Waldena was semaphoring Gaiety the finger.

They all bickered about parliamentary procedures until the two Koreans agreed to be one voter. I wasn't too clear on what needed to be decided beyond how I should be brought home and fed, so I stayed shut up.

Eventually the rules for the summit were determined: after Mini and her staff finished dinner, during which they would not be disturbed, we would come to the back patio, sober and weaponless, where we would solve our problems with all the wisdom and dignity that our respective civilizations represented. And sauna afterward, added Snorri.

I was looking forward to unloading the number-one bestselling unputdownable novel that was soon-to-be-made-into-a-major-motion-picture. It was developing a noumenal static charge, becoming a whatsis with more symbolic lumber than physical weight. The cover had torn an inch or so since Mr. Lucy gave it to me, but I wasn't going to tell anyone. I guess I had imagined handing it to Snorri like a dean dispensing a diploma. Neither of the Koreans had inscribed it, and it wasn't exactly gift-wrapped. Someone had used the title page to figure how to divide twenty-five by seven. The retail price had been magic-markered out; inside the cover it was listed for fifty cents. Tag sale, I concluded. The used bookstores that came and went on the island would have charged more. When I held the book nearly horizontally, I saw the vermiform topography of indented handwriting, but could read none of it.

I hadn't been paying close attention during much of the Thing. Snorri and Waldena had ethnonational differences with prehistoric roots that could only be expressed through epic and allegory, which they delusionally believed they were cogently expressing as necessary preambles to their specific, more topical conniptions. They also seemed to believe that we foreigners would appreciate the educational aspects of their intractabilities. Mineola, who had one vote, proposed we break. She had one of her Gaiety Myrmidons bring us a pitcher of iced sumac tea, which turned out to be drinkable with a minimum of six ice cubes and a heap of sugar.

Snorri handled the book handover with aplomb, happening to notice it, saying he'd heard of the book and had always been curious to read it in English. The rest was easy—I said it was indeed very good in English; however, it was not mine to loan. Snorri allowed Ill John to refuse to allow Snorri to borrow it, insisting Snorri must take possession of it as a token of friendship and memento of their time together here in the North American Northeast Atlantic Archipelago. Snorri tugged on an eyebrow, declared he was touched, and he'd begin it that very night.

That was it. I didn't fall in the ocean or anything. My albatross had finally rotted off.

Waldena saw the book and the exchange as perfect proof of the absolute idiocy of all involved. I wished I could disagree with her rattling rhetorical bullet points. As Waldena enumerated and castigated examples of our genetically ordained stupidity, Snorri's color and dudgeon rose. I knew from stories he'd told that somewhere in Finlindia, locked in an ancient cedar chest banded with brass and warded with long-forgotten incantations, was his family's bear shirt. Judging from the steam I could almost see shooting from his ears, I knew he must be thinking of it. If he were to throw back his patio chair and stomp off from our Thing, make a quick dash back across the Atlantic to Finlindia, grab the bear shirt and return—presuming of course that we stayed here biding our time—he would don the hide, suck in the stench of epic battles that clung to it like olfactory heraldry, and go berserk until fjords of blood flowed from our islands. His rage would be unquenchable, and he would fight until the entire nation of North American bears banded together to vanquish him.

As a demonstration of how Waldena's rant had pushed him to his apoplectic uttermost, he slammed his glass of iced sumac tea on his chair's wrought iron armrest, sent ice cubes skittering, and opened a nice gash in his palm. Waldena had drawn first blood without even standing up. Another break was declared; Snorri bloodied Eero's shirt while fending off his ministrations, asking Eero if he and his Varangian girlfriends stopped mid-battle for antiseptic ointments and stitches.

I watched the vein in Snorri's temple throb and the blood stain spread over his bandage as he endured Waldena's remonstration. She continued, "Snorri calls himself a whaler. The Finlindians fancy themselves a whaling people. Yet what his people consider whaling would shame even a little Estonindian boy with a homemade fishing pole and a pocket full of worms. It pains me to even hear him utter the word "whale"; it diminishes, demeans the noble leviathan. To think of those pallid dwarf minkes and inbred belugas listlessly bobbing for air in your rank fjords like so many bleating sheep in a paddock—it's so typically Finlindian. Bred for good behavior and obedience.

"See the world from the whale's point of view. Lords of the ocean in all of its dimensions—from the sunny surface to breathe, to unknowable depths to feed. Summer in the Arctic, winters off Baja, you have a prick the length of your body and cows waiting for you in every port. You have only two predators—clever apes with boats, and squid. One pokes you from the surface, the other grasps from below. Evade them and you will live nearly a century to see the world, visit your friends and allies in all the oceans, battle your rivals, and see your children grow.

"Your lineage is so ancient your ancestors knew the planet before the continents had moved. The stories of your voyages and battles are written in scars along your back, each creature an epic unto itself. Your voice travels hundreds of miles, your presence known to everyone but your prey. Even before you arrive at the breeding ground, the cows are quivery in anticipation; they've heard you singing your name and how hard you'll fuck them from miles away.

"If you don't live long enough for your corpse to descend to the benthonic plains, at least you will die nobly, fighting your greatest adversary—the Estonindian. Your flesh, oil, blubber, and bones will be in the hands of men and women who understand your dignity; a people who look upon you with awe and ferocity.

"Now consider the fate of a whale in Finlindia. Each generation of whale punier, more docile, fed on whale kribble grown in a lagoon. How long are you going to live? Ten years? Probably just long enough to have someone like Snorri jerk you off for your sperm before you're hauled out of the fjord and gutted. What talent does it take to harpoon a whale in a pen? What kind of life is it, isolated from the world to wallow in the same mucky fjord all your days, where everyone is your cousin? You weren't meant to be kept and herded. You weren't meant to live in a warm bath full of parasites and feculence. Your flesh wasn't meant to be flabby; you shouldn't have to listen to the nonsensical gabble of devolved pathological dwarves who can only moan and whistle songs of inbred decadence and despair.

"What kind of nation turns its back on millennia-old traditions? A people preparing to surrender their identity. To turn away from hunting—something so noble, so proper for our people—and take up herding? Should they just wear their pajamas all day? Join the European Union so you can spend your lives arguing about Brussels sprouts and cheese? Why not just sell yourselves to Sweden or Denmark and get it over with? Why bother going on as a Northern Indian?"

Waldena folded her arms and glared at Snorri. The rest of

us watched him too, to see how well his goat had been got. Her point had been made, evidently. Though the specifics still eluded me, I got the gist of her ire. She looked satisfied but still hungry. I wasn't going to be telling my fellow Thing members, but her speech had given me a bit of a hard-on; she must have floated some pheromones my way. I liked it when she was mad at other people; yet, I still felt implicated somehow. God knows I never tried to raise a whale. All I'd ever done was kill fish and eat them. I'd never even cleaned an aquarium before.

Maybe it was his age or the slantwise wisdom his angler fish-like eyebrows belied, but Snorri righted his temper and steered a straight course through Waldena's gale. Maybe it was the fact he'd already monkeywrenched the *Maiden*.

"*From the whale's perspective*, Waldena? Does the whale's umwelt need to include being chased to death by trigger-happy harpoonists who aren't slaked until they are soaked by the bloody flume from a jabbed whale's spew hole? Is there room in their umwelt for anything but terror and anguish? I've chased plenty of beings to their deaths. How noble am I now? You spoke about the ethos of our people; don't you think a people should tend to the creatures in their care? Who cares what kind of incantations you make to your prey when you jab it? Not your whale, I'm certain.

"I've seen so much blood flow in my life, on and off of Finlindian soil, don't you think I've learned something about cruelty? I don't need to apologize to my prey. I can dangle my legs over the fjord and yoik about the frisking minkes and the shimmering northern lights, and they will rise to the surface and join my song. And the waters are hardly full of feculence and incest. We breed our whales carefully to maintain stocks that are the whaling world's envy. No nation on Earth has our talent for it—the whales aren't puny, they are the optimal size for their lifestyle and ours. They spend their lives in the best whale water on earth. They have nothing ahead of them but safety and fellowship—no worries, no predators.

"And, perhaps, Waldena, you may have noticed your prized free rangers are a sorrier bunch of lone wolves every year. And it's not because the squid are getting grabbier. They stray into shipping lanes, they get swallowed by Japanese meat-grinder vessels, and if they manage to avoid all the iron leviathans on the surface long enough to grow to adulthood, along come the Estonindians looking to drive a spear through the skulls of the biggest, wisest bulls. And why? They're mostly blubber and chuck. Most of the meat goes to dog food. Landsmen gain little while whales lose their grandfathers and their links to cetological history. Just to give you all a thrill to make up for your disappointment that your nation cannot master captive whale breeding."

Mineola harrumphed. "You all set?"

"I am OK," said Chosen.

Snorri and Waldena, who could not be OK in the same room together, both gave him the stink eye.

"I think this Thing might need more a little more focus," said Mineola. "I move we foreshorten the historic expiation and cut to the chase."

"The bitch killed my whale."

"The bearfucker fouled the *Maiden*."

"She hag rode the poor creature to death, and she's proud of it."

"Snorri, that thing was literally out of its depth. What you did to that whale was a perversion of nature. They aren't meant to live that way."

"Oh, that's right. So kill it, huh?"

"At least at the bottom, it's fulfilling its natural purpose."

"Sure, I'd forgotten the Estonindians think a whale carcass gets protective status and the live ones deserve to die. That's a little self-serving, don't you think?"

"Whale carcasses are a vital part of the marine ecology!"

"Right, the ocean needs more dead whales."

"It does! You Finlindians refuse to accept what the rest of the world knows is foregone—whalefalls need to be distributed throughout the depths to foster new growth of the herds; they are like seed pods for future generations. You pen them up and haul their carcasses to rot on dry land, you are not only stinking up your own country but you're robbing the ocean of the raw material of evolution itself."

"Waldena, you're young, so I'll forgive your ignorance. That's not actually how whales reproduce."

I can't tell the difference between their native tongues, but I do know a reeling din when I hear one, and they were at it hammer and tongs. Snorri's snide comment was the last straw for constructive dialogue in English. The Koreans blew off English as well and were ignoring us. I looked to Mineola, my fellow Anglophone, for support. She just rolled her eyes.

"I could get a gavel," growled Mineola.

"No weapons," said Waldena.

"Gavels are ceremonial totems of justice carried by North American judges," said Snorri. "Little cudgels they wear under their vestments."

"No wigs, though," added Ill John.

Mineola rapped the wrought iron table with her knuckles, "I'm calling us to order. That means everyone shuts up. I think I can settle things between Waldena and Snorri quite easily. What we do is forget that business and move on to our own business. The promise of profit should balance out whatever miscarriages of justice you two have conceived."

The Northern Indians both grumbled, but Snorri looked pleased enough to be tamed by Mineola, and Waldena was smart enough not to argue with her in her own house. "You have all previously agreed to become a sub-directorship with limited liability of a joint-stock company administered from the top by a presiding council of Northern Indian Whaling Councils representing the nations concerned. Our own group here would be traditionally represented by a board of directors, but since there are no other members, we will simply be the board and I will be the chair.

"Our board has two functions. Snorri has been carrying out the first for over a year now. You know that he and his partners have implanted antennae in a sufficient number of whales to make the cell network feasible, and he is ready to begin road testing it, as it were. His partners were not made aware of the purpose of the antennae and believe that they were part of a scientific study."

Snorri nodded.

"We have nearly one hundred whales set up with these antennae; we have proof-of-concept that roving nodes are practicable. Next we just have to see if the network holds together as the nodes disperse—or collect, as the case may be."

Snorri said, "*Honeypaws* has. . . ."

Mineola pointed at him. "You've had your turn."

"But I. . . ."

Mini gave him a 'shut up' squint. He squinted back, but the 'shut up' held.

"The second function of our board is to assemble North

American investors," continued Mineola. "This will begin in earnest next year when we have hard data. This is contrary to typical business models, at least here in America, where we gather investors first and use their money. However we must do it this way, because secrecy is so important—right now, our whales and our intellectual property are very vulnerable and difficult to defend. This is possible due to the fiduciary enthusiasm these pan-national whaling councils have shown for this opportunity—we have a surprising amount of capital. Not only do these councils support the technical developments we are making, they are also eager to keep a good portion of their profits in extraterritorial scientific research, which limits the opprobrium they face in many ports."

Mini directed her comment about opprobrium to the two Northern Indians, who probably did need to be reminded that much of the world loathed whaling in all of its forms.

"Now that Snorri has begun the field testing, I want to review the roles we're playing in this endeavor. Waldena has been instrumental in liaising with Estonindian concerns; without their technology and enthusiasm for wild-water whaling, this project would never had got out of the bathtub. She and Snorri will, on the *Hammer Maiden* and *Honeypaws,* stay within the network during the testing period. We're just going to have to find out in the field, or at sea, whether the dispersal and migration models work out in practice. You know we chose this breed of whales for their predictable circumnavigation along the Gulf Stream, and it's a little too predictable. Waldena and Snorri will be doing a bit of police work, making sure they don't get poached.

"Chosen and Ill John have been integral to this since the project's inception. Since they first met Snorri last year, their insight into how to move money internationally without subjecting it to

the depredations of taxation has made this enterprise seawor-
thy, so to speak. Through their own network of floating fish
factory ships and continental Koreatowns, our investments will
metamorphose from several different forms of currency into
dollars that will become, eventually, our company's dividends."

I understood that Mineola was talking about money laundering, but I understood the concept about as well as I understood
whale fishery. Well, maybe a bit better, since most cash arrangements here on the island were conducted to escape federal and
state attention. Of the people on this island who were smart
enough to keep books, most were smart enough to keep two
sets. But that's not money laundering. Money only needs to be
washed when there's too much of it, and that's just laughable
on Bismuth. This was a sort of entrepreneurship I admired, but
I couldn't see myself convincing anyone at home they had too
much money and that I could get rid of it for them for a fee.

"Our Korean partners," Mineola continued, "will be leaving
soon but maintaining a presence here that will allow them to
account for a certain modest cash flow. They're also going to
continue working closely with me on the administration of the
company.

"Myself, through my own business and government contacts,
I have a good pool of investor stock to choose from. I will involve people of enough importance that they can provide capital
and yet keep quiet due the contentious nature and pending le-
gitimacy of this company. I'm going to have to give wide berth
to most of this, however. I am much too public a figure to play
an evident role in the company. By providing Gaiety as a base
I could actualize the network, but I'll have to keep things very
quiet. I'll need to work with people I can trust and who know
how to mind their own business. That's why we brought you in,

Orange."

I almost bust in to her speech to tell her how good I'd be at shutting up, but managed to restrain myself.

"Orange is going to play an important role for us if he can keep this all in his hat and his hat on his head."

"And his cat in his bag," said Chosen, eager to give an idiom some exercise.

"What we could really use here is someone who does not need a passport, someone who can come and go without suspicion. It's awfully hard for most members of our board to get much closer to the continent than Bismuth without attracting undue attention. Orange, you might be pleased, or maybe even disappointed to know that you are not on any sort of database or registry available to my research staff, and they have some good contacts. You're not on the no-fly; credit agencies have incomplete records for you; your phone number is listed under your father's name; your university records misspell your name; and you are not listed as owning anything taxable, not even an income."

"I am the silent ninja shadow."

"Don't get too impressed with yourself. You're no Buddha, there's a limit to what you can achieve by doing nothing. We're going to be asking a lot from you. In return. . . ." Mini handed me a black zippered document portfolio.

I opened it and found three healthy stacks of American currency, one of which was entirely hundreds. I blew my cool when my stomach growled loudly. "I promise. . . ."

"Actually, you don't need to promise anything. Let's just say I can make Bismuth so small, there will be no room left for you if you betray us."

What was I going to do, give her back the money? Her threat

was annoying, but only mildly so. Every Island imprecation ends with an unsaid 'and I know where you live.' Mini was being more gauche than insulting. I knew she was right about my lack of official accountability, but there was still a strange contradiction to it—here at home, everyone knew my employment status, my negligible romantic eligibility, not to mention my address. As long as I kept my troubles offisland, they would froth up a welter of deniability if the suits ever came a-knocking. I gave the stack of hundreds a riffle so I could savor the bouquet as it wafted, zipped the portfolio back up, and told her OK.

"Good. Now here's the next step. For the first half of September you're going to crew with Snorri on *Honeypaws*. That will give him a good opportunity to coach you on the network while you assist with monitoring the whales. He'll bring you back to the Bis this evening and then you'll set off later next week."

I saluted Snorri. "Skipper."

Snorri replied in Finlindian and added, "That's how we say 'first mate.'"

Waldena rolled her eyes. "More like Gilligan."

"This is important," said Mini, "you've got to go back home and establish a cover story. People need to hear that you're shipping off for a long run. Don't mention Snorri, since no one on Bismuth would believe he's a real fisher. I suggest you tell Donny Lucy that you're hard up for money and are going to work on a Korean processing ship for a couple of weeks. There's no chance that he'll keep his mouth shut, and he'll think Ill John and Chosen have hired you; that will help explain their presence here. You'll need to behave normally and don't let it slip that you're involved in anything else."

"You're going to tell me not to spend this all at once, aren't you?" I said, tapping the portfolio with the cash.

"I think maybe it might be for the best if I hold on to that for now; you won't be needing it on the *Honeypaws*."

"Nope, nope, I got it, OK." I took the portfolio from the table and held it on my lap.

CHAPTER TWENTY-EIGHT

The Double Shift

Even I had to work on Labor Day weekend, thanks to my new role as a sleeper agent on Bismuth. The tourists work very hard to make enough money to come here and give it to us, and it was our responsibility as Islanders to make sure the cash flowed with few obstructions and little value exchanged. I took the Saturday afternoon prep shift in the Topsoil kitchen, hoping to scoot out before the rush. Prepping is significantly cleaner and less frantic than line or dish work. People are still in a reasonable mood and you even have a chance of going home in the daylight.

I was just wiping down a table when the pretty Irish waitress here for the summer came back with a nice cold beer. She stood and chatted with me while I drank it, telling me a story about a sunburn she'd got earlier this week due to a slightly skimpier bathing suit than usual. I found the story riveting and forgot to storm off when she mentioned that Bob asked her to ask me to stick around to help for Saturday dinner.

Sometime around half-past dyspepsia, the heat and flickery fluorescence of the kitchen began to knot the muscles of my face into a painful grimace. The beer, the coffee, the angry cook, the fussy sous, the shrill waitstaff; all of them conspired to give me a headache worthy of Phineas Gage. Working a holiday weekend night in a tourist town restaurant is like working in an ER during a circus fire. It's hard to say whether we in the kitchen were the staff or the patients. My headache came to feel like a horseshoe crab clamped on my head, dry humping the nape of my neck. Cooks occasionally stick around to help the dishers at the end of the shift as an act of noblesse oblige; for me it was more grudging solidarity and tragic competence. Being the only person who knows how to snake the grease trap is not a source of pride. At least it earned me a few drags of a joint and two bottles of beer for my walk home.

When I got home, I smelled like hot garbage in a stagnant tidal pool. My bedroom upstairs was still too warm for sleeping. The sofa held an aroma of decade-old overheated parental shame. I couldn't remember having eaten anything all day, and the mota I'd smoked with a disher by the Topsoil Dumpster made me feel like I was wearing a scratchy hemp bag over my head. The TV was at its most blaringly banal. I couldn't bear most of the things I relied on when I couldn't bear most other things.

Late that night, Rover lost patience with me and yowled until I got up off the living room floor. I washed my face and hands and sucked some water up into my swollen sinus cavities. Took some aspirin that smelled like vinegar. I prepared to make a donation to the goddess Cloaca. Blessedly, my gorge settled. I resolved to walk down to the shore and let the cool breeze and negative ions lull me into some kind of comfort—or thoughtlessness, at least. Sunrise over the ocean was bound to have some kind of positive effect on me.

Dawn found me nearly suffocated with my own breath as I dozed at the kitchen table, my head sweaty from the cage I'd made for it with my arms.

CHAPTER TWENTY-NINE

Provisioning for the Voyage

I went down to Puffin Muffins for my coffee, a place most Islanders avoided scrupulously. I figured I might forget who I was and wind up on the ferry that afternoon, on my way back home, where my furniture and fulfilling life awaited me on the mainland. Sometimes it did me some good to see people vacationing on my island. It reminded me that novelty and happy surprises really do happen to some people. Right here, even. I watched the daytrippers gathering their gear and provisions they'd ransomed back from the ferry skipper who charged ten dollars a bag, even if it was just a purse. They'd be right there again in five hours, crotches full of sand, skin burnt, wallets thinned. I had no right to mock their baffling choices in island-appropriate clothing. The plastic clogs that made them look like night nurses. The jellybean-colored summer survival gear with detachable legs and plenty of straps and D-rings for securing the tourist in four-point restraints. I'd had to sniff my socks a few times this morning before I decided my feet would be better off without them.

I waved wanly to Islanders who quickened their pace when they saw me. It wasn't worth talking to them anyway. Either they were pathologically but vaguely busy—undergoing a uniquely stressful period in their otherwise seamlessly swell lives—or their kids were in urgent need of shuttling. Seeing me piss away time so flagrantly sent some people into a sort of rage I never fully understood. My simple existence must rot the pilings that hold up their sense of purpose.

At least as a single male adult islander, I was still allowed to smoke cigarettes, so I bummed one from the girl who sold me the coffee—a nymphette whose parents I sort of knew. It had the satisfying effect of inducing a scowl from a young woman who'd been arguing with her husband at a sidewalk table about how to properly deploy what could have been the ejection seat from a jet fighter, but was probably just a stroller. Children, of course, are the new gods. All must be made respectable and earnest before them. Persons such as myself were forbidden to enter their sacred groves. Only their priests—their parents—could interpret the cryptic commandments they uttered, but we all had to obey. Being a kid these days seemed too hard. I couldn't keep up.

I took my mope on the road and drifted dockward. I was pleased I had killed the morning; I hoped I could dispatch the afternoon with an equal lack of effort. Just to give me something to look at, a three-masted windjammer was moored outside of the harbor. Some of the rocks I stood on were said to be whilom ballast from English ships during the whaling days. People even said that about our gravestones. As if the island weren't mostly stone in the first place. I wondered what people of other ports said Bismuthians left behind, besides bastards. I had just realized the pain in my stomach was actually hunger when I noticed the *Princess Pea* tied alongside the *Wendy's Mom* a few docks down at the commercial wharfs. It was a bold and foolish spot for smuggling. A more careful look revealed a couple of guys with black hair and yellow foul weather pants stacking some pots. It had to be the Koreans; by the look of it, they'd finally been alobstering. I figured if they saw me, I'd be conscripted again, so I slunk.

Moira scared the Christ right out of me.

"How come you didn't come to karaoke night?" she said, having sidled up to me out of nowhere.

"You spooked me."

"You were standing there forever."

"Where's your mom?"

"She's in town, shopping."

"Aren't you supposed to be with her?"

"I don't have to. How come you weren't at karaoke night?" She pronounced it 'Carrie Okie,' like most of us.

"I was working." I hate karaoke. It's no news to me that my neighbors can't sing. I don't need empirical proof. "How come you were? It's late isn't it?"

"Everyone was there," she said, as if she were disappointed with me.

"What does your mom say about me?"

"Nothing. I have a new purse. For next year at school. But I probably won't bring it, but I could just leave it in my backpack. You want to see it? It just has some shells in it now. And some money."

Moira grubbed into her bag and showed me several dimes, around thirty cents worth of a sand dollar, some periwinkles, and a lot of sand.

"Nice," I said. "You going to buy me lunch?"

"Do you know what yoiking is? It's so stupid. Uncle Snorri yoiked at karaoke. You know how it's like video karaoke? He picked some song and didn't even sing it. He just wanted to look at the video. It was these people in bathing suits walking around and the sunset and stuff. He wasn't even singing words in any language. Dad said he was a strangled auk. First he made everybody be quiet, then he said we could yoik too, and the DJ said 'Thank you!' in a funny voice and everybody laughed."

"Did you sing?"

"I don't think kids are allowed to. My mom and Aunt Mini did that "Barracuda" song they always do. They're so good! My mom told me that this lady, Waldena, is your friend. She's pretty but kind of mean. She did a song that everyone knew but she did it really scary. And these two guys! They sang "Yellow Submarine" in Korean! I couldn't believe it!"

Moira sauntered off, purse exhibited, wild night described. I felt a little bit like I did when my mother called me to tell me about the exploits of people I hadn't seen since they were teenagers. Their difficult in-laws, the delighted grandparents—somehow I was left feeling sadly nostalgic for something I'd never wanted.

I spent the next week-and-a-half trying not to look too hard for the *Angie Baby* and suppressing my dread of being Snorri's mate. *Tharapita's Hammer Maiden* and *Honeypaws* were not in evidence, though I did see the *Princess Pea* around the harbor several times. I wouldn't have minded passing some time with Ill John and Chosen, but they seemed busy; maybe they had rented the franchise to someone's trap line. Lobstering was supposed to be good this season, but prices were down. That probably didn't much matter to those two. They were probably enjoying themselves just hauling up the bugs.

When it came time to depart with Snorri, I provisioned myself with beer, of course, and some good store-bought food so I wouldn't have to subsist on herring and shoe leather, or whatever it was that Snorri packed for extended picnics on the Atlantic. I paid too much for a quarter from Ricky, who now said maybe he would go back to school next week—he thought it would just be easier than a job and an apartment. He was very curious about Waldena, and I made him promise to jump overboard if he ever found himself alone with her. He looked at me almost as if I'd cuckolded him, but I let the impertinence pass, since our tacit pact to not mention her had served us well until now. Also, I told him she was seventy-eight years old and had several monstrous grandchildren his age and an angry husband. I traded an eighth of Ricky's weed with Mitchell to take care of Rover. I thought he'd say no, but he was a strong proponent of me taking a long ocean voyage. I wanted to ask him about Angie, but knew I'd only piss him off. It must have been bad enough for him to watch the *Angie Baby* make its rounds without wondering if I were on board too.

The day before we shipped off, I sat at the nearly empty raw bar upstairs at the Topsoil and drank my way through two bartender's shifts. I tried to watch the news so Snorri and I could discuss current events. I was too bleary to read the crawl on the TV bolted into the room's darkest corner. Afghanistan . . . Blood . . . Contested . . . it was always the same anyway. I doubted Snorri watched much American TV, or any other nation's for that matter. Finlindian state TV probably had herring for newscasters.

CHAPTER THIRTY

The Whale Network

I may not be as lazy as many people think. It's just as reasonable to believe that I oversleep because I am not yet done with my seizure of the previous day. Snorri did not share this point of view, but he was going to have me for the next two weeks, so I really didn't care. We shoved off well before lunch, at any rate. I didn't know anyone who had ever spent this much time alone with Snorri, and it seemed possible that no human being ever had; I was concerned about being his captive audience. I was just a bit giddy too, wondering when the last time a Whippey from Bismuth had boarded a whaling ship.

Honeypaws was an intimidating vessel, even with her harpoon gun shrouded under heavy Kevlar; pearl white and thick-skinned with armor, she lumbered like her namesake at low speed. Her hull looked tough enough to break ice and she was trimmed with wide gray rubber bumpers, which made it look like she did a lot of shoving. When she got up to speed on open water and up on her hydrofoils, she shrugged off the waves and vaulted along their peaks. This was no tug; she was a catcher boat, born and bred an Arctic predator.

Inside, she was clean and nearly spacious. She had berths for at least eight crew and a few more nautical versions of the Murphy bed. Her cabin did not carry the cannibal's crock pot aroma I was accustomed to on the Bismuth tubs, but it did carry several more bookshelves and hanging artwork than I'd ever seen on a fishing boat. I was disappointed to see that most of the texts were in Finlindian, a language that seemed to have more diacritical marks than letters in its alphabet.

What was truly intimidating about *Honeypaws* was being responsible for her. I had never piloted anything this big or fast and had only been on a boat up on its hydrofoils once on a high-speed ferry trip to Canada that had cost as much as a flight to South America. In easy weather, Snorri could set it on automatic pilot and get much of his work done, but he was eager to teach me. It was easier than I expected. I commented to Snorri that I was surprised by how high tech his controls were, and he reminded me his civilization was older than mine and that he was concerned that letting an ignoble savage such as myself take the wheel was less than wise. His highly civilized wheel was more of a hybrid of a steering wheel and a video game controller. I never did find out what half the buttons and gauges did, but I didn't need them for most of our work. Within a few days and with only a few incidents, I was commanding, "Make it so, thusly!" as I pushed forward on the lever that sprouted our hydrofoils. I came to enjoy it and doubted I'd ever get another chance to skipper anything with half this much power and speed as long as I remained on Bismuth.

Our job was, essentially, to play shepherd to invisible sheep. We had ninety-eight beluga whales to protect as we followed them on their slow migration, and they rarely showed themselves to us. These were the small white whales that Waldena mockingly called "melonheads." I couldn't imagine Waldena being much else but indignant that she had been employed as a whale herder. She was probably blasting all the other big game out of the water—the *Maiden* was probably crusty with swordfish blood. The networked belugas had been bred in open water and conditioned through the generations to be docile. The antennae implanted within them were nearly flat flexible strips of plastic with embedded wires and circuits. They were, according to Snorri, installed in quick painless procedures that could be done on a boat deck or in shallow water. Snorri considered this breed of whale to be sweet and kittenish, but not so bright. He said the obnoxious ones could actually spit buckets of water quite accurately and he disliked feeding their cousins in the Finlindian fjord whale pens. I had heard them on the underwater microphone, and they sounded like Tweety Bird imitating a dial-up modem.

Apart from spying a fluke here and there, we had to rely on the Whale Network itself and *Honeypaws's* sonar. Snorri had a handheld device that he would not share with me. He could access most of the boat's controls with his device, and could even pilot the boat with it remotely. I was allowed to use the boat's computer, which performed, I supposed, most of the same functions. Mostly, I used a big pictorial spreadsheet with an illustration of each whale on the network. Snorri had named each whale—Henriikka, Iiltaa, Jhalmarii, Kaijia, Lyyli—I couldn't pronounce any of them, except Mineola and Moira.

By selecting each whale, I could see its network status and the compass coordinates of its location. Another couple of mouse clicks and the location of each nearby whale was shown on a chart of our current coordinates. We more or less followed the main pod of belugas and took occasional excursions to see where the outliers had got to. We kept track of their positions and plotted their courses, along with rating the reception we got near each of them. What we wanted was adequate to excellent signal strength all along their projected migration route.

These little white whales were semi-domesticated and probably easy prey. The other, much more interesting aspect of our job was to protect their little selves. I had asked Snorri several times about weapons access, but he said they would only come out if needed. He said the same thing about his secure cabinet with the old milk, but I still had beer and was happy the noxious stuff was locked up. It wasn't so much that I wanted to shoot at anything, but having a shotgun handy would have made the enterprise seem more exciting. I couldn't think of any genuinely persuasive arguments that began with 'I have plenty of experience with firearms and liquor,' even though it was sort of true.

The North Atlantic was treating us well. There was a tropical depression somewhere near Africa according to the weather service, but no corresponding Arctic elation in our region. The water was calm and boring. The job was boring. I was boring. After the first few days, I'd run out of things to say to Snorri and depleted my reserves of listening energy—most of Snorri's stories began with a Northern Indian version of biblical begats, since it was so urgently important for me to know the ancestors of every person, creature, and significant object, fictional and historical, that could sustain a narrative.

One night, as I piloted *Honeypaws* from boring chart point A to tedious chart point B, and then halfway to featureless point C, but back again to tedious B, I imagined turning her about and taking her as far west as the water would carry her. I had to turn her into an RV to get us across the continent, but she bore the indignity. We were lost for weeks among the rotaries and expressways of the East as we explored Red Sox Nation. We cruised some coastal cities, our vehicle too huge to park among the countless, ever-spawning automobiles. My imagination found it difficult to conceive of the urban masses as anything other than post-apocalyptic zombies and marauders, so Snorri and I had to take turns with the harpoon gun on our armored RV's roof turret.

Farther west, in the continent's vast and spreading midsection, the people, like the buffaloes they replaced, were bigger and slower and better armed than their coastal cousins. People of the continent's heartbasket knew nothing of Bismuth, not even as a cheaper alternative to a weekend on one of the expensive islands. Most of them had never even seen an island or been behind the control of anything without wheels. Snorri and I served the brave and curious among them chowder and made them gifts of T-shirts from distant lands.

We found the middle of the continent's tragic flaw to be overabundance. From cholesterol to floodwaters, they were imperiled by proportions beyond human control. Today's archeologists still wondered whether the ancient mounds they found there were monuments or heaps of trash, and so would tomorrow's. I figured Snorri would save us from the middle-Americans. His experience with bears and whales would give him an intuitive sense of easily-spooked herding creatures. We would flee farther west into the forbidden zone, from whence no Bismuthian had ever returned with a coherent tale to tell. I couldn't tell the difference between the cities and states from what I'd seen on TV, and every story I'd ever heard was about sameness and distance.

As we crossed the Rockies, Snorri would be reminded of his days in the forest with the bears. He'd like it there and want to stay. I would have to remind him that I'd eat him right away if we got stranded in the snow. People from my island had done that before, so it wasn't an entirely empty threat.

Finally, we would reach the Left Coast, where we would see familiar ground—the Pacific. There would be whales but not as many islands. I knew of two versions of that coast. One was fully of jiggly boobs and beach volleyball. The other was of neon signs reflected on dark rainy streets. There were sharper racial and class divides here. And professions like style coach and time-management guru—I was from the relative Far East; maybe I could land a job telling people how to rearrange their furniture according to ancient Northeast island spiritual formulas that would make them feel lucky and me wealthy.

I stopped the *RV Honeypaws* before it became a boat again and took us toward Korea. Thinking about the continent was tiring; I opened a beer and faced east, just to put the landmass behind me.

CHAPTER THIRTY-ONE

A New Telephone

Several days out, I found myself with only a few beers left. I had mismanaged my supply. I couldn't even blame Snorri, since he thought my brand was swill. I tried to explain the advantages of buying beer by the thirty, as opposed to twenty-four pack, but he just turned the argument back on me, using it as an example of how his culture favored quality and mine, quantity, and I got stuck trying to make a patriotic point that I couldn't actually sustain. Sensing my inverse relationship between beer and surliness, or perhaps seizing on the prospect of my impending sobriety, Snorri asked me down into the cabin and said he had a gift for me. Mr. Lucy—my most frequent skipper—sometimes prefaced the assignment of an odious task with 'I got something for ya.' Snorri actually had a little box in crisp white wrapping paper with a lacy white bow. I shouted "Sampo!" in mock-triumph, like I was shouting "Goal!" at a soccer game. Snorri looked miffed, as if he thought I had peeked.

It was a rounded ivory rectangle, about half as thick as a pack of cigarettes with a bas-relief carving of a runic "O." Inside the circle was a cameo of a stylized eight-point mer-deer in profile with one staring saucer eye that immediately sought out my own. After hoofed forelegs, its body took the form of a coiled fish's tail. Snorri showed me how the device opened like a folding measuring stick. And then he slid and turned a section of it and unfolded it some more, and then some more, tessaract-style, until it resembled a nautilus. "Don't use it fully extended too often," he told me, "it saps power." He then refolded it back into its tile-shape and used his thumb to push forward on the mer-deer and slid the cover open. Inside was a smooth flat surface the color of old milk. Snorri touched the surface with his thumb and the word "sampo" appeared on it, as if it were being time-lapse scrimshawed. He shook it and a grid of tiny faces appeared on the screen. "That's the private Whale Network," he said.

Each face was a tobacco-tinged etching of a member of our joint-stock company, plus Moira and Rover, whom I assumed were not actually shareholders. The faces looked like they had been carved on baby teeth. He poked his own face and it grew to fill the screen, which was too narrow to accommodate his reaching eyebrows. A tiny whale began to sing in Snorri's shirt pocket. He handed me the device and pulled a similar one from his pocket and slid it open. On its screen was an etching of me. I looked OK, but a little startled. This was what I would look like if I were on money. "See? You're calling me."

We both put our phones to our ears.

"Hello?" Snorri answered.

"It's me, Orange," I said.

"Hello, how are you, Orange?"

"I'm fine, how are you?"

"Splendid."

"Uh, how do you hang up?"

Snorri demonstrated with his device, sliding and twisting it. "Waterproof. Very rugged. Clever, too. But still, don't force it."

I rubbed my thumb over it; it felt good, smooth but a little soapy. It smelled slightly sulfurous.

"I carved the mer-deer sigil for you Orange, that's your phone. Each of us has our own. We can only call each other on the Whale Network right now, but you can access any network you want with it, no matter the protocols."

"I thought ivory was illegal."

"Not for natives, not for ceremonial purposes."

"This is ceremonial?"

"The ceremony was held a century ago, when this ivory was consecrated to future generations, like myself, to make utensils they hadn't thought of yet. Look—" he took it, slid open a section, and held it to the sky. The open portion had a translucent yellowish inlay. "That's ambergris." Snorri slid and folded it some more until it looked like a batarang, then reconfigured it back into its natal slab shape and handed it back to me. "That's the self-winding mode, just keep it swinging." Somehow, now the mer-deer was facing left, when it had been facing right. It was still staring at me, though. Snorri looked at me expectantly.

I was baffled, well on the way to consternation.

"It has free minutes for life," he said. I was thinking I already had more minutes than I wanted when it started to take on the properties of my own arrhythmia, and I nearly fumbled it. "That's shudder mode," he said. "You have a message." It felt like a bumblebee in a matchbox. I handed it back to Snorri, who held it horizontally and pecked at the screen with his thumbs. He didn't seem to like the results. "Calluses," he said, holding up a thumb. "There. See? It's from me." It read, 'Welcome to the Whale Network.' Snorri handed it back to me again and gave me a look with his eyebrows arched so high, his hairline was pushed back a couple of inches. I realized finally that I was supposed to be grateful, not deeply intimidated.

"Wow?"

Snorri's face crinkled in a brief registration of frustration.

I considered it. I wasn't sure I could utter a credible "thank you." I discovered a small section of my brain that was concerned the device might be alive. The better-informed departments in my head knew how important craftsmanship was to Snorri and his people. But I barely knew what it was, and my pockets had special holes for important objects like this. It was worrisome, like a clock with an extra hour.

I tapped our faces. The etchings had a sameness to them that made me suspect software was the artist. When I had it set on Rover—it was strange to see such a young face rendered in virtual faux-scrimshaw—Snorri took the device from my hands, folded it into a right angle and returned it to me. Somehow it was displaying a three-dimensional illustration of Rover's head between the halves of the device. Poor little Rover's face instantly became the creepiest thing I'd seen in days. Still, though, it was fascinating. I looked at it from different angles but she kept looking at me like she was Andrew Jackson looking back at a cashier searching a bill for a watermark. I turned half of the device around so the mer-deer was on top again and folded it back into its rectangle. I was genuinely relieved that the cat's eidolon hadn't spoken to me. I told Snorri that it was like a piece of heirloom future.

He was pleased. "The best of the batch have a numinous puissance. They are each unique, but most of their functions are potentialities, at present."

"It doesn't work?"

"No, I think in business-English you would say it is 'beta.' Its full capacity may never be called upon. Just don't focus your eyes into the corners of the image projection for long or hold it at a thirty-seven degree angle while moving it in a horizontal plane."

"What?"

"Those might trigger functions that are reserved for the device itself to determine. It is a little more presumptive than intuitive right now."

"What would it do?"

"There is no real saying. Now all it can do is take different aspects of its programs and mix them together. We think future generations of the device will be able to get past randomness and into wrongness and falsity. From there they might be able start creating something meaningful."

"This isn't some kind of robot?"

"No, we just took the future into account when designing it. It's going to be a phone that might learn how to converse someday. Like how humans only use ten percent of their brains. This has room and some motivation. The more you use it, the more it will learn and adapt to its circumstances. The richer, more interesting your conversations, the more sophisticated your device will become. When there's no one to talk with, I have been telling mine the sagas."

"So that they're stored in its memory?"

"To give it something to listen to. To establish the cadences. I can tell it is working because the device keeps adding more detail to my portrait. I have even told yours a few stories. Don't worry, nothing too personal and not even in English."

I was very reluctant to keep this thing on my person. I slid it into my back pocket like it was a loaded mousetrap. I had an insight. "They talk to each other about us, don't they?"

Snorri smiled. "Yes, indeed. They are curious." He patted his crotch. "Here, keep it in your front pocket instead. It will keep you a little warmer on a raw day and the shudder mode is better experienced this way."

"This is sampo, isn't it? Not just brand sampo."

"You're learning!"

The first intrusive feature of the device I came to learn about was tattling. It ratted me out to the rest of the Whale Network shortly after I had stowed it in my pocket. "Snorri, it's poking me."

"Each caller in the Whale Network has their own vibrational signature. Someone is calling you."

I slid the top open. There was the money version of Moira. The phone was poking in a childishly insistent jab. I wondered if she had chosen her own vibration. I poked her illustration's nose, held the phone to my ear, and said hello.

"Hi! It's Moira!"

"How you doin', Moira?"

"Good. Snorri gave you your phone."

"Ayup."

"What are you doing?"

"I'm with Snorri on the *Honeypaws*. We're sort of whale-watching."

"I know. Your picture is on Sampo."

"That's what you're calling it?"

"It's written on it. I think that's its name. What's yours called?"

"I don't even know."

"Snorri will help you name it. I think my mom is going to talk to you soon. Because she didn't yell when I said you were on the Whale Network now."

"Can I talk to her? Is she there?"

"I . . . Mom can't come to the phone right now," she said, trying to get the euphemism right.

"Um, how come you're calling me?" I welcomed her bright voice, especially as an antidote to Snorri's superannuation, but she'd been weirdly quick on the draw, as if she'd been watching her phone, waiting for me to show.

"Your head started bumping up and down on Sampo, so I knew Snorri gave you yours."

"Well, uh, nice to hear from you. We'll be back tomorrow."

"I'm going to give you a ringtone now. You should give me a good one too. Bye."

I told Snorri it had been Moira, and he smiled. "Mineola says that Angie is making very good progress in trying to forgive you." He punched me lightly in the shoulder. It was a gesture my father called an "attaboy," and which I always hated.

The thing home phones must envy about mobile phones is that home phones attract very little attention when they aren't ringing. Mobile phones are like so many Yorricks to their Hamlets. People muse and ponder over them, waiting for their oracles to speak, or, as in my case, squint at them in perplexity. Yorrick might be a good name for a phone. Snorri would have something snide to say about Danes, though.

This time it rang instead of vibrated. A nearly real ring, too, almost like a little clapper and bell. I slid it open with my thumb; none of the network faces were jiggling. I asked Snorri what was going on. He said I had a phone call, which I'd already figured out. I told him there were no faces to poke.

"That tone means the call is from outside the Whale Network. Here in this box is 'caller identification' and that lists the name and number of the person calling you, as long as it's not blocked. See, it says 'Whippey.' I don't know the American area codes."

I did. Florida. Mom. Maybe Dad, but probably not; he'd only ever called me a few times in his life, and I could tell Mom was standing right next to him each time. "My mother? How?"

"Why don't you answer it?" he said and then showed me how.

I tried to clear my mind first. I didn't want Snorri or my mom to know how spooked I was by her ability to find this little ivory device in my pocket from across the continent. When I answered, she told me how proud she was that I'd finally got a phone and was impressed I had reception. I told her it was a new network, and tried to imply that I'd been on top of the whole cell thing for years and was just waiting for the technology to meet my exacting standards. I didn't mention the whales.

"How did you find this phone?"

"Your friend John told me."

"John?" There were several.

"Your Korean friend."

"How do you even know Ill John?"

"Mrs. Cruikshank—you know she got her real estate license last year, right?—she introduced us. Honey, I think you have his name backwards. You know Hezzie's—Mrs. Cruikshank's—daughter, Emily, right? She's down in Massachusetts and her husband. . . ."

I didn't, though I probably just didn't remember. My mother had a gossip network of her own with a trunk line that stretched along the Atlantic seaboard from their condo in Florida to Bismuth. She was always telling me about the illnesses and exploits of several generations of people and their offisland diaspora she presumed I knew and cared about. I never told her anything I might need to deny later.

". . . Ronald and Tabitha are moving back from Kittery

because they can't cover their taxes on Bismuth with renters. . . ."

The real purpose, I think, to my mother's calls was to make sure my little thread was woven into the Bismuthian social tapestry. She thought I did a terrible job of it myself and stitched me in like she was still patching the knees on my Toughskins all those years ago. I usually had trouble accounting for myself when we spoke and had to plan anecdotes about wholesome things I'd done ahead of time, so mostly I just listened passively to the strokes, children, and divorces, and typically failed the occasional pop quizzes she proctored.

The phone had a little stopwatch in a corner of the screen. It would be interesting if it could divide time up into karmic units; this much time has been wasted on the phone; this much time banked up so I don't die lonely. I had always been good at wasting time, but not so hot at enumerating it.

"Orange, Honey? I asked you if you knew the Hobbler house."

"No, which one?"

"You remember Jenny Hobbler, that girl that used to tease you in school? Her family's house. She's offisland now; she had two boys, I think. Deirdre, that's Jenny's mother, Mrs. Hobbler, still owns the house, since they wanted it for Jenny's family, but she's not coming back. But since Mr. Hobbler passed, she won't live there alone and has moved in with her sister just over on the mainland. She doesn't like it there. I don't think she and her sister ever got along that well. When they were girls. . . ."

"The house?" I asked, hoping the interruption would be taken as eager attentiveness and not impatience.

"Dear, as I've been trying to tell you for the last several minutes, the Korean boys are going to buy the Hobbler house. And listen to this—they talked about buying the Topsoil and the store too."

"Why?"

"Well, John said that he and his friend loved the island and they wanted to make investments in hospitality opportunities, or something like that, anyway." She lowered her voice: "I think they may be the B&B types." That was my mother's politest code for 'gay.' She was eager to meet more gay men; she had felt deprived throughout most of her life. I'd thought they were probably gay, too, but couldn't tell for certain. Maybe they just actually liked each other. That's easier to do if you don't have sex with each other.

"You know Orange, your father has said for years that we could sell the house to you for cheap. There'd be no mortgage and no sales tax—you would just have to pay the property tax." This was a conversation many Bismuthians of my age had with their parents. I'd had it several times with my mother. It's never been plush on the island, but these days, the houses are assessed for so much and there are so few jobs that even inheriting a free house was too expensive. But Ill John and Chosen were the men with tiger testes and whale phones and probably deep pockets in other peoples' pants. Property on Bismuth was probably nothing compared to their friends' crash pads in Bangkok or Dubai or wherever.

"So how come you were talking to John?"

"Hezzie—Mrs. Cruikshank—said that you were their only reference on the island."

"So? They're cool."

"She . . . felt that she wanted some more background."

"I would have told her whatever."

"I think, Honey, that Mrs. Cruikshank and I had more to talk about than you and she might."

It was possible that my mom was trying to imply that Mrs. C. had insinuated I might not be an entirely reliable character witness.

"So she calls you in Florida to vet these guys neither of you have met?"

"Well, I told Mrs. Cruikshank that I'd have to talk to the gentleman. And then John called me, and he was very polite. Did you know that his father met Mr. Lucy during the war?"

"Yeah, on a sub."

"He told me about his mother's kimchi and the hole they had for it in the yard. He was a dear. I'm going to buy some so your father can try it."

"I don't think he'd like it."

"I make cole slaw for him all the time. And he eats sauerkraut."

"Their slaw is like weaponized cabbage."

"At any rate, Dear, John and his friend want to buy someplace they can stay at next summer."

"Not year round?"

"No, I don't think they understand rentals here, they seem to think they'll be able to rent it out over the winter; he even mentioned you staying there. But I told him about how you were planning on buying the title for our house from us so you can just pay the taxes."

That wasn't actually part of any of my plans. My mother's new insistence on this enduring topic suggested she might have gleaned from Ill John that I had a bundle of cash on me. Part of her plan to weave me further into society with every phone call involved hinting that the world disapproved of my avoidance of crippling responsibility and debt. My mom would talk about food and taxes with anyone, though. Not enough and probably prepared wrong; and too much and definitely prepared wrong.

"But, Orange, this is what I didn't tell Hezzie: they were asking about seagum. Whether your father taught you to go seagumming; if you would take them to your patch."

And this is how even the most morally pristine of island mothers resembles a successful drug dealer: they are excellent enforcers of discretion. The wrong tone from a stranger and it's all over. Seagum patches are passed from father to son and are defended by threats of feud and sabotage that can only make sense to natives. "They probably don't know. I'll talk to him about it."

Our conversation ended like they usually do. Mom passed on instructions and warnings from Dad. Then she said she still loved me. If Snorri hadn't been standing there, I might have said the same back to her. I held the phone up to him and gave him a smug look to say, 'Hey, lookit, I just I just aced a phone call—with my mother, even.'

"You've got a problem," he said.

"What's wrong?"

"You have a message from Waldena."

I looked at the Brady Bunch-style grid of faces; Waldena's was scowling but not bobbing like Moira's. "Why's she making a face?"

Snorri smirked. "Your countrymen call it an 'app.' You should see what she does on mine."

I gave her image a little bip between the eyes and got her text message: "Come find me." Snorri saw it. "She sounds lonely."

"I think she threatened to kill me last time I saw her. Or maybe it was the time before that. Maybe she just wants to re-up the threat." I wondered . . . I wondered if there were a word in Finlindian for the perfect marriage of dread and desire.

Snorri gave me a look that suggested we'd all be better off

married to good Finlindian bears. I couldn't decide what to type back, even after Snorri showed me how to invoke the English keyboard, so I waved the phone around, hoping to shake off Waldena's summoning.

CHAPTER THIRTY-TWO

The Wrong Whale

"We're not towing anything, are we?"

Snorri said no.

"Well, Skipper, I believe it is my genetic destiny to inform you, thar she blows."

"It just breached?"

"Yeah, but it's been with us a while."

"Why didn't you tell me?"

"I thought I was probably hallucinating."

"You should have told me anyway."

"Yesterday a seagull said, 'Fish in limber clouds.'"

"You should know the difference from bird blather and a real whale."

"I should be home sleeping off a big lunch."

We watched a while. "It's spending too long on the surface," Snorri said.

"Is it OK? Wait, I think it's waving at us. Fuck, it's huge!" The whale had rolled onto its side and raised a fluke that seemed as large as the *Honeypaws*. It hit the water's surface with a tremendous beaver slap and then descended, leaving the water to our aft a rolling boil.

A minute later the boat bulged up under us, making us both nearly squat in compensation. Just below us, its image barely distorted by the water, was the biggest eye that had ever looked at me. I was transfixed as my measure was taken by the vastness. Then, staccato pops like a machine-gun cannonade that rose in pitch and frequency until it was the scream of a banking fighter jet. I fell back onto the deck and got tangled up in Snorri. My heart, and his too—I could feel it—were fluttering like the last brown leaves on a winter oak. I couldn't tell whether I was hearing a strangely-dopplered police siren or whether my ears were ringing. Snorri and I noticed we were holding each other and ungrappled ourselves. When I got to my knees and looked over the side, I could see that the boat was yawing in the vortex the whale had left as it dived again.

"I'll take the harpoon gun!" I yelled, unnecessarily, to Snorri, "You get the wheel!"

He caught my arm as I scrambled to the forward deck, "No!"

"It's going to kill us!"

Snorri was a very pale man at the moment—me too, probably, but Snorri appeared disturbed on an epic scale, whereas I was merely scared silly. "It already did not kill us."

"What?!" I wanted action. I had already not shit my breeches, nor barfed breakfast, and the cartilage in my knees was already firming back up. I knew I was nearly OD'ing on adrenaline and stupidity, but I wondered if I weren't actually bred for this moment—stabbing the whale—and if Snorri were thwarting my birthright. And besides, the nasty harpoon gun on the deck—what the hell else was it for?

Before I could mutiny, another spout erupted several boat lengths away and drenched us. It smelled foul. This time, when the whale breached, I got a better look at it, having been unable to look away from its eye when it was under the boat. It was smiling at me. And groaning. Its chinless face was a little like the bow of a ship and its recursive lips gave its grin the rueful droop of a seagum addict. I took this expression to mean, 'I'm going to enjoy mulching your little boat, even though I may bruise my forehead.' "It's gonna ram us!"

Snorri held me by my shoulder, much too hard. "I think I recognize that whale. Or rather I think maybe he recognizes me."

"So, it's back for revenge?"

"I think, I hope, it's just curious. Look at him. That's a big blackie. What do you islanders call these, right whales?"

"Right." Or wrong, really. If I had lived hundreds of years ago, this big black whale would have been swimming right off coast. My ancestors, and Snorri's too, used to hunt these guys in little boats launched from the shore. Properly stabbed to death, their corpses would float and could be towed in to get flensed right on the beach. Thus they were considered the "right" whale to hunt and thus they had been nearly exterminated. It wasn't until most of them had been boiled down into oil that North Atlantic whalers ventured to the South Pacific. It was the wrong whale for another reason too; this wasn't the species carrying Snorri's antennae. We hadn't been looking for this kind of whale.

So this whale shouldn't have been there. Or it should have had enough sense to stay away from human beings. Therefore it was here to kill us.

Snorri exclaimed in Finlindian. In English, he said, "I think the Whale Council's sonar is working too well!"

The *Honeypaws* came with the usual assortment of fishing and navigational tools, but his sonar was something special, as he had told me during the ceaseless orientation seminar our week-long whale-watching trip had become. Just because North Americans had quit whaling didn't mean we were done harassing them. Ever since the Industrial Revolution, we'd been doing our best to drive them insane by transforming the ocean into a clanging discordia of grinding propellors, sonic booms, cable buzz and every other sound we buried, unheard by human ears, in the ocean depths. In a mere generation or two for some of their species, we surface-dwelling hominids had filled the ocean with enough sonic pollution to effectively blind, deafen, starve, and madden all the remaining echolocutionists.

Snorri had explained that the Northern Indian whaling councils had developed a type of sonar that was supposed to be more euphonious, more cetacean, and that *Honeypaws* was among the first generation of whalers to use the system. He had told me the real tragedy was the callous destruction of the whales' oral culture, but by then I had tired of his own oral culture, and had stopped listening to his conjectures about the molecular transference of vibrational resonance of the one-stringed harp his ancestors played and its influence on cetacean telecommunication. He had a story about a thousand Finlindian greybeards yoiking and strumming their harps on the beach, summoning whales to deliver them from starvation and darkness.

Snorri didn't have a harp, but I knew it was only a matter of time before he began yoiking. "Listen to this," he said and went in the cabin, where he adjusted his council's special sonar song so that we could hear it onboard. It made me think of melancholic satellites whistling as their orbits decayed. While I and the gulls listened to that, Snorri hooked his phone up to Honeypaws' dashboard. "Now listen to this . . . no, wait. Wait a minute." Snorri advanced and reversed a recording of someone, possibly a human being, gargling and whooping. "Here, this is a recording of the summoning song I was telling you about."

"Song" was a poor descriptor for what I was hearing. There was a sort of rhythmic thwonging—the one-stringed harp—and the sound of a man who had smoked far too much opium being

310

startled to death slowly, while he occasionally hit himself in the windpipe. Then he played the "song," which he said was a recording of one of Finlindia's living yoiking legends at the peak of his improvisational form, along with the special sonar. "You hear it? The concordances? Not harmonies, but . . ." and then he started warbling along, making a rumble in his throat and a whistle in his nose.

I looked out at the dark leviathan. He was staring at us with the other eye now. I looked back at Snorri. His eyes were closed, and his Adam's apple was bobbing. Suddenly, I knew just what to do. I cupped my hand over my ear back-up singer-style and went at it like a sled dog staked out for the night in polar bear country. Somehow, it felt right to utter/sing a series of "wuh wuh wuh woos," in different speeds and tones. Snorri opened up his chant/wail to leave room for mine and we found ourselves in a sort of concordance and not harmony, just as Snorri had said. He moved close in to me and I began to lose sense of the cabin. While I worked the chant, stretching and goosing the syllables, Snorri whispered in my ear: "Think of distance, of time, how your voice can transcend them or make them unbearable." Then he stood right up against me and joined back in. We were sharing the same breath. I'd do the "wuh woos," which were coming to me in wave-like sounds, and he'd swallow them, replying with something like a squadron of distant geese. Snorri moved in even closer. Back-and-forth, nose-to-nose, we yoiked until I got fizzy, saw the stars we were singing about, and blacked out.

I was only down for a moment; Snorri and I had filled the cabin up with a weirdness and level of carbon dioxide that was beyond my tolerance. Snorri turned off the yoik and the sonar and I peeked back at the whale. Did whales blink? This one didn't seem to.

"What was. . . . "

"Anybody can yoik. You just did. You intuited whale speech. And the big blackie heard us. He's responding."

We listened to something like a giant copper cauldron being rolled across a rocky valley. "What's it saying?"

"I really do not know, though I wish I did. There are legends that Northern Indian ancients could sing with them, but they never wrote the language down, and it's long lost. Some of our scholars think that certain scrimshawed designs are actually a sort of sonic map to Northern waters, transliterated from whale speech, but other people think they're just scribbles. I don't know. I could understand my bearbride well enough, but we lived together for years. When I used to feed the little pink melonheads in my council's fjord, they'd be right there at the water's edge, chattering away to me. I don't know what they were saying, but I could tell it was mostly just trivial gossip about the pod—and begging for more kribble, of course. *More, more, more, now, now, now.* That's what all animals say when you're holding food."

We listened for a little while. The whale shifted from its epic rumbles to a goofier, though still stentorian series of meeps and fwoos. I told Snorri it sounded a little like Rover yowling at spiders in the cellar.

"Did you know most whales have millions of lice on them? The lice can be used to date the origin of a whale's species, since the insects reproduce so quickly. Many generations of lice live on a long-lived whale like this, and they form their own divisions of lice-species as they adapt to the particular whale's biological ecology."

"That's like what that Bags guy in the sub was saying about the whalefalls and his arcology fantasy."

"The lice might even have more of a story to tell us than the whales."

"You're not going to do a lice yoik, are you? I don't want to talk to them."

"Me neither. I only like to sing with heavy animals."

I scratched my head hard; it had been a long time since I'd showered.

"Brace yourself!" Snorri yelled. The whale had crossed the distance between us in a moment, and then *Honeypaws* was being butted along the water, her bow almost shipping from the speed. Snorri and I staggered into the wheelhouse, and he took the wheel to keep us pointing forward.

"Now?" I asked, pointing to the harpoon gun.

"No! If this were a serious attack, he would have used his tail. This is, I don't know, affectionate?"

"We're fucked!"

"You better hope not. These guys have the biggest testicles of any animal on the planet."

I had a headful of nearly insuppressible sarcasm, and a bolus of panic bobbled around my stomach and intestines. A thought of good old Rover came to me as unbidden as the whale was butting our stern. She did this too. In fact, most every domesticated creature I could think of had done this to me. Animals headbutt you when they want food.

"The kribble!" I said to Snorri.

He thought about it a moment and told me to fetch it from the forward hold. I dashed down the steps. We only had a few sacks of the dried krill and krill by-products, but they were fifty pounders. I humped them up to the stern deck and Snorri handed me his long knife. I slit the bags and heaved them over the stern, where they hit the whale on the back. It stopped shoving us and veered away. We coasted on another fifty yards or so; as we slowed, our bow rose to a safer level. Snorri started the engine he'd cut when we first saw the whale and took us out in a short arc. The whale was doing something similar; he circled back to the spreading cloud of kribble and came to a relative stop as he hoovered in the dried bugs, straining them through his long thin louvres of baleen.

"That's learned behavior," said Snorri. "The important question is; did he learn it from fellow whales or people?" With the boat under power and the whale occupied, it was safe for Snorri to leave the wheel for a moment. He twisted his phone a couple of times and then folded it back onto itself, sort of like cutting a deck of cards with one hand. Then he held it up at eye level as if he were saluting with it.

"What are you doing?"

"I'm photographing it. See? This configuration acts as a lens. A microphone, too; I've been recording it. Your phone does this too, but it doesn't have the same quality lens."

Snorri told me to pilot us around the whale slowly, now that it was relatively still. He wanted to see as much of it as possible. It was still watching me; I could tell.

"Set the wheel straight and let us drift a minute, I want you to see something." I made it so and joined him on the rear deck to watch the whale have his snack.

"You see that brindling?" he asked, pointing along the whale's length.

"Is it from lice?"

"No! That's a really desirable pattern, almost impossible to breed for. See, under the black there's a coruscating wavy pattern like ripples reflecting the night sky."

"Nobody breeds this species."

"Right, they're much too big and range too far, even if they weren't nearly extinct."

"And now it's following us. And we're out of kribble."

"This, I think, is a legendary whale. That brindle is a pattern from our distant history—it resembles a sequence of powerful runes. In some illuminated sagas, these whales swim on the margins with names and messages coded into their skin. My people have always known whales are the masters of long-distance travel and communications on this planet; we have folk tales about wizards who passed messages across the oceans with these whales."

"What, they wrote on them?"

"No they sang to them. Like our sonar does."

"What, exactly, is our sonar singing?"

"I had thought it was just a nice historic allusion, like that car with the flag on your TV show that plays 'Yankee Doodle' on its horn."

"That's not . . . never mind." There are nuances of North American popular culture that are not worth explaining in the presence of a whale.

"But now I think the whale councils might have a broader and deeper agenda. Maybe they are trying to summon these old boys back. If our ancestors really did know how to sing to whales, they never wrote the language down, and it's long lost to our culture. Maybe the councils want the whales to come back and teach us."

"Teach them what?"

"I don't know. I spent years learning more than I want to know about whale husbandry, but really, at heart, I'm a bear man. The whale councils are the oldest and most secretive institutions in our society. They have agendas that span history and nations. The European nonsense about the councils as smuggling syndicates is just the most recent attempt to smear them. Without the councils we wouldn't have crossed the Atlantic in prehistory."

Ignoring the fact that I knew with moral certainty that Snorri was a smuggler and that nothing much we'd done together recently would have been considered legal in North America, I asked about the writing on the whale instead.

"It's not necessarily runes," he said. "It might just be a fortuitous coincidence. Maybe they're code. It's organic though, nobody tattooed or branded them. Actually, I've never even seen one before. I doubt many people have."

"Because they were fished out."

"Yes, but if it weren't for the whale councils, this type here, the messenger whales, wouldn't even exist."

"I thought they couldn't be bred."

"They can't, they're like samurai crabs."

"Yeah, and ninja lobsters."

"No, really, Japanese fishermen throw back crabs that look like they have the faces of mythic drowned samurais on their shells. So after centuries, the samurai crabs lived to breed, while the others were eaten. It was the same with these big blackies with the runic brindles—Northern Indian whalers left them alone to continue cruising the coasts and even up the fjords and rivers. They probably even knew the individual whales by name and could count on seeing them at certain times of the year as they made their migrations."

"So why are they so rare now?"

"I didn't even think they still existed. The entire species is nearly extinct, not just this breed. You should know, Orange. It's your very ancestors that nearly killed them off. You Americans didn't even notice the patterns. All you wanted was casks and casks of blubber. Your people never considered the value of a creature that was done with dry land and had learned how to navigate and communicate across the entire planet long before our species evolved. Think of it! These creatures walked the earth for longer than Homo Sapiens has, then shoved off to explore the oceans before we could even stand up."

"People from the Northern Indies have killed more whales and casked up an awful lot more blubber than my ancestors ever did, and they're still doing it."

"Yes but we have relationships with whales; they've always been part of our culture."

This was an argument that people with much more conviction and education than myself had been having for a long time. I didn't stand a rhetorical chance in hell.

"And there's something else strange about this whale, too. He has beautiful skin. It doesn't make sense. He's obviously old, probably older than me even, but he doesn't have the scars he should have."

"From giant squid." Some whales ate itsy bits of krill, others hunted the invisible depths for unseen monsters.

"No, from propellors. Our shipping lanes are their old roads; just about the only time one ever sees what you call a right whale is when it's been injured by a ship. A whale like this—I don't see how it could live this long without some obvious damage. Which makes me wonder, where has it been all these years?"

"And how did it recognize the sonar?"

"Indeed!"

"We're being stalked by a pushy, loud wrong whale with a grudge against humanity."

"We are having a serendipitous encounter with a mythic

creature that seems as curious about us as we are about him."

"I'm not that curious, and I think it thinks we're just a soft touch for kribble."

"I know I told you before that our work on the Whale Network was making history, but we are actually making history right now. This is a very important interspecies moment. We will need to stay with this whale as long as possible, follow it where ever it goes."

"How are we going to do that? It's going to figure out we're out of snacks soon and then probably eat us just on principle."

"It would not eat us. And besides, they use their tails to smash boats; they only bash each other with their heads. We will have to follow this big old boy on the surface and then try to ping him with the sonar when he dives. We are going to have to stick close to him. It will be a sleigh ride straight out of the sagas!"

"You know, you promised to take me back home tomorrow."

"Think about where this whale could lead us! A sanctuary—a literal sort of school even! Somewhere, our friend here learned from his elders how to avoid the dangerous ships and how to cadge food from *Honeypaws* with her whale song sonar. Wait till the councils hear about this!

"Oh, hmm, they must already know—this sonar must be their way of scouting. These could be the very whales that teach us their language. Oh, this is historical. Deep, living history. Maybe the polar melt. . . ." Snorri guttered away into Finlindian raving.

"You think it's nearby?"

"What?"

"Whale Shangri-la."

"My best guess might be in the Arctic somewhere. Someplace where the floes are breaking up. A new Ultima Thule. There are myths older than my race; legends my people learned on their migration across the Arctic. You know the Norse Valhalla—their retirement home for old soldiers?"

"Yes, but I don't think that's how your pagan neighbors would have described it."

"Well, the idea is not theirs. 'Valhalla' has its foundations in our language group—it is a corruption of how we would say 'Whale Hall.' The Norse built their veterans' hospital over our own sacred foundation."

"So it's where your whales go to drink mead and feast on squid?"

"Many foreigners thought the exploration sagas we told were myths until anthropologists of the twentieth century began to see their literal and figurative truths. Why not this myth, too?"

"I'm not dressed for the North Pole."

"*Honeypaws* has plenty of storm gear."

"I want to go home."

"We cannot lose track of this whale. It is too important."

I summoned a good loud, sustained stare, straight up from my diaphragm, let it resonate in my sinus cavities, and then shot it out my eyeballs at Snorri.

"Don't be petulant. Moments ago you were on the cusp of a dramatic cultural awakening. Something distant and deep called to you and you responded in kind. This is your time to be a hero."

Our friendly nemesis, in all his black brindled bulk, was done waiting for us to toss more kribble. It chuffed and grunted and then brought its head down hard enough to splash and lurch us.

"Can we friend it?"

"It may be an ally, but we will have to get to know it first."

"No, I mean add it to the Whale Network. What I'm thinking

is we could shoot an antenna into it with the harpoon gun."

"Even if there were such a thing as the antenna javelin, I would never violate this . . . *harbinger*. This is a harbinger whale. A whale with safe harbor, here to tell us something. A whale with serious lineage."

"The Harbinger Whale. Well named, Snorri."

"Yes, and that's just in English."

"I'm not coming with you."

"We are not leaving this whale."

Our new friend, the Harbinger—the probable smasher of *Honeypaws*, likely consumer of my flesh—was frothing the water again, less than its own length from the boat. He was chuckling like Jimmy Durante, if Durante were an antediluvian titan.

"Fuck! Don't we have anything left to feed it?"

"Just your burritos." Snorri had mocked my diet throughout the trip and pretended not to have a microwave for our first day at sea. "He wouldn't want. . . ." We got soaked by a reeking geyser. The whale turned over, giving the churning water another slap with his fin, and looked at us with his other eye. He groaned and began snuffling the water right around the boat, as if he were vacuuming and our lazy feet were in the way. Snorri said the bumping would start again shortly and it was a good thing that *Honeypaws* was armored.

"You can't follow this whale anywhere if it wrecks us here, Snorri."

"Forbearance! And stay away from the sides."

Ignoring Snorri, I flicked a clump of spilled kribble over the side and watched it get sucked into one of the vortices swirling around us. I was not going down with this ship. I was not getting dragged to the Arctic. I had a small idea. "You said these phones talk to each other, right? They know where each other are?"

"Yes, but not like other phones. No GPS. That can be accessed through other networks, but not legally yet, so these phones are configured only to locate other members of the Whale Network. We won't incorporate GPS while our network is still in development to curtail espionage.

"I'm going to try for a little distance now. Too much whelm."

As Snorri started the props and motored us off a bit, I sent my first-ever text message, a reply to Waldena: "Call Snarri ASSP—Ornge." I had to leave the typos in, since the backspace key was too elusive.

It only took a moment for the whale to catch up to us. "We're not going to make it; we've got a pork chop tied around our neck or something."

Snorri looked puzzled. "Like an albatross?"

"No, I mean it's not going to stop fucking with us. We need more distance!"

"I cannot let it out of my sight."

This time our new friend-cum-assassin pushed a wave like a small hill at us, catching us broadside and tipping *Honeypaws* dangerously toward swamping. Snorri stayed in the wheelhouse, trying to keep the bow pointed at the whale. I went back out on the deck and gathered up what crumbs of kribble I could find. I unfolded the phone back into its self-winding mode, the batarang croissant, sloshed it around some water and sprinkled the kribble on it. It fell right off. I needed something sticky. I hurried past Snorri at the wheel and into the galley, where I got my peanut butter.

Snorri, whose native cuisine was entirely indefensible, had also mocked my peanut butter throughout the trip. He saw the jar and rolled his eyes. "This is a good time for a sandwich?"

"I'll just eat it out of the jar." Back on the rear deck, I smeared my now crescent-shaped phone with the peanut butter and then dredged it in the pile of kribble I'd made. Would the whale hear me if I shouted? I knew it could see me. I waved and shouted.

"I know, I know!" shouted back Snorri.

"No you don't!" I yelled and flung the phone at the whale. It bounced off his snout and began to sink right in front of him. I realized he couldn't see in front of himself, but before I could rue my pitch, the big bully sucked it right up.

Snorri ran out of the wheelhouse, "What have you done?!"

"Now the Harbinger is on the Network, right?"

"That was your phone!"

"Now it's his. My gift. He's on the Net."

Snorri's mouth hung open. "But . . . huh." He pulled at an eyebrow. "Huh."

"Right?"

"I had that phone made just for you."

"But you can track its signal now?"

"Yes," he said slowly, catching on to my idea.

"Then let's get the fuck outta here!"

Snorri stood still, watching the whale. "Huh," he said, yet again.

"We are completely out of kribble. Peanut butter too. We have to go now."

Snorri twiddled a long strand of eyebrow. "You know, if they all had phones, they could sing to each other without interference from longwave radio and propwash noise."

"That's. . . . "

Snorri punched me hard in the shoulder. "It might work!"

We stood watching the whale watch us. I thought about his massive tongue working the peanut butter out of his baleen slats. "Hey, I never knew my phone number."

An hour later, Snorri's phone squawked stridently. He scowled. "It's not the whale."

"My ride?"

"The witch," he said, reading his screen. "She sends her regards and will be here soon."

"Snorri, you can't expect me to come on a goo—whale chase to the North Pole. We've been out here for days and I've done my part already."

"You can do—were going to do—better than Waldena."

"Listen, we agreed. I get a ride home, you get to follow the whale anywhere you and he want."

"And Angie? You could make it work."

"Not from the Arctic Circle."

"What do you think she will have to say when she hears who you've been shipping with?"

"She's already not talking to me."

"You heard Moira, she's almost ready to begin forgiving you."

"I'm just hitching the only ride in town. You could take me."

"I cannot, I would be out of range soon—no antenna, remember?"

"My hands are tied."

Snorri said something in Finlindian that sounded scornful and conclusive.

While we waited for my taxi, I gathered up my gear and my big wads of money. I wrapped each of the three banded stacks in a couple plastic bags each and put them in my duffel with my clothes. I decided to leave my burritos and cans of Beefaroni for Snorri in case he got iced in up north. When I got back topside, Snorri had his binoculars out. "The whale?"

"I'm reading a heliogram from Waldena. A message sent by flashing a mirror in the sunlight. A very old and durable means of telecommunication."

"Why not use the phone?"

"She's being clever. She's sending a short, rude poem that rhymes our names with sex acts. Her and my countrymen used to yell things like this at each other during battles. I hope she shows some more decorum around the Harbinger."

I wondered what my name rhymed with in Estonindian.

Snorri had reversed roles, seemingly, with the whale. Now that he could track it, he had opened up some distance between us so he could stay nearby but not injure it with *Honeypaws's* props. Also so that the whale wouldn't sink us, but I knew he wouldn't cop to that. He probably wouldn't be up on the hydrofoils any time soon. I saw the flashes and then the *Hammer Maiden* about ten minutes out. I wondered if she had her crew with her. Ship-to-ship transfers are kind of tricky, but we had fine weather. We could use the harpoon gun to shoot a line to her and then, once we had it secured, I could slide over to her in a sort of harness. The danger is getting stuck between boats, dangling from the slack line. Snorri had returned to the wheel, grumbling. I waited until I could make out Waldena and waved to her. When she got close enough, Snorri came out and handed me a life vest and told me to put it on. "Are you certain, Orange?"

"Ayup," I said putting my arms through the holes.

"Got everything? Your money?"

"Ayup."

"Get up by the rail so you can make ready to secure her line. You are entirely sure?"

"Yeah thanks, I'm all set."

Snorri put his hand on the back of my vest and rubbed. "Be

heroic." Before I could turn to hug him, he hooked his boot between my ankles and gave me a shove overboard.

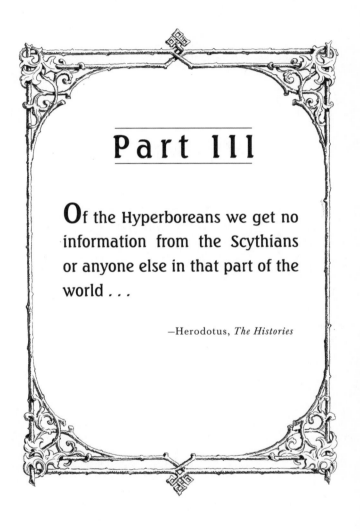

Part III

Of the Hyperboreans we get no information from the Scythians or anyone else in that part of the world . . .

—Herodotus, *The Histories*

CHAPTER THIRTY-THREE

The Spouter

There's a way to approach smokers without being too apparent a mooch. It's a certain kind of sidle that suggests a friendly complicity, a momentary rebellion to the main gathering. We used to lurk off to escape parental attention, but now things are mostly reversed. I had spotted a little eddy of young adults quietly spiraling off of the main pool of wedding guests; the girls appealingly clumsy in their dresses and heels, the guys looking unlikely to drone about the Patriots, despite their gelled-up crew cuts. I said Hey to them like I was supposed to know them, they said Hey back, like they were supposed to know me. I caught the joint twice as it swirled around the swaying vortex of tipsy post-teenagers. Soon, though, came the inevitable, "Who are you with?"

The girl who asked me, her heels were sinking into the grass I'd trimmed earlier that afternoon. She wasn't long for the vertical. She shouldn't have been smoking, but her girlfriend was shouldering her up and smirking at me. I was with myself, which I think was evident to her, but I don't think she'd sussed out my illegitimacy. If you're going to drift off into the bushes with an unattended male at a wedding, it's not supposed to be the help. I wasn't wearing the clean white shirt and black pants, not jeans, with black shoes that Chosen had asked me to bring to change into after I helped set up the tent and humped gear around for the caterer. They'd come with their own efficient and tidy servers, so I'd been surreptitiously set loose to wander among the guests for the evening like a dog behaving tolerably off his leash. I didn't even own a clean white shirt, not even an unstained white t-shirt. I would have just got in the way anyway. I was supposed to stay sober and out of trouble so I could help clean up later, so I stayed away from the keg and stuck with bottles of beer that stood conveniently upright in the inside pocket of my jean jacket.

I didn't want to wind up wondering whether I should offer a toot of tiger testes to this young woman who was already a few loops into her downward gyre, so I sidled away from their bubble and back into the walled garden of the Spouter, the B&B that Ill John and Chosen had bought while I was at sea with Snorri and Waldena. We'd worked on it all winter and spring; the paint was still fresh on Memorial Day. It was cute, I guess. Actually, there was one room, the Pineapple Room, that had given me a seizure. It was all the calico, I think. I'd spent too long in there staining the wainscot, and the patterns from the wallpaper and the nearly matching bedspread swirled into each other. My eyeballs stiffened, and my vision crazed with what seemed like pulsing afterimages of lightning jags. Electric colors dripped from auroral bursts that concussed my brain until it sloshed on its motor mounts. I couldn't see or stand straight, and I knew I was going to lose my stomach and maybe more soon. So I crawled into the mostly pattern-free bathroom and pulled towels down off the rack to nest on while I panted into my palms, letting my warm breath soothe my throbbing eyelids.

Towels are inordinately important to offislanders. The Spouter housed more towels than I'd ever seen in my life. I had always been secretly glad for bathroom floors, since they had reliably provided me with full stops to run-on descents. To find one-self on the bathroom floor means something painful and ugly is finally coming to an end. That afternoon when I was in post-calico recovery, I finally understood towels too. The wings of angels are best when they are a bit scratchy and smell of God's BO, which, as a mere mortal, I don't have enough scent receptors to discern.

I own my parents' towels and their house now. Or, they're mine now. I own my own. I paid off the last of their second mortgage with the bundles of cash I'd got from the WhaleNet dividend. The result of this was that I was just as poor as I'd always been and still lived where I always lived. And I had to talk to my mother more often. And the bank knew who I was, and presumably someone in some office somewhere in America would soon be wondering where their tax money was. The assessment was astonishing. How I could own something so entirely expensive, yet feel so poor wasn't something I'd worked out yet. It pleased my neighbors though. They liked that I was now suffering in a way they could understand. The transition from possession to ownership was both trivial and freighted with consequence. But mandatory, as far as my parents were concerned. I hoped I wasn't going to have to buy their condo in Florida.

After the house had become mine, all mine, Mitchell and Moira came over and we had an enthusiastic afternoon sketching out renovations and saying things like, "Opening out the non-retaining walls into the hearth area," and "No more shag." I still keep these noble goals in mind and will probably get to them after I finally buy a new TV. Besides, I was busy with the Spouter.

Ill John and Chosen were glad to have a guy who knew how to bring drywall over without having to pay the full ferry freight fee. They were offisland often during that offseason and trusted me to get much more work done at their new place than I'd ever conceived of doing. I got Mitchell some work as well as a few other guys, but not Donny, who seemed to be getting ready to inherit the *Wendy's Mom* from his dad. I had a new kind of credibility on Bismuth and I was sort of getting used to it. I never did really horn in on the seagum trade with the island's new innkeepers. Mr. Lucy kept that to himself and Donny felt he was gaining his own street cred because of it.

Since I'd sacrificed my WhaleNet phone to the Harbinger Whale last year, I'd actually owned a few more. I found out they were like gum and cigarettes in America—you could buy a phone almost anywhere that had a cash register. I lost two of them overboard, but had held onto the one that Angie gave me. It was Moira's old phone from before she got her WhaleNet phone from Snorri. Angie had joined the WhaleNet too. Moira's old phone was still gummy from the puffy stickers I had peeled off it. Unlike my lost, cheap phones, this one had a screen so I could see the WhaleNet icons again. It was interesting to see what they'd got up to. Mine was at the center; it still looked like me, but I had a better haircut, thanks to Angie. Despite the fact that the icons were all rendered in tobacco juice-colored scrimshaw-style, Angie's icon had red lipstick. Sometimes it appeared to smile, but I might be presuming, since she's not my girlfriend. Her icon circumnavigated around the rest of us. At first I took this to mean that she was the wanderer and I was the center of the solar system. Now I understand she's prescribing her territory—Bismuth is hers. She keeps me schooled in the center of the shoal so I'll stay out of trouble and out of her way. She's not my girlfriend, but I don't know who else she sees.

There's another icon on the WhaleNet I don't remember from

my first phone, one that's not on Moria's and Angie's phones. For weeks I thought it was just a little square of static. And then one day, when I'd been looking at Angie's icon for a while, I noticed the static square had certain forms—lines and swirls that looked like a fetal sonogram or a tiny hurricane. It was like a caricature of bad reception. Something seemed to be taking shape there; it was hard to look away from. Once, the icon inflated to cover the whole screen and my phone throbbed, not vibrated. It thumped from within my pocket once, then several seconds later again. A sort of *lub . . . dub.* Slow and heavy. I took the call, and whatever it had to say, it was beyond the capacity of my phone's speaker to render. All I heard was whooshing.

Snorri's icon was pulsing with imminence. I'd seen its eyes follow me a few times recently. He was due on Bismuth. I could tell by the color of the water, the taste of the air, and because Moira told me she saw him at her Aunt Mini's the other day. The last I'd seen of his flesh and blood form, I was sputtering in the cold Atlantic. He was still onboard, waving with his whole arm and pointing at me. All of my standard motherfucking imprecations had been shocked out of me by the plunge, and each time I tried to wave my fist at him, I sank some. My duffel straps kept shrugging off my arm and I wondered which would be stupider: losing my money and then drowning, or drowning while trying to keep my money. Unable to convincingly threaten Snorri's life, I turned to the *Hammer Maiden* to beg Waldena to rescue me. She also was waving and pointing. It didn't seem to me that Snorri was wishing me well on my journey, nor did I think Waldena was signaling how glad she was to see me. Utterly horrified, I realized they had the vantage of their gunwales to see the abominable shadow rising from below me, the Harbinger of Engulfment, the Big Blackie itself. I knew that in moments its sheer bulk would displace enough water to vacuum me under. I thought for a moment about loosening my hold on the duffel of money so I could grapple the whale's blowhole when I got the chance. Some whales launch themselves from the depths to shake loose and then crush the demonic lampreys burrowing into their hides. So too would the Harbinger Whale when I scrabbled for purchase on the rim of his blowhole. At the apex of his breach I'd be ejaculated skyward. In what would be my last sensible moment I'd give a good full wave goodbye to my Northern Indian friends before I splatted on the ocean's surface. The whale would give me a last whomping to demonstrate who was boss out here on the wide lonesome; what was left of me that wasn't bludgeoned into chummy paste would flutter downward into the predatory, teeming nowhere. Maybe I'd have time enough to bloat and return to the surface to have my eyeballs pecked out by the skua and gulls. More likely though, the sharks that attended the whale—the Harbinger's hench-sharks—would rend my corpse into stew-chunks before I even knew I was dead.

It had crept up upon me, my wet and final moment. But I hadn't been drained into a whale vortex. Instead, its enormous round blaze orange-rimmed eye ogled and speculated me. For far too long. In fact, it went from looking at me to looking an awful lot like a life buoy with a line back to the *Hammer Maiden* that Waldena had thrown me. The same orange life preserver they'd been pointing at. I feathered my ankles to check if my feet hadn't been bit off yet and paddled to the ring and let Waldena haul me in.

I learned things on the *Hammer Maiden*. I was taught things. Things about myself, even. Things that will vex me forever after, things that are none of anybody's business, that I wish weren't mine. Things that will never have any practical application on

Bismuth. I return to these things in my mind too often, the way my tongue returns to stroke a canker sore.

My phone rang. Or, it uttered a pleasant trill. That was Moira's ringtone, though it was neither a ring nor a tone. Each member of the WhaleNet has a ringtone. I think I could set them individually if I wanted, but I let the WhaleNet handle it. Moira called me more often than anyone else; her ringtones almost always connoted a cheery busyness. I'd never heard my own tone, but Moira said it had changed from sounding like a beached grampus to a sort of puzzled but interested bird, sort of like a raven's "Bok?" A grampus, she reminded me, was a small whale with a soft head.

Actually, I think maybe Ill John and Chosen were my most frequent callers. They had a lot of questions about Bismuth and a variety of, as Chosen liked to put it, opportunities that have risen. Their tones were pretty similar—both were a pair of watery barks, as if a dog were trying to tell you something while it was swimming and biting bubbles. It sounded something like my name: "Unh rij, unh rij."

Waldena texted me sometimes; I think just to spook me. It was never anything sinister—just lines of poetry, sometimes in Estonindian, and terse descriptions of sea creatures and ice floes. But my phone felt different in my hand when I read her messages.

Snorri rarely called to speak to me. His calls announced themselves with an inhuman yoik. He was, however, an epic texter, literally sending me epics and sagas and whole encyclopedias of information about, I don't know, anything on his mind, I suppose—I didn't usually read past the first screen. Most recently he'd had plenty to say about the King of Herrings, a nightmarish fish so long it could not fit on one screen of my phone, no matter how much the image was reduced. It was a snaky, despotic beast that had terrified the entire race of herring into subjugation. In addition to being mythically monstrous, it was also, evidently, real.

Angie most often used her phone to predict the future. She would call me and her tone would be like a roomful of canaries; she'd say, "I'll be there in five minutes," and then she was. Angie would look at her phone more often than anyone I knew. I would say something, she'd pull out the phone, thumb-type something, then look at me with a slightly anguished, "How could you have possibly been right about that?" expression.

After nearly a year, her sister Mineola's icon was still barely sketched in. I got the impression that Mini didn't want to be on the WhaleNet—or at least didn't want to be apparent on it. I don't think she and I ever spoke directly on the phone. I did get plenty of reports from her on WhaleNet business stuff, but it mostly went unread, although I didn't delete it. My mother, who was mercifully not on the Net, called often. She felt even more compelled to tell me what to do with the house now that I owned it. It turns out the list of things I still hadn't done to the house since they moved down to Florida was much more extensive than I ever knew. The house was fine though. Even if the uninformed eye did find it a bit rustic.

Moira, though, I took all her calls. She had enthusiasm and little regard for the myriad of inhibitions and confusions that lassoed their coils around me like a. . . . well, like a wall phone cord. It was a relief to chat with her sometimes. My phone again uttered its sharp but happy little "squee," which was its tone for Moira in her most result-seeking mode. I answered.

"Hi, it's me. We got here a few minutes ago," she said.

This was a habit I think she picked up from her mom. I didn't mind. It's nice that the youth of our island live a few more moments into the future than their elders. She said she and her mom were in the kitchen, and I went in to find them. Angie and Moira were here to help clean up too.

This was the Spouter's first wedding. In the small kitchen, Angie, Moira, Chosen, and I were entirely in the way of the poor caterer and her minions, but it was our island and our friend's B&B, even if it was someone else's wedding. Nothing really needed cleaning up yet. Or actually, there were vast and teetering towers of sauce and food-filled aluminum trays and pots that we were not going to clean up since we didn't work for the caterer. I specifically was employed to stay until the bitter end, in case guests needed hauling back to their various rented cabins and rooms and boats for the night. It was an ambitious operation, too big for Bismuth, really. The ferry had even been hired for an extra run to take back the caterer and the guests who weren't staying overnight. That ferry was leaving pretty soon and we really weren't helping by clogging up the kitchen. I was glad I was neither working for the caterer nor getting married. I think Moira was there out of excitement and curiosity, and Angie was there due to her congenital habit of supervising anything that occurred within her ken. I recognized the percussive rattling tone of the caterer's cookware and could tell she was near snapping. As a fellow kitchen worker, I did her a favor and shepherded our group of in-the-way islanders outside.

Moira surveyed the wedding guests. "How many sunglasses you think I'll get?" She had a good collection of lost glasses she'd been waiting to grow into for years.

"What do you think for phones?" I asked.

"Those scarfs the ladies are wearing are pretty," she observed.

Strangers leave a lot of stuff behind on the island, and it's not always trash. We were being quiet, since we didn't want Angie to overhear us.

We sat down at an empty table set up near the kitchen door that opened up on the back garden. The catering minions were snapping the folding chairs closed with peevish alacrity, signaling the end of their involvement and desire to get back on the ferry. We stayed planted in ours—they were island chairs anyway, I'd pushed them over on a wheeled rack built for neither sand nor cobblestones from under the stage of the Historical Society house where they were kept. Actually I was supposed to fold and stack them, but I wasn't going to mention it to them. Chosen went to get Moira a soda and to make Angie a gin and tonic. He hadn't asked me if I wanted anything. After he left, I took the bottle of beer out of my jacket pocket and put it on the table. I knew better than to light a cigarette in front of Moira, but would have liked to.

Angie said she'd seen Snorri at Mini's the other night and that he was coming over to Bismuth tomorrow. Last fall, I'd actually rehearsed some martial arts moves I'd worked out that were all about throwing the Finlindian into the drink the next time I saw him. I was less sore about it now since I'd come to realize that unless one of the boats is a Coast Guard cutter, there's no easy way to get a dry sailor from one ship to another— if neither ship were willing to be polite and tie up to the other, that is. He just wanted a friend to come with him as he followed a mythical whale to the Arctic. Was that so much to ask? And he really did know I was better off on Bismuth with Angie than on Waldena's wicked vessel. I knew his shove signaled his disappointment with me—I should have gone with him and allowed him to deliver me to Angie.

What really kept me off of my revenge fantasy, though, was the fact that I had been telling people for a year that the Harbinger Whale had rammed our boat so hard that Snorri had implored me to jump ship and save myself, since he was certain the *Honeypaws* was going to flounder. It was desperately important to him that someone survive and pass the news of the historic whale sighting along. I had pleaded with him to let me stay aboard and help fend off the monster, or to at least bring him with me to the *Hammer Maiden*, a ship neither of us wanted to board at all, ever, unless our continued existence was in question. The last I'd seen of Snorri, he was putting on his survival suit and manning the harpoon gun. He'd waved to Waldena and I, shouting, "You're a brave man, Orange! Remember me!" We both saluted him. "There goes a noble soul," I told Waldena, as he motored off to face his martyrdom, and she said with grudging but sincere respect that he loved his *Honeypaws* and that he would be honored by the Whale Council. Then Waldena and I, who were not attracted to each other at all, kept a mature and chaste distance from each other on the trip back to Bismuth, as two grown-up and civilized people would naturally do. Especially since I was so eager to return to Bismuth and make amends to Angie, who was someone I respected as a person, a mother, and as a beautiful woman.

Like the *Polk*, the target-practice boat I'd first met the Koreans on, my story was full of holes so big you could drive a boat through them, but it hadn't yet been questioned. Not in front of me, anyway. There was little chance that Angie believed me, but she'd let it go. We'd all managed to be on the same telephone for a while now. I was concerned what might happen if we were all in the same room together.

Angie and I talked about the eternal mysteries of offislanders and their strange ways. With the entire continent at their disposal, why get married here? I'm not even allowed to mention marriage to most married people my age. They're liable to scream, "We're fine!" and wave a fist in my face. I suppose some discontent at home is necessary to keep the men of Bismuth going down to the sea in ships.

"How come so many people take pictures of food?" I asked. The caterer had photographed everything she made with her telephone, and many of the guests photographed their plates before eating and then did the same with the table debris afterward.

"It's nice," said Angie. "They post the photos to share the stories of the night with their friends. The caterer is probably proud of her work, or wants to study it later."

"Is there a new stage in eating? It's like they're doing favors for anthropologists from the far future."

Angie didn't answer. I thought about an invention for telephones that would source local ingredients, choose a recipe, prepare the meal, do the dishes, donate the leftovers, and broadcast every step of it to the world. No actual eating or cleaning would be necessary.

"Do you remember Jellies?" asked Angie.

"When that gale pushed them all into the harbor?" I said. "That was beautiful. And disgusting."

"No, not the fish, the sandals."

"No."

"They came between Tevas and Crocs, I think. Years before flip flops. They were ugly. The sandals this year are nicer."

Angie was looking at the young women's sandals. I looked at hers. They were pretty and leather and would probably stay on if she broke into a run. She had painted her toenails. They were red, probably. It was dark under the table. She was wearing an Indian print skirt with a little fringe and a Bismuth Yacht Club hooded sweatshirt. I was wearing my clothes. She saw me thinking about her feet and let a sandal fall from her heel.

Chosen came back with Ill John and gin and tonics for all of us. Everywhere Moira looked, adults were drinking. She said she'd get a start on cleaning up but wanted to know first if she could keep some of the lacy/candle/faux-sea glass table decorations. Later, I risked a hand on Angie's knee, for the sake of conversational emphasis, and she let it stay. I can do that sometimes, even though she's not my girlfriend. It was a soft warm night and it never did get fully dark. I forgot to worry about Snorri until I was cinching one of the last trash bags.

CHAPTER THIRTY-FOUR

Hyperborea

I always thought that someday I'd stop being subject to other people's plans. I shouldn't, of course, they're probably the only thing that get me out of the house. I'm sure other people feel I should have better plans of my own, but it doesn't seem like I ever have the time. I don't need anyone's help to waste my own time, but someone's usually there to do it for me, since their plans might as well be my plans, and my time might as well be their time.

So Snorri's plans changed, and I had to join him on Gaeity, Mineola's island, two days after the wedding at the Spouter. I had plans the day after the wedding that involved some nice weed from Ricky—I was glad he'd signed on for another tour of duty as the Topsoil tender captain—the weight of Rover upon my belly, the leftovers I was sent home with, and the beer that found its way home with me too. It was good: Lemon chicken with capers, Asian-style noodle salad—there had been a cassoulet with lots of smoked bacon, but Angie and Moira ate it all that night. Ever since I'd been mooching meals off of Ill John and Chosen, I'd been eating better than I had in decades. So Rover and I were busy that next day and unable to come to the phone just right then, even if was actually in my pocket.

Mercury and Evinrude were in retrograde, or something like

that, Angie told me. Planets and stars were both auspiciously-and poorly-aligned, which augured confusing weather and an encounter between a foolish man and a demented wizard. Angie refused to predict whether I'd stay dry on the taxi ride she gave me to Gaiety on the *Angie Baby*. She played psychic for me sometimes. I liked palmistry the best, because there was touching involved. I liked it when she traced particular lines of biographical development up the inside of my wrist. She was good for freckle-constellations too.

I had thought we were going to have some kind of meeting of the WhaleNet executive council, but Angie said she was just going to her sister's to do laundry, and that it was no trouble at all to bring me with. I felt mildly miffed. I wanted to be some trouble, at least. But it was a good day—blue above, gray below, whitish in between—and I was grateful my shepherd was Angie and not one of her sister's glum Varangian guards. She had called in the morning to say I'd been summonsed by Snorri. I told her "summoned," and she told me to stop correcting her. Summonsed is worse. I wouldn't have come if that were the case, but I didn't tell her that.

I looked at Snorri's icon. It had gained ever more clarity over the past few days that he'd been on Gaiety. The longer he'd been around, the more lifelike his icon had become. It had gone from a faux-primitive scrimshaw etching, to *Wall Street Journal*-style illustration, to U.S. currency accuracy to a meticulous line drawing. This last image was nearly perfect in its representation of Snorri, yet it depicted his eyebrows as stretching beyond the frame, as if the phone were demonstrating its talent to portray and mock its subjects. Angie's icon was just a silhouette, as the WhaleNet icons were often when their subjects were nearby. I think that was the phone's way of telling me to quit looking at my phone and look around me instead.

Mini and Snorri were waiting for us at the floating dock. We tied up and waved. I held Angie's laundry bag and kept it between us when Snorri came in for a hug. I hadn't seen the whale-herder in the flesh in nearly a year. It looked like Mini had bought him some clothes. He was wearing a green light wool sweater that did not look like it had been passed down through the generations. Stiff blue American jeans, too. His graying hair had two thin braids that led back from his sideburns to his pony-tail. He looked good, actually—less obsession, more grooming.

"Orange Whippey, son of Bismuth! Scion of harpoonists, charter member of the Whale Network, Known Associate of the Harbinger. It is very good to see you, Sir."

Snorri wasn't going to let me by without physical contact, so I hoisted Angie's huge laundry bag to my shoulder and started to tip backward as a result. Snorri pulled me back into a hand-shake and hug and overcompensated for the bag. In order to keep upright, he wound up holding Angie's laundry. This wasn't quite the plank-walk for Snorri I'd fantasized about, but it was about time somebody else was left holding the bag, so I appreciated the moment and walked quickly to shore before Snorri could give it back. This seemed to amuse Mini, and she pecked me on the cheek. Gaiety seemed jolly so far.

Angie had been lured away by unlimited Internet bandwidth and an industrial-sized frontloader, no quarters necessary. Mini settled Snorri and I on the balcony off her living room and kitchen. We looked over the slantwise pines and arthritic oaks to see the waves horripilating into whitecaps—it was going to be a choppy ride back. She had nice snacks, which was good because I'd skipped breakfast. We had a lemony white wine that was too sweet, cold smoked mussels on ship's biscuits, seaweed salad I recognized from the Spouter fridge, and caviar and *crème fraiche* on slices of hard-boiled egg. Chicken egg, probably, I don't know; I didn't eat it, since I didn't like the idea of using the little spoon to lump fish eggs on the chicken egg.

Mini never did dress like an islander. She was always wearing clothes that would look wrong with axle grease and fish scales, which was probably right for her, since she was on camera a few times a week, instead of being pushed overboard a few times a week, like myself. "We have a lot to catch up on," she said, when I poured myself a second glass of wine. Snorri looked serious and sober. I must have looked like I was in trouble. What had I done?

"What?" I asked, wondering what to deny.

"You are becoming important," said Mineola.

"I'm sorry," I said.

"Wrong!" shouted Snorri. I grabbed my fork, prepared to defend myself. "That's not how a hero faces importance!"

"What?"

Snorri's eyes rolled back under the scrim of his reaching eyebrows. He sighed. He stroked an eyebrow strand and let his fingers continue down a braid that dangled along his head. "The Whale Council has taken an interest in you."

"Sorry," I said.

"It is not often the Whale Council turns its attention to an American," he said. "You do not have to apologize. You could even be proud, if you wanted."

"I think, maybe, I'd rather be home."

"Calm down. Just give Snorri a listen," said Mini.

"There's no way I'm giving the money back," I said.

Mini smiled gently and reached over to pat the back of my

hand. "They don't want your money. They might even give you some more. In fact, I'm certain they probably will."

"I'm calm," I said. "More money?"

"Snorri?" said Mini.

"Oh, certainly they might."

Well that was all right, I figured. We were at a subcommittee meeting of the WhaleNet joint-stock company. I was a decision-making vested member, probably. I guessed I could do a job for them or something. I could probably move some things around and make some time. We'd have to see. "What do I gotta do?"

"Just hear what Snorri has to say," said Mini.

Snorri straightened up in his chair and moved his little plate from his knee to a side table.

"Wait," I said. "Is there more wine? Different wine?"

"Do you mean beer?" she asked.

"Yes, please."

After Mini left, Snorri leaned across the arms of our patio chairs and stuck his face in mine. I checked to make sure I was a safe distance from the balcony rail. He gave me a long curious look. "So, Waldena?" He cocked an eyebrow, signaling his readiness for some whaleman-to-seaman confidences.

"No," I said, leaning away.

He shook his head slightly and looked to see if Mini had returned. "No, really."

"Really, no."

"Orange! Waldena?"

Snorri had no concept of where his business ended and others' began. "Leave it," I said.

"It is left," he said, but then winked, which was an expression he exceled at due to his branching eyebrows. Snorri could stare into the middle distance like no man I know, but I had special island-bred powers. I glared right through his eyeballs down his optic nerve with enough follow-through to reach the "shut up" region of his brain.

Mini interrupted my *coup d'oiel* with the beer. "Play nice and use the glass." She didn't pour it for me.

"Listen," said Snorri, "I was on the cold Atlantic too long last year. I was lucky to return. Icebergs are loosening from the Arctic like teeth from a jawbone. The frigid lagoons are booming with the lowing of the bergs. Boat-sized chunks of ice bob about like chess pieces knocked from a giant's table. The floating mountains are growing slushy and the residents are ready to riot."

"The Inuit?" I asked.

"No, they're ready to sue, though. I mean the real citizens of the icebergs: the grebes, auks, skua, the seals, the bears, the whales, the fish, the foxes, the squid. . . ."

"You don't have to go epic on us," I said.

"Son, I went epic before you were born, and you are interrupting. I'm telling something here."

I had half the beer left. Mini made a 'be nice and listen' gesture with her hands. One's fucking elders, one must respect.

"Change is afloat in the Arctic. It has been stirred like a wasp nest in a rotting rowboat. Just a few seasons from now, all the ways will be lost, especially for the animals. Do you know what will come next?" he said, pointing at me.

I wasn't going to interrupt again.

He pointed harder. "You. In your lifetime, Orange—well, maybe Moira's, or her daughters'—men will find new ways through the Arctic. The compass won't even point to the same places: North is on the move again. But men will explore and find ways and places that never existed before, or at least had not existed since before man. And those men will be islanders, sea-faring men from the very top of the world, where creatures adapt and evolve faster than anywhere else on the planet. Their neighbors will be new kinds of bears, don't you think? Bears that can swim farther and farther as they adapt to a world without ice shelves. Bears that will eventually only need to haul up on shore now and then to meet other bears. Bears that will need less and less fur and more and more fat to survive the cold sea. Bears that might decide to dive for their food—take some squid from where they live, instead of waiting for them to come up through ice holes."

I had to interrupt. "Squid come up through ice holes?"

"Why not? There are flying calamari in the South Seas."

I didn't like thinking about it.

"And the whales, of course. The baleens will be affected terribly. They feed on the tiny doomed animals that live in the cold water, the krill, the plankton. That's our Harbinger Whale, for instance. How will his people adapt? The toothed whales, though, they will have smorgasbord. No ice shelves to keep them from snatching seals from the rocks, and more and more species will take to the sea to feed. What do you think those polar bears will do to adapt? Not lose their talons and teeth, I am sure of that. No, they will only grow vaster and more ferocious. In time the leviathans of the north will be joined by a new lineage, and it will be a huge and fearsome predator."

Mini and I said it together: "Bearwhales!"

Snorri nodded sagely. "They might even outlast humanity. Two of the smartest, best-looking species on the planet; most deserving. The melting of the Arctic and the centuries-long diaspora of dispersing ice that will follow will be a planet-wide evolutionary catalyst. What new species will Ragnarok prepare for us? I would like you both to think about that—the world to come."

I did, I did think about it. Mostly, though, I was thinking about bearwhales. Mini was very sophisticated, cosmopolitan, even, in her island-bound way. She was probably thinking about bearwhales too. Was that enough, though, for Snorri to have summonsed me to Gaiety? To tell me ice was going to melt? Even with the thought sweetened, as it were, with bearwhales?

"There is going to be a new archipelago in the far north," Snorri continued. "Greenland will come to rival Australia in its deserted vastness, and, oh, what they are going to find under the permafrost plateaus when they melt! Artifacts from forgotten civilizations! Preserved creatures from before time! Meteorite craters mined for iron. Just like the Oregon Trail here on North America, we will find the very sled tracks left by the proto-Northern Indians! We'll follow them from right here on Bismuth to the very fjords of Finlindia! We will find their sleds made from mammoth bones, their kayaks of baleen and skin, their diving suits made from walrus intestines and flippers. Ancient sauna pits filled with rune stones. Funerary crypts vaulted with ivory ribbing waiting to be discovered under half a mile of ice."

Snorri half-stood and stretched so he could touch me on the knee with one hand and Mini on the thigh with the other. "We will seek what my ancestors sought, the greatest city the planet has ever known, the El Dorado of tusk and ivory, the icy Atlantis, the lost paradise of the pole. . . ."

"Hyperborea," Mini said with noticeably less bardic enthusiasm than Snorri.

"Well, yes, obviously," he said and sat back down.

Hyperborea, the mythical city at the North Pole, land beyond the north wind, is everything from the origin of civilization and home to ageless demigods, Frankenstein's monster's final resting place, the address of Santa's workshop, his elves' slave pens, the home of the frost giants, Superman's Fortress of Solitude, site of the shaft to the center of the hollow Earth, the Alexandrian Library of all lost Saknussemm lore, and object of Snorri's fascination. The chief item I knew about Hyperborea was its lack of substantiated existence, and I wondered if Snorri would acknowledge that fact.

Snorri continued, "The islands that will rise from the Arctic melt are the peaks of the ancient circumpolar continent. They are said to surround a mile-high lodestone mountain. What does that suggest to you two?"

Mini sighed and asked me if I wanted another beer. She came back with two bottles, already sipping one. I offered her my glass, she waved it away. Snorri, miffed at the distraction, crossed the room to put on a vest of some sort of marine mammal hide that was hanging from the back of a chair. He took his chair again and then pulled out a flask from the vest's inside pocket and had a swig of what had to be old milk. Mini rolled her eyes. I wanted to take my chance to fidget too, but Snorri started back up too soon.

"You're both right, of course," he said, "an impact crater."

"I didn't say that," I said.

"A vast caldera, maybe," said Snorri, "Maybe it is volcanic in origin, from within the earth. But an impact from an asteroid would explain much. At any rate, the top of the world began in fire, but it will not end in ice."

"But it is, right? Covered in ice?" I asked.

"That is now, but not the past nor the future."

"I've been meaning to ask, now that you mention it—'now,'

that is—what am I doing here right now?"

"At this present moment in history, Orange, you are not paying enough attention."

I really did not know what it was I was supposed to be paying attention to. Money had been mentioned but the topic hadn't come up again yet. Mini looked like she'd heard it before, but she was sticking around anyway. I supposed I could watch Snorri's Delphic head of steam come to a full boil, as long as we stayed out of the sauna. I gave him a contrite look so that he'd continue.

"This is Hyperborea I'm telling you about," he said. "Its possible origin, its future!"

Mineola cut in, "Snorri, Hyperborea? It's not a real place. The lodestone mountain, the ring of islands, those are mythical."

"Throughout history, entire nations have been absolutely certain of it. My own people, the Northern Indians, have been telling legends about it since before we crossed the Atlantic. The Inuit knew it was there, though for them it was a ring of crystal mountains. The fact is, Hyperborea is a cipher, a mirage. In the far north there is . . . I don't know if there is an English term. It is a sur-mirage, a mountain can appear to be upside down, balancing on its own peak, as if there were a vast mirror between them. Or entire cities can be seen to appear, fuzzy, squashed, or attenuated. This is how the Inuit knew of Trondheim, how when they first visited the Norwegian city, they already knew their way around the major streets. They'd been seeing the city for decades. Sometimes it's an island—the Faeroes are seen west of Greenland now and then. So imagine you are one of my grandest ancestors, too many millennia ago to count. You are part of a generations-long migration eastward. How could people of that time even conceive of having a destination another continent away? Especially when they did not know there were such things as continents? They had seen it, that is how. They had seen snow-free forests, islands, maybe even villages. Imagine looking at the horizon, when all is bleak and white around you, and seeing the aurora whoosh and arc around the sky like languid bioluminescent eels scouting from the dark deep. Imagine now seeing a warm forest full of game within the glowing loops of the aurora. How could you not believe that you had glimpsed a paradise? There's no reasonable way to get there—the compass would be no help, no seaway existed, no dog sled, no human legs could get someone across the unmappable wastes. So there was a paradise, a snowless forest, a city, an impossible mountain; my people always knew it was there, but had never visited. All was legend, but that legend was as matter-of-fact as Bismuth is from Gaiety—of course it is there, whether it can be seen or not. Some of our myths say our people had their origin there, but the rest of our stories, and now our research too, tells us we began right here on these Northeast islands of yours. Other myths say Hyperborea was our race's destination when we began our migration. History shows that what may have begun as a quest for Hyperborea became a voyage on the Northeastern Passage, a route that became legendary in its own right. We Northern Indians like to think of our people as having experienced a collective vision so powerful, it drew us across the planet. And I do not mean to disparage this vision, but what I began to learn when we met our friend, the Harbinger Whale, was that we had help from other creatures. The Whale Council's lore is meant to be their own mystery, but they have taken a very serious interest in my discovery of the Harbinger and shared some of the secret archives with me. They believe that not only did whales and other animals show us the way, but the whales may have even induced us to migrate, for their own unknowable whaleish reasons. The Whale Council suggests that when our people were spread along our migration route—a voyage that took centuries—the ancestors of the Harbinger Whale helped us communicate with each other. Messages could be sent from one continent to another, from tribes trudging and paddling the frozen nowheres to the seat of their new civilization. They could tell their relatives, "We saw your cairns; we will be arriving in a few decades. We hope you will be home."

Angie does that, I thought. She calls to say she's on her way.

"Carrier pigeon whales?" asked Mineola.

"Ha! The minkes are a bit pigeonish, but no, they were probably more like city buses. The migration routes and territorial patrols of some special whales were known to the people. It could well be that particular whales were fitted with boxes or slots in their blubber. Over the years this would heal over and not trouble the whale at all. Harpoon tips and all sorts of hardware have been found in whales many times; we still find centuries-old matériel in the big bulls and cows. Conceivably, a whale could even hold a bank of boxes, individual boxes for particular tribes. When the whale came to call, people would check their box or post something in another's box.

"By our standards, this would be slow, but for the ancients, this would be miraculous. No other culture on the planet would have possessed such advanced telecommunication skills."

"Were this all true," said Mini.

"It is speculative, I'll grant you, but it's supported by increasingly rich likelihood."

"A floating post office, like the islands in Kashmir," I said.

Snorri appraised me. "Worldly."

"I read it in a poem."

"A bookmobile," said Mini.

"Imagine an ark, a cultural repository," said Snorri, "a kit for starting a culture. If your tribe knew it was headed for danger or facing cultural stagnation, a Harbinger Whale could be loaded up like an arc and sent off into the future for further generations to find."

"Like the millennium vault on Svalbard," I said. "But you'll never find a whale with an ancient trove—they outlive us but not by millennia."

"No, you are right," said Snorri, "we met their descendant last summer. But discovering their lineage—or rather its discovery of us—is akin to finding the foundations of the Alexandrian Library. Even if a scroll were never found, just knowing the library was not a mere legend changes our civilization. Likewise for the Harbinger Whale. The Whale Council's archives are ancient beyond writing even. Just knowing the Harbingers existed allows for new interpretations of artifacts and relics. Maybe there were no pre-literate times for my people. It's quite possible they have had symbolic writing systems for eons. The ancient ivory platters, so ill-suited to any practical use, may not be covered with wear marks. This may be representational language. A disc of bone slotted into a whale may well be a schedule: This whale will be at such and such a place when the sun and the stars are at such and such a place. Each whale would carry a map of its route."

City buses were not native to Bismuth, but I knew what they looked like. I imagined people lined up on the beach, waiting for the whale, complaining about how late it always was.

Mini was more critical. "Why would a whale have anything to do with people? Especially your ancestors, Snorri. They'd all know you as killers, I'm sure."

"Whaleherding is not modern, Dear. We are thought of as old-fashioned even by our own people. A good whaleherd has a great deal of empathy for his subjects. What I learned as bear-groom, some of it I could use with whales. Whales, obviously, are much less personable and charismatic, harder to develop feelings for, but whaleherds are a guild that have been part of our culture—not so much Estonindian anymore, but Finlindian, certainly—since forever.

"What a whaleherd must do is take care of and watch over his whales. Protect them from predators, help them find grazing waters, groom them. Grooming is especially important. And it's not just aesthetic, though a handsome whale is a happy one. Whales get terrible parasites. Wars are fought on their backs between rival city-states of lice. The hagfish, the lamprey, the doctor and nurse fish, the crabs—you know we have to wind worms out of them? We lure them from their tunnels in the blubber with morsels and then twist them around a rod like a windlass ever-so-slowly to pull them out without breaking them and causing a terrible infection. It is crowded on a whale, even their reefs of barnacles have parasites of their own. So what is a poor whale to do? It has to scrape itself on shoals or slap itself silly by belly- and back-flopping just to scratch an itch. When I was a whalehand at the fjord, I spent hours every day scrubbing the little beasties off the minkes. They loved it! They titter when you tickle their bellies! They love their kribble too, but they just adore being plucked and preened. Sometimes just a quick wipe of tissue to clear the snot from its blowhole, other times it is more like surgery—sawing off corns from their flukes and chiseling away concretions of crustaceans.

"A whale simply cannot turn its head and nibble at a flea like Rover can. Some of them genuinely appreciate the grooming.

Who's to say it is not their idea? We humans are the ones bred for nit-picking and tick extraction. Maybe they are taking advantage of an instinctual compulsion of ours. There are fish grooming stations in the lagoons of archipelagoes across the oceans, everything from walruses to basking sharks get the treatment. On land, anything that stands still long enough will get its lice plucked by birds if they know where to go. This is a service we could have exchanged with whales for their messaging. This, the Whale Council and I believe may be the fundamental mystery of Hyperborea."

"They were whale scrubbers," I said, sensing an oncoming conscription into another foul job.

"Even for you," said Mineola, "this is odd."

"My bearbride would not have thought so, nor do the Whale Council. Interspecies grooming and cooperative hunting are not at all uncommon.

"If whales knew there were a protected place, a safe harbor, where for generations they could go to rid themselves of pests, they would exploit it, cooperate, even. The Council does not see these conjectural Hyperboreans as poolside attendants. Caring for the whales was crucial, of course, just as a postal worker lovingly cares for his vehicle."

"What?" said Mini.

"Oh, you know, the old postal pride—prompt, accurate delivery on gleaming steeds."

Mini and I looked at each other. The mail must be different in Finlindia. "We don't have a mail man." I told Snorri, "We go pick it up ourselves at the PO."

"This whole continent has such pretensions to the first-world economy," he said. "I forget sometimes that North America is still a developing country. No national education, no health care, a rudimentary rural postal service, no bandwidth to speak of outside of the cities. Everyone in debt to your own multinational versions of company stores."

"The whole continent is not like that," said Mini.

"Bismuth is," I said.

"My point is," said Snorri, "Hyperboreans took care of their whales. They were respectful, yes. However, these were work animals."

"Not servants?" said Mini, wearying of Snorri's pedantry and maybe a little defensive of the national economy that had served her so well.

"They were working men and working animals. They had a shared umwelt of purpose, a mutually advantageous symbiosis. They had reached an agreement, a compact. The Hyperboreans maintain their grooming station in perpetuity, and this attracts reliable whales; the whales, in turn, act as couriers for the Hyperboreans. Thus, a cultural empire that straddles the Northern Hemisphere."

"The working men of Hyperborea are the emperors of the North Pole?" Mini was mocking Snorri.

"No, though they might have thought so at some point in history. And 'empire' is the wrong word I think. The Hyperboreans may have allowed a culture to stay vital as it migrated for thousands of miles and thousands of years. They could have made long distance, high-speed communication possible. News and small objects could travel distances in weeks that would otherwise take years or be simply impossible. To put it in the terms of your people, it could be how we knew there was a there there, and we could get there from here." Snorri had tried a little Down East accent with his attempt at regional humor. I could imagine him practicing it, listening to Bert and I records.

Snorri seemed to feel as if he'd made an important point and settled back into his chair for a slow pull off his flask of old milk. I was still asea but tried to summarize what he'd been telling us, hoping to hasten this tale that began in deep history and supposedly promised money for me in its conclusion. "There's a bus station/post office/whale spa at the North Pole."

Snorri capped his leathern flask. "Say instead that it is the hub of the world . . . of ancient Northern civilization, at any rate."

Mini said, "I kind of like 'whale spa.'"

Snorri chuckled insincerely to humor her. He probably did not see any humor in whale scrubbing. He'd probably scrubbed too many himself. I don't know how I'd feel if he were talking about an ancient guild of dishwashers.

"Well," he said, "the grooming was probably not the most important element of what may have happened in Hyperborea. It is probably most significant for its likely geography. Obviously, whales are sea mammals and need to breathe air. Although the Arctic is principally a sea, in places the ice on top of it is higher than the water below is deep. Sea mammals simply cannot travel the distance from open water to the presumable location of Hyperborea without surfacing to breathe. If there were an isolated, protected patch of open water—an oasis—it would be an ideal wintering harbor for some whales, as long as they didn't spread the word too far and crowd themselves out of it. This harbor could have been bored through the ice by a meteor. It could be a volcanic or thermal vent from an undersea fissure. Most likely, though, is that it was a product of glacial melting, and it has been maintained by human hands—the Hyperboreans."

Mini asked whether she had already asked if the Hyperboreans were Northern Indians and what they had to do with the Inuit.

"That is an important question," said Snorri. "And we are not certain of the answer. There have been several waves of human immigration to the Arctic. The Northern Indians had more of a migration. The race was native to the Arctic for several generations, but is now concentrated in coastal Northern Europe. The Whale Council and other anthropologists do not think we were the only aboriginals in the region at the time. The most likely answer is that, as the Northern Indians passed through the Arctic territories on the Northeast Passage, we bestowed aspects of civilization to the local cultures. They came to admire and emulate us, and even though their histories have forsaken us, their cultural progenitors, we live on in their mythologies as ancient gods and heroes. So perhaps the Inuit were living in the Arctic as my people passed through. There may not be record of contact, but echoes and shadows of our passage linger in their culture."

"Oh, that's right," said Mineola sarcastically, "I'd forgotten it was your ancestors that had also built the pyramids and ziggurats. And taught farming to the Mesopotamians."

"I'm surprised you don't think my ancestors were influential," said Snorri, with mock offense.

"Whatever they were, it wasn't modest," she said.

"I bet they could explain the hell out of just about anything," I said.

"You are forgetting that you are directly involved, young man," said Snorri.

"You're right!" I said. "I've been sneaking up to Hyperborea every summer since college. Don't tell Angie, but I have a girlfriend up there."

"Angie's not your girlfriend," said Snorri.

"How would you know?"

"Mini."

She nodded.

"Well, anyway, about two hundred hours ago you started telling me a fish story about the top of the world and got me to keep listening by promising me some money. That was when I became involved. Not in prehistory. And I am never going to give a whale a bath."

"You said you wanted him over," Mineola told Snorri, "to prepare him, to set this in context. And you have, but we're not even into the Bronze Age yet. Tell him what the Whale Council told you."

"Orange," said the whaleherder, "would you explain 'off the hook' and 'on the hook' to me? I know they are both North Americanisms about busyness and fishing, but the nuances escape me."

"'Off the hook' is when a phone receiver is knocked off its cradle and nobody can call you because of the busy signal. But it doesn't really mean you are occupied; mostly it means you are having such a wild party that you can't hear the busy signal. I bet the kids who say it don't even have land lines or busy signals."

"It has nothing to do with fish?"

"No, that's just 'on the hook.' Which is also not really about fishing. It's like when someone believes a whopper and they swallow it 'hook, line, and sinker.' If you're on the hook, someone is reeling you in."

"And it is metaphorical."

"Ayup. Or I suppose. I don't do that kind of fishing. We use nets and dredges."

"And lastly, Captain Hook?"

"A legendary old island whaler with a boathook for a hand and a grudge against the fish that ate it. Nobody really knows how he got in *Peter Pan*."

"Snorri, you're drifting," said Mineola.

"I am just looking for the right phrasing, the right hook, to tell Orange the Whale Council wants him to follow the Harbinger Whale to the Arctic and find Hyperborea. They will fund the expedition. We will take *Honeypaws* and a few other vessels."

"That's off the hook!" I said.

"The Whale Council are not having a wild house party. Though they do have a trunk line grafted directly from the Transatlantic Cable."

"No I mean they want their hooks in me. That's off the hook." Snorri did not look edified. "'Off the hook' can mean a wild statement, too. Also, the entire idea is off the hook, in the sense that it's crazy."

"Nonetheless," said Snorri.

I directed my next question to Mini, whom I felt possessed the most rationality of the three of us: "What?"

"He's shit serious," she said.

"Why?"

"The Council," said Snorri, "believes you may be a natural-born whale sensitive. They want you to ask the Harbinger Whale for the directions to Hyperborea."

Up until this very moment, I had suspected Snorri's tale was going to conclude with some dealmaking for seagum. Me and the Lucy family were among the last of the Island seagum-mers and we had the Korean connection too. I figured until the Whale Network became profitable or had at least milked all the money it could from the Northern Indian Whale Council, seagum would solve some liquidity issues for them. I had also presumed that Snorri was working his way up to telling me the secret origin of seagum—that it was Harbinger Whale jism or something. I remembered a snide remark Waldena had made about Snorri being a "whale handler," and I thought I was going to be made to help induce its production. Thus, I was relieved to merely refuse to join Snorri on yet another trip northward.

"No," I said.

"Hold on, Orange, it gets kind of interesting from here," said Mini.

"It does indeed. Now the first whale sensitives known to the Council. . . ."

I tapped the pocket where I thought my phone might be. Took it out, and showed it to Snorri. "Angie says she needs me in the laundry room."

"I didn't hear it ring," said Snorri.

"It was a hyper audiotext mail. American phones have them." I bolted to find Angie before her sister and Snorri could reel me back in.

I was making balls from Moira's pink and purple socks. I was making sure not to mix them up, as instructed. Angie was telling me what a whale sensitive was.

"I have no idea, I've never heard of one," she said. "And don't drink all my beer."

I gave her back the bottle and she held it up to look at the tablespoon of backwash I'd left.

"Snorri's Whale Council says you're a whale sensitive?"

"The Harbinger Whale is supposed to give me directions."

"To where?"

"Hyperborea."

"Where's that?"

"The North Pole."

"People already know where the North Pole is, Orange."

I must have looked lost.

"Do you want me to talk to them with you?" she asked.

"Yes, please."

"A sensitive is an empath," said Snorri, "someone with an enhanced awareness of the umwelt of another. The Council suspects you are a whale sensitive—that you have a natural correspondence with the Harbinger Whale."

"Harbinger umwelt is sampo, isn't it?" I asked.

"Ayup," said Snorri with a credible island accent.

"Orange has a natural sensitivity?" Angie sounded doubtful.

"He's kind of oversensitive sometimes," said her sister.

"Tetchy," agreed Angie.

"A natural-born shirker," amplified Mini.

"They're right. The Council has the wrong man," I said.

"That was my first reaction as well," said Snorri. "but they wonder if you may have a special propensity for whalishness."

"Do you feel whalish?" Angie asked me.

I tried to self-assess my whalishness.

"You were eating squid at The Spouter," she said.

This was true. I had brought myself to eat Chosen's grilled squid with relaxing sauce. It was the old shoe to the old socks of their kimchi. "Not kribble, though," I said, remembering the Harbinger was a baleen.

"You don't feel like eating freeze-dried krill?" said Mini.

I patted my stomach. "Nope, not even a hankering."

"He doesn't look any more whalish than last summer," Mini said to her sister. "Skinnier, if anything."

Angie asked, "Can you hold your breath any longer? No, you

smoke too much. How about swimming? I don't think I've seen you swim yet this year. How about when you go out fishing with the Lucys, can you sense the currents? Can you hear fish swimming from miles away?"

Mini joined in. "Have you developed an aversion to harpoons? Any worries about orcas? Do you want Snorri to yoik for you while he rubs your belly?"

The Bombardier sisters were teasing me. It made me glad the Harbinger wasn't a sperm.

"The Council does not think he is becoming like a whale," said Snorri, trying to keep things from getting silly. "They believe he has a nascent ability to understand them."

"Like singing?" I asked.

"You're not going to give him yoiking lessons," said Angie, with a tone of menace. "Wait, why does your Whale Council even know who Orange is?"

"They know him from the WhaleNet, of course. They helped me make his telephone. They've been monitoring the WhaleNet since its inception."

"Monitoring? How so?" said Angie, with a heaping measure of dread.

"In all ways. You know we have been field testing the network for nearly a year now," said Snorri.

"Listening? Looking?"

"Of course."

Mini, the older, financially-triumphant sister and CNN's most popular proponent of privacy, blended tones of condescension and pity with Angie's name with such practice it belied a lifetime of expert sororal agitation. "Oh, Angie . . . to whom?"

Angie blanched then flushed. Her neck prickled with red hives that spread like the very opposite of frost on a window pane. "Nobody!" she said.

I just knew they had to be talking about sexting. I'd had phones for close to a year and nobody had yet sexted me. It was like living next to an invisible mountain. Who had Angie sexted, why hadn't she sexted me? Should I have sexted her first? Can one be sexted by one's girlfriend? If not, I was all set, since she was not my girlfriend. I felt as if I had waited my entire life for the invention of sexting, and now it had passed me by. Who had Angie sexted, and why wasn't it me? I tried to think of polite ways to elaborate on how I would like to be sexted. 'Angie, I too would also like to be sent a photograph of you unclad. The opportunities you have afforded me to form memories over the last year have been cherished and embellished, but the days at sea are long and the nights on my couch are boring and often my memory and imagination lead me to much duller places than I deserve and a naked picture of you would serve as an objective correlative, a lighthouse to guide my visual imagination to a warm snug harbor.' As usual, it was good that I did not speak what was on my mind. I tried to give Angie a non-leering, thoroughly supportive look, but it came out all wrong. There is probably no polite way to say you find someone's embarrassment provocative.

Snorri must have sensed some of this. Who knows what he'd photographed and forwarded. Maybe he was a sexting sensitive. Which is what I'd have much preferred over being a whale empath. He addressed himself to Mini and I, so Angie wouldn't feel too self-conscious. "As I learned how the Whalenet was being established, technicians told me cellular architectures they had worked on before often picked up babbling and crying children. These engineers were typically childless men with no last names, so they did not realize they were listening to the broadcasts of baby monitors throughout the Northern Indies."

Mini snorted. This sort of eavesdropping was the kernel of so many of her presentations on privacy.

"I suppose," Snorri continued, "the infants could have been scandals or state secrets themselves, but they were highly unlikely to utter anything worth overhearing."

"So our joint-stock company got its start peeping on babies," said Mini.

"No, no, I just brought that up because it was the first time I had heard of baby monitors and it is a fitting analogy. The Whale Council is only watching over the WhaleNet the way parents monitor their newborns from another room."

"That's creepy," said Angie.

"It is a very significant investment," he said.

"There's how many of us?" asked Mini.

I knew the screenful of icons well. "Seven people, one cat, and one hallucination."

"You are forgetting several dozen belugas at sea," said Snorri. "That is the Council's principal concern."

"They never call," I said.

"What some North American islanders have to say about each other is not important to them. They are not listening to your conversations. Or if they do, it is just to monitor quality assurance."

Angie uttered a groan that signaled embarrassment eroding into exasperation.

Mini said, "Why do you use the WhaleNet phone so much; we knew from the start how insecure it was."

"It's free. And I get access to just about everything. It's kind of weird," Angie said.

"You do not use yours much, outside of calling me, do you?"

Snorri asked Mini.

"No, but it's beautiful, Snorri, the legacy of so much craft and care. It's a wonderful accessory."

Snorri didn't seem to like her accessorizing with his cultural legacy, 'the heirloom from the future, I think he had once called it. "It is not a handbag."

"Oh, but it holds so much," said Mini. "So many memories, so much elegance and history. It is a badge of endearment. I look at this phone and can almost hear you whispering in my ear, and behind your voice, a chorus of your ancestors."

Snorri groomed an eyebrow. Angie and I looked at each other. Her sister sure could bullshit.

"You, though," Snorri said to me, "are a Chatty Cindy."

"That's Cathy, and no I'm not."

"Who do you call?" asked Angie, with a little suspicion.

"Almost nobody."

Snorri asked if he could see my phone, and I passed it to him. He opened it up and turned it on. His expression suggested my phone was in poor taste.

"What?" I asked.

"This is among the shoddiest plastic clamshells available!" He scoffed as he turned it over. "I am surprised it does not take double Ds."

"I think you mean D cells," said Mini.

Snorri asked, "May I?" and I nodded. He poked the green button and looked at the display screen. He frowned and waved his finger over the screen as if admonishing a tiny phone gremlin. Then he held the phone horizontally and frowned again. He squeezed the sides and the phone broke into a few pieces. "It is just the shit tab-and-slot plastic case. We can glue it."

"My numbers were in there, my icons too," I said.

"Snorri!" said Mini.

"This phone is indefensible," said Snorri. Sensing his harsh judgment of the phone had not been shared, Snorri tried reassembling it as if he were re-stacking a deck of cards. "See, it still works. Don't worry, there are many better devices in store for you," he told me.

I was thinking of lobsters and what mutilations they could survive. The phone did seem to still work. I could see the lighted display screen and most of the workings were still connected by tiny colored wires. Maybe it could grow a new shell.

Snorri was inspecting the screen. "You know that your cat Rover does not have her own telephone. This icon represents you."

I did know that, although I think I had forgotten it at some point. I had called her a number of times this winter and chided her for not answering.

"I do not know what this is, however," he said, tapping the ghost icon with the nail of his right little finger.

"You just called it," I said.

"What, or who?"

"I don't know, I thought it might be you—like an avatar."

"That is a nice idea, but no," he said.

"Who is it?" asked Angie.

I shrugged. "See if it answers. It doesn't usually. Sometimes it calls me though."

"A glitch, maybe? It just looks like electronic fuzz." said Mineola.

"Sometimes it calls me at night when I can't sleep," I said.

"What kind of ringtone does it have?" asked Snorri.

"It doesn't."

"How do you know when to answer?"

"It usually happens when I've been holding it and looking at the screen for a while."

"Then it rings?" he said.

"No, it's more like after a while I notice I've been talking . . . well, no, it's more like we just spend time together."

Snorri looked alarmed.

Angie looked concerned. "Tell me you're reading a novel or something with it."

"Why would I need a phone to read?"

"That's not . . . do you talk to it?" said Snorri.

"Not really. Usually I just watch the icon swirl around. I can sometimes hear whooshing and thumps and sometimes clicks and beeps. Once in a while there's a drone that lasts hours. I thought maybe it was picking up satellites or spy ships."

"Why?" said Angie.

"Maybe the whale antennae are receiving covert transmissions on the Atlantic; I could see how that would be possible," said Mini.

"No," said Angie, "I mean, Orange, why do you look at a gray blur and listen to your phone drone and thump?"

What disturbed me about this question is that I had never thought about it critically. Angie had a good point, though I was certainly never going to tell her that staring at a phone was among the least eccentric and most socially acceptable things I did when left alone too long in the winter. It was an odd thing to do—even watching infomercials all night was more reasonable. The smirch on the phone was soothing. I liked the whoosh, thump, and drone. I felt big and old and dark when I listened to it. Not that it was the only icon I watched. I also would not be telling Angie that I looked at hers quite a bit too. I had told myself that at times I could tell when she was looking at my icon too, but I didn't believe myself. I looked at Waldena's sometimes too. The first time it winked at me, I hid the phone under a sofa pillow. That ghostly smudge of electrons though, the one that looked like a thumbnail of a fetal sonogram, occasionally I felt like I'd been places with it. Where, I had no idea, but it was like transport without traveling. Sometimes the effect was more settling. It could make me feel like a goldfish in the best bowl ever: just the right polished quartz for gravel, a not overlarge plastic plant swaying in the bubbles, pleasant-tasting water at a perfect temperature. I felt as if I could sit in the bowl and watch a cat watch me all day long.

"Orange! You're doing it right now!" Angie said.

She was right. I hadn't even been aware I was looking at it. I had to take the image in my mind and iris it down to a tight beam and send it back into the phone. I did not literally do anything but blink stupidly, but that was the way I'd come up with to hang up the phone without giving myself the psychic equivalent of a slap to the face with a halibut, which is something I had genuinely experienced many times working with Donny on his dad's boat.

"Oof," I said.

"Oof?" repeated Angie, as if I'd just woofed.

They were all looking at me; I looked out the window at the water beyond the treetops so that I wouldn't look back at the phone.

"Remarkable," said Snorri. "I was watching the icon. I saw it too."

"Saw what?" asked Mini.

"I do not know. Maybe some of what Orange saw. Orange, what did you see?"

"Nothing, just the telephone. You're making too big a deal of this."

"Tell me honestly," he said, "What did you see? None of us heard anything. You did not hear anything did you? Can you tell me if you saw any sounds? Could you hear shapes in your mind's ear?"

I hadn't found words yet for the images in my mind. It had never occurred to me to think on it, and when I did now, I could only come up with an invisible, indescribable cavern, a place I knew intuitively like a goldfish knew the boundary of the bowl without seeing it.

Snorri was being too earnest for me to be sarcastic. I tried answering. "It's like a somewhere, but not a place? But I could tell you how to get from here to there within it? Cloud-sized silent cushions pressing me with reassuring news?"

Angie was massaging the bridge of her nose. Her sister was looking at my phone. Snorri was looking at me like I had a third eye. "Orange Whippey!" he said, startling all of us. "I should not have doubted the Whale Council. This is a shamanic trance you are describing. Powerful sampo," he added, solemnly.

"It's a fucking staring spell," said Angie.

"So he's a shaman now?" said Mini.

"It is absurd, is it not?" said Snorri. "But see it from the Whale Council's perspective. . . ."

"Don't you mean *umwelt*?" interrupted Angie, who was not taking the news of my ascension to spiritual leadership with wonderment and awe, but who did seem as if she were about to be bodily possessed by the great spirit of sarcasm.

Since I'd known him, Snorri had typically been insouciant with detractors of his spiritual world view; he was in tune with the infinite and felt free to mock the natterings of naysayers. But the opportunity to spread his culture usually triumphed and he was often a tolerant, though expository man. "The Whale Council is almost entirely human," he said, "their umwelt would be virtually the same as ours—their sensoriums only slightly altered by their cultural and. . . ."

Angie put her hands over her face and groaned another interruption.

"I think this is kind of interesting," I said, feeling sensitive and maybe whalish.

"Thank you," he said. "You have fire in your scrotum and the aurora in your eyes. A direct quotation from the Whale Council."

Angie snorted into her palms.

"You're gonna give him airs," warned Mini.

"Well, none of this made me comfortable either," said Snorri. "When the Council suggested Orange may be a shaman, a whale sensitive, I was shocked too. I was reminded though of the historic cultural role of the shaman. An outsider from within the community—a fool sometimes, othertimes a healer or an oracle. Occasionally, a real pest. Someone who can be an interlocutor between the animal world and the spiritual world."

"What about the human world?" asked Mini.

"That is the animal world. We are animals too. Shamans in the Arctic and in the Northern Indian tradition as well usually have spirit guides in the form of animals. The animals tell or show or somehow imply how a community should behave."

"The whale tells me what to tell the islanders?"

"In a sense."

I thought about it. I reached out to the whale. "The whale says, 'Hey,'" I told Mini and Angie, "and it says, 'Stop hunting us' to you," I told Snorri.

"We do not hunt whales, we herd," said Snorri.

"The whale gets you and the Estonindians confused some-times. The whale also says the shaman needs more beer."

"You will have to take the spiritual journey to the refrigerator yourself, Shaman," said Mineola.

Angie had been pushed too far. "I, the island of Bismuth, for that matter, do not need Orange any more abstruse or arrogant than he already is. This is like pouring diesel on a beach bonfire at three AM. The wrong way to enlightenment. Do you know the expression 'blowing smoke up someone's ass'?"

"Is it about beach fire, or sex?" asked Snorri.

Instead of answering, Angie glared at her sister.

"How'm I supposed to talk to whales, anyway?" I asked.

"You just showed us," said Snorri.

"I was making that up."

"No, I mean here," he said, pointing to the pieces of my telephone.

I still didn't get it.

"Orange, you have been in contact with the Harbinger Whale for close to a year now; you two chat on the phone almost daily."

"The phone?"

"There! That icon you call the ghost; it's the whale!"

I talked to a ghost whale every day? I felt unfamiliar with myself. The Shaman really did need a beer, so I got up and got him one.

"Why?" I asked Snorri when I returned.

"Get me one too," said Angie.

"Why?" I asked when I returned again with her bottle.

"We discussed this, the Council and I. There's no simple an-swer of course. Maybe it's your habitual use of seagum—you do not know what actually produces seagum do you?"

I said no.

"Well maybe it is something that inculcates a whalish propinquity."

Angie tittered into her beer.

"Or it is genetic. It could be your 'staring spells' as Angie calls them. One thing we are all certain about is that you sacrificed your WhaleNet phone to the Harbinger Whale."

"There was an exigency," I said.

"Whatever you feel your reason was, your offering was accepted. At first I thought what you had done was, frankly, idiotic. But you yourself convinced me quickly of the wisdom of the sacrifice. I had not grasped how the Council's interest in establishing the WhaleNet was so congruent with the mythology of the Harbinger Whale. I do not even know if they intended to look for it. I suspect, given the Whale Council's millennia-old history, they put many plans into operation long before the modern era, and, like their predecessors, the current councilors concocted a scheme to profit from whaling while attending to their own long-term plans. In this case, I think, even if the WhaleNet were a failed business venture, they would still have informants swimming the North Atlantic who could help them investigate the mythologies that the sagas and histories simply do not explain."

"They didn't know about the Harbinger Whale?" I asked.

"They suspected it. Our myths and legends had been proven historically accurate so often in the twentieth century that it has become worthwhile to sort out what might be metaphorical and what might be actual. Everything from the sasquatch to the Hyperboreans is being reconsidered. So the Harbinger might really be carrying news from the past about our future. Or perhaps the study of the whale will help the Whale Council re-learn how to navigate and exploit the Arctic after it melts.

"Human sources and historical documents are all the modern scholars have relied on. But in the past we were much more involved with other animals as collaborators. The Council's interest in the Harbinger signals a return to the older traditions of working more closely with our fellow creatures to prepare for our return to the Arctic."

"Let's say for a moment," said Mini, "that it is somehow possible to talk with a whale; why would it tell you anything—you're their worst predators."

"Our culture is their best caretaker. Your island ancestors were the predators."

"We don't use whale meat as dog food here."

"Well, too bad for the horses," he said, peevishly.

I had seen this argument burst into horrible conflagrations often enough. I think we all felt the Northern Indian preoccupation with sea mammals was something of a cultural affectation, but knew better than to mention it. We also knew that Snorri's people thought our people were a bunch of yahoos, and we didn't want to hear about it.

"How do you know the whales won't just lead you on; or really, why would what they have to say make any sense to you at all?"

Snorri wrapped a strand of eyebrow around his little finger. "That is an excellent question. As my fellow beargrooms used to say, just because a bear swears they are tasty, does not mean you should eat bees.

"Maybe it would be better to say that the Whale Council's approach is to simply listen for a while—to see what the whales have to say for themselves. But they have to find them first, and that is why they need you, Orange."

"It is still hard to imagine members of the Finlindian

parliament talking about myths and whales, let alone talking about Orange," said Angie.

"The Whale Council has no official role in the governments. They are an autarky within a representational democracy. That is how they have persisted over the years and are able to further the goals set by their ancestors and conceive of new plans to prepare our culture for the next leg of its migration."

"What leg?" asked Mini.

"The return."

"Where?"

"Here. The Arctic. We will head into the western lands when the islands return to the Arctic."

Once again I was trying to fish information about my immediate future from Snorri and he was going on about deep time. It made me surly. So did the beer and the late afternoon.

"Well, what the fuck did you go to Europe for?" I asked.

"We didn't emigrate, we migrated. Migrations continue in cycles. By the time North America is ready to be serious about civilization, we will be here to help and guide. This is one of the chief purposes of the Whale Council—to preserve our culture and to push it forward. They are progressive."

"And almost entirely made up of human beings, you said."

"Correct."

He was imperturbable on the subject. I tried to circle back to my chief interest: myself. "So, I'm a shaman."

"Correct, almost entirely a human being," he said, smiling.

"And your Council has deduced this because of the ghost smirch on my phone? They think this is proof I can talk to a whale? That I have psychic powers?"

"It is not just about you. It is somehow a correspondence between you, the whale, and the telephone itself. A quantum embranglement. A trinity. I do not know how to describe the technology within the WhaleNet phones I gave you all, but they have plenty of autonomy and potential for self-development. It may actually be that your phone, Orange, has initiated all of this on its own. Maybe the phone feels you should be in contact with the whale and it interceded by connecting the two of you."

"Maybe it knew it was for the whale, and not me before you even gave it to me."

"No I doubt that very much. That phone was made with your self, your personality, in mind. The Council did not know you then, but Mineola and I helped them develop it based on our knowledge of you."

I took a moment to congratulate myself on getting rid of that phone so quickly. But then I realized I hadn't. It had found me again almost the moment I got another phone. Also, if it were a trinity and the whale was the ghost and the phone got sacrificed like the son, that made me God. Unless being a shaman precluded that. I hadn't expected so much theology this afternoon.

Snorri interrupted my ascension to godhead by asking Mini to see her phone.

"Not a chance!" she said.

"I will be respectful and gentle," he said, making their exchange sound a smidge lurid.

"Use your own."

"I cannot, it has too many whales on it."

Mini slapped the tops of her knees to show she did not really want to get up, but would. "OK, fine, I'll get it."

After Mini left the room, Snorri said to Angie, "She doesn't even keep it in her pocket."

Angie bounced her empty beer bottle on the coffee table like a gavel. "We're going to have to leave pretty soon."

Mini came back with her WhaleNet phone and gave it to Snorri. It looked like the rest of the adult phones—Moira's was the only one that was bendy. Where mine had the sigil of the mer-deer, Mineola's was decorated with an inlaid design of a heart with a garland around it. Snorri stroked it with his finger, telling us that it was heritage whaletooth with a mammoth tusk inlay. Snorri drew his finger along the heart's border and the phone responded by glowing softly from within. We all smiled. It was romantic. He opened her phone like a reliquary, drew a heart on the touchscreen and showed it to us. This was Mini's personal display, he told us. There we all were, the members of the WhaleNet, rendered in scrimshaw-style illustrations, just like on the phone the whale ate. "Now look at Orange's," he said.

My phone looked like it might still work, despite being in pieces. We looked at the display on mine. What was immediately apparent was that Mini's phone was a beautiful artifact and mine looked like it deserved its fate. My phone's screen looked to be lit with an insectile flashlight, hers made our icons look like they hung on a gallery wall. Yet the icons on mine seemed to have much more dimensionality, more personality. On mine, Angie and Mini and Snorri were all just outlines, since they were in the room with me. "Look at Moira!" said Angie. Moira's icon's eyes were crossed and it was sticking out its tongue.

"She does that when you look at her too long," I told Angie.

"Not on mine," she said.

"Your icons," said Snorri, "are lively and subtly expressive."

"Moira's subtle?" said Angie.

"The icon is astonishingly good at representing her feelings about being observed by adults; that is actually quite subtle."

Angie made the same expression as her daughter. "Subtle," she said and left for the bathroom.

"The point I am trying to make is that Orange's phone is not capable of this, yet here it is. This is the disposable ball point pen of mobile phones. Never mind its utter lack of aesthetics, it does not have the memory, the processing power, or even the resolution to show images like this. Where's the charger?"

"I lost it. I thought it had self-winding mode, anyway, like the Batphone you gave me."

"You know it was a whale phone. And obviously you don't know that this phone can't 'wind itself.' But it does?"

"Ayup. I've never plugged anything into it."

"How did you import the icons of the WhaleNet? Did you sync with Angie?

I didn't want to say, here in front of her and her sister.

"He means the telephones," said Mini.

"Oh, no, I don't think so. When I first got it, I didn't know anyone's number, so I just called a few places in town like the store and the Topsoil. This used to be Moira's, right?" Angie, who had re-joined us in the living room, nodded. "You guys must have deleted everything on it. I tried entering some things but gave up. The next time I picked it up, there you all were waving back to me on the WhaleNet icons."

"Those are several more things this phone is incapable of. What you are describing is an emulation and an improvement upon something we all thought was induplicable. Are there any other surprises?"

"The ringtones change a lot, so do the vibrations."

"And I suppose you have never downloaded a ringtone?" said Snorri.

"Moira was gonna show me how, but we never did," I said.

"What about the phone you lost?"

"Phones. I had two before this one, not counting yours."

"They were on the WhaleNet too?"

"Yup. I thought they were roaming and found it themselves."

Snorri shook his head. "You cannot wander into the WhaleNet; you must be invited."

Mini asked if I'd communed with the whale on the other phones and I told her I hadn't owned them long enough to try. I couldn't remember if the ghost icon had been on those phones.

Snorri said to Mini, "I am so pleased you cherish your WhaleNet phone, but I am concerned it is languishing. These telephones were made to thrive on attention, and I worry that yours will be slower than its peers. This could be why the WhaleNet is so persistent in finding you, Orange. It is a scant but legitimate possibility that it felt lost and lonely in the whale's gut and it sought out you, the only person it ever knew."

"I didn't abandon it at the convent doorstep. I don't think I even had it for more than a few hours. I never even knew its number."

"It was made for you. It expected to be held in your hands, to learn by hearing your speech patterns."

"The poor thing," said Angie.

"Well," said Snorri, "perhaps instead of you, it was fostered by the Harbinger Whale. One possibility is that it received lots of environmental stimulation in the whale and that was enough to quicken its evolution. It is possible the phone does not consider itself to be a telephone any longer. Maybe the phone is sharing its Jonah-like impressions of its world with you; or it could be that the whale is somehow consciously or intuitively using the phone to call you up and you simply do not understand what it is saying.

"Most intriguing to me is the possibility that you, the Harbinger, and the telephone have formed a symbiotic gestalt umwelt, a trimurti combining your sensorium with the phone's network and the whale's echolocation."

Angie started to speak, but her sister gave her a look that said, 'Let it pass; you'll get home sooner.'

"There are members of the Whale Council who wonder if there is a quantum connection between Orange, the phone, and the whale. A simultaneity in their communications, no matter the distance. Can you imagine? Instant communication with a vessel that can hear in three dimensions? Think of the navigational applications! I could even see spaceships using this!"

"Orange and his magic phone," said Angie.

"Wasn't my idea."

"Or was it?" asked Snorri. "You quite deliberately prepared and sacrificed that telephone. I know, I know. You did not volunteer for any of this, but you were the one who was chosen."

"That's Chosen One, right there; I just talked to him yesterday." said Angie, tapping the Korean's icon on my broken phone.

"Duty calls, Orange," said Snorri.

Booty calls, I thought.

"So, what do you think?" Snorri asked.

Before I could answer, Angie stood up. "We can't stay any longer—I have to go and pick up Moira; she and her father are going to be at the dock in an hour."

"Call them and say you may be late," said Snorri.

"I did call them a few minutes ago—so that I won't get stuck here, late."

"We still have a great deal to discuss," said Snorri.

"You might, but I have a great deal of daughter to go get."

"Why don't you leave Orange here, I can bring him over on *Honeypaws* tomorrow."

I bugged my eyes at Angie, pleading silently to be taken home.

Corwin Ericson

"Let him go, you can talk to him tomorrow," Mini said to Snorri.

"Perhaps we should pause," he said. "This has been heady, I know. All right, I will call you tomorrow. All set?"

"Ayup." I pushed the parts of my phone into a pile so I could scoop them into my pocket.

"But there is one more thing," said Snorri.

"No there's not," said Angie.

"Hold on a second," said Mini.

"Oh, right, I forgot," said Angie.

"What?" I asked. They were all smiling.

Snorri had a present for me. It was a wooden box shaped like a small coffin. He pretended to find it on the floor and then brought it up as if it were surfacing. He pantomimed it popping out of the water and then floating over to me. "For you! From the depths, back to your pocket."

I opened the hinged box and inside it was a palm-sized dull metal slab, the color of a porpoise. It had a rough finish and was very heavy for its size. It was a telephone, of course.

"Show him how to use it," said Mini.

"Just let him a moment," said Snorri.

It opened like a book, with hinges on the long side. Each side of it had a black screen and there wasn't a single button or key on the whole thing.

"Stroke an O with your finger on the left screen," said Snorri.

I did. An ivory O appeared.

"Now blow into the circle."

This was stupid, but I did it anyway. We appeared—us members of the WhaleNet, rendered much the same way we appeared on Mini's phone. I didn't see the ghost icon. The phone was actually quite heavy and came with a lanyard attached to it by a brass clip.

"See, you can put it around your neck so you won't drop it!"

This was really stupid. I was the last person to have much of an opinion about fashion accessories, but even I knew wearing a phone around your neck was lame. I put it on anyway.

"It's made from meteoritic steel more than three thousand years old," said Snorri.

"Is it Damascus steel?" asked Angie, stroking it as it rested flat against my chest.

"The Syrians learned from the Vikings and the Vikings learned it from us. It's Northern Indian meteor steel from a sacred crater."

"It's really heavy," I said.

"That makes it harder to lose and more durable," he said. "Famous weapons with long names have been made from this very same steel."

It was so heavy, it felt like it would pull my pants down if I put it in my pocket. It was a brand-new albatross, an anchor dense with cultural lumber and demands from the future. I had to thank him for it. I weighed it in my hand. "It looks like it'll stop a bullet."

"Ha!" said Snorri, "Like a sheriff's badge. Here. . . ." Snorri took the phone, still leashed around my neck and pulled me forward with it. He opened the phone and tapped something inside. Then he held it up as if he were looking in a shaving mirror and growled. It strobed. "Did it come out?" he asked, blinking, holding it in my face. "I cannot see."

Snorri's had photographed himself; his image was overlit and his eyes were half shut. His teeth were bared in what looked like a grimace.

"It looks great," I said.

"That was my bullet-catching face," he said, pleased. "I will bite it out of the air." He closed the phone tenderly like a locket and let it drop against my chest.

Mini mimicked a lanyard around her neck, "It looks like you have credentials now. A suit and a haircut and they'll start letting you into buildings."

"What's its name?" I asked Snorri. "All the phones have names, right?"

Snorri glanced at Angie and Mini. He leaned in and whispered in my ear, "Odin's Bodkin." To all of us, he said, "There is much to tell you about this device," he said, poking it.

One thing I already hated about the phone was that it allowed people too many opportunities to poke me in the chest.

"Do I have a new phone number?" I asked.

Angie grabbed it next and pulled gently. "We have to go right now."

Snorri stood and hugged me hard enough for me to feel the phone pressed between our chests. "I will call you tomorrow!" he said.

"I know." I said.

We made short goodbyes, and I made promises. I would decide later if they were sincere. Down at the docks, Eero, one of Mini's Varangian guards, blocked my path. Angie didn't seem to notice and started to ready her boat to cast off. I had done so well, keeping out of the ocean. I just knew he was going to toss me in. I thought about whirling Odin's Bodkin on its tether over my head like a bull-roarer and whacking him in the skull. I tried to deke around him, but he put his big hand on my shoulder and said my name quietly and urgently.

"Do you have any cigarettes?" he asked.

I shook my head.

"I'll pay."

I really didn't. In fact, he gave me an intense desire to smoke one. I would have loved to stand on *Angie Baby's* prow, as she broke the waves and I smoked and thought shamanic thoughts.

He looked back at Mini's house, "She confiscates them." He wasn't ready to let me pass and seemed genuinely disappointed. I must have been his last hope for tobacco.

I grubbed around in my pockets until I found the foil-wrapped Chiclet-sized pieces of seagum I had and gave him one. "It's seagum," I told him, hoping I wouldn't have to explain it.

He watched me unwrap and chew my piece and then did the same. "This tastes awful!" he said.

"Yeah, but we don't have any cigarettes."

We had hours to go until sunset, but afternoon was functionally over. Angie and I were in the wheelhouse of her *Baby*, on our way back to Bismuth. She took the phone and lifted the lanyard from my neck, asking me if she could after she'd done it. We both laughed at Snorri's photo. I told her I didn't know how to forward it to her, and she said that was good. Angie asked if I didn't mind taking us the rest of the way in while she went belowdecks and washed up.

My head was so painfully stuffed with Snorri's stories and schemes I imagined it coldly burning with St. Elmo's fire. Gaiety was behind us, Bismuth was ahead, glowing pink in a sideways sun. Certainty was an unusual feeling for me, so I recognized it right away. I hadn't expected to know my own mind so quickly. Maybe it was the seagum I was still chewing. I spit it overboard. It did taste awful, but I'd known that since childhood. What I had realized was I didn't need to go with Snorri.

This was a familiar thought, of course. This time, however, my home island's rosy hue seemed righteously unironic. I did not need to accompany Snorri to find the Harbinger Whale. I knew I did not need to because I was certain as an ancient Hyperborean that the whale would come to me, and there was nothing I could do to elude it.

This was a slow sure thought I'd had, and I'd barely noticed passing through the granite forearms of Bismuth's breakwater. I dropped our speed and steered us slowly to Angie's mooring. After I'd caught the float and tied us up, I went below and knocked on Angie's cabin door.

"Orange?"

I said ayup as if I'd had to think about it, for the sake of comedy. I was actually starting to feel gloomy with our return to the full-scale ongoingness of island life.

"Look at the phone," Angie said from within her room.

It was hanging by its leash from the doorknob. I picked it up; it stuck briefly to the doorknob—Odin's Bodkin was magnetic. It was still heavy. It was a scale from a robotic dragon, a boreal gris-gris.

"Don't just stand there staring, open it!" she yelled.

A new photo had replaced Snorri's mug. It was Angie; it was all of Angie, washed out by the overbright strobe and weirdly foreshortened from holding the camera at arm's length, and she was a sea nymph who could chase whales right out of my brain with a flutter of her eyelashes. I knocked again.

"Come in," she sang.

Fin